Praise for #1 *New York Times* bestselling author

"A superb author… Ms. Roberts is an enormously
gifted writer whose incredible range and intensity
guarantee the very best of reading."
—*Rave Reviews*

"Nora Roberts is among the best."
—*The Washington Post Book World*

"The publishing world might be hard-pressed
to find an author with a more diverse style
or fertile imagination than Roberts."
—*Publishers Weekly*

"Roberts has a warm feel for her characters
and an eye for the evocative detail."
—*Chicago Tribune*

"Romance will never die as long as the
megaselling Roberts keeps writing it."
—*Kirkus Reviews*

"[Nora] Roberts is at the top of her game."
—*People*

"Roberts' bestselling novels are some of the best
in the romance genre. They are thoughtfully plotted,
well-written stories featuring fascinating characters."
—*USA TODAY*

"A consistently entertaining writer."
—*USA TODAY*

Dear Reader,

It's that time of year again! Time for a fresh blanket of snow to make everything look beautiful, and time for another charming holiday delight from Silhouette Books! We are pleased to bring you *First Impressions,* a classic tale from *New York Times* bestselling author Nora Roberts about how appearances can be deceiving—and how two people find someone to love them for who they truly are.

First Impressions is a story about a woman determined to do a good deed…only to have her kind offer of work thrown back in her face by the rudest unemployed man she's ever met. It's also a story about a man determined to retreat from the world…only to have his best intentions turned upside down by one of the most caring and beautiful women he's ever met. And in the end they both learn that first impressions aren't necessarily what they seem.…

And don't forget *Blithe Images,* an extra treat. Bombshell model Hilary Baxter is every photographer's muse—but what she really wants to inspire is love between her and fashion mogul Bret Bardoff. Yet how can she get him to see her as more than just a pretty face?

We hope you and yours enjoy a safe, wonderful holiday season, and that the New Year brings you all that you wish for!

Happy holidays!

The Editors
Silhouette Books

NORA ROBERTS

FIRST *Impressions*

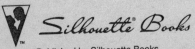
Silhouette Books

Published by Silhouette Books

America's Publisher of Contemporary Romance

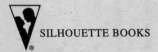

SILHOUETTE BOOKS
®

FIRST IMPRESSIONS

ISBN-13: 978-0-373-28571-6
ISBN-10:   0-373-28571-X

Copyright © 2008 by Harlequin Books S.A.

The publisher acknowledges the copyright holder of the individual works as follows:

FIRST IMPRESSIONS
Copyright © 1984 by Nora Roberts

BLITHE IMAGES
Copyright © 1982 by Nora Roberts

This edition published by arrangement with Harlequin Books S.A.

® and TM are trademarks of Harlequin Books S.A., used under license. Trademarks indicated with ® are registered in the United States Patent and Trademark Office, the Canadian Trade Marks Office and in other countries.

Visit Silhouette Books at www.eHarlequin.com

Printed in U.S.A.

CONTENTS

FIRST IMPRESSIONS

To Georgeann, neighbor and friend

Chapter 1

The morning sun shot shafts of light over the mountains. It picked up the hints of red and gold among the deep green leaves and had them glowing. From somewhere in the woods came a rustling as a rabbit darted back to its burrow, while overhead a bird chirped with an insistent cheerfulness. Clinging to the line of fences along the road were clumps of honeysuckle. The light scent from the few lingering blossoms wafted in the air. In a distant field a farmer and his son harvested the last of the summer hay. The rumble of the baler was steady and distinct.

Over the mile trek to town only one car passed. Its driver lifted his hand in a salute. Shane waved back. It was good to be home.

Walking on the grassy shoulder of the road, she plucked a blossom of honeysuckle and, as she had as a child, drew in the fleetingly sweet aroma. When she crushed the flower between her fingers, its fragrance briefly intensified. It was a scent she associated with summer, like barbecue smoke and new grass. But this was summer's end.

Shane looked forward to fall eagerly, when the mountains would be at their best. Then the colors were breathtaking and the air was clean and crisp. When the wind came, the world would be full of sound and flying leaves. It was the time of woodsmoke and fallen acorns.

Curiously, she felt as though she'd never been away. She might still have been twenty-one, walking from her grandmother's to Sharpsburg to buy a gallon of milk or a loaf of bread. The busy Baltimore streets, the sidewalks and crowds of the last four years might have been a dream. She might never have spent those four years teaching in an inner-city school, correcting exams and attending faculty meetings.

Yet four years had passed. Her grandmother's narrow two-story house was now Shane's. The uneven, wooded three acres of land were hers as well. And while the mountains and woods were the same, Shane was not.

Physically, she looked almost as she had when she had left western Maryland for the job in a Baltimore high school. She was small in height and frame, with a slender figure that had never developed the curves and roundness she'd hoped for. Her face was subtly triangular with its creamy skin touched with warm color. It had been called peaches and cream often enough to make Shane wince. There were dimples that flashed when she smiled, rather than the elegant cheekbones she had wished for. Her nose was small, dusted with freckles, tilted up at the end. Pert. Shane had suffered the word throughout her life.

Under thin arched brows, her eyes were large and dark. Whatever emotion she felt was mirrored in them. They were rarely cool. Habitually, she wore her hair short, and it curled naturally to frame her face in a deep honey blond. As her temperament was almost invariably happy, her face was usually animated, her small, sculpted mouth tilted up. The adjective used most to describe her was *cute*. Shane had grown to detest the word, but lived with it. Nothing could be done to alter sharp, vital attractiveness into sultry beauty.

As she rounded the last curve in the road before coming into town, she had a sudden flash of having done so before—as a child, as a teenager, as a girl on the brink of womanhood. It gave her a sense of security and belonging. Nothing in the city had ever given her the simple pleasure of being part of the whole.

Laughing, she took the final yards at a run, then burst through the door of the general store. The bells jingled fiercely before it slammed shut.

"Hi!"

"Hi, yourself." The woman behind the counter grinned at her. "You're out early this morning."

"When I woke up, I discovered I was out of coffee." Spotting the box of fresh doughnuts on the counter, Shane rolled her eyes and headed for them. "Oh, Donna, cream filled?"

"Yeah." Donna watched with an envious sigh as Shane chose one and bit into it. For the better part of twenty years, she'd seen Shane eat like a linebacker without gaining an ounce of fat.

Though they had grown up together, they were as different as night and day. Where Shane was fair, Donna was dark. Shane was small; Donna was tall and well rounded. For most of their lives, Donna had been content to play follower to Shane's leader. Shane was the adventurer. Donna had liked nothing better than to point out all the flaws in whatever plans she was hatching, then whole-heartedly fall in with it.

"So, how are you settling in?"

"Pretty well," Shane answered with her mouth full.

"You've hardly been in since you got back in town."

"There's been so much to do. Gran couldn't keep the place up the last few years." Both affection and grief came through in her voice. "She was always more interested in her gardening than a leaky roof. Maybe if I had stayed—"

"Oh, now don't start blaming yourself again." Donna cut her off, drawing her straight dark brows together. "You know she wanted you to take that teaching job. Faye Abbott lived to be ninety-four. That's more than a lot of people can hope for. And she was a feisty old devil right to the end."

Shane laughed. "You're absolutely right. Sometimes I'm sure she's sitting in her kitchen rocker making certain I wash up my dishes at night." The thought made her want to sigh for the childhood that was gone, but she pushed the mood away. "I saw Amos Messner out in the field with his son haying." After finishing off the doughnut, Shane dusted her hands on the seat of her pants. "I thought Bob was in the army."

"Got discharged last week. He's going to marry a girl he met in North Carolina."

"No kidding?"

Donna smiled smugly. It always pleased her, as proprietor of the general store, to be the ears and eyes of the town. "She's coming to visit next month. She's a legal secretary."

"How old is she?" Shane demanded, testing.

"Twenty-two."

Throwing back her head, Shane laughed in delight. "Oh, Donna, you're terrific. I feel as though I've never been away."

The familiar unrestricted laugh made Donna grin. "I'm glad you're back. We missed you."

Shane settled a hip against the counter. "Where's Benji?"

"Dave's got him upstairs." Donna preened a bit, thinking of her husband and son. "Letting that little devil loose down here's only asking for trouble. We'll switch off after lunch."

"That's the beauty of living on top of your business."

Finding the opening she had hoped for, Donna pounced on it. "Shane, are you still thinking about converting the house?"

"Not thinking," Shane corrected. "I'm going to do it." She hurried on, knowing what was about to follow. "There's always room for another small antique shop, and with the museum attached, it'll be distinctive."

"But it's such a risk," Donna pointed out. The excited gleam in Shane's eyes had her worrying all the more. She'd seen the same gleam before the beginning of any number of outrageous and wonderful plots. "The expense—"

"I have enough to set things up." Shane shrugged off the pessimism. "And most of my stock can come straight out of the house for now. I want to do it, Donna," she went on as her friend frowned at her. "My own place, my own business." She glanced around the compact, well-stocked store. "You should know what I mean."

"Yes, but I have Dave to help out, to lean on. I don't think I could face starting or managing a business all on my own."

"It's going to work." Her eyes drifted beyond Donna, fixed on their own vision. "I can already see how it's going to look when I'm finished."

"All the remodeling."

"The basic structure of the house will stay the same," Shane countered. "Modifications, repairs." She brushed them away with the back of her hand. "A great deal of it would have to be done if I were simply going to live there."

"Licenses, permits."

"I've applied for everything."

"Taxes."

"I've already seen an accountant." She grinned as Donna sighed. "I have a good location, a solid knowledge of antiques, and I can re-create every battle of the Civil War."

"And do at the least provocation."

"Be careful," Shane warned her, "or I'll give you another rundown on the Battle of Antietam."

When the bells on the door jingled again, Donna heaved an exaggerated sigh of relief. "Hi, Stu."

The next ten minutes were spent in light gossiping as Donna rang up and bagged dry goods. It would take little time to catch up on the news Shane had missed over the last four years.

Shane was accepted as an oddity—the hometown girl who had gone to the city and come back with big ideas. She knew that to the older residents of the town and countryside she would always be Faye Abbott's granddaughter. They were a proprietary people, and she was one of their own. She hadn't settled down and married Cy Trainer's boy as predicted, but she was back now.

"Stu never changes," Donna said when she was alone with Shane again. "Remember in high school when we were sophomores and he was a senior, captain of the football team and the best-looking hunk in a sweaty jersey?"

"And nothing much upstairs," Shane added dryly.

"You always did go for the intellectual type. Hey," she continued before Shane could retort, "I might just have one for you."

"Have one what?"

"An intellectual. At least that's how he strikes me. He's your neighbor too," she added with a growing smile.

"*My* neighbor?"

"He bought the old Farley place. Moved in early last week."

"The Farley place?" Shane's brows arched, giving Donna the satisfaction of knowing she was announcing fresh news. "The house was all but gutted by the fire. Who'd be fool enough to buy that ramshackle barn of a place?"

"Vance Banning," Donna told her. "He's from Washington, D.C."

After considering the implications of this, Shane shrugged. "Well, I suppose it's a choice piece of land even if the house should be condemned." Wandering to a shelf, she selected a pound can of coffee then set it on the counter without checking the price. "I guess he bought it for a tax shelter or something."

"I don't think so." Donna rang up the coffee and waited while Shane dug bills out of her back pocket. "He's fixing it up."

"The courageous type." Absently, she pocketed the loose change.

"All by himself too," Donna added, fussing with the display of candy bars on the counter. "I don't think he has a lot of money to spare. No job."

"Oh." Shane's sympathies were immediately aroused. The spreading problem of unemployment could hit anyone, she knew. Just the year before, the teaching staff at her school had been cut by three percent.

"I heard he's pretty handy though," Donna went on. "Archie Moler went by there a few days ago to take him some lumber. He said he's already replaced the old porch. But the guy's got practically no furniture. Boxes of books, but not much else." Shane was already wondering what she could spare from her own collection. She had a few extra chairs…

"And," Donna added warmly, "he's wonderful to look at."

"You're a married woman," Shane reminded her, clucking her tongue.

"I still like to look. He's tall." Donna sighed. At five foot eight, she appreciated tall men. "And dark with a sort of lived-in face. You know, creases, lots of bone. And shoulders."

"You always did go for shoulders."

Donna only grinned. "He's a little lean for my taste, but the face makes up for it. He keeps to himself, hardly says a word."

"It's hard being a stranger." She spoke from her own experience. "And being out of work too. What do you think—"

Her question was cut off by the jingle of bells. Glancing over, Shane forgot what she had been about to ask.

He was tall, as Donna had said. In the few seconds they

stared at each other, Shane absorbed every aspect of his physical appearance. Lean, yes, but his shoulders were broad, and the arms exposed by the rolled-up shirtsleeves were corded with muscle. His face was tanned, and it narrowed down to a trim, clipped jaw. Thick and straight, his black hair fell carelessly over a high forehead.

His mouth was beautiful. It was full and sharply sculpted, but she knew instinctively it could be cruel. And his eyes, a clear deep blue, were cool. She was certain they could turn to ice. She wouldn't have called it a lived-in face, but a remote one. There was an air of arrogant distance about him. Aloofness seemed to vie with an inner charge of energy.

The spontaneous physical pull was unexpected. In the past, Shane had been attracted to easygoing, good-natured men. This man was neither, she knew, but what she felt was undeniable. For a flash, all that was inside her leaned toward him in a knowledge that was as basic as chemistry and as insubstantial as dreams. Five seconds, it could have been no longer. It didn't need to be.

Shane smiled. He gave her the briefest of acknowledging nods, then walked to the back of the store.

"So, how soon do you think you'll have the place ready to open?" Donna asked Shane brightly with one eye trained toward the rear of the store.

"What?" Shane's mind was still on the man.

"Your place," Donna said meaningfully.

"Oh, three months, I suppose." She glanced blankly around the store as if she had just come in. "There's a lot of work to do."

He came back with a quart of milk and set it on the

counter, then reached for his wallet. Donna rang it up, shooting Shane a look from under her lashes before she gave him his change. He left the store without having spoken a word.

"That," Donna announced grandly, "was Vance Banning."

"Yes." Shane exhaled. "So I gathered."

"You see what I mean. Great to look at, but not exactly the friendly sort."

"No." Shane walked toward the door. "I'll see you later, Donna."

"Shane!" With a half laugh, Donna called after her. "You forgot your coffee."

"Hmm? Oh, no thanks," she murmured absently. "I'll have a cup later."

When the door swung shut, Donna stared at it, then at the can of coffee in her hand. "Now what got into her?" she wondered aloud.

As she walked home, Shane felt confused. Though emotional by nature, she could, when necessary, be very analytical. At the moment, she was dealing with the shock of what had happened to her in a few fleeting seconds. It had been much more than a feminine response to an attractive man.

She had felt, inexplicably, as though her whole life had been a waiting period for that quick, silent meeting. Recognition. The word came to her out of nowhere. She had recognized him, not from Donna's description, but from some deep inner knowledge of her own needs. *This was the man.*

Ridiculous, she told herself. Idiotic. She didn't know him, hadn't even heard him speak. No sensible person felt so strongly about a total stranger. More likely, her response had stemmed from the fact that she and Donna had been speaking of him as he had walked in.

Turning off the main road, she began to climb the steep lane that led to her house. He certainly hadn't been friendly, she thought. He hadn't answered her smile or made the slightest attempt at common courtesy. Something in the cool blue eyes had demanded distance. Shane didn't think he was the kind of man she usually liked. Then again, her reaction had been far removed from the calm emotion of liking.

As always when she saw the house, Shane felt a rush of pleasure. This was hers. The woods, thick and touched with the first breath of autumn; the narrow struggling creek; the rocks that worked their way through the ground everywhere—they were all hers.

Shane stood on the wooden bridge over the creek and looked at the house. It did need work. Some of the boards on the porch needed replacing, and the roof was a big problem. Still, it was a lovely little place, nestled comfortably before woods, rolling hills and distant blue mountains. It was more than a century old, fashioned from local stone. In the rain, the colors would burst out of the old rock and gleam like new. Now, in the sunlight, it was comfortably gray.

The architecture was simple—straight lines for durability rather than style. The walkway ran to the porch, where the first step sagged a bit. Shane's problem wouldn't be with the stone but with the wood. She overlooked the rough edges to take in the beauty of the familiar.

The last of the summer flowers were fading. The roses were brown and withered, while the first fall blooms were coming to life. Shane could hear the hiss of water traveling over rocks, the faint whisper of wind through leaves, and the lazy drone of bees.

Her grandmother had guarded her privacy. Shane could turn a full circle without seeing a sign of another house. She had only to walk a quarter mile if she wanted company, or stay at home if she didn't. After four years of crowded class-rooms and daily confinement, Shane was ready for solitude.

And with luck, she thought as she continued walking, she could have her shop open and ready for business before Christmas. Antietam Antiques and Museum. Very dignified and to the point, she decided. Once the outside repairs were accomplished, work could start on the interior. The picture was clear in her mind.

The first floor would be structured in two informal sections. The museum would be free, an inducement to lure people into the antique shop. Shane had enough from her family collection to begin stocking the museum, and six rooms of antique furniture to sort and list. She would have to go to a few auctions and estate sales to increase her in-ventory, but she felt her inheritance and savings would hold her for a while.

The house and land were hers free and clear, with only the yearly taxes to pay. Her car, for what it was worth, was paid for. Every spare penny could go into her projected business. She was going to be successful and indepen-dent—and the last was more important than the first.

As she walked toward the house, Shane paused and glanced down the overgrown logging trail, which led to the Farley property. She was curious to see what this Vance Banning was doing with the old place. And, she admitted, she wanted to see him again when she was prepared.

After all, they were going to be neighbors, she told herself as she hesitated. The least she could do was to introduce herself and start things off on the right foot. Shane set off into the woods.

She knew the trees intimately. Since childhood she had raced or walked among them. Some had fallen and lay aging and rotting on the ground among layers of old leaves. Overhead, branches arched together to form an intermittent roof pierced by streams of morning sunlight. Confidently she followed the narrow, winding path. She was still yards from the house when she heard the muffled echo of hammering.

Though it disturbed the stillness of the woods, Shane liked the sound. It meant work and progress. Quickening her pace, she headed toward it.

She was still in the cover of the trees when she saw him. He stood on the newly built porch of the old Farley place, hammering the supports for the railing. He'd stripped off his shirt, and his brown skin glistened with a light film of sweat. The dark hair on his chest tapered down, then disappeared into the waistband of worn, snug jeans.

As he lifted the heavy top rail into place, the muscles of his back and shoulders rippled. Totally intent on his work, Vance was unaware of the woman who stood at the edge of the woods and watched. For all his physical exertion, he was relaxed. There was no hardness around his mouth now or frost in his eyes.

When she stepped into the clearing, Vance's head shot up. His eyes instantly filled with annoyance and suspicion. Overlooking it, Shane went to him.

"Hi." Her quick friendly smile had her dimples

flashing. "I'm Shane Abbott. I own the house at the other end of the path."

His brow lifted in acknowledgment as he watched her. What the hell does she want? he wondered, and set his hammer on the rail.

Shane smiled again, then took a long, thorough look at the house. "You've got your work cut out for you," she commented amiably, sticking her hands into the back pockets of her jeans. "Such a big place. They say it was beautiful once. I think there used to be a balcony around the second story."

She glanced up. "It's a shame the fire did so much damage to the inside—and then all the years of neglect." She looked at him then with dark, interested eyes. "Are you a carpenter?"

Vance hesitated briefly, then shrugged. It was close to the truth. "Yes."

"That's handy then." Shane accepted the answer, attributing his hesitation to embarrassment at being out of work. "After D.C. you must find the mountains a change." His mobile brow lifted again and Shane grinned. "I'm sorry. It's the curse of small towns. Word gets around quickly, especially when a flatlander moves in."

"Flatlander?" Vance leaned against the post of the railing.

"You're from the city, so that's what you are." She laughed, a quick bubbling sound. "If you stay for twenty years, you'll still be a flatlander, and this will always be the old Farley place."

"It hardly matters what it's called," he said coldly.

The faintest of frowns shadowed her eyes at his response. Looking at the proud, set face, Shane decided he would never accept open charity. "I'm doing some work on my place too," she began. "My grandmother loved clutter. I don't suppose you could use a couple of chairs? I'm going to have to haul them up to the attic unless someone takes them off my hands."

His eyes stayed level on hers with no change of expression. "I have all I need for now."

Because it was the answer she had expected, Shane treated it lightly. "If you change your mind, they'll be gathering dust in the attic. You've got a good piece of land," she commented, gazing over at the section of pasture in the distance. There were several outbuildings, though most were in desperate need of repair. She wondered if he would see to them before winter set in. "Are you going to have livestock?"

Vance frowned, watching her eyes roam over his property. "Why?"

The question was cold and unfriendly. Shane tried to overlook that. "I can remember when I was a kid, before the fire. I used to lie in bed at night in the summer with the windows open. I could hear the Farley cows as clearly as if they were in my grandmother's garden. It was nice."

"I don't have any plans for livestock," he told her shortly, and picked up his hammer again. The gesture of dismissal was crystal clear.

Puzzled, Shane studied him. Not shy, she concluded. Rude. He was plainly and simply rude. "I'm sorry I disturbed your work," she said coolly. "Since you're a flatlander, I'll give you some advice. You should post your property lines if you don't want trespassers."

Indignantly, Shane strode back to the path to disappear among the trees.

Chapter 2

Little twit, Vance thought as he gently tapped the hammer against his palm. He knew he'd been rude, but felt no particular regret. He hadn't bought an isolated plot of land on the outskirts of a dot on the map because he wanted to entertain. Company he could do without, particularly the blond cheerleader type with big brown eyes and dimples.

What the hell had she been after? he wondered as he drew a nail from the pouch on his hip. A cozy chat? A tour of the house? He gave a quick, mirthless laugh. Very neighborly. Vance pounded the nail through the wood in three sure strokes. He didn't want neighbors. What he wanted, what he intended to have, was time to himself. It had been too many years since he had taken that luxury.

Drawing another nail out of the pouch, he moved down the rail. He set it, then hammered it swiftly into place. In particular, he hadn't cared for the one moment of attraction he had felt when he had seen her in the general store. Women, he thought grimly, had an uncanny habit of taking advantage of a weakness like that. He didn't intend for it to happen to him again. He had plenty of scars to remind him what went on behind big, guileless eyes.

So now I'm a carpenter, he mused. With a sardonic grin, Vance turned his hands palms up and examined them. They were hard and calloused. For too many years, he mused, they had been smooth, used to signing contracts or writing checks. Now for a time, he was back where he had started—with wood. Yes, until he was ready to sit behind a desk again, he was a carpenter.

The house, and the very fact that it was falling to pieces, gave him the sense of purpose that had slipped from him over the last couple of years. He understood pressure, success, duty, but the meaning of simple enjoyment had become lost somewhere beneath the rest.

Let the vice-president of Riverton Construction, Inc., run the show for a few months, he mused. He was on vacation. And let the little blonde with her puppy-dog eyes keep on her own land, he added, pounding in another nail. He didn't want any part of the good-neighbor policy.

When he heard leaves rustling underfoot, Vance turned. Seeing Shane striding back up the path, he muttered a long stream of curses in a low voice. With the exaggerated care of a man greatly aggravated, he set down his hammer.

"Well?" He aimed cold blue eyes and waited.

Shane didn't pause until she had reached the foot of the steps. She was through being intimidated. "I realize you're *extremely* busy," she began, matching his coolness ice for ice, "but I thought you might be interested in knowing there's a nest of copperheads very close to the footpath. On *your* edge of the property," she added.

Vance gave her a narrowed glance, weighing the possibility of her fabricating the snakes to annoy him. She didn't budge under the scrutiny, but paused just long enough to let the silence hang before she turned. She'd gone no more than two more yards when Vance let out an impatient breath and called her back.

"Just a minute. You'll have to show me."

"I don't *have* to do anything," Shane began, but found herself impotently talking to the swinging screen door. Briefly, she wished that she'd never seen the nest, or had simply ignored it and continued down the path to her own home. Then, of course, if he'd been bitten, she would have blamed herself.

Well, you'll do your good deed, she told herself, and that will be that. She kicked a rock with the toe of her shoe and thought how simple it would have been if she'd stayed home that morning.

The screen door shut with a bang. Looking up, Shane watched Vance come down the steps with a well-oiled rifle in his hands. The sleek, elegant weapon suited him. "Let's go," he said shortly, starting off without her. Gritting her teeth, Shane followed.

The light dappled over them once they moved under the cover of trees. The scent of earth and sun-warmed leaves warred with the gun oil. Without a word, Shane skirted around him to take the lead. Pausing, she pointed to a pile of rocks and brown, dried leaves.

"There."

After taking a step closer, Vance spotted the hourglass-shaped crossbands on the snakes. If she hadn't shown him the exact spot, he never would have noticed the nest…unless, of course, he'd stepped right on it. An unpleasant thought, he mused, calculating its proximity to the footpath. Shane said nothing, watching as he found a thick stick and overturned the rocks. Immediately the hissing sounded.

With her eyes trained on the angry snakes, she didn't see Vance heft the rifle to his shoulder. The first shot jolted her. Her heart hammered during the ensuing four, her eyes riveted to the scene.

"That should do it," Vance muttered, lowering the gun. After switching on the safety, he turned to Shane. She'd turned a light shade of green. "What's the matter?"

"You might have warned me," she said shakily. "I wish I'd looked away."

Vance glanced back to the gruesome mess on the side of the path. That, he told himself grimly, had been incredibly stupid. Silently, he cursed her, then himself, before he took her arm.

"Come back and sit down."

"I'll be all right in a minute." Embarrassed and annoyed, Shane tried to pull away. "I don't want your gracious hospitality."

"I don't want you fainting on my land," he returned, drawing her into the clearing. "You didn't have to stay once you'd shown me the nest."

"Oh, you're very welcome," she managed as she placed a hand on her rolling stomach. "You are the most ill-mannered, unfriendly man I've ever met."

"And I thought I was on my best behavior," he

murmured, opening the screen door. After pulling Shane inside, Vance led her through the huge empty room toward the kitchen.

After a glance at the dingy walls and uncovered floor, Shane sent him what passed as a smile. "You must give me the name of your decorator."

She thought he laughed, but could have been mistaken.

The kitchen, in direct contrast to the rest of the house, was bright and clean. The walls had been papered, the counters and cabinets refinished.

"Well, this is nice," she said as he nudged her into a chair. "You do good work."

Without responding, Vance set a kettle on the stove. "I'll fix you some coffee."

"Thank you."

Shane concentrated on the kitchen, determined to forget what she'd just seen. The windows had been reframed, the wood stained and lacquered to match the grooved trim along the floor and ceiling. He had left the beams exposed and polished the wood to a dull gleam. The original oak floor had been sanded and sealed and waxed. Vance Banning knew how to use wood, Shane decided. The porch was basic mechanics, but the kitchen showed a sense of style and an appreciation for fine detail.

It seemed unfair to her that a man with such talent should be out of work. Shane concluded that he had used his savings to put a down payment on the property. Even if the house had sold cheaply, the land was prime. Remembering the barrenness of the rest of the first floor, she couldn't prevent her sympathies from being aroused again. Her eyes wandered to his.

"This really is a lovely room," she said, smiling. The faintest hint of color had seeped back into her cheeks. Vance turned his back to her to take a mug from a hook.

"You'll have to settle for instant," he told her.

Shane sighed. "Mr. Banning… Vance," she decided, and waited for him to turn. "Maybe we got off on the wrong foot. I'm not a nosy, prying neighbor—at least not obnoxiously so. I was curious to see what you were doing to the house and what you were like. I know everyone within three miles of here." With a shrug, she rose. "I didn't mean to bother you."

As she started to brush by him, Vance took her arm. Her skin was still chilled. "Sit down…Shane," he said.

For a moment, she studied his face. It was cool and unyielding, but she sensed some glimmer of suppressed kindness. In response to it, her eyes warmed. "I disguise my coffee with milk and sugar," she warned. "Three spoonsful."

A reluctant smile tugged at his mouth. "That's disgusting."

"Yes, I know. Do you have any?"

"On the counter."

Vance poured the boiling water, and after a moment's hesitation, took down a second mug for himself. Carrying them both, he joined Shane at the drop-leaf table.

"This really is a lovely piece." Before reaching for the milk, she ran her fingers over the table's surface. "Once it's refinished, you'll have a real gem." Shane added three generous spoons of sugar to her mug. Wincing a little, Vance sipped his own black coffee. "Do you know anything about antiques?"

"Not really."

"They're a passion of mine. In fact, I'm planning on opening a shop." Shane brushed absently at the hair that fell over her forehead, then leaned back. "As it turns out, we're both settling in at the same time. I've been living in Baltimore for the last four years, teaching U.S. history."

"You're giving up teaching?" Her hands, Vance noted, were small like the rest of her. The light trail of blue veins under the pale skin made her seem very delicate. Her wrists were narrow, her fingers slender.

"Too many rules and regulations," Shane claimed, gesturing with the hands that had captured his attention.

"You don't like rules and regulations?"

"Only when they're mine." Laughing, she shook her head. "I was a pretty good teacher, really. My problem was discipline." She gave him a rueful grin as she reached for her coffee. "I'm the worst disciplinarian on record."

"And your students took advantage of that?"

Shane rolled her eyes. "Whenever possible."

"But you stuck with it for four years?"

"I had to give it my best shot." Leaning her elbow on the table, Shane rested her chin on her palm. "Like a lot of people who grow up in a small, rural town, I thought the city was my pot of gold. Bright lights, crowds, hustle-bustle. I wanted excitement with a capital *E*. I had four years of it. That was enough." She picked up her coffee again. "Then there are people from the city who think their answer is to move to the country and raise a few goats and can some tomatoes." She laughed into her cup. "The grass is always greener."

"I've heard it said," he murmured, watching her. There were tiny gold flecks in her eyes. How had he missed them before?

"Why did you choose Sharpsburg?"

Vance shrugged negligently. Questions about himself were to be evaded. "I've done some work in Hagerstown. I like the area."

"Living this far back from the main road can be inconvenient, especially in the winter, but I've never minded being snowed in. We lost power once for thirty-two hours. Gran and I kept the woodstove going, taking shifts, and we cooked soup on top of it. The phone lines were down too. We might have been the only two people in the world."

"You enjoyed that?"

"For thirty-two hours," she told him with a friendly grin. "I'm not a hermit. Some people are city people, some are beach people."

"And you're a mountain person."

Shane brought her eyes back to him. "Yes."

The smile she had started to give him never formed. Something in the meeting of their eyes was reminiscent of the moment in the store. It was only an echo, but somehow more disturbing. Shane understood it was bound to happen again and again. She needed time to decide just what she was going to do about it. Rising, she walked to the sink to rinse out her mug.

Intrigued by her reaction, Vance decided to test her. "You're a very attractive woman." He knew how to make his voice softly flattering.

Laughing, Shane turned back to him. "The perfect face for advertising granola bars, right?" Her smile was devilish and appealing. "I'd rather be sexy, but I settled for wholesome." She gave the word a pained emphasis as she came back to the table.

There was no guile in her manner or her expression. What, Vance wondered again, was her angle? Shane was involved in studying the details of the kitchen and didn't see him frown at her.

"I do admire your work." Inspired, she turned back to him. "Hey listen, I've got a lot of remodeling and renovating to do before I can open. I can paint and do some of the minor stuff myself, but there's a lot of carpentry work."

Here it is, Vance reflected coolly. What she wanted was some free labor. She would pull the helpless-female routine and count on his ego to take over.

"I have my own house to renovate," he reminded her coolly as he stood and turned toward the sink.

"Oh, I know you wouldn't be able to give me a lot of time, but we might be able to work something out." Excited by the idea, she followed him. Her thoughts were already racing ahead. "I wouldn't be able to pay what you could make in the city," she continued. "Maybe five dollars an hour. If you could manage ten or fifteen hours a week…" She chewed on her bottom lip. It seemed a paltry amount to offer, but it was all she could spare at the moment.

Incredulous, Vance turned off the water he had been running, then faced her. "Are you offering me a job?"

Shane flushed a bit, afraid she'd embarrassed him. "Well, only part-time, if you're interested. I know you can make more somewhere else, and if you find something, I wouldn't expect you to keep on, but in the meantime…" She trailed off, not certain how he would react to her knowing he was out of work.

"You're serious?" Vance demanded after a moment.

"Well…yes."

"Why?"

"I need a carpenter. You're a carpenter. There's a lot of work. You might decide you don't want any part of it. But why don't you think about it, drop by tomorrow and take a look?" She turned to leave, but paused for an instant with her hand on the knob. "Thanks for the coffee."

For several minutes, Vance stared at the door she had closed behind her. Abruptly, he burst into deep, appreciative laughter. This, he thought, was one for the books.

Shane rose early the next morning. She had plans and was determined to begin systematically. Organization didn't come naturally to her. It was one more reason why teaching hadn't suited her. If she was to plan a business, however, Shane knew an inventory was a primary factor— what she had, what she could bear to sell, what she should pack away for the museum.

Having decided to start downstairs and work her way up, Shane stood in the center of the living room and took stock of the situation. There was a good Chippendale fireplace seat in mahogany and a gateleg table that needed no refinishing, a ladderback chair that needed new caning in the seat, a pair of Aladdin lamps, and a tufted sofa that would require upholstering. On a Sheridan coffee table was a porcelain pitcher, circa 1830, that held a spray of flowers Shane's grandmother had dried. She touched them once briefly before she picked up her clipboard. There was too much of her childhood there to allow herself the luxury of thinking of any of it. If her grandmother had been alive, she would have told Shane to be certain what she did was right, then do it. Shane was certain she was right.

Systematically, she listed items in two columns: one for items that would need repairs; one for stock she could sell as it was. Everything would have to be priced, which would be a huge job in itself. Already she was spending her evenings poring through catalogs and making notations. There wasn't an antique shop within a radius of thirty miles she hadn't visited. Shane had taken careful account of pricing and procedure. She would incorporate what appealed to her and disregard what didn't. Whatever else her shop would be, she was determined it would be her own.

On one wall of the living room was a catchall shelf that had been built before she'd been born. Moving to it, Shane began a fresh sheet of items she designated for the museum.

An ancestor's Civil War cap and belt buckle, a glass jar filled with spent shells, a dented bugle, a cavalry officer's sabre, a canteen with the initials JDA scratched into the metal—these were only a few pieces of the memorabilia that had been passed down to her. Shane knew there was a trunk in the attic filled with uniforms and old dresses. There was a scrawled journal that had been kept by one of her great-great-uncles during the three years he fought for the South, and letters written to an ancestral aunt by her father, who had served the North. Every item would be listed, dated, then put behind glass.

Shane might have inherited her grandmother's fascination for the relics of history, but not her casualness. It was time the old photos and objects came down from the shelf. But as always when she examined or handled the pieces, Shane became caught up in them.

What had the man been like who had first blown that bugle? It would have been shiny then, and undented. A boy, she thought, with peach fuzz on his face. Had he been frightened? Exhilarated? Fresh off the farm, she imagined, and sure his cause was the right one. Whichever side he had fought for, he had blown the bugle into battle.

With a sigh, she took it down and set it in a packing box. Carefully, Shane wrapped and packed until the shelves were clear, but for the highest one. Standing back, she calculated how she would reach the pieces that sat several feet above her head. Not bothering to move the heavy ladder from across the room, she dragged over a nearby chair. As she stood on the seat, a knock sounded at the back door.

"Yes, come in," she called, stretching one arm up while balancing herself with a hand on one of the lower shelves. She swore and muttered as her reach still fell short. Just as she stood on tiptoe, teetering, someone grabbed her arm. Gasping as she overbalanced, Shane found herself gripped firmly by Vance Banning. "You scared me to death!" she accused.

"Don't you know better than to use a chair like that?" He kept his hands firmly at her waist as he lifted her down. Then, though he'd had every intention of doing so, he didn't release her. There was a smudge of dust on her cheek, and her hair was tousled. Her small, narrow hands rested on his arms while she smiled up at him. Without thinking, Vance lowered his mouth to hers.

Shane didn't struggle, but felt a jolt of surprise. Then she relaxed. Though she hadn't expected the kiss then, she had known the time would come. She let the first stream of pure pleasure run its course.

His mouth was hard on hers, with no gentleness, no trace of what kissing meant to her—a gesture of affection, love or comfort. Yet instinct told her he was capable of tenderness. Lifting a hand to his cheek, Shane sought to soothe the turbulence she sensed. Immediately, he released her. The touch of her hand had been too intimate.

Something told Shane to treat it lightly no matter how her body ached to be held again. Tilting her head, she gave him a mischievous smile. "Good morning."

"Good morning," he said carefully.

"I'm taking inventory," she told him with a sweeping gesture of the room. "I want to list everything before I haul it upstairs for storage. I plan to use this room for the museum and the rest of the first floor for the shop. Could you get those things off the top shelf for me?" she asked, looking around for her clipboard.

In silence, Vance moved the ladder and complied. The fact that she'd made no mention of the turbulent kiss disconcerted him.

"Most of the work will be gutting the kitchen and putting one in upstairs," Shane went on, giving her lists another glance. She knew Vance was watching her for some sort of reaction. She was just as determined to give him none. "Of course, some walls will have to be taken out, doorways widened. But I don't want to lose the flavor of the house in the remodeling."

"You seem to have it all plotted out." Was she really so cool? he wondered.

"I hope so." Shane pressed the clipboard to her breasts as she looked around the room. "I've applied for all the necessary permits. What a headache. I don't have any natural business sense, so I'll have to work twice as hard learning. It's a big chance." Then her voice changed, became firm and determined. "I'm going to make it work."

"When do you plan to open?"

"I'm shooting for the first part of December, but…" Shane shrugged. "It depends on how the work goes and how soon I can beef up my inventory. I'll show you the rest of the place. Then you can decide if you want to take it on."

Without waiting for his consent, Shane walked to the rear of the house. "The kitchen's a fairly good size, particularly if you include the pantry." Opening a door, she revealed a large shelved closet. "Taking out the counters and appliances should give me plenty of room. Then if this doorway is widened," she continued as she pushed open a swinging door, "and left as an archway, it would give more space in the main showroom."

They entered the dining room with its long diamond-paned windows. She moved quickly, he noted, and knew precisely what she wanted.

"The fireplace hasn't been used in years. I don't know whether it still works." Walking over, Shane ran a finger down the surface of the dining table. "This was my grandmother's prize. It was brought over from England more than a hundred years ago." The cherrywood stroked by sunlight, gleamed under her fingers. "The chairs are from the original set. Hepplewhite." Shane caressed the heart-shaped back of one of the remaining six chairs. "I hate to sell this, she loved it so, but…" Her voice was wistful as she unnecessarily straightened a chair. "I won't have anywhere to keep it, and I can't afford the luxury of storing it for myself." Shane turned away. "The china cabinet is from the same period," she continued.

"You could keep this and leave the house as it is if you took a job in the local high school," Vance interrupted.

There was something valiant and touching in the way she kept her shoulders straight while her voice trembled.

"No." Shane shook her head, then turned back to him. "I haven't the character for it. It wouldn't take long before I'd be cutting classes just like my students. They deserve a better example than that. I love history." Her face brightened again. "*This* kind of history," she said as she walked back to the table. "Who first sat in this chair? What did she talk about over dinner? What kind of dress did she wear? Did they discuss politics and the upstart colonies? Maybe one of them knew Ben Franklin and was a secret sympathizer of the Revolution." She broke off laughing. "That's not the sort of thing you're supposed to teach in second-period eleventh-grade history."

"It sounds more interesting than reciting names and dates."

"Maybe. Anyway, I'm not going back to that." Pausing, Shane watched Vance steadily. "Did you ever find yourself caught up in something you were good at, something you'd been certain was the right thing for you, then woke up one morning with the feeling you were locked in a cage?"

The words hit home, and he nodded affirmatively.

"Then you know why I have to choose between something I love and my sanity." She touched the table again. After a deep breath, Shane took a circle around the room. "I don't want to change the architecture of this room except for the doorways. My great-grandfather built the chair rail." She watched Vance walk over to examine it. "He was a mason by trade," she told him, "but he must have been handy with wood as well."

"It's a beautiful job," Vance agreed, admiring the workmanship and detail. "I'd have a hard time duplicating this quality with modern tools. You wouldn't want to touch this, or any of the woodwork in this room."

In spite of himself he was becoming interested in the project. It would be a challenge—a different sort than the house he had chosen to test himself on. Sensing his change of attitude, Shane pressed her advantage.

"There's a small summer parlor through there." Indicating another door, she took Vance's arm to draw him with her. "It adjoins the living room, so I plan to make it the entrance to the shop, with the dining room as the main showroom."

The parlor was no more than twelve by twelve with faded wallpaper and a scarred wooden floor. Still, Vance recognized a few good pieces of Duncan Phyfe and a Morris chair. On the brief tour, he had seen no furniture less than a hundred years old, and unless they were excellent copies, a few pieces of Wedgwood. The furniture's worth a small fortune, he mused, and the back door's coming off the hinges.

"There's a lot of work here," Shane commented, moving over to open a window and dispel the faint mustiness. "This room's taken a beating over the years. I suppose you'd have a better idea than I would exactly what it needs to whip it into shape."

She watched his frowning survey of chipped floorboards and cracked trim. It was obvious to her that his professional eye missed little. It was also obvious the state of disrepair annoyed him. And, she thought, faintly amused, he hadn't seen anything yet.

"Maybe I shouldn't press my luck and take you upstairs just yet," she commented.

A quizzical brow shot up as he turned to her. "Why?"

"Because the second floor needs twice the attention this does, and I really want you to take the job."

"You sure as hell need somebody to do it," he muttered. His own place needed a major overhaul. Heavy physical work and a lot of time. This, on the other hand, needed a shrewd craftsman who could work with what was already there. Again, he felt the pull of the challenge.

"Vance…" After a moment's hesitation, Shane decided to take a chance. "I could make it six dollars an hour, throw in your lunches and all the coffee you can drink. The people who come in here will see the quality of your work. It could lead to bigger jobs."

He surprised her by grinning. Her heart leaped into her throat. More than the tempestuous kiss, the quick boyish grin drew her to him.

"All right, Shane," Vance agreed on impulse. "You've got a deal."

Chapter 3

Pleased with herself and Vance's abrupt good humor, Shane decided to show him the second floor. Taking his hand, she led him up the straight, steep stairway. Though she had no notion of what had prompted the amused gleam or sudden grin, Shane wanted to keep him with her while his mood lasted.

Against his work-hardened hand, her palm was baby soft. It made Vance wonder how the rest of her would feel—the slope of her shoulder, the length of her thigh, the underside of her breast. She wasn't his type, he reminded himself, and glanced at the hairline crack in the wall to his left.

"There are three bedrooms," Shane told him as they came to the top landing. "I want to keep my own room, and turn the master into a sitting room and the third into my kitchen. I can handle the painting and papering after the initial work is done." With her hand on the knob of the master bedroom door, she turned to him. "Do you know anything about drywall?"

"A bit." Without thinking, Vance lifted a finger and ran it down her nose. Their eyes met in mutual surprise. "You've dust on your face," he mumbled.

"Oh." Laughing, Shane brushed at it herself.

"Here." Vance traced the rough skin of his thumb down her cheekbone. Her skin felt as it looked: soft, creamy. It would taste the same, he mused, allowing his thumb to linger. "And here," he said, caught up in his own imagination. Lightly he ran a fingertip along her jawline. He felt her slight tremor as his gaze swept over her lips.

Her eyes were wide and fixed unblinkingly on his. Abruptly, Vance dropped his hand, shattering the mood but not the tension. Clearing her throat, Shane pushed open the door.

"This—umm…" Frantically, Shane gathered her scattered thoughts. "This is the master," she continued, combing nervous fingers through her hair. "I know the floor's in bad shape, and I'd like to skin whoever painted that oak trim." She let out a long breath as her pulse began to level. "I'm going to see if it can be refinished." Idly, she touched a section of peeling wallpaper. "My grandmother didn't like changes. This room hasn't altered one bit in thirty years. That's when her husband died," she added softly. "The windows stick, the roof leaks, the fireplace smokes. Basically, the house, except for the dining room, is in a general state of disrepair. She never had the inclination to do more than a patch job here and there."

"When did she die?"

"Three months ago." Shane lifted a corner of the patch-work coverlet, then let it fall. "She just didn't wake up one morning. I was committed to teaching a summer course and couldn't move back permanently until last week."

Clearly, he heard the sting of guilt in her words. "Could you have changed anything if you had?" he asked.

"No." Shane wandered to a window. "But she wouldn't have died alone."

Vance opened his mouth, then closed it again. It wasn't wise to offer personal advice to strangers. Framed against the window, she looked very small and defenseless.

"What about the walls in here?" he asked.

"What?" Years and miles away, Shane turned back to him.

"The walls," he repeated. "Do you want any of them taken down?"

For a moment, she stared blankly at the faded roses on the wallpaper. "No... No," she repeated more firmly. "I'd thought to take out the door and enlarge the entrance." Vance nodded, noting she had won what must be a continuing battle with her emotions. "If the woodwork cleans off well," she continued, "the entrance could be framed in oak to match."

Vance walked over to examine it. "Is this a bearing wall?"

Shane made a face at him. "I haven't the slightest idea. How do—" She broke off, hearing a knock at the front door. "Damn. Well, can you look around up here for a few minutes? You'll probably get the lay of things just as well without me." With this, Shane was dashing down the steps. Shrugging, Vance took a rule out of his back pocket and began to take measurements.

Shane's instinctively friendly smile faded instantly when she opened the door.

"Shane."

"Cy."

His expression became faintly censorious. "Aren't you going to ask me in?"

"Of course." With a restraint unnatural to her, Shane stepped back. Very carefully, she shut the door behind him, but moved no farther into the room. "How are you, Cy?"

"Fine, just fine."

Of course he was, Shane thought, annoyed. Cy Trainer Jr., was always fine—permanent-pressed and groomed. And prosperous now, she added, giving his smart-but-discreet suit a glance.

"And you, Shane?"

"Fine, just fine," she said, knowing the sarcasm was both petty and wasted. He'd never notice.

"I'm sorry I didn't get by last week. Things have been hectic."

"Business is good?" she asked without any intonation of interest. He failed to notice that too.

"Money's loosening up." He straightened his tie unnecessarily. "People are buying houses. Country property's always a good investment." He gave her a quick nod. "The real estate business is solid."

Money was still first, Shane noticed with irony. "And your father?"

"Doing well. Semiretired now, you know."

"No," she said mildly. "I didn't." If Cy Trainer Sr. relinquished the reins to Trainer Real Estate six months after he was dead, it would have surprised Shane. The old man would always run the show, no matter what his son liked to think.

"He likes to keep busy," Cy told her. "He'd love to see you though. You'll have to drop by the office." Shane said nothing to that. "So…" Cy paused as he was wont to do before a big statement. "You're settling in."

Shane lifted a brow as she watched him glance around at her packing cases. "Slowly," she agreed. Though she knew it was deliberately rude, she didn't ask him to sit. They remained standing, just inside the door.

"You know, Shane, this house isn't in the best of shape, but it is a prime location." He gave her a light, condescending smile that set her teeth on edge. "I'm sure I could get you a good price for it."

"I'm not interested in selling, Cy. Is that why you came by? To do an appraisal?"

He looked suitably shocked. "Shane!"

"Was there something else?" she asked evenly.

"I just dropped by to see how you were." The distress in both his voice and eyes had an apology forming on her lips. "I heard some crazy story about your trying to start an antique shop."

The apology slipped away. "It's not a story, crazy or otherwise, Cy. I am going to start one."

He sighed and gave her what she termed his paternal look. She gritted her teeth. "Shane, have you any idea how difficult, how risky it is to start a business in today's economy?"

"I'm sure you'll tell me," she muttered.

"My dear," he said in calm tones, making her blood pressure rise alarmingly. "You're a certified teacher with four years' experience. It's just nonsense to toss away a good career for a fanciful little fling."

"I've always been good at nonsense, haven't I, Cy?" Her

eyes chilled. "You never hesitated to point it out to me even when we were supposed to be madly in love."

"Now, Shane, it was because I cared that I tried to curb your…impulses."

"Curb my impulses!" More astonished than angry, Shane ran her fingers through her hair. Later, she told herself, later she would be able to laugh. Now she wanted to scream. "You haven't changed. You haven't changed a whit. I bet you still roll your socks into those neat little balls and carry an extra handkerchief."

He stiffened a bit. "If you'd ever learned the value of practicality—" he began.

"You wouldn't have dumped me two months before the wedding?" she finished furiously.

"Really, Shane, you can hardly call it that. You know I was only thinking of what was best for you."

"Best for me," she muttered between clenched teeth. "Well, let me tell you something." She poked a dusty finger at his muted striped tie. "You can stuff your practicality, Cy, right along with your balanced checkbook and shoe trees. I might have thought you hurt me at the time, but you did me a big favor. I *hate* practicality and rooms that smell like pine and toothpaste tubes that are rolled up from the bottom."

"I hardly see what that has to do with this discussion."

"It has *everything* to do with this discussion," she flared back. "You don't see anything unless it's listed in neat columns and balanced. And I'll tell you something else," she continued when he would have spoken. "I'm going to have my shop, and even if it doesn't make me a fortune, it's going to be fun."

"Fun?" Cy shook his head hopelessly. "That's a poor basis for starting a business."

"It's mine," she retorted. "I don't need a six-digit income to be happy."

He gave her a small, deprecating smile. "You haven't changed."

Flinging open the door, Shane glared at him. "Go sell a house," she suggested. With a dignity she envied and despised, Cy walked through the door. She slammed it after him, then gave in to temper and slammed her hand against the wall.

"Damn!" Putting her wounded knuckles to her mouth, she whirled. It was then she spotted Vance at the foot of the stairs. His face was still and serious as their eyes met. With angry embarrassment, Shane's cheeks flamed. "Enjoy the show?" she demanded, then stormed back to the kitchen.

She gave vent to her frustration by banging through the cupboards. She didn't hear Vance follow her. When he touched her shoulder, she spun around, ready to rage.

"Let me see your hand," he said quietly. Ignoring her jerk of protest, he took it in both of his.

"It's nothing."

Gently, he flexed it, then pressed down on her knuckles with his fingers. Involuntarily, she caught her breath at the quick pain. "You didn't manage to break it," he murmured, "but you'll have a bruise." He was forced to control a sudden rage that she had damaged that small, soft hand.

"Just don't say anything," she ordered through gritted teeth. "I'm not stupid. I *know* when I've made a fool of myself."

He took a moment to bend and straighten her fingers

again. "I apologize," he said. "I should have let you know I was there."

After letting out a deep breath, Shane drew her hand from his slackened hold. The light throbbing gave her a perverse pleasure. "It doesn't matter," she muttered as she turned to make tea.

He frowned at her averted face. "I don't enjoy embarrassing you."

"If you live here for any amount of time, you'll hear about Cy and me anyway." She tried to make a casual shrug, but the quick jerkiness of the movement showed only more agitation. "This way you just got the picture quicker."

But he didn't have the full picture. Vance realized, with some discomfort, that he wanted to know. Before he could speak, Shane slammed the lid onto the kettle.

"He always makes me feel like a fool!"

"Why?"

"He always dots his *i*'s and crosses his *t*'s." With an angry tug, she pulled open a cabinet. "He carries an umbrella in the trunk of his car," she said wrathfully.

"That should do it," Vance murmured, watching her quick, jerky movements.

"He never, never, *never* makes a mistake. He's always reasonable," she added witheringly as she slammed two cups down on the counter. "Did he shout at me just now?" she demanded as she whirled on Vance. "Did he swear or lose his temper? He doesn't *have* a temper!" she shouted in frustration. "I swear, the man doesn't even sweat."

"Did you love him?"

For a moment, Shane merely stared; then she let out a small broken sigh. "Yes. Yes, I really did. I was sixteen when we started dating." As she went to the refrigerator, Vance turned the gas on under the kettle, which she had forgotten to do. "He was so perfect, so smart and, oh…so articulate." Pulling out the milk, Shane smiled a little. "Cy's a born salesman. He can talk about anything."

Vance felt a quick, unreasonable dislike for him. As Shane set a large ceramic sugar bowl on the table, sunlight shot into her hair. The curls and waves of her hair shimmered briefly in the brilliance before she moved away. With an odd tingling at the base of his spine, Vance found himself staring after her.

"I was crazy about him," Shane continued, and Vance had to shake himself mentally to concentrate on her words. The subtle movements of her body beneath the snug T-shirt had begun to distract him. "When I turned eighteen, he asked me to marry him. We were both going to college, and Cy thought a year's engagement was proper. He's very proper," she added ruefully.

Or a cold-blooded fool, Vance thought, glancing at the faint outline of her nipples against the thin cotton. Annoyed, he brought his eyes back to her face. But the warmth in his own blood remained.

"I wanted to get married right away, but he told me, as always, that I was too impulsive. Marriage was a big step. Things had to be planned out. When I suggested we live together for a while, he was shocked." Shane set the milk on the table with a little bang. "I was young and in love, and I wanted him. He felt it his duty to control my more…primitive urges."

"He's a damn fool," Vance muttered under the hissing of the kettle.

"Through that last year, he molded me, and I tried to be what he wanted: dignified, sensible. I was a complete failure." Shane shook her head at the memory of that long, frustrating year. "If I wanted to go out for pizza with a bunch of other students, he'd remind me we had to watch our pennies. He already had his eye on this little house outside of Boonsboro. His father said it was a good investment."

"And you hated it," Vance commented.

Surprised, Shane looked back at him. "I despised it. It was the perfect little rancher with white aluminum siding and a hedge. When I told Cy I'd smother there, he laughed and patted my head."

"Why didn't you tell him to get lost?" he demanded.

Shane shot him a brief look. "Haven't you ever been in love?" she murmured. It was her answer, not a question, and Vance remained silent. "We were constantly at odds that year," she went on. "I kept thinking it was just the jitters of a long engagement, but more and more, the basic personality conflicts came up. He'd always say I'd feel differently once we were settled. Usually, I'd believe him."

"He sounds like a boring jackass."

Though the icy contempt in Vance's voice surprised her, Shane smiled. "Maybe, but he could be gentle and sweet." When Vance gave a derisive snort, she only shrugged. "I'd forget how rigid he was. Then he'd get more critical. I'd get angry, but I could never win a fight because he never lost control. The final break came over the plans for the honeymoon. I wanted to go to Fiji."

"Fiji?" Vance repeated.

"Yes," she said defiantly. "It's different, exotic, romantic. I was barely nineteen." On a fresh wave of fury,

Shane slammed down her spoon. "He had plans for this—this plastic little resort hotel in Pennsylvania. The kind of place where they plan your activities, have contests and an indoor pool. Shuffleboard." She rolled her eyes before she gulped down tea. "It was a package deal—three days, two nights, meals included. He'd inherited a substantial sum from his mother, and I had some savings, but he didn't want to waste money. He'd already outlined a retirement plan. I couldn't stand it!"

Vance sipped his own tea where he stood and studied her. "So you called off the wedding." He wondered if she would take the opportunity he was giving her to claim the break had been her idea.

"No." Shane pushed her cup aside. "We had a terrible fight, and I stormed off to spend the rest of the evening with friends at this little club near the college. I had told Cy I wouldn't spend my first night as a married woman watching a tacky floor show or playing bingo."

Vance's lips twitched but he managed to control his grin. "That sounds remarkably sensible," he murmured.

On a weak laugh, Shane shook her head. "After I'd calmed down, I decided where we went wasn't important, but that we'd finally be together. I told myself Cy was right. I was immature and irresponsible. We needed to save money. I still had two more years of college and he was just starting in his father's firm. I was being frivolous. That was one of his favorite adjectives for me."

Shane frowned down at her cup but didn't drink. "I went by his house ready to apologize. That's when he very reasonably, very calmly jilted me."

There was a long moment of silence before Vance came

to the table to join her. "I thought you told me he never made mistakes."

Shane stared at him a moment, then laughed. It was a quick, pure sound of appreciation. "I needed that." Impulsively, she leaned her head against his shoulder. The anger had vanished in the telling, the self-pity with the laugh.

The tenderness that invaded him made Vance cautious. Still, he didn't resist the urge to stroke his hand down her disordered cap of hair. The texture of her hair was thick and unruly. And incredibly soft. He wasn't even aware that he twisted a curl around his finger.

"Do you still love him?" he heard himself ask.

"No," Shane answered before he could retract the question. "But he still makes me feel like an irresponsible romantic."

"Are you?"

She shrugged. "Most of the time."

"What you said to him out there was right, you know." Forgetting caution in simple wanting, he drew her closer.

"I said a lot of things."

"That he'd done you a favor," Vance murmured as his fingers roamed to the back of her neck. Shane sighed, but he couldn't tell if the sound came from pleasure or agreement. "You'd have gone crazy rolling up his socks in those little balls."

Shane was laughing as she tilted her head back to look at his face. She kissed him lightly in gratitude, then again for herself.

Her mouth was small and very tempting. Wanting his fill, Vance cupped his hand firmly on the back of her neck to keep her there. There was nothing shy or hesitant in her response to the increased pressure. She parted her lips and invited.

On a tiny moan of pleasure, her tongue met his. Suddenly hot, suddenly urgent, his mouth moved over hers. He needed her sweetness, her uncomplicated generosity. He wanted to saturate himself with the fresh, clean passion she offered so willingly. When his mouth crushed down harder, she only yielded; when his teeth nipped painfully at her lip, she only drew him closer.

"Vance," she murmured, leaning toward him.

He rose quickly, leaving her blinking in surprise. "I've got work to do," he said shortly. "I'll make a list of the materials I'll need to start. I'll be in touch." He was out the back door before Shane could form any response.

For several moments, she stared at the screen door. What had she done to cause that anger in his eyes? How was it possible that he could passionately kiss her one second and turn his back on her the next? Miserably, she looked down at her clenched hands. She had always made too much of things, she reminded herself. A romantic? Yes, and a dreamer, her grandmother had called her. For too long she'd been waiting for the right man to come into her life, to complete it. She wanted to be cherished, respected, adored.

Perhaps, she mused, she was looking for the impossible—to keep her independence and to share her dreams, to stand on her own and have a strong hand to hold. Over and over she had warned herself to stop looking for that one perfect love. But her spirit defied her mind.

From the first instant, she had sensed something different about Vance. For the flash of a second when their eyes had first held, her heart had opened and shouted. *Here he is!* But that was nonsense, Shane reminded herself. Love meant understanding, knowledge. She neither knew nor understood Vance Banning.

With a jolt, she realized she might have offended him. She was going to be his employer, and the way she had kissed him…he might think she wanted more than carpentry for her money. He might think she intended to seduce him while dangling a few much-needed dollars under his nose.

Abruptly, she burst into laughter. As her mirth grew, she threw back her head and pounded both fists on the table. Shane Abbott, seductress. Oh Lord! she thought, wiping tears of hilarity from her eyes. That was rich. After all, what red-blooded man could withstand a woman with dirt on her face who tries to punch holes in walls?

She sighed with the effort of laughing. Her imagination, she decided, needed a rest. Shane went back to her inventory.

Chapter 4

Vance couldn't sleep. He had worked until late in the evening, sweating off anger and frustrated desire. The anger didn't worry him. He knew that emotion too well to lose sleep over it. Neither was he a stranger to desire, but having to acknowledge he felt it for a snippy little history buff infuriated him…and made him restless.

He should never have agreed to take the job, he told himself yet again. What devil had provoked him into doing it? Annoyed with himself, Vance wandered outside to stand on the porch.

The air had cooled considerably with nightfall. Overhead, the stars were spread in a wide, brilliant pattern around a white half-moon. Venus was as clear as he'd ever seen it. An army of crickets sent out their high, monotonous signal while fireflies danced, tiny yellow lights, over the fallow field to his right. When he looked straight ahead, he could see to the edge of the trees but no farther. The woods were dark, mysterious, secret. Shane slept on the other side in a room with faded wallpaper and a Jenny Lind bed.

He imagined her cuddled under the wedding-ring quilt he'd seen on the bed. Her window would be open to let in the sounds and scents of night. Did she sleep in one of those fussy cotton nightgowns that would cover her from neck to feet, he wondered, or would she slip under the quilt in solitary nakedness?

Furious with the direction of his thoughts, Vance cursed himself. No, he should never have taken the damn job. It had appealed to his ego and his humor. Six dollars an hour. He laughed shortly, startling an owl in a nearby tree. Leaning on a post, he continued to stare into the woods, seeing nothing but silhouettes and shadows.

When was the last time he'd worked for an hourly wage? To answer his own question, Vance looked back, trying to remember. Fifteen years? Good God, he thought with a shake of his head. Had so much time passed?

He'd been a teenager starting out at the bottom of his mother's highly successful construction firm. "Learn the ropes," she had told him, and he'd eagerly agreed. Vance had wanted nothing more than to work with his hands, and with wood. He'd had his share of youthful confidence—and youthful arrogance. Administration was for old men in business suits who wouldn't know how to miter a corner. He'd wanted no part of their stuffy business meetings or complicated contract negotiations. Shuffle papers? No, he was too clever to fall into that trap.

How long had it taken before he had been pulled in—

chained behind a desk? Five years? he thought. Six? With a shrug, he decided it didn't matter. He'd gone beyond the time when a year made much difference.

Sighing, Vance walked the length of the porch. Under his hand, the rail he had built himself was rough and sturdy. What choice had there been? he asked himself. There had been his mother's sudden stroke and long painful recovery. She had begged him to take over as president of Riverton. As a widow with only one child, she had been desperate not to see her business run by strangers. It had mattered to her, perhaps too much, that the firm she had inherited, had struggled to keep during the lean years, stay in the family. Vance knew that she had fought prejudices, taken chances and worked nearly half her life to turn a mediocre firm into an exemplary one. Then she had been all but helpless, and asking him.

If he had been a failure at it, he could have delegated the responsibilities and stayed a figurehead without a qualm. He could have picked up his tools again. But he hadn't been a failure—there was too much of his mother in him.

Riverton Construction had thrived and expanded under his leadership. It had grown beyond the prestigious Washington concern into a national conglomerate. It was his own misfortune that he had the same knack with administration that he had with a hammer. He had bolted the lock on his own cage.

Then there had been Amelia. Vance's mouth tightened into a cynical smile. Soft, sexy Amelia, he mused, with hair like a sunset and a quiet Virginia drawl. She had kept him yapping at her heels for months, drawing him in, holding him off, until he had been mad to have her. Mad, Vance thought again. A very apt word. If he had been sane, he would have seen through that beautiful, cultured mask to the calculating scrambler she had been—before he had put the ring on her finger.

Not for the first time, he wondered how many men had envied him his lovely, dignified wife. But they hadn't seen the face unmasked—the perfect face with a rotted shell beneath. Cold. In all of his experience, Vance had known no one as cold as Amelia Ryce Banning.

The owl in the oak to his left set up a steady hooting: two short calls then a long—two short, then a long. Vance listened to the monotonous sound as he thought over the years of his marriage.

Amelia had spent his money lavishly those first months—clothes, furs, cars. That had mattered little to him as he had felt her unearthly beauty demanded the finest. And he had loved her—or the woman he had thought she'd been. He had thought she was a woman made for diamonds, for soft, exotic furs and silks. It had pleased him to surround her with them, to see her sulky beauty glow. For the most part, he had ignored the excessive bills, paying them without a murmur. Once or twice he had commented on her extravagance and had received her sweet distress and apologies. He'd hardly noticed that the bills had continued to flow in.

Then he had discovered she was draining his bank account to feed her brother's teetering construction firm in Richmond. Amelia had been tearful and helpless when confronted with it. She had pleaded prettily for her brother. She had claimed she couldn't bear to have him almost facing bankruptcy while she lived so well.

Because he'd believed her familial concern, Vance had agreed to a personal loan, but he'd refused to siphon money from Riverton into an unstable and mishandled company. Amelia had been far from satisfied, had pouted and cajoled. Then when he'd remained adamant, she had attacked him like a crazed tigress, raking his face with her well-manicured nails, spewing out obscenities through her tinted cupid's-bow mouth. Her anger had driven her to strike out and tell him why she had married him—for his money and position, and what both could do for her and her own family business. Then Vance had looked beneath the beauty and the careful charm to see what she was. It had been only the first of many shocks and disillusionments.

Her warm passion had become frigidity; her adoring smiles had become sneers. She had refused to consider having children. It would have spoiled her figure and restricted her freedom. For more than two years Vance had struggled to save his failing marriage, to salvage something of the life he had planned to have with Amelia. But he had come to know that the woman he thought he had married was an illusion.

Ultimately, he'd demanded a divorce and Amelia had laughed and agreed. She would happily give him his freedom for half of everything he owned—including his share of Riverton. She had promised him an ugly court battle and plenty of publicity. After pointing out that she would be the injured party, Amelia had vowed to play her part of the cast-off wife to the hilt.

Trapped, Vance had lived with her for another year, keeping up the pretense of marriage in public, avoiding her privately. When he had discovered Amelia was taking lovers, he'd seen the first ray of hope.

He had felt no pain on being betrayed, for there had been no emotion in him for her. Slowly, discreetly, Vance had begun to compile the evidence that would give him his freedom. He was willing to face the humiliation and publicity of a messy court battle to free himself and his company. Then there had been no more need. One of Amelia's discarded lovers put a bullet through her heart and ended it.

It had been due to Vance's wealth and influence that the publicity hadn't been worse than it had been. Still, the whispers and speculation had been ugly enough. Yet there had been a staggering relief in him rather than grief. The guilt this had brought had caused him to bury himself even more in his work. There were condominiums to be built in Florida, a large medical complex in Minnesota, an addition to a university in Texas. But there had been no peace for him.

Determined to find Vance Banning again, he'd bought the dilapidated house in the mountains and had taken an extended leave of absence. Time, solitude and the work he loved had been his prescription. Then, just when he had thought he had found the answer, he had met Shane Abbott.

She was no smoldering hothouse beauty as Amelia had been, no poised sophisticate as were the women he had taken to his bed over the last two years. She was fresh and vital. Instinctively, he was attracted to her good-natured generosity. But his wife's legacy to him had been cynicism and distrust. Vance knew that only a fool fell for the innocent act twice. And he was no fool.

He had taken the job with Shane on impulse, and now he would see it through. It would be a challenge to learn if he was still capable of the fine precision work she required. And he knew how to be cautious with a woman now. It was true her fresh looks and artless charm had appealed to him. He admired her way of dealing with her former fiancé. She'd been hurt, yet she had held her own and booted Cy out the door.

It might be interesting, he decided, to spend his vacation remodeling Shane's house and learning what she hid under her mask. Everyone wore masks, he thought grimly. Life was one long masquerade. It wouldn't take long to discover what went on behind her big brown eyes and bubbling laugh.

With a sound of disgust, Vance hurled himself back into the house. He wasn't going to lose any sleep over a woman. Nevertheless, he tossed and turned much of the night.

It was a perfect morning. In the west, the mountains rose into a paintbrush blue sky. Birds chattered in noisy jubilation as Shane tossed open the windows. The air that rushed in was warm, laced with the scent of zinnias. It was all but impossible for one of her nature to remain inside on such a day, cooped up with dust and a clipboard. But there were ways, Shane decided as she leaned on the windowsill, of doing her duty *and* having fun.

After dressing in an old T-shirt and faded red shorts, she rummaged through the basement storage closet and unearthed a can of white paint and a roller. The front porch, she knew, needed more repair than her meager talents could provide, but the back was still sturdy enough. All it required was a coat or two of paint to make it bright and cheerful again.

Picking up a portable radio on her way, Shane headed outside. She fiddled with the tuner until she found a station that matched her mood; then, after turning the volume up, she went to work.

In thirty minutes, the porch was swept clean and hosed down. In the bright sun, it dried quickly while Shane pried the lid off the paint can. She stirred it, enjoying the day and the prospect of work. Once or twice, she glanced toward the old logging path, wondering when Vance would "keep in touch." She would have liked to have seen him coming down the path toward her. He had a long, loose-limbed stride she admired, and a way of looking as though he were in complete command of himself and anything that might get in his way. Shane liked that—the confidence, the hint of controlled power.

She had always admired people of strength. Her grandmother, through all her hardships and disappointments, had remained a strong woman right to the end. Shane would have admitted, for all their disagreements, that Cy was a strong man. What he lacked, in her opinion, was the underlying kindness that balanced strength and kept it from being hard. She sensed there was kindness in Vance, though he was far from easy with it. But the fact that the trait existed at all made the difference for Shane.

Turning away from the path, she took her bucket, roller and pan to the end of the porch. She poured, knelt, then took a deep breath and began to paint.

When Vance came to the end of the path, he stopped to watch her. She had nearly a third of the porch done. Her arms were splattered with tiny specks of white. The radio blared, and she sang exuberantly along with it. Her hips kept the beat. As she moved, the thin, faded material of her shorts strained over her bottom. That she was having a marvelous time with the homey chore was as obvious as her lack of skill. A smile tugged at his mouth when Shane leaned over for the bucket and rested her palm on the wet paint. Cheerfully, she swore, then wiped her hand haphazardly on the back of her shorts.

"I thought you said you could paint," Vance commented.

Shane started, nearly upsetting the contents of the bucket as she turned. Still on all fours, she smiled at him. "I said I could paint. I didn't say I was neat." Lifting her hand, she shielded her eyes against the sun and watched him walk to her. "Did you come to supervise?"

He looked down at her and shook his head. "No, I think it's already too late for that."

Shane lifted a brow. "It's going to be just fine when I've finished."

Vance made a noncommittal sound. "I've got a list of materials for you, but I need to make a few more measurements."

"That was quick." Shane sat back on her haunches. Vance shrugged, not wanting to admit he'd written it out in the middle of the night when sleep had eluded him. "There was something else," she continued, stretching her back muscles. Leaning over, she turned down the volume on the radio so that it was only a soft murmur. "The front porch."

Vance glanced down at her handiwork. "Have you painted that too?"

Correctly reading his impression of her talents, Shane made a face. "No, I didn't paint that too."

"That's a blessing. What stopped you?"

"It's falling apart. Maybe you can suggest what I should do about it. Oh, look!" Shane grabbed his hand, forgetting the paint as she spotted a family of quail bobbing single file across the path behind them. "They're the first I've seen since I've been home." Captivated, she watched them until they were out of sight. "There's deer too. I've seen the signs, but I haven't been able to catch sight of any yet." She gave a contented sigh as the quail rustled in the woods. All at once, she remembered the condition of her hand.

"Oh, Vance, I'm sorry!" Releasing him, she jumped to her feet. "Did I get any on you?"

For an answer, he turned his palm up, studying the white smear ironically.

"I really am sorry," she managed, choking on a giggle. He shot her a look as she struggled to swallow the irrepressible laughter. "No, really I am. Here." Taking the hem of her T-shirt, Shane lifted it to rub unsuccessfully at his palm. Her stab at assistance exposed the pale, smooth skin of her midriff.

"You're rubbing it in," Vance said mildly, trying not to be affected by the flash of skin or the glimpse of her narrow waist.

"It'll come off," she assured him while she fought a desperate battle with laughter. "I must have some turpentine or something." Though Shane pressed the back of her hand against her mouth, the giggle escaped. "I *am* sorry," she claimed, then dropped her forehead on his chest. "And I wouldn't laugh if you'd stop looking at me that way."

"What way?"

"Patiently."

"Does patience usually send you into uncontrollable laughter?" he asked. Her hair carried the scent of her shampoo, a faint tang of lemon. It was odd that he would think just then of the honey-sweetness of her mouth.

"Too many things do," she admitted in a strangled voice. "It's a curse." She drew a deep breath, but left her hand on his chest as she tried to compose herself. "One of my students drew a deadly caricature of his biology teacher. When I saw it, I had to leave the room for fifteen minutes before I could pretend I disapproved."

Vance drew her away, unnerved by his unwanted, unreasonable response to her. "Didn't you?"

"Disapprove?" Grinning, Shane shook her head. "I wanted to, but it was so good. I took it home and framed it."

Suddenly, she became aware that he was holding her arms, that his thumbs were caressing her bare skin while his eyes watched her in the deep, guarded way he had. Looking at him, Shane was certain he was unaware of the gentle, intimate gesture. There was nothing gentle in his eyes. If she had followed her first instinct, she would have risen to her toes and kissed him. It was what she wanted—what she sensed he wanted as well. Something warned her against making the move. Instead, she stood still. Her eyes met his calmly, with no secrets to be seen in them. All of the secrets were his, and at that moment, they both knew it.

Vance would have been more comfortable with secrets than candor. When he realized that he was holding her, that he wanted to go on holding her, he released her.

"You'd better get back to your painting," he said. "I'll take those measurements."

"All right." Shane watched him walk to the door. "There's hot water in the kitchen if you want some tea."

What a strange man, she thought, frowning after him. Unconsciously, she lifted a finger to the warm spot on her arm where his flesh had touched hers. What had he been looking for, she wondered, when he had searched her eyes so deeply? What did he expect to find? It would be so much simpler if he would only ask her the questions he had. Shrugging, Shane went back to her painting.

Vance paused by the foot of the stairs and glanced at the living room. Surprised, he walked in for a closer look. It was clean as a whistle, with every vase, lamp and knick-knack packed away in labeled boxes.

She must have really worked, he thought. That compact little body stored a heavyweight energy. She had ambition, he concluded, and the guts to carry it through. Whatever her former fiancé termed her, Vance would hardly characterize Shane Abbott as frivolous. Not from what he had seen so far, he reminded himself. He felt another flash of admiration for her as he mounted the stairs.

She'd been at work on the second floor as well, Vance discovered. She must move like a whirlwind, he concluded as he looked at the labeled boxes in the master bedroom. After taking his measurements and notations, he moved into Shane's room.

It was a beehive of activity, with none of the meticulous organization he had found in the other rooms. Papers, lists, notes, scrawled tablets and bills sat heaped on the open slant top of a Governor Winthrop desk. They fluttered a bit from the breeze through the open windows. On the floor beside it were dozens of catalogs on antiques. A night-gown—not the one he had envisioned her in, but a thigh-length chemise—was tossed inside out over a chair. A pair of worn sneakers sat propped against the closet as if they had been kicked there then forgotten.

In the center of the room was a large box of books,

which he remembered seeing the day before. Then they had been in the third bedroom. Obviously, Shane had dragged them into her own room the night before to sort through them. Several were piled precariously on the floor; others littered her nightstand. It was apparent that her style of working and style of living were completely at variance.

Oddly, Vance thought of Amelia and the elegant order of her private rooms. They had been decorated in pinks and ivories, without the barest trace of dust or clutter. Even the army of bottles of creams and scents on her vanity had been carefully arranged. Shane had no vanity at all, and the bureau top held only a small enameled box, a framed photo and a single bottle of scent. He noted the photo was a color snapshot of a teenaged Shane beside a very erect, white-haired woman.

So this is the grandmother, Vance mused. She had a prim, proper smile on her face, but he was certain her eyes were laughing out of the lined face. He observed none of the softness of old age about her, but a rather leathery toughness that contrasted well with the girl beside her.

They stood on the summer grass, their backs to the creek. The grandmother wore a flowered housedress, the girl a yellow T-shirt and cut-off jeans. This Shane was hardly different from the woman outside. Her hair was longer, her frame thinner, but the look of unbridled amusement was there. Though her arm was hooked through the old woman's, the impression was of camaraderie, not of support.

She was more attractive with her hair short, Vance decided as he studied her. The way it curled and clung to the shape of her face accented the smoothness of her skin, and the way her jaw tapered…

He found himself wondering if Cy had taken the picture and was immediately annoyed with the idea. He disliked Cy on principle, though he'd certainly employed a good many men like him over the years. They plotted their way through life as though it were a tax return.

What the hell had she seen in him? Vance thought in disgust as he turned away to take more measurements. If she had tied herself up with him, she would be living in some stuffy house in the suburbs with 2.3 children, the Ladies Auxiliary on Wednesdays and a two-week vacation in a rented beach cottage every year. Fine for some, he thought, but not for a woman who liked to paint porches and wanted to see Fiji.

That buttoned-down jerk would have picked on her for the rest of her life, Vance concluded before he headed back downstairs. She'd had a lucky escape. Vance thought it was a pity he hadn't had one himself. Instead he had spent an intolerable four years wishing his wife out of existence and another two dealing with the guilt of having his wish come true.

Shaking off the mood, Vance walked outside to take a look at Shane's front porch.

Later, when he was measuring and muttering, Shane came out with a mug of tea in each hand. "Pretty bad, huh?"

Vance looked up with an expression of disgust. "It's a wonder someone hasn't broken a leg on this thing."

"No one uses it much." Shane shrugged as she worked her way expertly around the uncertain boards. "Gran always used the back door. So does anyone who comes to visit."

"Your boyfriend didn't."

Shane shot him a dry look. "Cy wouldn't use the back

door, and he's not my boyfriend. What do you think I should do about it?"

"I thought you'd already done it," he returned, and pocketed his rule. "And very well."

Shane eyed him a moment, then laughed. "No, not about Cy, about the porch."

"Tear the damn thing down."

"Oh." Gingerly, Shane sat on the top step. "All of it? I was hoping to replace the worst boards, and—"

"The whole thing's going to collapse if three people stand on it at the same time," Vance cut in, frowning at the sagging wood. "I can't understand how anyone could let something get into this condition."

"All right, don't get riled up," she advised as she held out a mug of tea. "How much do you think it'll cost me?"

Vance calculated a moment, then named a price. He saw the flicker of dismay before Shane sighed.

"Okay." It killed her last hope of holding on to her grandmother's dining-room set. "If it has to be done. I suppose it's first priority. The weather might turn cold anytime." She managed a halfhearted smile. "I wouldn't want my first customer to fall through the porch and sue me."

"Shane." Vance stood in front of her. As she sat on the top step, their faces were almost level. Her look was direct and open, yet still he hesitated before speaking. "How much do you have? Money," he added bluntly when she gave him a blank look.

She drew her brows together at the question. "Enough to get by," she said, then made a sound of annoyance as he continued to stare at her. "Barely," she admitted. "But it'll hold until my business makes a few dollars. I've got so much budgeted for the house, so much for buying stock. Gran left me a nest egg, and I had my own savings."

Vance hesitated again. He had promised himself not to become involved, yet he was being drawn in every time he saw her. "I hate to sound like your boyfriend," he began.

"Then don't," Shane said quickly. "And he's not."

"All right." Vance frowned down at his mug. It was one thing to take on a job as a lark, and another to take money from a woman who was obviously counting her pennies. He sipped, trying to find a reasonable way out of his hourly wage. "Shane, about my salary—"

"Oh, Vance, I can't make it any more right now." Distress flew into her eyes. "Later, after I've gotten started…"

"No." Embarrassed and annoyed, he put a hand on hers to stop her. "No, I wasn't going to ask you to raise it."

"But—" Shane stopped. Realization filled her eyes. Tears followed it. Swiftly, she set down the mug and rose. Shaking her head, she descended the stairs. "No, no, that's very kind of you," she managed as she walked away from him. "I—I appreciate it, really, but it's not necessary. I didn't mean to make it sound as though—" Breaking off, she stared at the surrounding mountains. For a moment there was only the sound of the creek bubbling on its way behind them.

Cursing himself, Vance went to her. After a brief hesitation, he put his hands on her shoulders. "Shane, listen—"

"No, please." Swiftly, she turned to face him. Though the tears hadn't brimmed over, her eyes still swam with them. When she lifted her hands to his forearms, he found her fingers surprisingly strong. "It's very kind of you to offer."

"No, it's not," Vance snapped. Frustration, guilt and something more ran through him. He resented all of it. "Damn it, Shane, you don't understand. The money isn't—"

"I understand you're a very sweet man," she interrupted. Vance felt himself become tangled deeper when she put her arms around him, pressing her cheek to his chest.

"No, I'm not," he muttered. Intending to push her away and find a way out of the mess he'd gotten himself into, Vance put his hands back on her shoulders. The last thing he wanted was misplaced gratitude. But his hands found their way into her hair.

He didn't want to push her away, he realized. No, by God, he didn't. Not when her small firm breasts were pressed against him. Not when her hair curled riotously around his fingers. It was soft, so soft, and the color of wild honey. Her mouth was soft, he remembered, aching. Surrendering to need, Vance buried his face in her hair, murmuring her name.

Something in the tone, the hint of desperation, made Shane long to comfort him. She didn't yet sense his desire for her, only his trouble. She pressed closer, wanting to ease it while she ran soothing hands over his back. At her touch, his blood leaped. In a swift, almost brutal move, Vance pulled her head back to savage her mouth with his.

Shane's instinctive cry of alarm was silenced. Her struggles went unnoticed. A fire consumed him—so great, so unbearably hot, he had no thought but to quench it. She felt fear, then, greater than fear, passion. The fire spread, engulfing her until her mouth answered his wildly.

No one, nothing had ever brought her to this—this madness of need, terror of desire. She moaned in panicked excitement as his teeth nipped into her bottom lip. Along her skin, quick thrills raced to confuse and inflame. There was never a thought to deny him. She knew she was already his.

He thought he would go mad if he didn't touch her, learn just one of the secrets of her small, slim body. For countless hours the night before, his imagination had tormented him. Now, he had to satisfy it. Never stopping his assault on her mouth, he reached beneath her shirt to find her breast. Her heart pounded beneath his hand. She was firm and small. His appetite only increased, making him groan while his thumb and finger worked the already erect peak.

Colors exploded inside her head like a blinding, brilliant rainbow. Shane clutched at him, afraid, enthralled, while her lips and tongue continued with a demand equal to his. Against her smooth skin his palm was rough and callused. His thumb scraped her, lifting her to a delirium of excitement. There was no smoothness, no softness in him. His mouth was hard and hot with the stormy taste of anger. Crushed to hers, his body was taut and tense. Some raw, turbulent passion seemed to pour out of him to dare her to match it.

She felt his arms tighten around her convulsively; then she was free so quickly she staggered, grabbing his arm to steady herself.

In her eyes, Vance saw the clouds of passion, the lights of fear. Her mouth was bruised and swollen from the fierceness of his. He frowned at it. Never before had he been rough with a woman. For the most part, he was a considerate lover, perhaps indifferent at times but never ungentle. He took a step back from her. "I'm sorry," he said stiffly.

Shane lifted her fingers to her still-tender lips in a nervous gesture. Her reaction, much more than Vance's technique, had left her shaken. Where had all that fire and feeling been hiding all this time? she wondered. "I don't…" Shane had to clear her throat to manage more than a whisper. "I don't want you to be sorry."

Vance studied her steadily for a moment. "It would be better all around if you did." Reaching in his back pocket, he drew out a list. "Here are the materials you'll need. Let me know when they're delivered."

"All right." Shane accepted the list. When he started to walk away, she drew up all of her courage. "Vance…" He paused and turned back to her. "I'm not sorry," she told him quietly.

He didn't answer, but walked around the side of the house and disappeared.

Chapter 5

Shane decided she had worked harder over the following three days than she had ever worked in her life. The spare bedroom and dining room were loaded with packing boxes, labeled and listed and sealed. The house had been scrubbed and swept and dusted from top to bottom. She had pored through catalogs on antiques until the words ran together. Every item she owned was listed systematically. The dating and pricing was more grueling for her than the manual work and often kept her up until the early hours of the morning. She would be up to start again the moment the sunlight woke her. Yet her energy never flagged. With each step of progress she made, the excitement grew, pushing her to make more.

As the time passed, she became more convinced, and more confident, that what she was doing was right. It *felt* right. She needed to find her own way—the sacrifices and the financial risk were necessary. She didn't intend to fail.

For her, the shop would be not only a business but an adventure. Though Shane was impatient for the adventure to begin, as always, the planning and anticipation were just as stimulating to her. She had contracted with a roofer and a plumber, and had chosen her paints and stains. Just that afternoon, in a torrent of rain, the materials she had ordered from Vance's list had been delivered. The mundane, practical occurrences had given her a thrill of accomplishment. Somehow, the lumber, nails and bolts had been tangible evidence that she was on her way. Shane told herself that Antietam Antiques and Museum became a reality when the first board was set in place.

Excited, she had phoned Vance, and if he were true to his word, he would begin work the next morning.

Over a solitary cup of cocoa in the kitchen, Shane listened to the constant drumming rain and thought of him. He had been brief and businesslike on the phone. She hadn't been offended. She had come to realize that moodiness was part of his character. This made him only more attractive.

The windows were dark as she stared out, with a ghostly reflection of the kitchen light on the wet panes. She thought idly about starting a fire to chase away the damp chill, but she had little inclination to move. Instead, she rubbed the bottom of one bare foot over the top of the other and decided it was too bad her socks were all the way upstairs.

Sluggishly, a drip fell from the ceiling into a pot on the floor. It gave a surprising ping now and again. There were several other pots set at strategic places throughout the house. Shane didn't mind the rain or the isolation. The sensation of true loneliness was almost foreign to her. Content with her own company, the activity of her own mind, she craved no companionship at that moment, nor would she have shunned it. Yet she thought of Vance, wondering if he sat watching the rain through a darkened window.

Yes, she admitted, she was very much attracted to him. And it was more than a physical response when he held her, when he kissed her in that sudden, terrifyingly exciting way. Just being in his presence was stimulating—sensing the storm beneath the calm. There was an amazing drive in him. The drive of a man uncomfortable, even impatient, with idleness. The lack of a job, she thought with a sympathetic sigh, must frustrate him terribly.

Shane understood his need to produce, to be active, although her own spurts of frantic energy were patchworked with periods of unapologetic laziness. She moved fast but didn't rush. She could work for hours without tiring, or sleep until noon without the least blush of guilt. Whichever she did, she did wholeheartedly. It was vital to her to find some way to enjoy the most menial or exhausting task. She concluded that while Vance would work tirelessly, he would find the enjoyment unnecessary.

The basic difference in their temperaments didn't trouble her. Her interest in history, plus her teaching experience, had given her insight into the variety of human nature. It wasn't necessary to her that Vance's thoughts and moods flow along the same stream as hers. Such comfortable compatibility would offer little excitement and no surprises at all. Absolute harmony, she mused, could be lovely, rather sweet and very bland. There were more… interesting things.

She'd seen a spark of humor in him, perhaps an almost forgotten sense of the ridiculous. And he was far from cold. While she accepted his faults and their differences, these qualities caused her to accept her own attraction to him.

What she had felt from the first meeting had only intensified. There was no logic in it, no sense, but her heart had known instantly that he was the man she'd waited for. Though she'd told herself it was impossible, Shane knew the impossible had an uncanny habit of happening just the same. Love at first sight? Ridiculous. But…

Impossible or not, ridiculous or not, Shane's heart was set. It was true she gave her affections easily, but she didn't give them lightly. The love she had felt for Cy had been a young, impressionable love, but it had been very real. It had taken her a long time to get over it.

Shane had no illusions about Vance Banning. He was a difficult man. Even with spurts of kindness and humor, he would never be anything else. There was too much anger in him, too much drive. And while Shane could accept the phenomenon of love at first sight on her part, she was practical enough to know it wasn't being reciprocated.

He desired her. She might puzzle over this, never having thought of herself as a woman to attract desire, but she recognized it. Yet, though he wanted her, he kept his distance. This was the reserve in him, she decided, the studied caution that warred with the passion.

Idly, she sipped her drink and stared out into the rain. The problem as Shane saw it was to work her way through the barrier. She had loved before and faced pain and emp-

tiness. She could accept pain again, but she was determined not to face emptiness a second time. She wanted
Vance Banning. Now all she had to do was to make him
want her. Smiling a little, Shane set down her cup. She'd
been raised to succeed.

The glare of headlights against the window surprised
her. Rising, Shane went to the back door to see who'd come
visiting in the rain. Cupping her hands on either side of her
face, she peered through the wet glass. She recognized the
car and immediately threw open the door. Cold rain hurled
itself into her face, but she laughed, watching Donna
scramble around puddles with her head lowered.

"Hi!" Still laughing, Shane stepped back as her friend
dashed through the door. "You got a little wet," she observed.

"Very funny." Donna stripped off her raincoat to hang
it over a peg near the back door. With the casualness of an
old friend, she stepped out of her wet loafers. "I figured
you were hibernating. Here." She handed Shane a pound
can of coffee.

"A welcome home present?" Shane asked, turning the
can over curiously. "Or a hint that you'd like some?"

"Neither." Shaking her head, Donna ran her fingers
through her wet hair. "You bought it the other day, then left
it at the store."

"I did?" Shane thought about it a moment, then laughed.
"Oh, that's right. Thanks. Who's minding the store while
you're out making deliveries?" Turning, she popped the
can into a cupboard.

"Dave." With a sigh, Donna plopped onto a kitchen
chair. "His sister's baby-sitting, so he kicked me out."

"Aw, out in the storm."

"He knew I was restless." She glanced out the window. "It doesn't seem as though this rain's ever going to let up." With a shiver, she frowned at Shane's bare feet. "Aren't you cold?"

"I thought about starting a fire," she said absently, then grinned. "It seemed like an awful lot of trouble."

"So's the flu."

"The cocoa's still warm," Shane told her, automatically reaching for another cup. "Want some?"

"Yes, thanks." Donna ran her fingers through her hair again, then folded her hands, but she couldn't keep them still. Suddenly, she gave Shane a glowing smile. "I have to tell you before I burst."

Mildly curious, Shane looked over her shoulder. "Tell me what?"

"I'm having another baby."

"Oh, Donna, that's wonderful!" Shane felt a twinge of envy. Hurriedly dismissing it, she went to hug her friend. "When?"

"Not for another seven months." Laughing, Donna wiped the rain from her face. "I'm just as excited as I was the first time. Dave is too, though he's trying to be very nonchalant." She sent Shane a beaming look. "He's managed to mention it, very casually, to everyone who came into the store this afternoon."

Shane gave her another quick hug. "You know how lucky you are?"

"Yes, I do." A little sheepishly, she grinned. "I've spent all day thinking up names. What do you think of Charlotte and Samuel?"

"Very distinguished." Shane moved back to the stove.

After pouring cocoa, she brought two cups to the table. "Here's to little Charlotte or Samuel."

"Or Andrew or Justine," Donna said as they touched rims.

"How many kids are you planning to have?" Shane asked wryly.

"Just one at a time." Donna gave her stomach a proud little pat.

The gesture made Shane smile. "Did you say Dave's sister was watching Benji? Isn't she still in school?"

"No, she graduated this summer. Right now she's hunting for a new job." With a contented sigh, Donna sat back. "She was planning to go to college part-time, but money's tight and the hours she's working right now make it next to impossible." Her brow creased in sympathy. "The best she can manage this term is a couple of night classes twice a week. At that rate it's going to take her a long time to earn a degree."

"Hmm." Shane stared into her cocoa. "Pat was a very bright girl as I remember."

"Bright and pretty as a picture."

Shane nodded. "Tell her to come see me."

"You?"

"After the shop's set up, I'm going to need some part-time help." She glanced over absently as the wind hurled rain at the windows. "I wouldn't be able to do anything for her for a month or so, but if she's still interested, we should be able to work something out."

"Shane, she'll be thrilled. But are you sure you can afford to hire someone?"

With a toss of her head, Shane lifted her drink. "I'll know within the first six months if I'm going to make it."

As she considered, she twisted a curl around her finger—a gesture Donna recognized as nerves. She drew her brows together but said nothing. "I want to keep the place open seven days a week," Shane continued. "Weekends are bound to be the busiest time if I manage to lure in any tourists. Between sales and bookkeeping, inventory and the buying I have to do, I won't be able to manage alone. If I'm going down," she murmured, "I'm going down big."

"I've never known you to do anything halfway," Donna observed with a trace of admiration vying with concern. "I'd be scared to death."

"I am a little scared," Shane admitted. "Sometimes I imagine this place the way it's going to look, and I see customers coming in to handle merchandise. I see all the rooms and records I'm going to have to keep..." She rolled her eyes to the ceiling. "What makes me think I can handle all that?"

"As long as I can remember, you've handled everything that came your way." Donna paused a moment as she considered Shane carefully. "You're going to try this no matter how many pitfalls I point out?"

A grin had Shane's dimples deepening. "Yes."

"Then I won't point out any," Donna said with a wry smile. "What I will say is that if anyone can make it work, you can."

After frowning into her cocoa, Shane raised her eyes to Donna's. "Why?"

"Because you'll give it everything you've got."

The simplicity of the answer made Shane laugh. "You're sure that'll be enough?"

"Yes," Donna said so seriously that Shane sobered.

"I hope you're right," Shane murmured, then shook off the doubts. "It's a little late in the game to start worrying about it now. So," she continued in a lighter tone, "what's new besides Justine or Samuel?"

After a moment's hesitation, Donna plunged ahead. "Shane, I saw Cy the other day."

"Did you?" Shane lifted a brow as she sipped. "So did I."

Donna moistened her lips. "He seemed very...ah, concerned about your plans."

"Critical and concerned are entirely different things," Shane pointed out, then smiled as the color in Donna's cheeks deepened. "Oh, don't worry about it, Donna. Cy's never approved of any of my ideas. It doesn't bother me anymore. In fact, the less he approves," she continued slowly, "the more I'm sure it's the right thing to do. I don't think he's ever taken a chance in his entire life." Noting that Donna was busy gnawing on her bottom lip, Shane fixed her with a straight look. "Okay, what else?"

"Shane." Donna paused, then began running her fingertip around and around the rim of her cup. Shane recognized the stalling gesture and kept silent. "I think I should tell you before—well, before you hear it from someone else. Cy..."

Shane waited patiently for a few seconds. "Cy what?" she demanded. Miserably, Donna looked up.

"He's been seeing quite a lot of Laurie MacAfee." Seeing Shane's eyes widen, Donna continued in a rush. "I'm sorry, Shane, so sorry, but I did think you should know. And I figured it might be easier hearing it from me. I think...well, I'm afraid it's serious."

"Laurie..." Shane broke off and seemed to stare, fascinated, at the water dripping into the pot. *"Laurie MacAfee?"* she managed after a strangled moment.

"Yes," Donna said quietly, and she stared down at the

table. "Rumor is they'll be married next summer." Donna waited, unhappily, for Shane's reaction. When she heard the burst of wild laughter, she looked up, fearing hysterics.

"Laurie MacAfee!" Shane pounded her palms on the table and laughed until she thought she would burst. "Oh, it's wonderful, it's perfect! Oh God. Oh God, what an *admirable* couple!"

"Shane…" Concerned with the damp eyes and rollicking laughter, Donna searched for the right thing to say.

"Oh, I wish I had known before so I could have congratulated him." Almost beside herself with delight, Shane laid her forehead on the table. Taking this as a sign of a broken heart, Donna put a comforting hand on her hair.

"Shane, you mustn't take on so." Her own eyes filled as she gently stroked Shane's hair. "Cy isn't for you. You deserve better."

The statement sent Shane into a fresh peal of laughter. "*Oh, Donna!* Oh, Donna, do you remember how she always wore those neat little coordinates to school? And she got straight A's in home economics." Shane was forced to take deep breaths before she could continue. "She did a term paper on planning household budgets."

"Please, darling, don't think about it." Donna cast her eyes around the kitchen, wondering if there were any medicinal brandy in the house.

"She'll have her own shoe trees," Shane said weakly. "I just know it. And she'll label them so they don't get them mixed up. Oh, Cy!" On a new round of giggles, she pounded a fist on the table. "Laurie. Laurie MacAfee!"

Almost frantic with concern, Donna gently lifted Shane's face. "Shane, I…" With a jolt she saw that rather than being devastated, her friend was simply overcome with amusement. For a moment, Donna stared into round dancing eyes. "Well," she said dryly, "I knew you'd be upset."

Shane howled with laughter. "I'm going to give them a Victorian whatnot as a wedding present. Donna," she added with grinning gratitude, "you've made my day. Absolutely made it."

"I knew you'd take it badly," Donna said with a baffled smile. "Just try not to weep in public."

"I'll keep my chin up," Shane promised, then smiled. "You're sweet. Did you really think I was carrying a torch for Cy?"

"I wasn't sure," Donna admitted. "You were…well, an item for so long, and I knew how crushed you were when the two of you broke up. You'd never talk about it after that."

"I needed some time to lick my wounds," Shane told her. "They've been healed over for a long while. I was in love with him, but I got over it. He put a large dent in my pride. I survived."

"I could have killed him at the time," Donna muttered darkly. "Two months before the wedding."

"Better than two months after," Shane pointed out logically. "We would never have made a go of it. But now, Cy and Laurie MacAfee…"

This time they both broke out into laughter.

"Shane." Donna gave her a sudden sober look. "A lot of people are going to be thinking you still care for Cy."

Shane shrugged it off. "You can't do anything about what people think."

"Or what they say," Donna murmured.

"They'll find something more interesting to talk about

before long," Shane returned carelessly. "Besides, I have too much to do to be worried about it."

"So I noticed from the pile of stuff on the porch. What's under that tarp?"

"Lumber and materials."

"Just what are you going to do with it?"

"Nothing. Vance Banning's going to do it. Want some more cocoa."

"Vance Banning!" Stunned, then fascinated, Donna leaned forward. "Tell me."

"There's not much to tell. You didn't answer me," Shane reminded her.

"What? No, no, I don't want any more." Impatiently, she brushed the offer away. "Shane, what is Vance Banning going to do with your lumber and materials?"

"The carpentry work."

"Why?"

"I hired him to do it."

Donna gritted her teeth. "Why?"

"Because he's a carpenter."

"Shane!"

Valiantly, Shane controlled a grin. "Look, he's out of work, he's talented, I needed someone who'd work under union scale, so…" She spread her hands.

"What have you found out about him?" Donna demanded the right to fresh news.

"Not much." Shane wrinkled her nose. "Nothing, really. He doesn't say much."

Donna gave her a knowing smirk. "I already knew that."

A quick grin was Shane's response. "Well, he can be downright rude when he wants to. He has a lot of pride and a marvelous smile that he doesn't use nearly enough. Strong hands," she murmured, then brought herself back. "And a streak of reluctant kindness. I think he can laugh at himself but he's forgotten how. I know he's a workhorse because when the wind's right I can hear him hammering and sawing at all hours." She glanced out the window in the direction of the path. "I'm in love with him."

"Yes, but what—" Donna caught her breath and choked on it. *"What!"*

"I'm in love with him," Shane repeated with an amused smile. "Would you like some water?"

For nearly a full minute, Donna only stared at her. *She's joking,* she told herself. But by Shane's expression, she saw her friend was perfectly serious. It was her duty, Donna decided, as a married woman starting on her second child, to point out the dangers of this kind of thinking.

"Shane," she began in a patient, maternal tone, "you only just met the man. Now—"

"I knew it the minute I set my eyes on him," Shane interrupted calmly. "I'm going to marry him."

"Marry him!" Beyond words, Donna could only come up with sputters. Indulgently, Shane rose to pour her some water. "He—he asked you to marry him?"

"No, of course not." Shane chuckled at the idea as she handed Donna a glass. "He only just met me."

In an attempt to understand Shane's logic, Donna closed her eyes and concentrated. "I'm confused," she said at length.

"I said I was going to marry him," Shane explained, taking her seat again. "He doesn't know it yet. First I have to wait for him to fall in love with me."

After setting the untouched water aside, Donna gave her

a stern look. "Shane, I think you're under more strain than you realize."

"I've been giving this a lot of thought," Shane answered, ignoring Donna's comment. "Number one, why would I have fallen in love with him in the blink of an eye if it wasn't right? It must be right, so number two, sooner or later he's going to fall in love with me."

Donna followed the pattern of thought and found it filled with snags. "And how are you going to make him do that?"

"Oh, I can't make him," Shane said reasonably. Her voice was both serene and confident. "He'll have to fall in love with me just as I am and in his own time—the same way I fell in love with him."

"Well, you've had some nutty ideas before, Shane Abbott, but this is the top." Donna folded her arms over her chest. "You're planning on marrying a man you've known barely a week who doesn't know he's going to marry you, and you're just going to sit patiently by until he gets the idea."

Shane thought for a moment, then nodded. "That's about it."

"It's the most ridiculous thing I've ever heard," Donna stated, then let out a surprised laugh. "And knowing you, it'll probably work."

"I'm counting on it."

Leaning forward, Donna took Shane's hands in hers. "Why do you love him, Shane?"

"I don't know," she answered immediately. "That's another reason I'm sure it's right. I know almost nothing about him except he's not a comfortable man. He'll hurt me and make me cry."

"Then why—"

"He'll make me laugh too," Shane interrupted. "And make me furious." She smiled a little, but her eyes were very serious. "I don't think he'll ever make me feel—inadequate. And when I'm near him, I *know*. That's enough for me."

"Yes." Donna nodded, giving Shane's hands a squeeze. "It would be. You're the most loving person I've ever known. And the most trusting. Those are wonderful traits, Shane, and—well, dangerous. I only wish we knew more about him," she added in a mutter.

"He has secrets," Shane murmured, and Donna's eyes sharpened. "They're his until he's ready to tell me about them."

"Shane…" Donna's fingers tightened on hers. "Be careful, please."

A little surprised by the tone, Shane smiled. "I will. Don't worry. Maybe I am more trusting than most, but I have my defenses. I'm not going to make a fool of myself." Unconsciously, she glanced out the window again, seeing the path to his house in her mind's eye. "He's not a simple man, Donna, but he is a good one. That much I'm sure of."

"All right," Donna agreed. Silently, she vowed to keep a close eye on Vance Banning.

For a long time after Donna left, Shane sat in the kitchen. The rain continued to pound. The steady drip from the ceiling plopped musically into the pan. She was aware of how reckless her words to Donna had been, yet she felt better having said them out loud.

No, she wasn't as blindly confident as she appeared. Inside, she was terrified by the knowledge that she loved so irrationally. She was trusting, yes, but not naive. She understood there was a price to pay for trust, and that often it was a dear one. Yet she knew her choice had already been made—or perhaps she'd never had one.

Rising, Shane switched off the lights and began to wander through the darkened house. She knew its every twist and turn, every board that creaked. It was everything familiar and comforting to her. She loved it. She knew none of Vance's twists and turns, none of his secret corners. He was everything strange and disturbing. She loved him.

If it had been a quiet, gentle love, she could have accepted it easily. But there was nothing quiet in the storm churning inside her. For all her energy and love of adventure, Shane had grown up in a slow, peaceful world where excitement was a run through the woods or a ride on the back of a tractor at haymaking. To fall suddenly in love with a stranger might seem romantic and wonderful in a story, but when it happened in real life, it was simply terrifying.

Shane walked upstairs, habitually avoiding the steps that creaked or groaned. The rain was a hollow, drumming sound all around her, whipped up occasionally by the wind to fly at the windows. Her bare feet met bare wood with a quiet patter. A small bucket caught the drip in the center of the hall. Expertly, she skirted around it.

Who was she to think all she had to do was to sit patiently by until Vance fell in love with her? she asked herself. After flipping on the light in her room, she went to stare at herself in the mirror. Was she beautiful? Shane asked her reflection. Alluring? With a half laugh, she rested her elbows on the dresser to look closer.

She saw the dash of freckles, the large dark eyes and cap of hair. She didn't see the stunning vitality, the temptingly smooth skin, the surprisingly sensual mouth.

Was that a face to send a man into raptures? she asked herself. The thought amused her so, that the reflection grinned back with quick good humor. Hardly, Shane decided, but she wouldn't want a man who looked only for a perfect face. No, she hadn't the face or figure to lure a man into love had she wanted to. She had only herself and the love in her heart.

Shane flashed the mirror a smile before she turned away to prepare for bed. She'd always thought love the ultimate adventure.

Chapter 6

Weak sunlight filtered through the bad-tempered clouds. The creek was swollen from the rainfall so that it ran its course noisily, hissing and complaining as it rounded the bend at the side of Shane's house. Shane was doing some complaining of her own.

The day before, she had moved her car out of the narrow driveway so that the delivery truck could have easy access to the back porch. Not wanting to ruin the grass, she had parked in the small square of dirt her grandmother had used as a vegetable garden. Once the car had been moved, Shane had become involved with the unloading of lumber and had promptly forgotten it. Now, it was sunk deep in mud, firmly resisting all efforts to get it out.

She pressed the gas lightly, tried forward, then reverse. She gunned the engine and swore. Slamming out of the driver's side, Shane sloshed ankle-deep in mire as she stomped back to the rear tire. She gave it an accusing stare, then kicked it.

"That's not going to help," Vance commented. He had been watching her for the last few minutes, torn somewhere between amusement and exasperation. And pleasure. There was a simple pleasure in just seeing her. He'd stopped counting the times over the last few days that he'd thought of her.

Out of patience, Shane turned to him, hands on hips. Her predicament was annoying enough without the added benefit of an audience. "You might have let me know you were there."

"You were…involved," he said, glancing pointedly at her mired car.

She sent him a cool look. "You've got a better idea, I suppose."

"A few," he agreed, moving across the lawn to join her. Her eyes snapped with temper while her mouth pouted. Her boots were caked with mud past the ankle. Her jeans, rolled up to the calf, had fared little better. She looked ready to boil over at the first wrong word. A cautious man would have said nothing.

"Who the hell parked it in this mud hole?" Vance demanded.

"*I* parked it in this mud hole." Shane gave the tire another fierce kick. "And it wasn't a mud hole when I did."

He lifted a brow. "I suppose you noticed it rained all night."

"Oh, get out of my way." Incensed, Shane pushed him aside and stomped back to the driver's seat. She turned on the ignition, shoved the shift into first, then stepped heavily on the gas. Mud flew like rain. The car groaned and sank deeper.

For a moment, Shane could only pound on the steering wheel in enraged impotence. She would have dearly loved to tell Vance that she didn't require any assistance. There was nothing more infuriating than an amused, superior male…especially when you needed one. Forcing herself to take a deep breath, she climbed back out of the car to meet Vance's grin with icy composure. "What's the first of your few ideas?" she asked coolly.

"Got a couple of planks?"

Even more annoyed that she hadn't thought of it herself, Shane went to the shed and found two long, thin boards. Without fuss or conversation, Vance took them and secured them just under the front wheels. Shane folded her arms and tapped one muddy boot as she watched him.

"I'd have thought of that in a minute," she muttered.

"Maybe." Vance stood again to walk to the rear of the car. "But you wouldn't get anywhere the way your back wheels are stuck."

Shane waited for him to make some comment on feminine stupidity. Then she would have an excuse to give him the full force of her temper. He merely studied her flushed face and furious eyes. "So?" she said at length.

Something suspiciously like a smile tugged at his mouth. Shane's eyes narrowed. "So, get back in and I'll push," he said, then put a restraining hand on her arm. "Gentle on the gas this time, hot rod. Just put it in Drive and easy does it."

"It's a four-speed," she told him with dignity.

"I beg your pardon." Vance waited until she had waded

her way back to the front of the car. For the first time in months, perhaps years, he had to make a concentrated effort to control laughter. "Let the clutch out slow," he instructed after clearing his throat.

"I know how to drive," she snapped, and slammed the door smartly. Frowning into the rearview mirror, Shane watched him until he gave her a nod. With meticulous care, she engaged the clutch and gently pressed on the gas. The front wheels crept slowly onto the planks. The back tires slid, then stuck, then ponderously moved again. Shane kept the speed slow and even. It was humiliating, she thought, glaring straight ahead, absolutely humiliating that he was going to get her out without a hitch.

"Just a little more," Vance called to her, shifting his weight. "Keep it slow."

"What?" Shane rolled down the window, then stuck her head out to hear his answer. As she did, her foot slipped and fell heavily on the gas. The car shot out of the mud like a banana squeezed from its peel. With a gasp, Shane hit the brake, rocking to an abrupt halt.

Closing her eyes, she sat for a moment and considered making a run for it. She didn't dare glance in the rearview mirror now. It wouldn't be difficult, she reflected, to make a U-turn, then keep right on going. But cowardice wasn't her way. She swallowed, bit her lip, then climbed out of the car to face the music.

Vance was kneeling in the mud. He was thoroughly splattered and hopping mad. *"You idiot!"* he shouted before Shane could say a word. Even as she started to agree with him, he continued. "What the hell did you think you were doing? Pea-brained little twit, I told you to take it *slow.*"

He didn't stop there. He swore at length, and fluently, but Shane lost track of the content. It was enough to know he was in a justifiable high rage, while she was fighting a desperate battle with laughter. She did her best, her very best, to keep her face composed and penitent. Feeling it would be unwise, as well as useless to interrupt with apologies, she folded her lips, bit the bottom one and swallowed repeatedly.

At first she concentrated on keeping her eyes directly on his, hoping the fury there would kill the urge to giggle. But the sight of his mud-splattered face had her sides aching with restrained mirth. She hung her head, ostensibly from shame.

"I'd like to know who the hell told you you could drive," Vance went on furiously. "And what person with a brain cell working would have parked the car in a swamp to begin with?"

"It was my grandmother's garden," Shane managed in a strangled voice. "But you're right. You're absolutely right. I'm so sorry, really…" She broke off here as a gurgle of laughter rose dangerously. Clearing her throat, she hurried on. "Sorry, Vance. It was very—" she had to look over his head in order to compose herself "—careless of me."

"Careless!"

"Stupid," she amended quickly, thinking that might placate him. "Absolutely stupid. I'm really sorry." Helplessly, she pressed both hands to her mouth, but the giggles came through. "I *am* sorry," she insisted, giving up as he glared at her. "I don't mean to laugh. It's terrible." Dizzy with the effort of trying to hold back, Shane bent over double. "Really awful," she added on a howl of laughter.

"Since you think it looks like fun..." he muttered grimly, and grabbed her hand. Shane landed on her seat with a gentle splash and kept on laughing.

"I didn't—I didn't thank you," she said on a peal of giggles, "for getting my car out."

"Think nothing of it." Most women, he mused, would have been infuriated to find themselves sitting in a pile of mud. Shane was laughing just as hard at herself as she had at him. His grin was completely unexpected and spontaneous. "Brat," he accused, but Shane shook her head.

"Oh no, no I'm not, really." She pressed the back of her hand to her mouth. "It's just this terrible habit of laughing at the wrong time. Because I really am sorry." The last word was drowned in a flood of laughter.

"I can see you are."

"Anyway, I didn't get it *all* over you." Scooping up some mud, she wiped it across his cheek. "I missed that part right there." She made a little choking sound in her throat. "That's much better," she approved.

"You aren't wearing nearly enough," Vance returned. He trailed both muddy palms down her face. Trying to avoid him, Shane slid, ending up flat on her back. Vance's boom of laughter broke into her shriek. "Much better," he agreed, then spotting the handful of mud she was about to heave, he made a grab for her arm. "Oh, no, you don't!"

As he laughed, she shifted. Vance landed half on his chest, half on his side. With a muttered curse, he propped himself up, studying her out of narrowed eyes.

"City boy," she mocked on a whoop of appreciation. "Probably never been in a mud fight in your life." She was too pleased with her maneuver to see the next one coming.

In a flash, Vance had her by the shoulders. Rolling her over, he straddled her, holding a hand to the back of her head. Lying full length, Shane looked wide-eyed at the mud inches away from her face.

"Oh, Vance, you *wouldn't!*" The helpless laughter bubbled still as she struggled.

"The hell I wouldn't." He pushed her face an inch closer.

"Vance!" Though she was slippery as an eel by this time, Vance held her firmly, clamping his knees around her while his hand urged her down. As the distance between revenge and her nose lessened, Shane closed her eyes and held her breath.

"Give?" he demanded.

Cautiously, Shane opened one eye. She hesitated a moment, torn between the desire to win and the image of having her face pushed into the mud. She didn't doubt he'd do it. "Give," she said reluctantly.

Abruptly, Vance rolled her over so that she lay in his lap. "City boy, huh?"

"You wouldn't have won if I weren't out of practice," she told him. "It was just beginner's luck."

Her eyes were mocking him. Her face was streaked with mud from his own fingers. The hands pressed against his chest were slippery with it. The grip on the back of her neck lightened until it was a caress. The hand at her hip roamed absently down her thigh as he lowered his eyes to her mouth. Slowly, without any conscious thought of doing so, Vance began to draw her closer.

Shane saw the change in his eyes and was suddenly afraid. Did she really have the defenses she had bragged to Donna about? Now that she was certain she loved him, could there be any defense? It was too fast, she thought frantically. It was all happening too fast. Breathless from the race of her heart, she scrambled up.

"I'll beat you to the creek," she challenged, then was off in a flash.

Pondering on her abrupt retreat, Vance watched her run around the side of the house. Normally, he would have considered it a ploy, but he found it didn't fit this time. Nothing about her fit, he concluded as he rose. Oddly, he realized he didn't seem to fit either. He hadn't realized he could find anything amusing or enjoyable about wrestling in the mud. Nor had he realized he could find a woman like Shane Abbott both intriguing and desirable. Trying to organize his thoughts, Vance walked around the side of the house to find her.

She had stripped off her boots and was wading knee-deep in the rushing creek water. "It's freezing!" she called out, then lowered herself to her waist. At the shock of cold, she sucked in her breath. "If it was warmer, we could walk down to Molly's Hole and take a quick swim."

"Molly's Hole?" Watching her, Vance sat on the grass to pull off his own boots.

"Right around the bend." She pointed vaguely in the direction of the main road. "Great swimming hole. Fishing too." Shivering a bit, she rubbed at the front of her shirt to help the water take off the worst of the mud. "We're lucky it rained, or else the creek wouldn't be high enough to do any good."

"If it hadn't rained, your car wouldn't have been stuck in the mud."

Shane shot him a grin. "That's beside the point." She watched him step into the water. "Cold?" she said sweetly when he winced.

"I should have pushed your face in," he decided. Stripping off his shirt, Vance tossed it on the grassy bank before scrubbing at his hands and arms.

"You'd have felt really bad if you had." Shane rubbed her face with creek water.

"No, I wouldn't have."

Glancing up, Shane laughed. "I like you, Vance. Gran would have called you a scoundrel."

He lifted a brow. "Is that praise?"

"Her highest," Shane agreed, rising to rub at the thighs of her jeans. They were plastered against her, molding her legs while her shirt clung wetly to her breasts. The cold had her nipples taut, straining against the thin cotton. Involved with cleaning off her clothes, she chattered, sublimely unaware they left her as good as naked.

"She loved scoundrels," Shane continued. "I suppose that's why she put up with me. I was always getting into one scrape or another."

"What kind?" Vance's torso was wet, cleaned of mud now, but he stayed where he was. Her body was exquisitely formed. He wondered how he hadn't noted before how perfectly scaled it was—small round breasts, wasp-thin waist, narrow hips, lean thighs.

"I don't like to brag." Shane worked the mud from the slippery sleeves of her shirt. "But I can show you the best way into old man Trippet's orchard if you want to snitch a few green apples. And I used to have a great time riding Mr. Poffenburger's dairy cows." Shane sloshed over to him. "Here, you haven't got it all off your face." Cupping some water in her hand, she lifted it and began to clean his face herself. "I tore my britches on every farmer's fence for three miles," she went on. "Gran would patch them up saying she despaired of my being any more than a hooligan."

With one small, smooth hand, she methodically scrubbed Vance's face. The other she held balanced against his naked chest. He made no protest, but stood still, watching her.

"'That Abbot girl,' they'd say," Shane told him, rubbing at a spot on his jawline. "Now I have to convince them I'm an upstanding citizen so they'll forget I filched their apples and buy my antiques. No one takes a hooligan very seriously. There, that's better." Satisfied, Shane started to lower her hand. Vance caught it in his. Her eyes didn't waver from his, but she became very still.

Without speaking, he began to wash the few lingering traces of mud from her face. He worked in very slow, very deliberate circles, his eyes fixed on hers. Though his palm was rough, his touch was gentle. Shane's lips trembled apart. With something like curiosity, Vance took a damp finger to trace their shape. He felt her quick, convulsive shudder. Still slow, still inquisitive, he ran his fingertip along the inside of her bottom lip. Under his thumb, the pulse in her wrist began to hammer. The sun broke briefly through the clouds, so that the light shifted and brightened before it dimmed again. He watched it play over her face.

"You won't run away this time, Shane," he murmured, as if to himself.

She said nothing, afraid to speak while his finger lingered on her lips. Slowly, he traced it down, over her chin, over the throbbing pulse in her throat. He paused there a moment, as if gauging and enjoying her response to him. Then he allowed his fingertip to sweep up over the swell of her breast and lie lightly on the erect peak covered only by the thin wet shirt.

Heat and cold shot through her; her skin was chilled from the water, her blood flamed at his touch. Vance watched the color drain from her face while her eyes grew impossibly large and dark. Yet she didn't draw away or protest the intimacy. He heard the sharp intake of her breath, then the slow, ragged expulsion.

"Are you afraid of me?" he asked, bringing his hand up to cup the back of her neck.

"No," she whispered. "Of me."

Puzzled, he drew his brows together. For a moment he looked hard and very fierce. Though his eyes weren't cold, they were piercing—full of questions, full of suspicion. Still Shane felt no fear of him, only of the needs and longing running through her. "An odd answer, Shane," he murmured thoughtfully. "You're an odd woman." With his fingers, he kneaded the back of her neck while he searched her face for answers. "Is that why you excite me?"

"I don't know," she said, struggling for breath. "I don't want to know. Just kiss me."

He lowered his lips, but only tested hers with the same lightness as his fingertip. "I wonder," he said softly against her mouth, "what it is about you I can't quite shake. Your taste?" He dug his teeth almost experimentally into her bottom lip. A low moan of pleasure was wrenched from her. "Fresh as rain one minute and honey soaked the next." Lightly, languidly, he traced her lips with his tongue. "Is it the way you feel? That skin of yours…like the underside of a rose petal." He ran his hands down her arms, then up again, gradually bringing her to him until she was caught close. The thud of her heart sounded like thunder in her ears.

"Why do you have to know?" The question was low and shaky. "Feeling's enough." They might have been naked, pressed body to body with only wet clinging clothes between them. "Kiss me, Vance, just kiss me. It's enough."

"You smell like rain now," he murmured, telling himself to resist her but knowing he wouldn't. "Pure and honest. When I look in your eyes, I'd swear there isn't a lie in you. Is there?" he demanded, but he crushed his mouth to hers before she could answer.

Shane reeled from the impact. Even as she gasped, his tongue was probing and exploring. The anger she had sensed in him before was now pure passion. Hunger, the rawness of his hunger, thrilled her. The water ran swiftly, grumbling as it hurried on its way to the river, but Shane heard only her own heartbeat. She no longer felt the stinging cold, only the warmth of his hand as it ran up her spine and down again.

He wasn't content with only her lips now, but took his own wild journey of her face. It was still wet, tasting of the cold freshness of the creek. But wherever his kisses wandered, he was drawn back again to the soft sweet taste of her mouth. It seemed always to be waiting for him, ready to open, invite, demand. Beneath the pliancy, beneath the willingness was a passion as great as his own and a strength he was just beginning to measure.

Vance told himself he needed a woman. That was why he was so desperate for Shane. He needed a woman's softness and flavor, and she was here. There was no exclusivity to it. How could there be? Yet there was something about her slight body, her fascinatingly different taste that drove every other woman to some dark corner of his mind, leaving only Shane in the light.

He could take her now, on the bank of the creek, in the dim daylight on the rain-damp grass. As her mouth moved, moist and warm under his, Vance could imagine how it would be to take full possession of her body. Her energy and hunger would match his own. There would be no false, foolish pretense of seduction, but an honest meeting of desires.

Her small round breasts pressed into his naked chest. Vance thought he could feel the aching need in them—or was it his own need? It raged in him, drove at him, until she was all he craved. Her mouth was small too, but avid, never retreating from the savageness of his. Instead, she matched it, propelling him further and further, pulling him closer and closer. All women or one woman, he was no longer certain, but she was overpowering him.

Somehow he knew that if he took her, he would never walk away easily. The reasons might not be fully clear yet, but she wasn't like the other women he had known and bedded. He was afraid her eager hands and mouth could hold him—and he wasn't yet ready to chance it.

Vance drew her away, but Shane dropped her head on his chest. There was something vulnerable in the gesture though the arms around his waist were strong. The contrast aroused him, as did the lightning fast beat of her heart. For a moment, he stood holding her while the water ran cold and fast around their legs and hazy sunlight drifted through the trees.

She'd once told him that a snowfall had made her feel a complete isolation. Vance felt it now. There might have been nothing, no one beyond the rushing creek and fringe of trees. And to his own confusion, he felt a need for none. He wanted only her. Perhaps they were alone… The thought both excited and disturbed him. Perhaps there was nothing beyond that forgotten little spot, and no reason not to take what he wanted.

Shane shivered, making him realize she must be chilled to the bone. It brought him back to reality in a rush. His arms dropped away from her.

"Come on," he muttered. "You should get inside." Vance pulled her up the slippery bank.

Shane bent over to pick up her boots. When she was certain she could do so calmly, she met his eyes. "You're not coming in." It wasn't a question. She had sensed all too well his change of attitude.

"No." His tone was cool again though his blood still throbbed for her. "I'll go change, then come back and get started on the porch."

Shane had known he would bring her pain, but she hadn't thought it would be so soon. The old wounds of rejection opened again. "All right. If I'm not here, just do whatever you have to do."

Vance could feel the hurt, yet she met his eyes and her voice was steady. Recriminations he could have dealt with easily. Anger he would have welcomed. For the first time in years, he was completely baffled by a woman.

"You know what would happen if I came in now." The words were rough with impatience. Vance found himself wanting to shake her.

"Yes."

"Is that what you want?"

Shane said nothing for a moment. When she smiled, the

light didn't reach her eyes. "It's not what you want," she said quietly. Turning, she started back to the house, but Vance caught her arm, spinning her around. He was furious now, all the more furious when he saw the effort her composure was costing her.

"Damn it, Shane, you're a fool if you think I don't want you."

"You don't want to want me," she returned evenly. "That's more important to me."

"What difference does it make?" he ground out impatiently. Frustrated by the calmness of her answer, he did shake her. How could she look at him with those big quiet eyes when she'd driven him to the wall only moments before? "You know how close I came to taking you right here on the ground. Isn't it enough to know you can push me to that? What more do you want?"

She gave him a long searching look. "Push you to it," she repeated quietly. "Is that really how you see it?"

The conflict raged in him. He wanted badly to get away from her. "Yes," he said bitterly. "How else?"

"How else," she agreed with a shaky laugh that started a new ache moving in him. "I suppose for some that might be a compliment of sorts."

"If you like," he said curtly as he picked up his shirt.

"I don't," she murmured. "But then, you said I was odd." With a sigh, she stared into his eyes. "You've cut yourself off from your feelings, Vance, and it eats at you."

"You don't know a damn thing," he tossed back, only more enraged to hear her speak the truth.

As he glared at her, Shane heard a bird set up a strident song in the woods behind her. The high, piercing notes suited the air of tension and anger. "You're not nearly as hard or cold as you'd like to think," she said calmly.

"You don't know anything about me," he countered furiously, grabbing her arms again.

"And it infuriates you when the guard slips," Shane continued without breaking rhythm. "It infuriates you even more that you might actually feel something for me." His fingers loosened on her arms, and Shane drew away. "I don't push you, but something else certainly does. No, I don't know what it is, but you do." She took a long steadying breath as she studied him. "You've got to fight your own tug-of-war, Vance."

Turning, she walked to the house, leaving him staring after her.

Chapter 7

He couldn't stop thinking of her. In the weeks that passed, the mountains became a riot of color. The air took on the nip of fall. Twice, Vance spotted deer through his own kitchen window. And he couldn't stop thinking of her.

He split his time between the two houses. His own was taking shape slowly. Vance calculated he would be ready to start the more detailed inside work by winter.

Shane's was progressing more quickly. Between roofers and plumbers, the house had been bedlam for more than a week. The old kitchen had been gutted and stood waiting for new paint and trim. Shane had waited patiently for rain after the roof had been repaired. Then she had checked all the familiar spots for signs of leaks. Oddly, she found herself a trifle sad that she didn't have to set out a single pan or bucket.

The museum area was completely finished. While Vance worked elsewhere, Shane busied herself arranging and filling the display cases that had been delivered.

At times she would be gone for hours, hunting up treasures at auctions and estate sales. He always knew the moment she returned because the house would spring to life again. In the basement, she'd set up a workroom where she refinished certain pieces or stored others. He saw her dash out, or dash in. He saw her carting tables, dragging packing boxes, climbing ladders. He never saw her idle.

Her attitude toward him was just as it had been from the first—friendly and open. Not once did she mention what had happened between them. It took all of his strength of will not to touch her. She laughed, brought him coffee and gave him amusing accounts of her adventures at auctions. He wanted her more every time he looked at her.

Now, as he finished up the trim on what had been the summer parlor, Vance knew she was downstairs. He went over his work critically, checking for flaws, while the simple awareness of her played havoc with his concentration. It might be wise, he thought, to take a trip back to Washington. So far, he had handled everything pertaining to his company by phone or mail. There was nothing urgent that required his attention, but he wondered if it wouldn't be wise to have a week of distance. She was haunting him. Plaguing him, Vance corrected. On a wave of frustration he packed his tools. The woman was trouble, he decided. Nothing but trouble.

Still, as he got ready to leave, Vance detoured to the basement steps. He hesitated, cursed himself, then started down.

Dressed in baggy cord jeans and a hip-length sweater, she was working on a tilt-top table. Vance had seen the table when Shane had first brought it in. It had been scarred and scratched and dull. Flushed with excitement, she had claimed to have bought it for a song, then had hustled it off to the basement. Now, the grain of mahogany gleamed through the thin coats of clear lacquer she had applied. She was industriously buffing it with paste wax. The basement smelled of tung oil and lemon.

Vance would have turned to go back upstairs, but Shane raised her head and saw him. "Hi!" Her smile welcomed him before she gestured him over. "Come take a look. You're the expert on wood." As he crossed the room, Shane stood back to survey her work. "The hardest thing now," she muttered as she twisted a curl around her finger, "is going to be parting with it. I'll make a nice profit. I only paid a fraction of its worth."

Vance ran a fingertip over the surface. It was baby smooth and flawless. His mother had a similar piece in the drawing room of her Washington estate. Since he had purchased it for her himself, he knew the value. He also knew the difference between an amateur job of refinishing and an expert one. This hadn't been done haphazardly. "Your time's worth something," he commented. "And your talent. It would have cost a good deal to have this done."

"Yes, but I enjoy it, so it doesn't count."

Vance lifted his eyes. "You're in business to make money, aren't you?"

"Yes, of course." Shane snapped the lid back on the can of paste wax. "I love the smell of this stuff."

"You won't make a lot of money if you don't consider your own time and labor."

"I don't need to make a lot of money." She placed the can on a shelf, then examined the ladder-back chair, which needed recaning. "I need to pay bills and stock my shop and have a bit left over to play with." Turning the chair upside down, she frowned at the frayed hole in the center of the seat. "I wouldn't know what to do with a lot of money."

"You'd find something," Vance said dryly. "Clothes, furs."

Shane glanced up, saw he was serious, then burst out laughing. "Furs? Oh, yes, I can see myself waltzing into the general store to buy milk in a mink. Vance, you're a riot."

"I've never known a woman who didn't appreciate a mink," he countered.

"Then you've known the wrong women," she said lightly as she set the chair upright again. "I know this man in Boonsboro who does caning and rushing. I'll have to give him a call. Even if I had the time, I wouldn't know where to begin on this."

"What kind of woman are you?"

Shane's thoughts came back from her ladder-back chair. When she looked at him again, she noted that Vance's expression was cynical. She sighed. "Vance, why do you always look for complications?"

"Because they're always there," he returned.

She shook her head, keeping her hands on the top rung of the chair's back. "I'm exactly the kind of woman I seem to be. Perhaps that's too simple for you, but it's true."

"The kind who's content to work twelve hours a day just for enough money to get by on?" Vance demanded. "The kind who's willing to slave away hour after hour—"

"I don't slave," Shane interrupted testily.

"The hell you don't. I've watched you. Dragging furniture, lugging boxes, scrubbing on your hands and knees." Remembering only made him angrier. She was too small to labor the way he had seen over the past weeks. The fact that he wanted to insist she stop only infuriated him further. "Damn it, Shane, it's too much for you to handle by yourself."

"I know what I'm capable of," she tossed back, springing to her own defense. "I'm not a child."

"No, you're a woman who doesn't crave furs or all the niceties an attractive female can have if she plays her cards right." The words were cool with sarcasm.

Temper sprang into Shane's eyes. Struggling not to explode, she turned away from him. "Do you think everyone has a game to play, Vance?"

"And some play better than others" was his response.

"Oh, I feel sorry for you," she said tightly. "Really very sorry."

"Why?" he demanded. "Because I know that grabbing all they can get is what motivates people? Only a fool settles for less."

"I wonder if you really believe that," she murmured. "I wonder if you really could."

"I wonder why you pretend to believe otherwise," he retorted.

"I'm going to tell you a little story." When she turned back, her eyes were dark with anger. "A man like you will probably find it corny and a bit boring, but you'll just have to listen anyway." Stuffing her hands into her pockets, she paced the low-ceilinged room until she was certain she could continue.

"Do you see these?" Shane demanded, indicating a row of shelves that held filled mason jars. "My grandmother— technically, she was my great-grandmother—canned these. Putting by, she always called it. She'd dig and hoe and plant and weed, then spend hours in a hot, steamy kitchen canning. Putting by," Shane repeated more quietly as she studied the colorful glass jars. "When she was sixteen, she lived in a mansion in southern Maryland. Her family was very wealthy. They still are," Shane added with a shrug. "The Bristols. The Leonardtown Bristols. You might have heard of them."

He had, and though his eyes registered surprise, he said nothing. Bristols Department Stores were scattered strategically all over the country. It was a very old, very prestigious firm that catered to the wealthy and the prominent. Even now, Vance's firm was contracted to build another branch in Chicago.

"In any case," Shane continued, "she was a young, beautiful, pampered girl who could have had anything. She'd been educated in Europe, and there were plans for her to be finished in Paris before a London debut. If she had followed her parents' plans, she would have married well, had her own mansion and her own staff of servants. The closest she would have come to planting would have been watching her gardener prune a rosebush."

Shane gave a little laugh as though the thought both amused and baffled her. "She didn't follow the plan, though. She fell in love with William Abbott, an apprentice mason who had been hired to do some stonework on the estate. Of course, her family would have none of it. They were already planning the groundwork for a marriage between Gran and the heir to some steel company. The moment they got wind of what was happening, they fired him. To keep it brief, Gran made her choice and married him. They disowned her. Very dramatic and Victorian. The I-have-no-daughter sort of thing you read in a standard Gothic."

Vance said nothing as she stared at him, almost daring him to comment. "They moved here, back with his family," Shane continued. "They had to share this house with his parents because there wasn't enough money for one of their own. When his father died, they cared for his mother. Gran never regretted giving up all the *niceties*. She had such tiny hands," she murmured, looking down at her own. "You wouldn't have thought they could be so strong." She shook off the mood and turned away. "They were poor by the standards she had grown up with. What horses they had were for pulling a plow. Some of your land was hers at one time, but with the taxes and no one to work it…" She trailed off, lifting down a mason jar, then setting it back. "The only gesture her parents ever made was when her mother left Gran the dining-room set and a few pieces of china. Even that was done through lawyers after her mother had died." Shane plucked up her polishing cloth and began to run it through her hands.

"Gran had five children, lost two in childhood, another in the war. One daughter moved to Oklahoma and died childless about forty years ago. Her youngest son settled here, married and had one daughter. Both he and his wife were killed when the daughter was five." She paused a moment, brooding up at the small window set near the ceiling. Light poured through it to lie in a patch on the concrete floor. "I wonder if you can appreciate how a mother feels when she outlives every one of her children."

Vance said nothing, only continued to watch as Shane moved agitatedly around the room. "She raised her grand-daughter, Anne. Gran loved her. Maybe part of the love was grief, I don't know. My mother was a beautiful child—there are pictures of her upstairs—but she was never content. The stories I've heard came mostly from people in town, though once or twice Gran talked to me. Anne hated living here, hated not having enough. She wanted to be an actress. When she was seventeen, she got pregnant."

Shane's voice altered subtly, but he heard the change. It was flat now, devoid of emotion. He'd never heard that tone from her before. "She didn't know—or wouldn't admit—who the father was," she said simply. "As soon as I was born, she took off and left me with Gran. From time to time, she came back, spent a few days and talked Gran out of more money. At last count she's been married three times. I've seen her in furs. They don't seem to make her happy. She's still beautiful, still selfish, still discontented."

Shane turned and looked at Vance for the first time since she had begun. "My grandmother only grabbed for one thing in her life, and that was love. She spoke French beau-tifully, read Shakespeare and tilled a garden. And she was happy. The only thing my mother ever taught me was that *things* meant nothing. Once you have a *thing,* you're too busy looking for the next one to be happy with it. You're too worried that someone might have a better one to be able to enjoy it. All the games my mother played never brought anything but pain to the people who loved her. I don't have the time or the skill for those games."

As she started to walk to the stairs, Vance stepped in front of her to bar her way. She lifted her chin to stare with eyes that glittered with anger and tears. "You should have told me to go to hell," he said quietly.

Shane swallowed. "Go to hell then," she muttered, and tried to move past him again.

Vance took her shoulders, holding her firmly at arm's length. "Are you angry with me, Shane, or with yourself for telling me something that was none of my business?" he asked.

After taking a deep breath, Shane stared at him, dry-eyed. "I'm angry because you're cynical, and I've never been able to understand cynicism."

"Any more than I understand an idealist."

"I'm not an idealist," she countered. "I simply don't automatically assume there's someone waiting to take advantage of me." She felt calmer suddenly, and sadder. "I think you miss a lot more by not trusting people than you risk by trusting them."

"What happens when the trust is violated?"

"Then you pick up and go on," she told him simply. "You're only a victim if you choose to be."

His brows drew together. Is that what he considered himself? A victim? Was he continuing to allow Amelia to blight his life two years after she'd died? And how much longer would he look over his shoulder for the next betrayal?

Shane felt his fingers relax, saw the puzzled consideration on his face. She lifted a hand to touch his shoulder. "Were you hurt very badly?" she asked him.

Vance focused on her again, then released her. "I was...disillusioned."

"That's the worst kind of hurt, I think." In compassion, she laid a hand on his arm. "When someone you love or care for turns out to be dishonest, or an ideal turns to glass, it's difficult to accept. I always set my ideals high. If they're going to crumble, I'd just as soon take the long fall." She smiled, slipping her hand down so it linked with his. "Let's go for a drive."

His thoughts were so bound up in her words, it took him a moment to understand the suggestion. "A drive?" he repeated.

"We've been cooped up for weeks," Shane stated as she pulled him toward the stairs. "I don't know about you, but I haven't done anything but work until I tumbled into bed. It's a beautiful day, maybe the last of Indian summer." She shut the basement door behind them. "And I bet you haven't had a tour of the battlefield yet. Certainly not with an expert guide."

"Are you," he asked with the beginnings of a smile, "an expert guide?"

"The best," she said without modesty. As she had hoped, the tension went out of the fingers that were laced with hers. "There's nothing about the battle I can't tell you, or as some of my critics would claim, won't tell you."

"As long as I don't have to take a quiz afterward," Vance agreed as she pulled him out the back door.

"I'm retired," she reminded him primly.

"The Battle of Antietam," Shane began as she drove down a narrow, winding road lined with monuments, "though claimed as a clear victory for neither side, resulted in the repulse of Lee's first effort to invade the North." Vance gave a quick grin at her faintly lecturing tone, but didn't interrupt. "Near Antietam Creek here in Sharpsburg," she continued, "on September 17, 1862, Lee and McClellan engaged in the bloodiest single day of the Civil War. That's Dunker Church." Shane pointed to a tiny white building set off the road. "Some of the heaviest fighting went on there. I have some pretty good prints for the museum."

Vance glanced back at the peaceful little spot as Shane drove by. "Looks quiet enough now," he commented, and earned a mild look.

"Lee divided his forces," she went on, ignoring him, "sending Jackson to capture Harper's Ferry. A Union soldier picked up a copy of Lee's orders, giving McClellan an advantage, but he didn't move fast enough. Even when he engaged Lee's much smaller army in Sharpsburg, he failed to smash through the line before Jackson returned with support. Lee lost a quarter of his army and withdrew. McClellan still didn't capitalize on his advantage. Even so, twenty-six thousand men were lost."

"For a retired schoolteacher, you don't seem to have forgotten the facts," Vance remarked.

Shane laughed, taking a bend in the road competently. "My ancestors fought here. Gran didn't let me forget it."

"For which side?"

"Both." She gave a small shrug. "Wasn't that the worst of it really? The choosing sides, the disintegration of families. This is a border state. Though it went for the North, sympathies this far south leaned heavily toward the Confederacy as well. It isn't difficult to imagine a number of people from this area cheering secretly or openly for the Stars and Bars."

"And with this section being caught between Virginia and West Virginia—"

"Exactly," she said, very much like a teacher approving of a bright student. Vance chuckled but she didn't seem to notice. Shane pulled off the side of the road into a small parking area. "Come on, let's walk. It's beautiful here."

Around them mountains circled in the full glory of fall. A few leaves whipped by—orange, scarlet, amber—to be caught by the wind and carried off. There were rolling hills, gold in the slanting sunlight, and fields with dried, withering stalks of corn. The air was cooler now as the sun dropped toward the peaks of the western mountains. Without thinking, Vance linked his hand with hers.

"Bloody Lane," Shane said, bringing his attention to a long, narrow trench. "Gruesome name, but apt. They came at each other from across the fields. Rebs from the north. Yanks from the south. Artillery set up there—" she pointed "—and there. This trench is where most of them lay after it was over. Of course, there were engagements all around—at the Burnside Bridge, the Dunker Church—but this…"

Vance shot her a curious look. "War really fascinates you, doesn't it?"

Shane looked out over the field. "It's the only true obscenity. The only time killing's glorified rather than condemned. Men become statistics. I wonder if there's anything more dehumanizing." Her voice became more thoughtful. "Haven't you ever found it odd that to kill one to one is considered man's ultimate crime, but the more a man kills during war, the more he's honored? So many of these were farm boys," she continued before Vance could form an answer. "Children who'd never shot at anything more than a weasel in the henhouse. They put on a uniform, blue or gray, and marched into battle. I doubt if a fraction of them had any idea what it was really going to be like. I'll tell you what fascinates me." Shane looked back at Vance, too wrapped up in her own thoughts to note how intensely he watched her. "Who were they really? The sixteen-year-old Pennsylvania farm boy who rushed across this field to kill a sixteen-year-old boy from a Georgia plantation—did they start out looking for adventure? Were they on a quest? How many pictured themselves sitting around a campfire like men and raising some hell away from their mothers?"

"A great many, I imagine," Vance murmured. Affected by the image she projected, he slipped an arm around her shoulders as he looked out over the field. "Too many."

"Even the ones who got back whole would never be boys again."

"Then why history, Shane, when it's riddled with wars?"

"For the people." She tossed back her head to look at him. The lowering sun shining on her eyes seemed to accentuate the tiny gold flecks that he sometimes couldn't see at all. "For the boy I can imagine who came across that field in September more than a hundred and twenty years ago. He was seventeen." She turned back to the field as if she could indeed see him. "He'd had his first whiskey, but not his first woman. He came running across that field full of terror and glory. The bugles were blaring, the shells exploding, so that the noise was so huge, he never heard his own fear. He killed an enemy that was so obscure to him it had no face. And when the battle was over, when the war was over, he went home a man, tired and aching for his own land."

"What happened to him?" Vance murmured.

"He married his childhood sweetheart, raised ten kids

and told his grandchildren about his charge to Bloody Lane in 1862."

Vance drew her closer, not in passion, but in camaraderie. "You must have been a hell of a teacher," he said quietly.

That made Shane laugh. "I was a hell of a storyteller," she corrected.

"Why do you do that?" he demanded. "Why do you underrate yourself?"

She shook her head. "No, I know my capabilities and my limitations. And," she added, "I'm willing to stretch them both a bit to get what I want. It's much smarter than thinking you're something you're not." Before he could speak, she laughed, giving him a friendly hug. "No, no more philosophizing. I've done my share for the day. Come on, let's go up in the tower. The view's wonderful from there." She was off in a sprint, pulling Vance with her. "You can see for miles," she told him as they climbed the narrow iron steps.

The light was dim though the sun shot through the small slits set in the sides of the stone tower. It grew brighter as they climbed, then poured through the opening at the top. "This is the part I like best," she told him, while a few annoyed pigeons fluttered away from their roost in the roof. She leaned over the wide stone, pleased to let the wind buffet her face. "Oh, it's beautiful, the perfect day for it. Look at those colors!" She drew Vance beside her, wanting to share. "Do you see? That's our mountain."

Our mountain. Vance smiled as he followed the direction of her hand. The way she said it, it might have belonged to the two of them exclusively. Beyond the tree-thick hills, the more distant mountains were cast in blue from the falling afternoon light. Farmhouses and barns were set here and there, with the more closely structured surrounding towns quiet in the early evening hush. Just barely, he could hear the whiz of a car on the highway. As he looked over a cornfield, he saw three enormous crows take flight. They argued, taunting each other as they glided across the sky. The air was very still after they passed, so quiet he could hear the breeze whisper in the dry stalks of corn.

Then he saw the buck. It stood poised no more than ten yards from where Shane had parked her car. It was still as a statue, head up, ears pricked. Vance turned to Shane and pointed.

In silence, hands linked, they watched. Vance felt something move inside him, a sudden sense of belonging. He wouldn't have been amused now if Shane had said "our mountain." Remnants of bitterness washed from him as he realized his answer had been staring him in the face. He'd kept himself a victim, just as Shane had said, because it was easier to be angry than to let go.

The buck moved quickly, bounding over the grassy hill, taking a low stone fence with a graceful leap before he darted out of sight. Vance felt rather than heard Shane's long, slow sigh.

"I never get used to it," she murmured. "Every time I see one, I'm struck dumb."

Shane turned her face up to his. It seemed natural to kiss her here, with the mountains and fields around them, with the feeling of something shared still on both of them. Above their heads a pigeon cooed softly, content now that the intruders were quiet.

Here was the tenderness Shane had sensed but had not been sure of. His mouth was firm but not demanding, his hands strong but not bruising. Her heart seemed to flutter to her throat. Everything warm and sweet poured through her until she was limp and pliant in his arms. She had been waiting for this—this final assurance of what she knew he held trapped inside him: a gentle goodness she would respect as much as his strength and confidence. Her sigh was not of surrender but of joy in knowing she could admire what she already loved.

Vance drew her closer, changing the angle of the kiss, reluctant to break the moment. Emotions seeped into him, through the cracks in the wall he had built so long ago. He felt the soft give of her mouth, tasted its moist generosity. With care, he let his fingertips reacquaint themselves with the texture of her skin.

Could she have been there all along, he wondered, waiting for him to stumble onto her through a curtain of bitterness and suspicion?

Vance drew her against his chest, holding her tightly with both arms as if she might vanish. Was it too late for him to fall in love? he wondered. Or to win a woman who already knew the worst of him and had no notion of his material advantages? Closing his eyes, he rested his cheek on her hair. If it wasn't too late, should he take the chance and tell her who and what he was? If he told her now, he might never be fully certain, if she came to him, that she came only to him. He needed that—to be taken for himself without the Riverton Banning fortune or power. He hesitated, torn and indecisive. That alone shook him. Vance was a man who ruled a multimillion-dollar company by being decisive. Now a slip of a woman whose hair curled chaotically under his cheek was changing the order of his life.

"Shane." Vance drew her away to kiss her brow.

"Vance." Laughing, she kissed him soundly, more like a friend than a lover. "You look so serious."

"Have dinner with me." It came out too swiftly and he cursed himself. What had become of his finesse with women?

Shane pushed at her windblown hair. "All right. I can fix us something at the house."

"No, I want to take you out."

"Out?" Shane frowned, thinking of the expense.

"Nothing fancy," he told her, thinking she was worried about her bulky sweater and jeans. "As you said, neither of us has done anything but work in weeks." He brushed his knuckles over the back of her cheek. "Come with me."

She smiled, pleasing him. "I know a nice little place just over the border in West Virginia."

Shane chose the tiny, out-of-the-way restaurant because it was inexpensive and she had some fond memories of an abbreviated career as a waitress there. She'd worked the summer after her high school graduation in order to earn extra money for college.

After they had settled into a cramped booth with a sputtering candle between them, she shot him a grin. "I knew you'd love it."

Vance glanced around at the painted landscapes in vivid colors and plastic frames. The air smelled ever so faintly of onion. "Next time, I choose."

"They used to serve a great spaghetti here. It was Thursday's special, all you can eat for—"

"It's not Thursday," Vance pointed out, dubiously opening the plastic-coated menu. "Wine?"

"I think they probably have it." Shane smiled at him

when he peered over the top of the menu. "We could go next door and get a whole bottle for two ninety-seven."

"Good vintage?"

"Just last week," she assured him.

"We'll take our chances here." He decided next time he would take her somewhere he could buy her champagne.

"I'll have the chili," Shane announced, bringing his thoughts back.

"Chili?" Vance frowned at the menu again. "Is it any good?"

"Oh, no!"

"Then why are you—" He broke off as he lowered his menu and saw Shane buried behind her own. "Shane, what—"

"They just came in," she hissed, turning her menu toward the entrance and peeping around the side of it.

Curiously, he glanced over. Vance spotted Cy Trainer with a trim brunette in a severely tailored tan suit and sensible pumps. His first reaction was annoyance; then, looking the woman over again and noting the way her hand rested on Cy's arm, he turned back to Shane. She was fully hidden behind the menu.

"Shane, I know it must upset you, but you're bound to run into him from time to time and…" He heard a muffled sound from behind the plastic-coated cardboard. Instinctively, Vance reached for her hand. "We could go somewhere else, but we can't leave now without his seeing you."

"It's Laurie MacAfee." She squeezed Vance's fingers convulsively. He returned the pressure, furious that she still had feelings for the man who had hurt her.

"Shane, you've got to face this and not let him see you make a fool of yourself."

"I know, but it's so hard." Cautiously, she tilted the menu to the side. With a jolt, Vance saw she was convulsed not with tears but with laughter. "As soon as he sees us," she began confidentially, "he's going to come over and be polite."

"I can see that's going to cause you a lot of pain."

"Oh, it is," she agreed. "Because you've got to promise to kick me under the table or stomp on my foot the minute you see I'm going to laugh."

"My pleasure," he assured her.

"Laurie used to keep her dolls lined up according to height and she sewed little name tags on all their clothes," Shane explained, taking deep breaths to prepare herself.

"That certainly clears everything up."

"Okay, now I'm going to put the menu down." She swallowed, lowering her voice a bit more. "Whatever you do, don't look at them."

"I wouldn't dream of it."

After a final cleansing breath, Shane set the menu on the table. "Chili?" she said in a normal tone. "Yes, it's always been good here. I believe I'll have it too."

"You're an idiot."

"Oh yes, I agree." Smiling, she picked up her water glass. Out of the corner of her eye, she spotted Cy and Laurie crossing the room toward them. To kill the first bubble of laughter, she cleared her throat violently.

"Shane, how nice to see you."

Looking up, Shane managed to feign surprise. "Hello, Cy. Hello, Laurie. How've you been?"

"Very well," Laurie answered in her carefully modulated voice. She's really very pretty, Shane thought. Even if her eyes are just a fraction too close together.

"I don't think you know Vance," she continued. "Vance, this is Cy Trainer and Laurie MacAfee, old school friends of mine. Vance is my neighbor."

"Ah, of course, the old Farley place." Cy extended his hand. Vance found it soft. The grip was correctly firm and brief. "I hear you're fixing the place up."

"A bit." Vance allowed himself to study Cy's face. He was passable, Vance decided, considering he had a weak jaw.

"You must be the carpenter who's helping Shane set up her little shop," Laurie put in. Her glance slipped over his work clothes before it shifted to Shane's sweater. "I must say, I was surprised when Cy told me your plans."

Seeing Shane's lip quiver, Vance set his foot firmly on top of hers. "Were you?" Shane said as she reached for her water again. Her eyes danced with suppressed amusement as they met Vance's over the rim. "Well, I've always liked to surprise people."

"We couldn't imagine you with your own business, could we, Cy?" Laurie went on without giving him a chance to answer. "Of course, we wish you the very best of luck, Shane, and you can count on both of us to buy something to help you get started."

The laughter was a pain in her stomach. Shane had to press a hand against it while Vance increased the pressure on her foot. "Thank you, Laurie. I can't tell you what that means to me…I really can't."

"Anything for an old friend, right, Cy? You know we wish you every success, Shane. I'll be sure to tell everyone

I know about your little shop. That should help bring a few people in. Though of course," she sighed apologetically, "the selling's up to you."

"Y-yes. Thank you."

"We'll just be running along now. We want to order before it gets too crowded. So nice meeting you." Laurie sent Vance a brief smile and drew Cy away.

"Oh, God, I think I'm going to burst!" Shane drank down the whole glass of water without a breath.

"Your boyfriend got just what he deserved," Vance murmured, glancing after them. "She'll regiment everything right down to their sex life." Thoughtfully, he looked after them. "Do you think they have one yet?"

"Oh, stop," Shane begged, savaging her lip in defense. "I'll be hysterical in a minute."

"Do you suppose she picked out that tie he's wearing?" Vance asked.

Giving up, Shane burst into laughter. "Oh, damn you, Vance," she whispered when Laurie turned her head. "I was doing so well too."

"Want to give them something to talk about over dinner?" Before she could answer, Vance pulled her across the narrow booth and planted a long, lingering kiss on her lips. To keep Shane from ending it too soon, he caught her chin in his hand and held her still. He drew her away for only seconds, tilting her head, then pressing his mouth to hers again at a fresh angle. He heard her give a tiny moan of distress. Though she lifted a hand to his shoulder to push him away, when he deepened the kiss, she allowed it to lie unresisting until he took his lips from hers.

"Now you've done it," she said when she gathered her

wits again. "By noon tomorrow it'll be all over Sharpsburg that we're lovers."

"Will it?" Smiling, he lifted her hand to his lips, then slowly kissed her fingers one by one. It satisfied him to feel the faint tremor of arousal.

"Yes," Shane answered breathlessly, "and I don't..." she trailed off when he turned her palm up to press another long kiss in its center.

"Don't what?" he asked softly, taking his lips to the inside of her wrist. Her pulse pounded against the light trace of his tongue.

"Think it's—it's wise," she managed, forgetting the restaurant and Cy and Laurie and everything else.

"That we're lovers or that it's all over Sharpsburg?" Vance enjoyed the confusion in her eyes and the knowledge that he had put it there.

Her pulse beat jerkily. He was different. Reckless? she thought, and felt a fresh thrill race down her spine. Smooth? How could he be both at once? Yet he was. The recklessness was in his eyes, but the romantic moves were smooth with experience.

She hadn't been afraid of the hard, angry man she had met, but she felt a skip of fear for the one who even now traced his thumb over the speeding pulse at her wrist.

"I'm going to have to give that some thought," she murmured.

"Do that," he said agreeably.

Chapter 8

Shane opened the doors of Antietam Antiques and Museum the first week of December. As she had expected, for the first few days the shop and museum were crowded, for the most part with people she knew. They had come to buy or browse out of curiosity or affection. Others came to see what "that Abbott girl" had up her sleeve this time. It amused Shane to hear her past crimes discussed as though they had taken place the day before. Cy's name was dropped a time or two, causing her to force back a chuckle and change the subject. Still, after the initial novelty had worn off, she had a steady trickle of customers. That was enough to satisfy her.

As planned, she hired Donna's sister-in-law, Pat, on a part-time basis. The girl was eager and willing, and not opposed to giving Shane weekend hours. Shane considered the additional expense well worth it when Pat, flushed with triumph, rang up her first sale. With her coaching, and Pat's own enthusiastic studying, Shane's assistant had learned enough to classify certain articles in the shop and to handle questions in the museum section.

Shane found herself busier than ever, managing the shop, watching for ads for estate sales and overseeing the remodeling still under way on the second floor. The long, chaotic hours stimulated her, and helped her deal with the slow but steady loss of her grandmother's treasures. It was business, Shane reminded herself again and again as she sold a corner cabinet or candle holder. It was necessary. The bills in her desk had mounted over the weeks of prep-aration, and they had to be paid.

She saw Vance almost daily as he came to hammer and saw and trim on the second floor. Though he wasn't as withdrawn as he once had been, the intimacy they had shared for an afternoon and evening had faded. He treated her as a casual friend, not a woman whose palm he would kiss in a restaurant.

Shane concluded that he had taken on a loverlike aspect for Cy's benefit, and now it was back to business as usual. She wasn't discouraged. In fact, the man she had dined with had made her nervous and uncertain. She was more confident with Vance's temper than with soft words and tender caresses. Knowing herself well, Shane was aware it would be difficult not to make a fool of herself over him if he continued to treat her with gentleness. She had little defense against romance.

Daily, her love for him grew. It only made her more certain than ever that he was the only man for her. It would only be a matter of time, she decided, before he realized she was the woman for him.

It was late afternoon when Shane carried her latest acquisition up the new front steps and into the shop. She was flushed with cold and highly pleased with herself. She was learning to be ruthless when bargaining. After pushing the door open with her bottom, she carried the table through the entrance sideways.

"Just look what I've got!" she said to Pat before she closed the door behind her. "It's a Sheridan. Not a scratch on it either."

Pat stopped washing the glass on the display case. "Shane, you were supposed to take the afternoon off." Automatically she polished off a lingering smear before giving Shane her full attention. "You've got to take some time for yourself," she reminded her with a hint of exasperation. "That's why you hired me."

"Yes, of course," Shane said distractedly. "There's a mantel clock in the car and a complete set of cut-glass salt-cellars." Pat sighed, smart enough to know when she was being ignored, and followed Shane into the main showroom.

"Don't you ever quit?" she demanded.

"Uh-uh." After setting the table beside a Hitchcock chair, Shane stepped back to view the results. "I don't know," she said slowly. "It might look better in the front room, right under the window. Well, I want to polish it first anyway." She darted to the work counter, rummaging for the furniture polish. "How'd we do today?"

Pat shook her head. The first thing she had learned on the job was that Shane Abbott was a powerhouse. "I'll do that," she said, taking the polish and rag from Shane's hands. Shane grinned at Pat's weighty sigh but said nothing. "You had seven people come through the museum," Pat told her as she began to polish the Sheridan. "I sold some postcards and a print of the Burnside Bridge. A woman from Hagerstown bought the little table with the fluted edges."

Shane stopped unbuttoning her coat. "The rosewood piecrust?" It had sat in the summer parlor for as long as she could remember.

"Yes. And she was interested in the bentwood rocker." Pat tucked a strand of hair behind her ear while Shane struggled to be pleased. "I think she'll be back."

"Good."

"Oh, and you had a nibble on Uncle Festus."

"Really?" Shane grinned, thinking of the portrait of a dour Victorian man she'd been unable to resist. She had bought it because it amused her, though she had had little hope of selling it. "Well, I'll be sorry to lose him. He gives the place dignity."

"He gives me the creeps," Pat said baldly as Shane headed for the front door to fetch the rest of her new stock. "Oh, I nearly forgot. You didn't tell me you'd sold the dining-room set."

"What?" Puzzled, Shane stopped with her hand on the knob.

"The dining-room set with the heart-shaped chairs," Pat explained. "The Hepplewhite," she added, pleased that she was beginning to remember makes and periods. "I nearly sold it again."

"Again?" Shane released the knob and faced Pat fully. "What are you talking about?"

"There were some people in here a few hours ago who wanted it. It seems their daughter's getting married, and they were going to buy it as a wedding gift. They must be rich," she added with feeling. "The reception's going to be at a Baltimore country club...with an orchestra." She began to daydream about this a bit, but then she noted Shane's hard look. "Anyway," she continued quickly, "I'd nearly finalized the sale when Vance came downstairs and explained it was taken already."

Shane's eyes narrowed. "Vance? Vance said it was already sold?"

"Well, yes," Pat agreed, puzzled by the tone. If she had known Shane better, she would have recognized the beginnings of rage. Innocently, she continued. "It was a lucky thing too, or else they'd have bought it and arranged for the shipping right then and there. I guess you'd have been in a fix."

"A fix," Shane repeated between set teeth. "Yeah, somebody's in a fix all right." Abruptly, she turned to stride toward the rear of the shop while Pat looked after her, wide-eyed.

"Shane? Shane, what's wrong?" Confused, she trotted after her. "Where are you going?"

"To settle some business," she said tightly. "Get the rest of the stuff out of my car, will you?" she called back without slackening her pace. "And lock up. This might take a while."

"Sure, but..." Pat trailed off when she heard the back door slam. She puzzled a moment, shrugged, then went to follow orders.

"A fix," Shane muttered as she crushed dead leaves

underfoot. "Lucky thing he came down." Furiously, she kicked at a fallen branch and sent it skidding ahead of her, waiting to be kicked again. Grinding her teeth, she stormed purposefully down the path between denuded trees. "Already taken!" Enraged, she made a dangerous sound in her throat. A hapless squirrel started across the path, then dashed in the other direction.

Through the bare trees, she could see his house, with smoke puffing from the chimney to struggle up into a hard blue sky. Shane set her jaw and increased her pace. Into the quiet came a steady thump, pause, thump. Without hesitation, she skirted around to the back of the house.

Vance put another log on the tree stump he used as a chopping block, then bore down with his axe to split it neatly in two. Without a pause in rhythm, he set a new log. Shane took no time to admire the precision or grace of the movement.

"You!" she spat, and stuck her fists on her hips.

Vance checked his next swing. Glancing over, he saw Shane glaring at him with glittering eyes and a flushed face. He thought idly that she looked her best when in a temper, then followed through. The next log split to fall in two pieces on either side of the stump. The generous pile was evidence that he had been working for some time.

"Hello, Shane."

"Don't you 'hello Shane' me," she snapped, closing the distance between them in three quick strides. "How dare you?"

"Most people consider it an acceptable greeting," he countered as he bent down for another log. Shane knocked it off the stump with a sweep of her hand.

"You had no right to interfere, no right to cost me a sale. An important sale," she added furiously. Her breath puffed out visibly in the frigid air. "Just who the hell do you think you are, telling my customers something's already taken? Even if it had been, which it wasn't, it's hardly your place to add your two cents."

Calmly, Vance picked up the log again. He had been expecting her—and her anger. He had acted on impulse but didn't regret it. Very clearly, he could recall the look on her face when she had first shown him her grandmother's pride and joy. There was no way he was going to stand by and do nothing while she watched it being carted out the door.

"You don't want to sell it, Shane."

Her eyes only became more furious. "It's none of your business what I want to do. I have to sell it. I'm *going* to sell it. If you hadn't opened your big mouth, I *would* have sold it."

"And spent several hours hating yourself and crying over the invoice," he tossed back, slamming the blade of the axe into the stump before he faced her. "The money isn't worth it."

"Don't you tell me what it's worth," she retorted, and poked a finger into his chest. "You don't know how I feel. You don't know what I have to do. *I* do. I need the money, damn it."

With strained calm, he curled his hand around the finger that dug into his chest, held it aloft a moment, then let it drop. "You don't need it enough to give up something that's important to you."

"Sentiment doesn't pay bills." The color in her cheeks heightened. "I've got a desk full of them."

"Sell something else," he shouted back at her. Her face was lifted to his, her eyes glowing with anger. He felt conflicting urges to protect her and to throttle her. "You've got the damn place packed with junk as it is."

"Junk!" He had just declared war. *"Junk!"* Her voice rose.

"Unload some of the other stuff you've got piled in there," he advised with a coolness that would have rattled his business associates. A dangerous hissing sound escaped through Shane's teeth.

"You don't know the first thing about it," she fumed, poking him again so that he stepped back. "I stock the very best pieces I can find, and *you*—" she poked again "—you don't know a Hepplewhite from a—a piece of pressboard. You keep your city nose out of my affairs, Vance Banning, and play with your planes and drill bits. I don't need some flatlander to hand out empty advice."

"That's it," he said grimly. In one swift move, he swept Shane off her feet and dumped her over his shoulder.

"What the hell do you think you're doing?" she screamed, thrashing and pounding him with her fists.

"I'm taking you inside to make love to you," he stated between his teeth. "I've had enough."

In absolute astonishment, Shane stopped thrashing. "You're *what?*"

"You heard me."

"You're crazy!" More furious than frantic, she renewed her efforts to inflict pain wherever she could land a hit. Vance continued through the back door. "You're not taking me inside," she raged, even as he carted her through the kitchen. "I'm not going with you."

"You're going exactly where I take you," he countered.

"Oh, you're going to pay for this, Vance," she promised as she pounded against his back.

"I don't doubt that," he muttered, starting up the stairs.

"You put me down this minute. I'm not putting up with this."

Weary of being kicked, he pulled off her shoes, tossed them over the banister, then tightened an arm around the back of her knees. "You're going to put up with a hell of a lot more in a few minutes."

With her legs effectively pinned, she wiggled uselessly as he continued up the stairs. "I'm telling you, you're in big trouble. I'll get you for this," she warned, beating furiously against him as he strode down the hall and into a bedroom. "If you don't put me down this minute, *right this minute,* you're fired!" Shane let out a shriek as she tumbled through the air, then a whoosh as she thudded heavily on the bed. Breathless and infuriated, she scrambled to her knees. "You idiot!" she raged, puffing a bit. "Just what do you think you're doing?"

"I told you what I was doing." Vance stripped off his jacket and tossed it aside.

"If you think for one minute you can toss me over your shoulder like a bale of hay and get away with it, you're sadly mistaken." Shane watched with mounting fury as he unbuttoned his shirt. "And you stop that right now. You can't *make* me make love with you."

"Watch me." Vance peeled off his shirt.

"Oh no, you don't." Though she stuck her hands on her hips, the indignant pose lost something as she knelt on the bed. "Just put that right back on."

Watching her coolly, Vance dropped it to the floor, then bent to pull off his boots.

Shane glared at him. "You think you can just dump me on the bed and that's all there is to it?"

"I haven't even started yet," he informed her as the second boot dropped with a clatter.

"You simpleminded clod," she returned, heaving a pillow at him. "I wouldn't let you touch me if—" She searched for something original and scathing but settled on the standby. "If you were the last man on earth!"

Vance sent her a long, glittering look before he unbuckled his belt.

"I told you to stop that." Shane pointed a warning finger. "I mean it. Don't you dare take another thing off. Vance!" she added threateningly as he reached for the snap of his jeans. "I'm serious." The word ended on a giggle. His hands paused; his eyes narrowed. "Put your clothes back on this minute," she ordered, but pressed the back of her hand to her mouth. Over it, her eyes were wide and brilliant with amusement.

"What the hell's so funny?" he demanded.

"Nothing, not a thing." With this, Shane collapsed on her back, helpless with laughter. "Funny? No, no, this is a very grave situation." Convulsed with giggles, she pounded her fists on the bed. "The man is standing there, pulling off his clothes and looking fit for murder. Nothing could be more serious."

Shane glanced over at him, then covered her mouth with both hands. "*That* is the face of a man overcome by lust and desire." She laughed until tears came to her eyes.

Damn her, Vance thought as a grin tugged at his mouth.

He crossed to the bed; then, sitting beside her, he planted his hands on either side of her head. The harder she tried to control her amusement, the more her eyes laughed at him. "Glad you're having a good time," he commented.

She swallowed a chuckle. "Oh no, I'm furious, absolutely furious, but it was *so* romantic."

"Was it?" His grin widened as he considered her.

"Oh yes, why you just swept me off my feet." Her laughter rang through the room. "I don't know when I've been more *aroused*," she managed.

"Is that so?" Vance murmured as Shane gave herself wholly to mirth. Very deliberately, he lowered his lips to brush her chin.

"Yes, unless it was when Billy Huffman pushed me into the briars in second grade. Obviously I inflame males into violent seizures of passion."

"Obviously," Vance agreed, tucking her hair behind her ear. "I've had several since I tangled with you." Her fit of giggles ceased abruptly when he caught her earlobe between his teeth. "I think I'm bound to have several more," he murmured, moving down to her neck.

"Vance—"

"Soon," he added against her throat. "Any minute."

"I have to get back," she began breathlessly. As she attempted to sit up, he pressed a hand to her shoulder to keep her still.

"I wonder what else might arouse you." He nibbled at the cord of her neck. "This?"

"No, I…"

"No?" He gave a deep, quiet laugh, feeling her pulse hammer against his lips. "Something else then." Her coat was unzipped, and deftly he loosened the range of buttons on her blouse. "This?" Very gently, he touched the tip of her breast with his tongue.

On a gasp, Shane arched against him. Vance drew her nipple into his mouth to let her taste seep through him. He savored it a moment as Shane dug her nails into his bare shoulders. But when the heat shot into him, he knew he had to pull back before he took her too quickly. He'd been careful since the night they had dined together to keep some space between them. He hadn't wanted to rush her. Now that he had her in his bed, he intended to savor every moment.

Vance lifted his head and looked down at her. Her eyes were wide and fixed on his. For a moment, they both looked for answers. Very slowly, Shane smiled. "This," she whispered, and drew his mouth down to hers.

She hadn't been prepared for the sweetness of the kiss. His lips moved gently over hers. Their breath merged and matched rhythm. With light kisses he roamed her face, only to return over and over to her waiting mouth. To linger, to savor, to make each moment, each taste last; that was his only thought. The fiery needs were banked by the simple knowledge that she was his to touch, to kiss, to love. For the first time in his memory, he wanted to bring a woman pleasure much more than he wanted to take his own. He could give her that with the slow kisses that made his own blood thunder. Until he sensed she craved more, he used only his lips and tongue to arouse her.

Hardly touching her, Vance drew her jacket over her shoulders and arms, lifting her slightly to slip it from under her. His touch was so sure, so gentle, she remained unaware of his inner conflict between passion and tenderness. Without hurry, he drew off her shirt, following its progress over her shoulders with his lips. Shane sighed as his kisses ranged down her arm to nibble at the inside of her elbow. Fighting the growing need to rush, Vance trailed his lips down to her wrist.

If the wind still blew outside the windows, if leaves still rustled along the ground, Shane was unaware. There was only the play of Vance's fingertips, only the warm trace of his mouth. Content, almost sleepy, she ran her fingers through his thick mane of hair as his teeth tugged lightly at the cord of her neck. The lazy friction of his skin against hers had her pulse beating thickly. She felt she could stay forever, floating in a world halfway between passion and serenity.

He began the downward journey slowly, hardly seeming to move at all. With kisses and light love bites, he circled her breast, moving inward until he captured the peak. It grew hot and hard in his mouth while she began to move under him. He suckled, using his tongue to bring them both to the edge of delirium. Her breathing was as raspy as his. Now he could feel the energy flowing from her, pouring out in passion and urgency. Moaning his name, she pressed him closer to her.

But there was so much more to give, so much more to take. With deliberate care, Vance repeated the same aching journey around her other breast, feeling her shudders, listening to the storm of her heartbeat under his hungry, seeking lips.

"So soft," he murmured. "So beautiful." For a moment he merely buried his face against her breast, struggling to hang on to his control. On a moan of need, Shane reached for him as if to bring his mouth back to hers, but he slipped lower.

Taking her arching hips in his hands, Vance traced his tongue down her quivering skin. Shane felt her jeans loosen at the waist and shifted to help him. But he only pressed his mouth deep into the vee of exposed flesh. Again she shifted, curving her back to offer herself, but he lingered, tracing lazy circles with his tongue.

When he worked the jeans over her hips, she felt each searing brush of his fingers. Down her thighs he journeyed, pausing to caress their soft inner flesh, over her calves to nibble gently at the taut muscles, then to her ankles, sending a devastating flush of heat up her body with a quick flick of his tongue.

He found points of pleasure she had been unaware existed. Then he was at the core of her, his tongue stabbing inside her to catapult her beyond all bounds of reason. She moaned his name, moving with him, moving for him, with mind and body tormented by dark, pulsing delights.

Vance heard his name come huskily through her lips and thrilled to it. Her energy, her wellspring of passion inflamed him, driving him to take her deeper before he took all. The sweet, sweet taste of her made him greedy. Somewhere in the back of his clouded mind he knew he was no longer gentle with her, but needs whipped at him.

Madness overcame him. His mouth roamed wildly over her body as his fingers took her from peak to staggering peak. Her breath was heaving when he found her breast. If she had been capable of words, Shane would have pleaded with him to take her. Her world was spinning at a terrifying speed, a speed far beyond the scope of her imagination. When his mouth crushed hers, she answered blindly. He thrust into her.

The flow of energy came from nowhere—a power, a strength that hurled her beyond the reasonable and into the impossible. One fed the other, driving higher and faster until they found the apex. Together, they clung to it, shuddering.

How long he lay still, Vance was unsure. Perhaps he even dozed. When his mind began to clear, he found his mouth nuzzled against Shane's throat, her arms wrapped around him. He was still inside her and could feel the light pulses of lingering passion deep within her. For a moment longer he kept his eyes closed, wondering how it was possible to be both sated and exhilarated. When he started to move, thinking of her comfort, Shane tightened her hold to keep him close.

"No," she murmured. "Just a little longer."

He laughed as his lips grazed her ear. "Can you breathe?"

"I'll breathe later."

Content, he snuggled back into the curve of her neck. "I like the way you taste. I've had a problem with that since the first time I kissed you."

"A problem?" she said lazily, running experimental fingers over the muscles of his back. "That doesn't sound much like a compliment to me."

"Would you like one?" He pressed his mouth to her skin. "You're the most exquisite creature I've ever seen."

Shane received this news with a snort of laughter. "Your first compliment was a bit more credible."

Vance lifted his head and looked down at her. Though her eyes were still sleepy with passion, they were amused. "You really don't see it, do you?" he said thoughtfully. Did she really have no notion what big velvet eyes and satin skin could do to a man when combined with her kind of vivacity?

Didn't she realize the kind of power there was in striking innocence when it was offset by a sensual mouth and an open, honest sexuality? "You might lose it if you did," he said half to himself. "What if I said I liked your nose?"

She eyed him warily for a moment. "If you say I'm cute, I'll hit you."

He chuckled, then kissed both dimpled cheeks. "Do you know how long I've wanted you like this?"

"From the first moment in the general store." She smiled when he lifted his head to stare down at her. "I felt it too. It was as though I'd been expecting you."

Vance laid his forehead on hers. "I was furious."

"I was stunned. I forgot my coffee."

They laughed before their mouths met. "You were terribly rude that day," she remembered.

"I meant to be." He lured her lips back to his. "I wanted to get rid of you."

"Did you really think you could?" Chuckling, she nipped at his bottom lip. "Don't you know a determined woman when you see one?"

"I *would* have gotten rid of you if I'd been able to close my eyes at night without seeing you."

"Did you really? Poor Vance." She gave him a sympathetic kiss.

"I'm sure you're very sorry I lost sleep over you."

She made a suspicious sound. Vance lifted his head again to see her bottom lip caught firmly between her teeth. "I would be sorry," she assured him, "if I didn't think it was wonderful."

"I often wanted to strangle you at three o'clock in the morning."

"I'm sure you did," she returned soberly. "Why don't you kiss me instead?"

He did, roughly, as banked passions began to smolder again. "That day when you sat in the mud, laughing like a fool, I wanted you so badly I hurt. Damn you, Shane, I haven't been able to think straight for weeks." His mouth crushed down on hers again with a touch of the anger she remembered. She soothed the back of his neck with her fingers.

When he lifted his head, their eyes met in a long, deep look. Shane lifted her palm to his cheek.

So much turbulence, she thought. So many secrets.

So much sweetness, he thought. So much honesty.

"I love you," they said together, then stared at each other in amazement. For a moment, they neither moved nor spoke. It seemed even their breathing had halted at the same instant. Then, as one, they reached out, clinging heart to heart, mouth to mouth. What started as a desperate meeting of lips softened, then sweetened, then promised.

Vance closed his eyes on waves of relief and towering pleasure. When he felt Shane's shudders he drew his arms tighter around her. "You're trembling. Why?"

"It's too perfect," she said in a voice that shook. "It frightens me. If I were to lose you now—"

"Shh." He cut her off with a kiss. "It *is* perfect."

"Oh, Vance, I love you so much. I've been waiting all these weeks for you to love me back, and now…" She took his face in her hands and shook her head. "Now that you do, I'm scared."

Looking down at her, he felt a surge of passion and possession. She was his now; nothing was going to change it.

No more mistakes, no more disillusionments. He heard her breath catch then shudder.

"I love you," he said fiercely. "I'm going to keep you, do you understand? We belong together. We both know it. Nothing, by God, nothing's going to interfere with that."

He took her on a wild surge of need and desperation, ignoring the shadow of trepidation that watched over his shoulder.

Chapter 9

It was dark when Shane woke. She had no idea of time or place, only of deep inner contentment and security. The weight of an arm around her waist meant love; the quiet breathing near her ear meant her lover slept beside her. She needed nothing more.

Idly, she wondered how long they had slept. The sun had been setting when she had closed her eyes. The moon was up now. Its cool white light filtered in through the windows to slant across the bed. Shifting slightly, Shane tilted her head back to look at Vance's face. In the dim light, she could make out the sweep of cheekbone and outline of jaw, the strong straight nose. With a fingertip, she traced his mouth gently, not wanting to wake him. As long as he slept, she could look her fill.

It was a strong face, even a hard one, she mused, with its

sharp angles and dark coloring. His mouth could be cruel, his eyes cold. Even in his loving there was a ruthless sort of power in him. While a woman might feel safe in his arms, she would never be completely comfortable. A life with him would be full of constant demands, arguments, passion.

And he loves me, Shane thought in a kind of terrified wonder.

In sleep, Vance shifted, drawing her closer. As their naked bodies pressed intimately close, a dull throb of need moved through her. Her skin heated against his, tingling with the contact. Against the slow, steady beat of his heart, hers began to thud erratically. Desire had never seemed more demanding, yet he did nothing more than lie quietly beside her, deep in his own dreams.

It would always be like this, she realized as she settled her head in the crook of his shoulder. He would give her very little peace. Though she was a woman who had always taken peace for granted, Shane would now forfeit it cheerfully. He was her fate; she had known it from the first instant. Now, she felt as bound to him as if she had been his wife for decades.

For a long time she lay awake, listening to him sleep, feeling the steady rise and fall of his chest against her breasts. This would never change, she told herself. This need to hold each other. She burrowed against him for a moment, filling herself with his scent. As long as she lived, Shane knew she would remember every second, every word spoken during their first time together. She would need no diary to remind her of young, churning fires when she was old. No passage of time would dull her memory or her feelings.

With a sigh, she brushed a whisper of a kiss over his lips. He didn't stir, but she wondered if he dreamed of her. She wanted him to, and closing her eyes, she willed him to. Carefully, she drew away from him, then moving lightly, slipped from the bed. Their clothes were in scattered heaps. Finding Vance's shirt, Shane slipped it on before she left the room.

Her scent lingered on the pillowcase. It was the first thing to penetrate Vance's senses as he drifted awake. It suited her so, the fresh, clean fragrance with a suggestion of lemon. Lazily, he allowed it to seep into him. Even in sleep, his mind was full of her. There was a slight stiffness in his shoulder where her head had rested. Vance flexed it before reaching out to bring her back to him. He found himself alone. Opening his eyes, Vance whispered her name.

He experienced the same sense of time disorientation that Shane had. The room was dim with moonlight, so that for a moment he thought he must have dreamed it all. But the sheets were still warm from her, and her scent still lingered. No dream. The relief he felt overwhelmed him. Softly, he called her name. It was then he smelled the bacon. In the dark, he grinned foolishly and settled back. As he lay quietly, he could just hear Shane's voice as she sang some silly popular song.

She was in the kitchen, he thought. Vance stayed where he was, listening. She was rooting through the cupboards, clattering something. Water was running. The scent of bacon grew stronger. How long, he wondered, had he waited to feel this way? *Complete.* He hadn't known he had been waiting, but he did know what he had found. She filled the emptiness that had nagged at him for years, healed an old, festering wound. She was all the answers to all the questions.

And what would he bring her? his conscience demanded. Vance closed his eyes. He knew himself too well to pretend he would give her a smooth, serene life. His temper was too volatile, his responsibilities too intrusive. Even with adjustments to both, he could paint her no soft pastoral scene. His life, past, present and future, had too many complications. Even this, their first night together, would have to be marred by one of his ghosts. He had to tell her about Amelia. There was a burst of rage followed by a prickle of fear.

No, he wouldn't accept the fear, he told himself as he rose quickly from the bed. Nothing, no one was going to interfere with him. No shadow of a dead wife or demands of a hungry business were going to take her from him. She was strong, he reminded himself, trying to override the apprehension. He could make her see his past as it was— something that had happened before her. It might shock her to learn he was president of a multimillion-dollar firm, but she could hardly be displeased once it was out in the open. He would tell Shane everything and wipe the slate clean. When it was done, he could ask her to marry him. If he had to make professional adjustments, he'd make them. He had sacrificed his own youthful dream for the good of the company, but he wouldn't sacrifice Shane.

As he pulled on his jeans, Vance tried to work out the best way to tell her and, perhaps more important, to explain why he had yet to tell her.

Shane added a dash of thyme to the canned soup she was heating. She rose on her bare toes to reach for a bowl on the shelf, the hem of Vance's shirt skimming her naked thighs. Her hair was tousled, her cheeks flushed. Vance stood for a moment in the doorway watching her.

Then in three strides, he was behind her, wrapping his arms around her waist and burying his face in the curve of her neck. "I love you," he murmured in a low, fierce whisper. "God, how I love you."

Before she could answer, he spun her around to take her mouth with his. Both stunned and aroused, Shane clung to him as her knees buckled. But she met the kiss with equal passion with soft, willing lips until he slowly drew her away. As the flame mellowed to a glow, Vance looked down at her and smiled.

"Any time you want to drive me crazy, just put on one of my shirts."

"If I'd known the kind of results I'd get, I'd have done it weeks ago." Returning his smile, Shane clasped her hands around his neck. "I thought you'd be hungry. It's after eight."

"I smelled food," he said with a grin. "That's why I came down."

"Oh." Shane lifted a brow. "Is that the only reason?"

"What else?"

Her retort ended on a laugh as he nuzzled her neck. "You could make something up," she suggested.

"If it makes you feel better, I could pretend it was because I couldn't keep away from you." He kissed her until she was limp and breathless. "That I woke up reaching for you, then lay listening to your clattering in the kitchen and knew I'd never been happier in my life. Will that do?"

"Yes, I…" She sighed as his hands slid down to caress beneath the loose shirt. Behind her, bacon popped and hissed. "If you don't stop, the food's going to burn."

"What food?" He chuckled, pleased that she was flushed and breathing unsteadily when she struggled away from him.

"My own specially doctored tomato soup and prize-winning BLTs."

He pulled her back to nuzzle her neck another moment. "Mmm, it does smell pretty good. So do you."

"It's your shirt," she claimed as she wiggled out of his arms again. "It smells like wood chips." Deftly, Shane took the sizzling bacon from the frying pan to let it drain. "If you want coffee, the water's still hot."

Vance watched her finish preparing the simple meal. She did more than fill the kitchen with the scents and sounds of cooking. He'd done that himself often enough in the past weeks. Shane filled it with life. He may have repaired and renovated and remodeled, but the house had always been empty. Vance realized now that without her, it would have always been unfinished.

There would be no living there without her—no living anywhere. Fleetingly, he thought of the large white house in an exclusive Washington suburb—the house he had bought for Amelia. There was an oval swimming pool sheltered by a white brick wall, a formal rose garden with flagstone paths, a clay tennis court. Two maids, a gardener and a cook. When Amelia had been alive there had been yet another maid to tend to her personally. Her dressing room alone had been larger than the kitchen where Shane was now fixing soup and sandwiches. There was a parlor with a rosewood cabinet Shane would adore, and heavy damask drapes she would detest.

No, Vance thought, he wouldn't go back there now, nor would he ask Shane to share his ghosts. He had no right to ask her to cope with something he was only beginning to resolve himself. But he would have to tell her something of his former marriage, and of his work, before yesterday could be buried.

"Shane…"

"Sit down," she ordered, busily pouring soup into bowls. "I'm starving. I skipped lunch this afternoon bargaining for this wonderful Sheridan table. I paid a bit more for the clock than I should have, but made it up on the table and the saltcellars."

"Shane, I have to talk to you."

Deftly, she sliced a sandwich in half. "Okay, I can talk and eat at the same time. I'm going to have some milk. Even I can tell that instant coffee's dreadful."

She was bustling here and there, putting bowls and plates on the table, poking into the refrigerator. Vance was suddenly struck with the picture of his life before she had come into it—the rush, the demands, the work that had ultimately added up to nothing. If he lost her… He couldn't bear thinking about it.

"Shane." He stopped her abruptly, taking both of her arms in a strong grip. Looking up, she was surprised by the fierceness in his eyes. "I love you. Do you believe it?" His grip tightened painfully on the question, but she made no protest.

"Yes, I believe it."

"Will you take me just as I am?" he demanded.

"Yes." There was no hesitation in her, no wavering. Vance pulled her toward him.

A few hours, he thought, squeezing his eyes tight. Just a few hours with no questions, no past. It's not too much to ask.

"There are things I have to tell you, Shane, but not

tonight." As the tension drained, he loosened his hold to a caress. "Tonight, I only want to tell you that I love you."

Sensing turmoil and wanting to soothe it, Shane tilted her face back to his. "Tonight it's all I need to know. I love you, Vance. Nothing you tell me will change that." She pressed her lips to his cheek and felt some of the tightness in his body loosen. Part of her wanted to coax him to tell her what caused the storm inside him, but she was conscious of the same need for isolation that Vance had. This was their night. Problems were for the practical, for the daytime. "Come on," she said lightly, "the food's getting cold." The fierce hug she gave him made him laugh. "When I fix a gourmet meal, I expect it to be properly appreciated."

"I do," he assured her, kissing her nose.

"Do what?"

"Appreciate it. And you." He dropped a second kiss on her mouth. "Let's go into the living room."

"Living room?" Her brow creased, then cleared. "Oh, I suppose it would be warmer."

"Exactly what I had in mind," he murmured.

"I tossed a couple of logs onto the fire when I came downstairs."

"You're a clever soul, Shane," Vance said admiringly as he took her arm and steered her from the room.

"Vance, we have to take the food."

"What food?"

Shane laughed and started to turn back, but he propelled her into the sparsely furnished, firelit room. "Vance, the soup'll have to be reheated in a minute."

"It'll be terrific," he told her as he began to unbutton the oversize shirt she wore.

"Vance!" Shane brushed his fingers away. "Be serious."

"I am," he said reasonably, even as he pulled her down on the oval braided rug. "Deadly."

"Well, *I'm* not going to reheat it," she promised huffily while he leaned on an elbow to undo the rest of the buttons.

"No one would blame you," he told her as he parted the shirt. "It'll be fine cold."

She gave a snort. "It'll be dreadful cold."

"Hungry?" he asked lightly, cupping her breast.

Shane looked up at him. He saw the dimples flash. "Yes!" In a quick move, she was lying across his chest, her mouth fixed greedily on his.

The verve and speed of her passion stunned him. He had meant to tease her, to stoke her desires slowly, but she was suddenly and completely in command. Her mouth was avid, demanding, with her small teeth nibbling, her quick tongue arousing him so quickly he would have rolled her over and taken her at once had his limbs not been so strangely weak. Her weight was nothing, yet he couldn't move her when she shifted to do clever, torturous things to his ear. Her hands were busy too, stroking through his hair, skimming over his shoulders and chest to find and exploit small, devastating points of pleasure.

He reached to pull off her shirt, too dazed to realize his fingers shook, but he fumbled, dragging at it. High on her own power, Shane gave a quick, almost nervous laugh. "Too soon," she whispered into his ear. "Much too soon."

He swore, but the curse ended on a groan when she pressed her lips to his throat. She burned even as he did, but she was driven to heighten his pleasure to the fullest. It spun through her mind until she was giddy that her touch, her kisses were enough to make him weak and vulnerable. Under her roaming mouth, his skin grew hot and damp. He stroked her where he could reach, but there was something dreamlike in the touch, as though he had passed the first feeling of desperation. For all his strength and power, he had surrendered to hers.

The light shifted and jumped with the crackling of the fire. A log broke apart, crumbling in a shower of sparks. The wind picked up, pushing a sluggish puff of smoke back down the chimney so that it struggled halfheartedly into the room to vie with the lingering scent of fried bacon. Neither of them was aware.

Shane heard the thunderous beat of his heart under her ear, the shallow, ragged sound of his breathing. Taking his mouth again, she kissed him deeply, filling herself on him, knowing she drained him. She luxuriated in him, experimenting with angles, allowing her tongue to twine with his. Then she began the journey down his throat.

Once, he murmured her name as though he were dreaming. She grew bolder. With firm, quick kisses, she ranged down his chest to the taut flat stomach. Vance jolted as though he had been scorched. Shane pressed her lips to the heated skin, wrenching a moan from him, then circled almost lazily with her tongue.

Her excitement was almost unbearable. He was hers, and she was learning his secrets. Her body felt weightless and capable of anything. The gnawing hunger in the pit of her stomach was growing, but the need to learn, to explore was greater. With a kind of greedy wonder, she took her hands and lips over him, reveling in a man's taste—*her* man's taste. The hair on his chest tapered down. Shane followed it.

Slowly, with a light touch, she loosened his jeans and began to draw them over his hips. Curious, Shane moved her lips over his hipbone and down to his thigh.

She heard him call out to her, hoarse, desperate, but she found the corded muscles of his thighs fascinating. So strong, she thought as her heart began to thud painfully. She ran fingers down his leg, aroused by the lean firmness and straining sinews. Testing, she replaced her fingers with her tongue, then her teeth. Vance shifted under her, murmuring something between his short, ragged breaths. His taste was everything male and mysterious. Shane felt she would never get her fill of him.

But he was on the point of madness. Her slender fingers, her curious tongue had him plunging down and rocketing up so that each breath he drew was an agony of effort. His body was alive with pleasure and pain, his blood swimming with passion that was both tantalized and frustrated. He wanted her to go on touching him, driving him mad. He wanted to take her quickly before he lost his mind. Then slowly, her small avid mouth roamed back up over his stomach, so that his skin quivered with fresh dampness. The heat was unbearable and more wonderful than anything he had ever known. Her breasts with their hard, erect points brushed over him, making him long to taste them. She gave him her mouth instead. Lying full length on his, her body was furnace hot and agile.

"Shane, in the name of God," he breathed, groping for her. Then she slid down, taking him inside her with a shuddering sigh of triumph.

His sanity shattered. Not knowing what he did, Vance seized her shoulders, rolling her over roughly, driving inside her with all the fierce, desperate strength that was pent up in him. Passion hammered through his core. Need was delirium.

She cried out as her hips arched to meet him, but he was far beyond any control. Harder and faster he took her, never feeling the bite of her nails on his flesh, barely hearing her harsh, quick breathing. She dragged him closer when he could get no closer. He drove her, drove himself to a crest that was dangerously high. Even the plummet was a shattering thrill.

She was shuddering beneath him, dazed, weak, powerful. Experimentally, Vance ran a hand over her arm, then linked his fingers around it. His thumb and forefinger met. "You're so small," he murmured. "I didn't mean to be rough."

Shane brushed a hand through his hair. "Were you?"

His sigh ended on a chuckle. "Shane, you make me crazy. I don't usually toss women around."

"I don't think this is a good time to go into that," she said dryly.

Shifting, he supported himself on his elbow so he could look down at her. "Would it be better to tell you that you inflame me into violent seizures of passion?"

"Infinitely."

"It appears to be true," he murmured.

She smiled at him, running her hand down his shoulder to the arm taut with muscle. "Would you rather I didn't?"

"No," he said definitely, then covered her laughing lips with his.

"Actually," she began in a considering tone, "since you do the same to me, it's only fair."

He liked seeing her with the sleepy, just-loved look on her face. Her eyes were soft and heavy, her mouth slightly swollen. With shifting shadows and a red glow, firelight danced over her skin. "I like your logic." Gently, he traced the shape of her face with a fingertip, imagining what it would be like to wake beside her every morning. Shane captured his hand, pressing his palm to her lips.

"I love you," she said softly. "Will you get tired of hearing that?"

"No." He kissed her brow, then her temple. Slipping an arm under her, he drew her close. "No," he said again on a sigh.

Shane snuggled, running a casual hand over his chest. "The fire's getting low," she murmured.

"Mmm."

"We should put some more wood on."

"Mmm-hmm."

"Vance." She tilted her face to look up at him. His eyes were closed. "Don't you dare go to sleep. I'm hungry."

"God, the woman's insatiable." After a long sigh, he cupped her breast. "I might find the energy with the right incentive."

"I want my dinner," she said firmly, but made no move to stop his caressing hand. *"You're* going to reheat the soup."

"Oh." Vance considered that a moment, running a lazy finger over the peak of her breast. "Aren't you afraid I might interfere with that special touch you have?"

"No," she told him flatly. "I have every confidence in you."

"I thought you might," he said as he sat up to tug on his jeans. Leaning over, he planted a quick kiss on her mouth. *"You* can toss some logs in the fire."

But after he had gone to the kitchen, Shane lay dreaming

a moment. The hiss of the fire was comforting. She drew the soft flannel of Vance's shirt closer around her, smiling as his scent stayed with her. Could it really be true that he needed her so much? she wondered sleepily. Love, yes, and desire, but she had a deep, innate knowledge that he very simply needed her. Not just for lovemaking, for holding, but to *be* there. Though she was unsure what it was, Shane knew there was something she had—or something she was—that Vance needed. Whatever she brought to him, it was enough to balance his anger, his mistrust. Fleetingly, she wondered again what had caused him to retreat behind cynicism. Disillusioned, he had said. Who or what had disillusioned him? A woman, a friend, an ideal?

Shane watched the sizzling red coals in the fire and wondered. The anger was still there. She had sensed it when he had demanded to know if she would take him just as he was. Patience, she told herself. She had to be patient until he was ready to share his secrets with her. But it was difficult for Shane to love and not try to help. Shaking her head, she sat up to rebutton her shirt. She'd promised him that love was enough for tonight; she had to abide by it. Tomorrow would be soon enough for problems. Expertly, she arranged more wood on the coals before she went to the kitchen.

"About time," Vance said coolly as she walked in. "There's nothing I hate more than having food get cold."

Shane shot him a look. "How inconsiderate of me."

After setting the bowls back on the table, Vance shrugged. "Well, no harm done," he told her in a forgiving tone. His eyes brimmed with amusement as Shane sat. "Coffee?"

"Not yours," she said witheringly. "It's terrible."

"I suppose if someone really cared, they'd see to it that I had decent coffee in the morning."

"You're right." Shane lifted her spoon. "I'll buy you a percolater." Grinning, she began to eat. The soup was hot and tangy, causing her to close her eyes in appreciation. "Good grief, I'm starving!"

"You should know better than to miss meals," Vance commented before applying himself to the meal. He quickly discovered he was famished.

"It was worth it." Shane shot him another grin. "The Sheridan I bought is fabulous." When he only lifted a brow, she chuckled. "Then I had intended to have an early dinner…but I was distracted."

Vance reached over to take her hand. Gently, he lifted it to his lips, then bit her knuckle. "Ow!" Shane snatched her hand away as she picked up his sandwich. "I didn't say it wasn't an enjoyable distraction," she added after a moment. "Even if you did make me furious."

"The feeling was mutual," he assured her mildly.

"At least I control my temper," she said primly. She eyed him coolly as he choked over his soup. "I *wanted* to punch you," she explained. "Hard."

"Again the feeling was mutual."

"You're not a gentleman," she accused with her mouth full.

"Good God, no," he agreed. For a moment, he hesitated, wanting to choose his words carefully. "Shane, will you hold off for a little while on that dining-room set?"

"Vance," she began, but he took her hand again.

"Don't tell me I shouldn't have interfered. I love you." Shane stirred her soup, frowning down at it. She didn't want to tell him how pressing her bills were. In the first place, she had every confidence that between her current stock and the small amount of capital she had left, she could straighten out her finances. And more, she simply didn't want to heap her problems on him.

"I know you did what you did because you cared," she began slowly. "I appreciate that, really. But it's important to me to make the shop work." She lifted her eyes now to meet the frown in his. "I didn't fail as a teacher, but I didn't succeed either. I have to make a go of this."

"By selling the one tangible thing you have left of your grandmother's?" Immediately, he saw he had hit a nerve. He tightened his fingers around hers. "Shane…"

"No. It is hard for me, I won't pretend it isn't." Wearily, she let out a long breath. "I'm not basically a practical person, but in this case I have to be. I have no place to keep that set and it's very valuable. The money it'll bring into the shop will keep me going for quite a while. And more than that…" She broke off with a little shake of her head. "If you can understand, it's more difficult for me having it there, knowing it has to be sold, than if it were already done."

"Let me buy it. I could—"

"No!"

"Shane, listen to me."

"*No!*" Pulling her hand from his, she rose to lean against the sink. For a moment she stared hard out the window at the trees splattered with moonlight. "Please, it's very sweet of you, but I couldn't allow it."

Frustrated, Vance rose, taking her shoulders, he drew Shane back against him. And how, he wondered, was he going to begin to explain? "Shane, you don't understand.

I can't bear watching you hurting, watching you work so hard when I could—"

"Please, Vance." Shane turned to him. Though her eyes were dry, they were eloquent. "I'm doing what I have to do, and what I want." She took his hands tightly in hers. "It's not that I don't love you even more for wanting to help. I do."

"Then let me help," he began. "If it's just a matter of the money right now—"

"It wouldn't make any difference if you were a millionaire," she said, giving him a little shake. "I'd still say no."

Not knowing whether to laugh or swear, Vance pulled her against him. "Stubborn little twit, I could make it easier for you. Let me try to explain."

"I don't want anyone, not even you, to make it easier." She gave him a fierce squeeze. "Please understand. All of my life I've been cute little Shane Abbott, Faye's sweet, slightly odd granddaughter. I need to prove something."

Remembering how frustrating it had been to be known as Miriam Riverton Banning's son, Vance sighed. Yes, he understood. And the understanding made him keep his silence on how simple it would be for him to help. "Well," he said, wanting to hear her laugh, "you are kind of cute."

"Oh, Vance," she moaned.

"And sweet," he added, tilting her face up for a kiss. "And slightly odd."

"That's no way to endear yourself to me," she warned. "I'll wash, you dry."

"Wash what?"

"The dishes."

He pulled her closer, wrapping his arms firmly around

her waist. "I don't see any dishes. You have wonderful eyes, just like a cocker spaniel."

"Watch it, Vance," she said threateningly.

"I like your freckles." He placed a light kiss on the bridge of her nose. "I've always thought that Becky Thatcher had freckles."

"You're heading for trouble," she told him, narrowing her eyes.

"And your dimples," he continued blithely. "She probably had dimples too, don't you think?"

Shane bit her lips to hold back a smile. "Shut up, Vance."

"Yes," he continued, beaming down at her, "I'd say that's definitely a cute little face."

"Okay, that does it." Putting a good deal of effort into it, Shane tried to wiggle out of his hold.

"Going somewhere?"

"Home," she told him grandly. "You can do your own dishes."

He sighed. "I guess I have to get tough again."

Anticipating him, Shane began to struggle in earnest. "If you throw me over your shoulder again, you really are fired!"

Hooking an arm behind her knees, Vance swept her up. "How's this?"

She circled his neck. "Better," she said grudgingly. The smile was becoming impossible to control.

"And this?" Softly, he placed his lips on hers, letting the kiss deepen until he heard her sigh.

"Much better," she murmured as he carried her from the room. "Where are we going?"

"Upstairs," he told her. "I want my shirt back."

Chapter 10

"**Y**es, of course you could convert it," Shane agreed, passing her fingertip over the porcelain base of a delicate oil lamp.

"That's just what I thought." Mrs. Trip, her potential customer, nodded her carefully groomed white head. "And my husband's very handy with electrical things too."

Shane managed a smile for Mr. Trip's prowess. It broke her heart to think that the sweet little lamp would be tampered with. "You know," she began, trying another tactic, "an oil lamp is a smart thing to have around in case of power failure. I keep a couple myself."

"Well yes, dear," Mrs. Trip said placidly, "but I have candles for that. This lamp's going to go right next to my rocker. That's where I do my crocheting."

Though she knew the value of a sale, Shane couldn't stop

herself from adding, "If you really want an electric lamp, Mrs. Trip, you could buy a good reproduction much cheaper."

Mrs. Trip sent her a vague smile. "But it wouldn't be a real antique then, would it? Do you have a box I can carry it in?"

"Yes, of course," Shane murmured, seeing it was useless to repeat that converting the lamp would decrease both its value and its charm. Resigned, she wrote out the sales slip, comforting herself with the thought that the profit from the lamp would help pay her own electric bill.

"Oh my, I didn't see this!"

Glancing up, Shane noted that Mrs. Trip was admiring a tea set in cobalt blue. The sun slanting in the windows fell generously on the dark, rich glass. There was a contrast of delicate gold leaf painted around the rim of each cup and the edge of each saucer.

"It's lovely, isn't it," Shane agreed, though she bit the underside of her lip as the lady began to handle the sugar bowl. When she found the discreet price tag, she lifted a brow. "It goes as a complete set," Shane began, knowing the price would seem staggering to someone unacquainted with valuable glass. "It's late nineteenth century and…"

"I must have it," Mrs. Trip said decisively, cutting off Shane's explanation. "It's just the thing for my corner cabinet." She sent a surprised Shane a grin. "I'll tell my husband he's just bought me a Christmas present."

"I'll wrap it for you," Shane decided, as pleased as Mrs. Trip with the idea.

"You have a lovely shop," the woman told her as Shane began to box the glass. "I must say, I only stopped in because the sign at the bottom of the hill intrigued me. I wondered what in the world I would find. But it wasn't a big barn of a place with nonsense packed around like a yard sale." She pursed her lips, glancing around again. "You've done very well." Shane laughed at the description and thanked her. "And it's so nice to have the little museum too," she went on. "A very clever idea, and so tidy. I believe I'll bring my nephew by the next time I'm in the area. Are you married, dear?"

Shane sent her a look of wary amusement. "No, ma'am."

"He's a doctor," Mrs. Trip disclosed. "Internal medicine."

Clearing her throat, Shane sealed the box. "That's very nice."

"A good boy," Mrs. Trip assured her as Shane adjusted the sales ticket to include the tea set. "Dedicated." She dug out her checkbook, pulling her wallet along with it. "I have a picture of him right here."

Politely, Shane examined the snapshot of a young, attractive man with serious eyes. "He's very good-looking," she told his aunt. "You must be proud of him."

"Yes," she said wistfully, tucking the wallet back into her purse. "Such a pity he hasn't found the right girl yet. I'm going to be sure to bring him by." Without a blink for the amount, Mrs. Trip wrote out a check.

It wasn't easy, but Shane maintained her composure until the door shut behind her customer. With a shout of laughter, she dropped into a button-back chair. Though she was uncertain if the nephew should be congratulated or pitied for having such a dedicated aunt, she did know what appealed to her sense of humor. Her next thought was how Vance would try not to grin when she told him of the lady's matchmaking attempts.

He'd lift a brow, Shane thought, and make some dry

comment about her charming the old ladies so that they'd dangle their nephews under her nose. She was beginning to know him very well. Most of him, Shane corrected with a considering smile. The rest would come.

She checked her watch, finding herself impatient that two hours remained before he would be with her. She'd promised him dinner—a more elaborate dinner than the soup and sandwiches they had eaten the night before. Even now, the small rib roast was cooking gently in the oven upstairs. She considered closing early, calculating she had just about enough time to whip up some outrageous, elaborate dessert before he arrived. As the thought passed through her head, the door opened again.

Laurie MacAfee stepped in, buttoned to the neck in a long tan coat. "Shane," she said, observing her casual posture in the chair. "Not busy I see."

Though she smiled in greeting, some demon kept her seated. "Not at the moment. How are you, Laurie?"

"Just fine. I took off work early to go to the dentist, so I thought I'd drop by afterward."

Shane waited, half expecting Laurie to comment on her good checkup. "I'm glad you did," she said at length. "Would you like a tour?"

"I'd love to browse," Laurie told her, glancing around. "What sweet things you have."

Shane swallowed a retort and rose. "Thank you," she said with a humility Laurie never noticed. Shane thought again how well suited she was to Cy.

"I must say, the place looks so much different." In her slow, measured step, Laurie began to wander the old summer parlor. Though she hadn't expected to approve, she could find nothing to condemn in Shane's taste. The room was small, but light and airy with its ivory-toned walls, and the gleaming natural wood floor was scattered with hand-hooked rugs. Furniture was set to advantage, with accessories carefully arranged to give the appearance of a tidy, rather comfortable room instead of a store. Loosening the first few buttons of her coat, she roamed to the main showroom, then stood perusing it from the doorway.

"Why, you've hardly changed this at all?" she exclaimed. "Not even the wallpaper."

"No," Shane agreed, unable to keep her eyes from skimming over the dining-room set. "I didn't want to. Of course, I had to set more stock in here, and widen the doorways, but I loved the room as it was."

"Well, I'll confess I'm surprised," Laurie commented as she wandered through to what had been the kitchen. "It's so organized, not jumbled up at all. Your bedroom was always a disaster."

"It still is," Shane replied dryly.

Laurie gave what passed for a laugh before continuing into the museum. "Yes, this I might have expected." She gave a quick nod. "You always were a whiz at this sort of thing. I could never understand it."

"Because I wasn't a whiz at anything else?"

"Oh, Shane." Laurie flushed, revealing how close Shane's words had been to her thoughts.

"I'm sorry." Immediately contrite, Shane patted her arm. "I was only teasing you. I'd show you the upstairs, Laurie, but it's not quite finished, and I shouldn't leave the shop in any case. Pat has classes this afternoon."

Mollified, Laurie strolled back into the shop. "I'd heard

she was working for you. It was very kind of you to give her the job."

"She's been a big help. I couldn't manage it seven days a week all alone." Shane felt a twinge of impatience as Laurie began to browse again. There wasn't going to be time to whip up anything more than instant chocolate pudding at this rate.

"Oh well, this is very nice." Laurie's voice held the first true ring of admiration as she studied the Sheridan table Shane had bought the day before. "It doesn't look old at all."

That was too much for Shane. She gave a burst of appreciative laughter. "No, I'm sorry," she assured Laurie when she turned to frown at her. "You'd be surprised how many people think antiques should look moldy or dented. It's quite old, really, and it is lovely."

"And expensive," Laurie added, squinting at the price. "Still, it would look rather nice with the chair Cy and I just bought. Oh…" Turning, she gave Shane a quick, guilty look. "I wonder if you'd heard—that is, I'd been meaning to have a talk with you."

"About Cy?" Shane controlled the smile, noting Laurie was truly uncomfortable. "I know you're seeing quite a lot of each other."

"Yes." Hesitating, Laurie brushed some fictitious lint from her coat. "It's a bit more than that really. You see, we're—actually…" She cleared her throat. "Shane, we're planning to be married next June."

"Congratulations," Shane said so simply that Laurie's eyes widened.

"I hope you're not upset." Laurie began to twist the strap of her purse. "I know that you and Cy…well, it was quite a few years ago, but still, you were…"

"Very young," Shane said kindly. "I really do wish you the best, Laurie." But a demon of mischief had her adding, "You suit him much better than I ever could."

"I appreciate your saying that, Shane. I was afraid you might…" She flushed again. "Well, Cy's such a wonderful man."

She means it, Shane noted with some surprise. She really loves him. She felt simultaneous tugs of shame and amusement. "I hope you're happy, Laurie, both of you."

"We will be." Laurie gave her a beaming smile. "And I'm going to buy this table," she added recklessly.

"No," Shane corrected her. "You're going to take the table as an early wedding present."

Comically, Laurie's mouth dropped open. "Oh, I couldn't! It's so expensive."

"Laurie, we've known each other a long time, and Cy was a very important part of my—" she searched for the proper phrase "—growing up years. I'd like to give it to both of you."

"Well, I—thank you." Such uncomplicated generosity baffled her. "Cy will be so pleased."

"You're welcome." Laurie's flustered appreciation made her smile. "Can I help you out to the car with it?"

"No, no, I can manage." Laurie lifted the small table, then paused. "Shane, I really hope you have a tremendous success here. I really do." She stood awkwardly at the door a moment. "Goodbye."

"Bye, Laurie."

Shane closed the door with a smile, then immediately put Laurie and Cy out of her mind. After a glance at her watch, she noted that she had barely more than an hour now before

Vance would be there. She hurried around to lock up the museum entrance. If she moved fast, she would have time to... The sound of an approaching car had her swearing.

Business is business, she reminded herself, and unlocked the door again. If Vance wanted dessert, he'd have to settle for a bag of store-bought cookies. Hearing the sound of footsteps on the porch, she opened the door with a ready smile. It faded instantly, as did her color.

"Anne," she managed in a voice unlike her own.

"Darling!" Anne bent down for a quick brush of cheeks. "What a greeting. Anyone would think you weren't glad to see me."

It took only a few seconds to see that her mother was as lovely as ever. Her pale, heart-shaped face was unlined, her eyes the same deep china blue, her hair a glorious sweeping blond. She wore a casual, expensive blue fox stroller belted at the waist with black leather, and silk slacks unsuitable for an Eastern winter. Her beauty, as always, sent the same surges of love and resentment through her daughter.

"You look lovely, Anne."

"Oh, thank you, though I know I must look a wreck after that dreadful drive from the airport. This place is in the middle of nowhere. Shane, dear, when are you going to do something about your hair?" She cast a critical eye over it before breezing past. "I'll never understand why... Oh, my Lord, what *have* you done!"

Stunned, she gazed around the room, taking in the display cases, the shelves, the racks of postcards. With a trill of laughter, she set down her exquisite leather bag. "Don't tell me you've opened a Civil War museum right in the living room. I don't believe it!"

Shane folded her hands in front of her, feeling foolish. "Didn't you see the sign?"

"Sign? No—or perhaps I did but didn't pay any attention." Her eyes slid, sharp and amused around the room. "Shane, what *have* you been up to?"

Determined not to be intimidated, she straightened her shoulders. "I've started a business," she said boldly.

"You?" Delighted, Anne laughed again. "But, darling, surely you're joking."

Stabbed by the utter incredulity in Anne's voice, Shane angled her chin. "No."

"Well, for heaven's sake." She gave a pretty chuckle and eyed Shane's dented bugle. "But what happened to your teaching job?"

"I resigned."

"Well, I can hardly blame you for that. It must have been a terrible bore." She brushed away Shane's former career as a matter of indifference. "But why in God's name did you come back here and bury yourself in Hicksville?"

"It's my home."

With a mild *hmm* for the temper in Shane's eyes, Anne spun the rack of postcards. "Everyone to his own taste. Well, what have you done with the rest of the place?" Before Shane could answer, Anne swept through the doorway and into the shop. "Oh, no, don't tell me, an antique shop! Very quaint and tasteful. Shane, how clever of you." Her eye was sharp enough to recognize a few very good pieces. She began to wonder if her daughter wasn't quite the fool she'd always considered her. "Well…" Anne unbelted her fur and dropped it carelessly over a chair. "How long has this been going on?"

"Not long." Shane stood rigid, knowing part of herself was drawn, as it always was, to the strange, beautiful woman who was her mother. Knowing too that Anne was deadly.

"And?" Anne prompted.

"And what?"

"Shane, don't be difficult." Masking quick annoyance, Anne gave her a charming smile. She was an actress. Though she had never made the splash she had hoped for, she wrangled a bit part now and again. She felt she knew her trade well enough to handle Shane with a friendly smile. "Naturally I'm concerned, darling. I only want to know how you're doing?"

Uncomfortable with her own manners, Shane unbent. "Well enough, though I haven't been open long. I wasn't happy with teaching. Not bored," she explained, "just not suited for it. I am happy with this."

"Darling, that's wonderful." She crossed her nylon-clad legs and looked around again. It occurred to her that Shane might be useful after all. It had taken brains and determination to set up this kind of establishment. Perhaps it was time she started to take a little more interest in the daughter she had always thought of as a mild annoyance. "It helps to know you're settling your life, especially since mine's such a mess at the moment." Noting the wariness in Shane's eyes, she sent her a sad smile. If memory served her, the girl was very susceptible to an unhappy story. "I divorced Leslie."

"Oh?" Shane only lifted a brow.

Momentarily set back by Shane's coolness, Anne continued. "I can't tell you how mistaken I was in him, how foolish it feels to know I was deceived into thinking he was a kind, charming man." She didn't add that he had failed, again and again, to get her the kind of parts that would lead to the fame she craved—or that she'd already begun to cultivate a certain producer she felt would be more successful. In any event, Leslie had begun to bore her to distraction. "There's nothing more devastating than to have failed in love."

You've had practice, Shane thought, but held her tongue.

"These past few months," Anne added on a sigh, "haven't been easy."

"For any of us," Shane agreed, understanding Anne too well. "Gran died six months ago. You didn't even bother to come to the funeral."

She'd been ready for this. With a tiny sigh, she dropped her eyes to her soft, pampered hands. "You must know how badly I felt, Shane. I was finishing a film. I couldn't be spared."

"You couldn't find the time for a card, a phone call?" Shane asked. "You never even bothered to answer my letter."

As if on cue, Anne's lovely eyes filled with tears. "Darling, don't be cruel. I couldn't—I just couldn't put the words down on a piece of paper." She drew a delicate swatch of silk from her breast pocket. "Even though she was old, somehow I felt she would just live forever, always be here." Mindful of her mascara, she dabbed at the tears. "When I got your letter telling me she was…I was so devastated." She lifted beautifully drenched eyes to Shane's, waiting while a single tear trickled gently down her cheek. "You of all people must know how I feel. She raised me." A little sob caught in her throat. "I still can't believe she's not in the kitchen, fussing over the stove."

Because the image tore at her own grief, Shane knelt at

her mother's feet. She'd had no family to mourn with her, no one to help her through the wrenching, aching hours after the numbness had passed. If she had been unable to share anything else with her mother throughout her life, perhaps they could share this. "I know," she managed in a thick voice. "I still miss her terribly."

Anne began to think the little scene had a great deal of possibility. "Shane, please forgive me." Anne gripped her hands, concentrating on adding a tremor to her voice. "I know it was wrong of me not to come, wrong to make excuses. I just wasn't strong enough to face it. Even now, when I thought I could…" She trailed off, bringing Shane's hand to her damp cheek.

"I understand. Gran would have understood too."

"She was so good to me always. If I could only see her one more time."

"You mustn't dwell on it." Those very thoughts had haunted Shane's mind a dozen times after the funeral. "I felt the same way, but it's better to remember all the good times. She was so happy here in this house, doing her gardening, her canning."

"She did love the house," Anne murmured, casting a nostalgic eye around the old summer parlor. "And I imagine she'd have been pleased with what you're doing here."

"Do you think so?" Earnestly, Shane looked up into her mother's damp eyes. "I was so sure, but still sometimes…" Trailing off, she glanced at the freshly painted walls.

"Of course she would," Anne said briskly. "I suppose she left the house to you?"

"Yes." Shane was looking around the room, remembering how it had been.

"There was a will then?"

"A will?" Distracted, Shane glanced back at her. "Yes, Gran had a will drawn up years ago. She had Floyd Arnette's son do it after he passed the bar. She was his first client." Shane smiled, thinking how proud Gran had been of the fancy legal terms that "sassy Arnette boy" had come up with.

"And the rest of the estate?" Anne prompted, attempting to curb her impatience.

"There was the house and land of course," Shane answered, still looking back. "Some stocks I sold to pay the taxes and the funeral expenses."

"She left everything to you?"

The tightness in Anne's voice didn't penetrate. "Yes. There was enough cash in her savings to handle most of the repairs on the place, and—"

"You're lying!" Anne shoved at her as she sprung to her feet. Shane grabbed the arm of the chair to keep from toppling; then, too stunned to move, she stayed on the floor. "She wouldn't have cut me off without a penny!" Anne exploded, glaring down at her.

The blue eyes were hard and glittery now, the lovely face white with fury. Once or twice before, Shane had seen her mother in this sort of rage—when her grandmother hadn't given her precisely what she had wanted. Slowly, she rose to face her. Anne's tantrums, she knew, had to be handled carefully before they turned violent.

"Gran would never have thought of it as cutting you off, Anne," Shane said with a calm she was far from feeling. "She knew you'd have no interest in the house or land, and there weren't that many extra pennies after taxes."

"What kind of fool do you think I am?" Anne demanded in a harsh, bitter voice. It was her temper more than a lack of talent that had snagged her career. Too often, she had let it rake over directors and other actors. Even now, when patience and the right words would have ensured success, she lashed out. "I know damn well she had money socked away, molding in some bank. I had to pry every penny I got out of her when she was alive. I'm going to have my share."

"She gave you what she could," Shane began.

"What the hell do you know? Do you think I'm so stupid I don't know this property is worth a tidy sum on the market?" She glanced around once in disgust. "You want the place, keep it. Just give me the cash."

"There isn't any to give. She didn't—"

"Don't hand me that." Anne shoved her aside and strode toward the stairs.

For a moment, Shane stood still, caught in a turmoil of disbelief. How was it possible anyone could be so unfeeling? And how, she asked herself, was it possible for her to be taken in again and again? Well, she would end it this time, once and for all. On her own wave of fury, she raced after her mother.

She found Anne in her bedroom, pulling papers out of her desk. Without hesitation, Shane dashed across the room and slammed the desk lid shut. "Don't you touch my things," she said in a dangerous voice. "Don't you ever touch what belongs to me."

"I want to see the bankbooks, and this so-called will." Anne turned to leave the room, but Shane grabbed her arm in a surprisingly strong grip.

"You'll see nothing in this house. This is mine."

"There *is* money," Anne said furiously, then jerked away. "You're trying to hide it."

"I don't have to hide anything from you." Rage raced through Shane, fed by years of cast-aside love. "If you want to see the will and the status of the estate, get yourself a lawyer. But I own this house, and everything in it. I won't have you going through my papers."

"Well…" Anne's blue eyes became slits. "Not such a sweet simpleton after all, are you?"

"You've never known what I am," Shane said evenly. "You've never cared enough to find out. It didn't matter, because I had Gran. I don't need you." Though saying the words was a relief, they didn't bank her fury. "There were times I thought I did, when you came sweeping in, so beautiful I hardly believed you were real. That was closer to the truth than I knew, because there's nothing real about you. You never cared about her. She knew that and she loved you anyway. But I don't." Her breathing was coming quickly, but she was unaware of how close it was to sobbing. "I can't even work up a hate. I just want to be rid of you."

Turning, she pulled open the desk and drew out her checkbook. Quickly, she wrote out a check for half of the capital she had left. "Here." She held it out to Anne. "Take it; consider it from Gran. You'll never get anything from me."

After snatching the check, Anne scanned the amount with a smirk. "If you think I'll be satisfied with this, you're wrong." Still, she folded the check neatly, then slipped it into her pocket. She knew better than to press her luck, and her own financial status was far from solid. "I'll get that lawyer," she promised, though she had no intention of wasting her money on the slim chance of getting more.

"And I'll contest the will. We'll just see how much I get from you, Shane."

"Do what you like," Shane said wearily. "Just stay away from me."

Anne tossed back her hair with a harsh laugh. "Don't think I'll spend any more time in this ridiculous house than I have to. I've always wondered how the hell you could possibly be my daughter."

Shane pressed a hand to her throbbing temple. "So have I," she murmured.

"You'll hear from my lawyer," Anne told her. Turning on her heel, she glided from the room, exiting gracefully.

Shane stood beside the desk until she heard the slam of the front door. Bursting into tears, she crumpled into a chair.

Chapter 11

Vance sat in the one decent chair he had in the living room. Impatiently, he checked his watch. He should have been with Shane ten minutes ago. And would have been, he thought with a glance at the front door, if the phone hadn't caught him as he'd been leaving the house. Resigned, he listened to the problems listed by the manager of his Washington branch. Though it wasn't said in words, Vance was aware there was some grumbling in the ranks that the boss had taken a sabbatical.

"...and with the union dispute, the construction on the Wolfe project is three weeks behind schedule," the manager continued. "I've been informed that there will be a delay in delivery of the steel on the Rheinstone site—possibly a lengthy one. I'm sorry to bother you with this, Mr. Banning, but as these two projects are of paramount importance to the firm, particularly with the bids going out on the shopping mall Rheinstone is planning, I felt…"

"Yes, I understand." Vance cut off what promised to be a detailed explanation. "Put a double shift on the Wolfe project until we're back on schedule."

"A double shift? But—"

"We contracted for completion by April first," Vance said mildly. "The increase in payroll will be less than the payment of the penalty clause, or the damage to the firm's reputation."

"Yes, sir."

"And have Liebewitz check into the steel delivery. If it's not taken care of satisfactorily by Monday, I'll handle it from here." Picking up a pencil, Vance made a scrawled note on a pad. "As to the Rheinstone bid, I looked it over myself last week. I see no problem." He scowled at the floor a moment. "Set up a meeting with the department heads for the end of next week. I'll be in. In the meantime," he added slowly, "send someone…Masterson," he decided, "up here to scout out locations for a new branch."

"New branch? Up there, Mr. Banning?"

The tone had a smile tugging at his mouth. "Have him concentrate on the Hagerstown area and give me a report. I want a list of viable locations in two weeks." He checked his watch again. "Is there anything else?"

"No, sir."

"Good. I'll be in next week." Without waiting for a reply, Vance broke the connection.

His last orders, he thought ruefully, would put them into quite a stir. Well, he reflected, Riverton had expanded before; it was going to expand again. For the first time in years, the company was going to bring him some personal happiness. He would be able to settle down with the woman he loved, where he chose to settle down, and still keep a firm rein on his business. If he had to justify the new branch to the board, which he would certainly have to do, he would point out that Hagerstown was the largest city in Maryland. There was also its proximity to Pennsylvania to consider…and to West Virginia. Yes, he mused, the expansion could be justified to the board easily enough. His track record would go a long way toward swaying them.

Rising, Vance shrugged back into his coat. All he had left to do now was to talk to Shane. Not for the first time, he speculated on her reaction. She was bound to be a bit stunned when he told her he wasn't precisely the unemployed carpenter she had taken him for. And he hadn't discounted the possibility that she might be angry with him for allowing her to go on believing him to be one. Vance felt a slight tug of apprehension as he stepped out into the cold, clear night.

There was a stiff breeze whipping in from the west. It sent stiff, dead leaves scattering and smelled faintly of snow. With his mind fully occupied, Vance never noticed the old stag fifty yards to his right, scenting the air and watching him.

He'd never set out to deceive her, he reminded himself. When they had first met, it had been none of Shane's business who he was. More, he added thoughtfully, he had simply wanted to shake loose of his company title for a while and be exactly what she had perceived him to be. Had there been any way of knowing she would become more important to him than anything else in his life? Could he

have guessed that weeks after he met her he would be
planning to ask her to marry him, finding himself ready to
toss his company into a frenzy of rush and preparation so
that she wouldn't have to give up her home or the life she
had chosen for herself?

Once he'd explained the circumstances, Vance told
himself as he crunched through frosted leaves, she'd understand. One of Shane's most endearing qualities was understanding. And she loved him. If he was sure of nothing else,
he was sure of that. She loved him without questions,
without demands. No one had ever given him so much for
so little. He intended to spend the rest of his life showing
her just what that meant to him.

He imagined that once the surprise of what he had to
tell her had worn off, she would laugh. The money, the
position he could offer her would mean nothing. She would
probably find it funny that the president of Riverton had
cut and hammered the trim in her kitchen.

Telling her about Amelia would be more difficult, but
it would be done—completely. He wouldn't pass over his
first marriage, but would tell her everything and rely on her
to understand. He wanted to tell her that she had been responsible for softening his guilt, lightening his bitterness.
Loving her was the only genuine emotion he'd felt in years.
Tonight, he would open up his past long enough to let the
air in; then he would ask Shane to share his future.

Still, Vance felt a twinge of apprehension as he approached her house. He might have ignored it if it hadn't
been for the sudden realization that all the windows were
dark. It was odd, he thought, unconsciously increasing his
pace. She was certainly home, not only because her car was

there, but because he knew she was expecting him. But why in God's name, he wondered, wasn't there a single light on? Vance tried to push away a flood of pure anxiety as he reached the back door.

It was unlocked. Though he entered without knocking, he called her name immediately. The house remained dark and silent. Hitting a switch, Vance flooded the rear showroom with light. A quick glance showed him nothing amiss before he continued through the first floor.

"Shane?"

The quiet was beginning to disturb him even more than the darkness. After making a quick circle of the lower floor, he went upstairs. At once he caught the scent of cooking. But the kitchen was empty. Absently turning off the oven, Vance went back into the hall. The thought struck him that she might have lain down after closing the shop and had simply fallen asleep. Amused more than concerned now, he walked quietly into her bedroom. All the amusement fled when he saw her curled up in the chair.

Though the room was in darkness, there was enough moonlight to make her out clearly. She wasn't asleep, but was curled up tightly with her head resting on the arm of the chair. He'd never seen her like that. His first thought was that she looked lost; then he corrected himself. Stricken. There was no innate vivacity in her eyes, and her face glowed palely in the silvery light of the moon. He might have thought her ill, but something told him that even in illness Shane wouldn't lose all of her spark. The thought ran through his mind in only seconds before he crossed the room to her. She made no sign that she saw him, nor was there any response when he spoke her name again. Vance knelt in front of her and took her chilled hands.

"Shane."

For a moment, she stared at him blankly. Then, as though a dam had burst, desperate emotion flooded her eyes. "Vance," she said brokenly, throwing her arms around his neck. "Oh, Vance."

She trembled violently, but didn't weep. The tears were dry as stone inside her. With her face pressed into his shoulder, she clung to him, breaking out of the numbed shock which had followed her earlier bout of tears. It was the warmth of him that made her realize how cold she had been. Without questions, with both strength and sweetness he held her to him.

"Vance, I'm so glad you're here. I need you."

The words struck him more forcibly than even her declaration of love. Up to that moment he had been almost uncomfortably aware that his needs far outweighed hers. Now it seemed there was something he could do for her, if it was only to listen.

"What happened, Shane?" Gently he drew her away only far enough to look into her eyes. "Can you tell me?"

She drew a raw breath, making him eloquently aware of the effort it cost her to speak. "My mother."

With his fingertips, he brushed the tousled hair from her cheeks. "Is she ill?"

"No!" It was a quick, furious explosion. The violence of the denial surprised him, but he took her agitated hands in his.

"Tell me what happened."

"She came," Shane managed, then fought to compose herself.

"Your mother came here?" he prompted.

"Near closing time. I didn't expect… She didn't come for the funeral or answer my letter." Her hands twisted in his, but Vance kept them in a gentle grip.

"This is the first time you've seen her since your grandmother died?" he asked. His voice was calm and quiet. Shane's eyes were still for a moment as she met his eyes directly.

"I haven't seen Anne in over two years," she said flatly. "Since she married her publicity agent. They're divorced now, so she came back." Shaking her head, Shane drew in a breath. "She almost made me believe she cared. I thought we could talk to each other. Really talk." She squeezed her eyes shut. "It was all an act, all the tears and grief. She sat there begging me to understand, and I believed—" Breaking off again, she shuddered with the effort of continuing. "She didn't come because of Gran or because of me." When she opened her eyes again Vance saw they were dull with pain. With a savage effort he kept his voice calm.

"Why did she come, Shane?"

Because her breathing was jerky again, she took a moment to answer. "Money," she said flatly. "She thought there would be money. She was furious that Gran left everything to me, and she wouldn't believe me when I told her how little there had been. I should have known!" she said in a quick rage, which then almost immediately subsided. "I did know." Her shoulders slumped as though she bore an intolerable weight. "I've always known. She's never cared about anyone. I'd hoped there might be some feeling in her for Gran, but… When she came running up here to paw through my papers, I said horrible things. I can't be sorry that I did." Tears sprang to her eyes, only to be swiftly controlled. "I gave her half of what's left and made her leave."

"You gave her money?" Vance demanded, incredulous enough to interrupt.

Shane gave him a weary look. "Gran would have given it to her. She's still my mother."

Disgust and rage rose in his throat. It took all the will-power he had not to give in to it. His anger wouldn't help Shane. "She's not your mother, Shane," he said matter-of-factly. When she opened her mouth to speak, he shook his head and continued. "Biologically, yes, but you're too smart to think that means anything. Cats have kittens too, Shane." He tightened his grip when he saw the flicker of pain on her face. "I'm sorry, I don't want to hurt you."

"No. No, you're right." Her hands went limp again as she let out a sigh. "The truth is, I very rarely think of her. Whatever feelings I have for her are mostly because Gran loved her. And yet…"

"And yet," he finished, "you make yourself sick with guilt."

"How can it be natural to want her to stay away?" Shane demanded in a rush. "Gran—"

"Your grandmother might have felt differently, might have given her money out of a sense of obligation. But think, who did she leave everything to? Everything important to her?"

"Yes, yes, I know, but…"

"When you think of the meaning of 'mother,' Shane, who comes to your mind?"

She stared at him. This time when the tears gathered,

they brimmed over. Without a word, she dropped her head back onto his shoulder. "I told her I didn't love her. I meant it, but…"

"You don't owe her anything." He drew her closer. "I know something about guilt, Shane, about letting it tear at you. I won't let you do that to yourself."

"I told her to stay away from me." She gave a long, weary sigh. "I don't think she will."

Vance remained silent for a moment. "Is that what you want?"

"Oh God, yes."

He pressed his lips to her temple before lifting her into his arms. "Come on, you're exhausted. Lie down for a while and sleep."

"No, I'm not tired," she lied as her lids fluttered down. "I just have a headache. And dinner's—"

"I turned off the oven," he told her as he carried her to the bed. "We'll eat later." After flipping down the quilt, he bent to lay Shane between the cool sheets. "I'll go get you some aspirin." He slipped off her shoes, but as he started to pull the quilt over her, Shane took his hand.

"Vance, would you just…stay with me?"

Touching the back of his hand to her cheek, he smiled at her. "Sure." As soon as he had pulled off his boots, he slipped into bed beside her. "Try to sleep," he murmured, gathering her close. "I'll be right here."

He heard her long, quiet sigh, then felt the feather-brush of her lashes against his shoulder as her eyes shut.

How long they lay still, he had no idea. Though the grandfather clock which stood in Shane's sitting room struck the hour once, Vance paid no attention. She wasn't trembling anymore, nor was her skin chilled. Her breathing was slow and even. The fingers that absently soothed at her temple were gentle, but his thoughts were not.

No one, nothing, was ever going to put that look on Shane's face again. He would see to it. He lay staring at the ceiling as he thought out the best way to deal with Anne Abbott. He'd let the money go, because that's the way Shane wanted it. But he couldn't resign himself to allowing her to deal with a constant emotional drain. Nothing had ever wrenched at him like the sight of her pale, shocked face or pain-filled eyes.

He should have known that anyone with as open a heart as Shane's could be hurt just as deeply as she could be made happy. And how, he wondered, could anyone who had dealt with that kind of pain since childhood be so generous and full of joy? The trial of a careless mother, the embarrassment and hurt of a broken engagement, the loss of the one constant family member she had known—none of it had broken her spirit, or her simple kindness.

But tonight she needed an arm around her. It would be his tonight—and whenever she needed him. Unconsciously he drew her closer as if to shield her from anything and everything that could hurt.

"Vance."

He thought she spoke his name in sleep and brushed a light kiss over her hair.

"Vance," Shane said again, so that he looked down to see the glint of her eyes against the darkness. "Make love with me."

It was a quiet, simple request that asked for comfort rather than passion. The love he already thought infinite tripled. So did his concern that he might not be gentle enough. Very softly, cupping the shape of her face in one hand, he touched his lips to hers.

Shane let herself float. She was too physically and emotionally drained to feel stinging desire, but he seemed to know what she asked for. Never had she felt such tenderness from him. His mouth was warm, and softer than she had thought possible. Minute after minute, he kissed her—and only kissed her. His fingers stroked soothingly over her face, then moved to the base of her neck as if he knew the dull, throbbing ache that centered there. Lovingly, patiently, he drew the quiet response from her, never asking for more than she could give. She relaxed and let him guide her.

With slow care, he roamed her face with kisses, touching his lips lightly to her closed lids as he shifted the gentle massage to her shoulders. There was a concentrated sweetness in his touch that was more kind than loverlike. When his mouth came back to hers, he used only the softest pressure, taking the kiss deep without fire or fury. With a sigh, she answered it, letting her needs pour out.

Passively, she let him undress her. His hands were deft and slow and undemanding. With a sensitivity neither of them had been aware he possessed, he made no attempt to arouse. Even when they were naked, he did nothing more than kiss her and hold her close. She knew she was taking without giving any in return, and murmuring, reached for him.

"Shh." He kissed her palm before turning her gently onto her stomach. With his fingertips only at first, he stroked and soothed, running them down her back, over her shoulders. She hadn't known love could be so compassionate or unselfish. With a sigh, she closed her eyes again and let her mind empty.

He was drawing out the pain, bringing back the warmth. As she lay quietly, Shane felt herself settle and balance. There was no need to think, and no need to feel anything but Vance's strong, sure hands. All of her trust was his. Knowing this, he took even more care not to abuse it.

The old bed swayed slightly as he bent to kiss the back of her neck. Shane felt the first stir of desire. It was mild and wonderfully easy. Content, she remained still to allow herself the full enjoyment of being treasured. He was treating her like something fragile and precious. She wallowed in the new experience as he ranged soft kisses down her spine. Tension and tears were a world away from the Jenny Lind bed with a sagging mattress and worn linen sheets. The only reality now was Vance's sweet loving and the growing response of her pampered body.

He heard the subtle change in her breathing, the faint quickening, which meant relaxation was becoming desire. Still, he kept his hands easy, not wanting to rush her. The clock in the sitting room struck the hour again with low, ponderous bongs. Creakily the house settled around them with moans and groans. Vance heard little but Shane's deepening breathing.

The moonlight shivered over her skin, seeming to chase after his roaming hands. It only made him see more clearly how slender her back was, how slight the flare of her hips. Pressing his lips to her shoulder, he could smell the familiar lemon tang of her hair mixed with the lavender sachet lingering on the sheets. The room was washed in shadows.

Her cheek rested on the pillow, giving him a clear view of her profile. She might have been sleeping had it not been for the breath hurrying between her lips and the subtle movements her body was beginning to make. Still gentle, he turned her onto her back to press his mouth to hers.

Shane moaned, so lost in him she noticed no sound, no scent that didn't come from him. But his pace never altered, remaining slow and unhurried. He wanted her, God, yes, but felt no fierce, consuming drive. Love, much more than desire, pulled him to her. When he lowered his mouth to her breast, it was with such infinite tenderness that she felt a warmth, half glow, half ache, pour into her. His tongue began to turn the warmth into heat. She rose up, but seemed to take the journey on a cloud.

With the same infinite care, he took his lips and hands over her. Her skin hummed at his touch, but softly. There was no sweet pain in the passion he brought her, but such pleasure, such comfort, she desired him all the more. Her thoughts became wholly centered on her own body and the quiet delights he had awakened.

Though his lips might stray from hers to taste her neck or her cheek, they returned again and again. Her mindless answer, the husky breath that trembled into his mouth, had the fires roaring inside him. But he banked them. Tonight, she was porcelain. She was as fragile as the moonlight. He wouldn't allow his own passion and needs to overtake him, then find he had treated her roughly. Tonight he would forget her energy and strength and only think of her frailty.

And when he took her, the tenderness made her weep.

Chapter 12

In a thick, steady curtain, the snow fell. Already the road surface was slick. Trees had been quickly transformed from dark and stark to glittery. Vance's windshield wipers swept back and forth with the monotonous swish of rubber on glass. The snow brought him neither annoyance nor pleasure. He barely noticed it.

With a few phone calls and casual inquiries, he had learned enough about Anne Abbott—or Anna Cross, as she called herself professionally—to make his anger of the night before intensify. Shane's description had been too kind.

Anne had been through three turbulent marriages. Each had been a contact in the film industry. She had coolly bled each husband for as much as she could get before jumping into the next relationship. Her latest, Leslie Stuart, had proven a bit too clever for her—or his attorney had. She'd come out of her last marriage with nothing more than she had gone into it. And, as she had a penchant for the finer things, she was already badly in debt.

She worked sporadically—bit parts, walk-ons, an occasional commercial. Her talent was nominal, but her face had earned her a few lines in a couple of legitimate films. It might have earned her more had her temper and self-importance not interfered. She was tolerated more than liked by Hollywood society. Even the tolerance, it seemed, was due more to her various husbands and intermittent lovers than to herself. Vance's contacts had painted a picture of a beautiful, scheming woman with a streak of viciousness. He felt he already knew her.

As he drove through the rapidly falling snow, his thoughts centered on Shane. He'd held her through the night, soothing her when she became restless, listening when she needed to talk. The shattered expression in her eyes would remain with him for a long time to come. Even that morning, though she had tried to be cheerful, there'd been an underlying listlessness. And he sensed her unspoken fear that Anne would come back and put her through another emotional storm. Vance couldn't change what had happened, but he could take steps to protect her in the future. That was precisely what he intended to do.

Vance turned into the lot of the roadside motel and parked. For a moment, he only sat, watching the snow accumulate on the windshield. He had considered telling Shane he intended to see her mother, then had rejected the idea. She'd been so pale that morning. In any case, he didn't doubt she would have been against it—even violently opposed to it. She was a woman who insisted on solving her own problems. Vance respected that, even admired it, but in this instance he was going to ignore it.

Stepping out of the car, he walked across the slippery parking lot to find the office and the information he needed. Ten minutes later, he knocked on Anne Abbott's door.

The crease of annoyance between her brows altered into an expression of consideration when she saw Vance. He was certainly a very pleasant surprise. Vance eyed her coolly, discovering that Shane's description hadn't been exaggerated. She was lovely. Her face had a delicacy of bone and complexion complemented by the very deep blue eyes and mane of blond hair. Her body, clad in a clinging pink dressing gown, was ripe and rounded. Though her glittery fairness was the direct opposite of Amelia's sultry beauty, Vance knew instantly they were women of the same mold.

"Well, hello." Her voice was languid and sulky, her eyes amused and appraising. Though he looked for it, Vance found not the slightest resemblance to her daughter. Overcoming a wave of disgust, he smiled in return. He had to get in the door.

"Hello, Ms. Cross."

He saw instantly that the use of her stage name had been a wise move. She flashed him the full-power smile that was one of her best tools. "Do I know you?" She touched the pink tip of her tongue to her top lip. "There is something familiar about you, but I can't believe I'd forget your face."

"Vance Banning, Ms. Cross," he said, keeping his eyes on hers. "We have some mutual friends, the Hourbacks."

"Oh, Tod and Sheila!" Though she couldn't abide them, Anne infused her voice with rich pleasure. "Isn't that marvelous! Oh, but you must come in. It's freezing out there.

Appalling Eastern weather." She closed the door behind him, then stood leaning back against it a moment. Perhaps, she mused, the hometown visit wouldn't be so boring after all. This was the best-looking thing to knock at her door for quite some time. And, if he knew the stuffy Hourbacks, chances were he'd have a few dollars as well. "Well, well, isn't it a small world," she murmured, gently tucking a strand of delicate blond hair behind her ear. "How are Tod and Sheila? I haven't seen them for an age."

"Fine when I last spoke to them." Well aware where her thoughts were traveling, Vance smiled again, this time with cold amusement. "They mentioned that you were in town. I couldn't resist looking you up, Ms. Cross."

"Oh, Anna, please," she said graciously. With a sigh, she gave the room a despairing glance. "I must apologize for my accommodations, but I have some business nearby, and…" She gave a tiny shrug. "I'm forced to make do. I can offer you a drink, however, if you'll take bourbon."

It was barely eleven, but Vance answered smoothly, "If it's not too much trouble."

"None at all." Anne glided to a small table. She felt particularly grateful that she had packed the silk dressing gown and hadn't yet drummed up the energy to change. It was, she knew, both becoming and alluring. A quick glance in the mirror as she poured assured her she looked perfect. Thank God she'd just finished putting on her makeup. "But tell me, Vance," she continued, "what in the world are you doing in this dull little place? You're not a hometown boy, are you?"

"Business," he said simply, nodding his thanks as she handed him a neat bourbon.

Anne's eyes narrowed a moment, then widened. "Oh,

of course. How could I be so foolish!" She beamed at him as the wheels began to spin in her head. "I've heard Tod speak of you. Riverton Construction, right?"

"Right."

"My, my, I am impressed." Her tongue ran lightly over her teeth as she considered. "It's about the biggest in the country."

"So I'm told," he answered mildly, watching her eye him over the rim of her glass. Without much interest, he wondered how much bait she would toss out before she tried to reel him in. If it hadn't been for Shane, he might have enjoyed letting her make a fool of herself.

With her carefully languid grace, Anne sat on the edge of the bed. As she sipped again, she wondered how soon he would try to sleep with her and how much resistance she should feign before she obliged him. "Well, Vance, what can I do for you?"

Vance swirled the bourbon without drinking. He sent her a cool, direct stare. "Leave Shane alone."

The change in her expression might have been comical under any other circumstances. She forgot herself long enough to gape at him. "What are you talking about?"

"Shane," he repeated. "Your daughter."

"I know who Shane is," Anne said sharply. "What has she to do with you?"

"I'm going to marry her."

Shock covered her face, then dissolved with her burst of laughter. "Little Shane? Oh, that's too funny. Don't tell me my cute little daughter caught herself a live one! I've underestimated her." Tossing her head, she sent Vance a shrewed glance. "Or I overestimated you."

Though his fingers tightened on the glass, he controlled his temper. When he spoke, his voice was dangerously mild. "Be careful, Anne."

The look in his eye checked her laughter. "Well," she continued with an unconcerned shrug, "so you want to marry Shane. What's that to me?"

"Not a damn thing."

Masking both apprehension and irritation, Anne rose gracefully. "I suppose I should go congratulate my little girl on her luck."

Vance took her arm. Though he applied no pressure, the meaning was very clear. "You'll do nothing of the kind. What you're going to do is pack your bags and get out."

Enraged, Anne jerked away from him. "Who the hell do you think you are? You can't order me to leave."

"Advise," Vance corrected. "You'd be wise to take the suggestion."

"I don't like the tone of your suggestion," she retorted. "I intend to see my daughter—"

"Why?" Vance stopped her cold without raising his voice. "You won't get another dime, I promise you."

"I haven't any idea what you're talking about," Anne claimed with frigid dignity. "I don't know what nonsense Shane's been telling you, but—"

"You'd be wise to think carefully before you say any more," Vance warned quietly. "I saw Shane shortly after you left her last night. She had to tell me very little before I got the picture." He gave her a long, hard look. "I know you, Anne, every bit as well as you know yourself. There'll be no more money," he continued when Anne fell silent. "You'd be smarter to cut your losses and go back to California. It would be a simple matter to stop payment on the check she's already given you."

That annoyed her. Anne cursed herself for not getting up early and cashing the check before Shane thought better of it. "I have every intention of seeing my daughter." She gave him a glittering smile. "And when I do, I'll have a few words to say to her about her choice of lovers."

His eyes neither heated nor chilled, but became faintly bored. Nothing could have infuriated her more. "You won't see Shane again," he corrected.

Under the silk, her lovely bust heaved. "You can't keep me from seeing my own daughter."

"I can," Vance countered, "and I will. If you contact her, if you try to wheedle another dollar out of her or hurt her in any way, I'll deal with you myself."

Anne felt the first prickle of physical fear. Warily, she stepped back from him. "You wouldn't dare touch me."

Vance gave a mirthless laugh. "Don't be too sure. I don't think it'll come to that though." Casually, he set down the glass of liquor. "I have a number of contacts in the movie industry, Anne. Old friends, business associates, clients. A few words in the right ears, and what little career you have is out the window."

"How dare you threaten me," she began, both furious and afraid.

"Not a threat," he assured her. "A promise. Hurt Shane again and you'll pay for it. You're getting the best of the deal, Anne," he added. "She doesn't have anything you want."

Smoldering, she took a step toward him. "I have a right to my share. Whatever my grandmother had should be split fifty-fifty between Shane and me."

He lifted a brow in speculation. "Fifty-fifty," he said thoughtfully. "You must be desperate if you're willing to settle for that." Without pity, he shrugged off her problems. "I won't waste my time arguing legalities with you, much less morals or ethics. Just accept that what Shane gave you yesterday is all you'll ever get." With this he turned toward the door. In a last-ditch effort, Anne sank down on the bed and began to weep.

"Oh, Vance, you can't be so cruel." She lifted an already tear-drenched face to his. "You can't mean to keep me from seeing my own daughter, my only child."

He studied the beautiful tragic face, then gave a slight nod of approval. "Very good," he commented. "You're a better actress than they give you credit for." As he pulled the door to behind him, he heard the sound of smashing glass on the wood.

Springing up, Anne grabbed the second glass, then hurled it as well. No one, *no one,* she determined, was going to threaten her. Or mock her, she fumed, remembering the cool amusement in his eyes. She'd see he paid for it. Sitting back on the bed, she clenched her fists until she could bring her temper to order. She had to think. There had to be a way to get to Vance Banning. *Riverton Construction,* she reflected, closing her eyes as she concentrated. Had there been any scandal connected with the firm? Frustrated, she hurled her pillow across the room. She could think of nothing. What did she know about a stupid firm that built shopping centers and hospitals? It was all so boring, she thought furiously.

Grabbing the second pillow, she started to toss it as well when a sudden glimmer of memory arrested her. Scandal, she repeated. But not about the firm. There had been something…something a few years back. Just a few whispers at a party or two. *Damn!* she swore silently when her recollection took her no further. Sheila Hourback, Anne thought, tightening her lips. Maybe the stuffy old bird could be useful. Scrambling over the unmade bed, Anne reached for the phone.

Shane was busy detailing a skirmish of the Battle of Antietam for three eager boys when Vance walked in. She smiled at him, and he heard enthusiasm in her voice as she spoke, but she was still pale. That alone brushed away any doubts that he had done the right thing. She'd bounce back, he told himself as he wandered into the antique shop, because it was her nature to do so. But even someone as intrinsically strong as Shane could take only so much. Spotting Pat dusting glassware, he went over to her.

"Hi, Vance." She sent him a quick, friendly grin. "How're you doing?"

"I'm fine." He cast a look over his shoulder to be certain Shane was still occupied. "Listen, Pat, I wanted to talk to you about that dining-room set."

"Oh yeah. There was some mix-up about that. I still haven't gotten it straight. Shane said—"

"I'm going to buy it."

"You?" Her initial surprise turned into embarrassment. Vance grinned at her, however, and her cheeks cooled.

"For Shane," he explained. "For Christmas."

"Oh, that's so sweet!" The romance of it appealed to her immediately. "It was her grandmother's, you know. She just loves it."

"I know, and she's determined to sell it." Idly, he picked up a china demitasse cup. "I'm just as determined to buy it for her. She won't let me." He gave Pat a conspirator's wink. "But she can hardly turn down a Christmas present, can she?"

"No." Appreciating his cleverness, Pat beamed at him. So the rumors were true, she thought, pleased and interested. There was something going on between them. "She sure couldn't. It'll mean so much to her, Vance. It just about kills her to have to sell some of these things, but that's the hardest. It's…ah, it's awfully expensive though."

"That's all right. I'm going to give you a check for it today." It occurred to him that it would soon be all over town that he had a great deal of money to spend. He would have to talk to Shane very soon. "Put a Sold sign on it." He glanced back again, seeing Shane's three visitors were preparing to leave. "Just don't say anything to her unless she asks."

"I won't," Pat promised, pleased to be in on the surprise. "And if she does, I'll just say the person who bought it wants it held until Christmas."

"Clever girl," he complimented. "Thanks."

"Vance." She lowered her voice to a whisper. "She looks kind of down today. Maybe you could take her out for a while and cheer her up. Oh, Shane," she continued quickly in a normal tone, "how did you manage to keep those little monsters quiet for twenty minutes? Those are Clint Drummond's boys," she explained to Vance with a shudder. "I nearly ran out the back door when they came in."

"They were thrilled that school was called off because of the snow." Instinctively, she reached for Vance's hand as she came in. "What they wanted was to work out the fine details of a few engagements so they could have their own Battle of Antietam with snowballs."

"Get your coat," Vance told her, planting a kiss on her brow.

"What?"

"And a hat. It's cold outside."

Laughing, Shane gave his hand a squeeze. "I know it's cold outside, fool. There's already six inches of snow."

"Then we'd better get started." He gave her a friendly swat on the seat. "You'll need boots too, I suppose. Just don't take all day."

"Vance, it's the middle of the day. I can't leave."

"It's business," he told her gravely. "You have to get your Christmas tree."

"Christmas tree?" With a chuckle, she picked up the duster Pat had set down. "It's too early in the season."

"Early?" Vance sent Pat a grin. "You've got just over two weeks until Christmas, and no tree. Most self-respecting stores are decked out by Thanksgiving."

"Well, I know, but—"

"But nothing," he interrupted, taking the duster from her and handing it back to Pat. "Where's your holiday spirit? Not to mention your sales strategy. According to the most recent poll, people spend an additional twelve and a half percent in a store decorated for the holidays."

Shane gave him a narrow glance. "What poll?"

"The Retail Sale and Seasonal Atmosphere Survey," he said glibly.

The first genuine laugh in nearly twenty-four hours burst from her. "That's a terrible lie."

"Certainly not," he disagreed. "It's a very good one. Now go get your coat."

"But, Vance—"

"Oh, don't be silly, Shane," Pat interrupted, giving her a push toward the stairs. "I can handle the shop. We're not likely to have customers pouring in with all this snow. Besides," she added, shrewd enough to know her employer, "I'd really love a tree. I'll make a place for it right in front of this window." Without waiting for a reply, Pat began to rearrange furniture.

"Gloves too," Vance added as Shane hesitated.

"All right," she said, surrendering. "I'll be back in a minute."

In little more than ten, she was sitting beside Vance in the cab of his small pickup. "Oh, it's beautiful out here!" she exclaimed, trying to look everywhere at once. "I love the first snow. Look, there're the Drummond boys."

Vance glanced in the direction she indicated and saw three boys pelting each other violently with snow.

"The battle's under way," he murmured.

"General Burnside's having his problems," Shane observed, then turned back to Vance. "By the way, what did you and Pat have your heads together about when I went upstairs to get my things?"

Vance lifted a brow. "Oh," he said complacently, "I was trying to make a date with her. She's cute."

"Really?" Shane drew out the word as she eyed him. "It would be a shame for her to be fired this close to Christmas."

"I was only trying to develop good employee relations," he explained, pulling up at a stop sign. Taking her by surprise, he pulled her into his arms and kissed her thoroughly. "I love that little choking sound you make when you try not to laugh. Do it again."

Breathless, she pulled away from him. "Firing a trusted employee is no laughing matter," she told him primly, and adjusted her ski hat. "Turn right here." Instead of obeying, he kissed her again. The rude blast of a horn had her struggling out of his arms a second time. "Now you've done it." She ruined the severity of the lecture with a smothered chuckle. "The sheriff's going to arrest you for obstructing traffic."

"One disgruntled man in a Buick isn't traffic," Vance disagreed as he made a right turn. "Do you know where you're going?"

"Certainly. There's a place a few miles down where you can dig your own tree."

"Dig?" Vance repeated, shooting her a look. Shane met it placidly.

"Dig," she repeated. "According to the latest conservation poll—"

"Dig," he agreed, cutting her off.

Laughing, Shane leaned over to kiss his shoulder. "I love you, Vance."

By the time they arrived at the tree farm, the snow had slowed to a gentle mist. Shane dragged him from tree to tree, examining each one minutely before rejecting it. Though he knew the color in her face was a result of the cold, the spark was back. Even if he sensed some of the energy was a product of nerves, he was satisfied that she was bouncing back. The simple pleasure of choosing a Christmas tree was enough to put the laughter back in her eyes.

"This one!" Shane exclaimed, stopping in front of a short-needle pine. "It's exactly right."

"It doesn't look much different from the other five hundred trees we've looked at," Vance grumbled, slicing the point of his shovel into the snow.

"That's because you don't have a connoisseur's eye," she said condescendingly. He scooped up a handful of snow and rubbed it into her face. "Be that as it may," Shane continued with remarkable aplomb, "this is the one. Dig," she instructed, and stepping back, folded her arms.

"Yes, ma'am," he said meekly, bending to the task. "You know," he said a few moments later, "it suddenly occurs to me that you're going to expect me to dig a hole to put this thing in after Christmas."

Shane sent him a guileless smile. "What a good idea. I know just the place too. You'll probably need a pick though. There are an awful lot of rocks." Ignoring Vance's rude rejoinder, she waved over an attendant. With the roots carefully wrapped in burlap and the tree itself paid for—by Shane over Vance's objection—they headed home.

"Damn it, Shane," he said in exasperation. "I wanted to buy the tree for you." The truck rumbled over the narrow wooden bridge.

"The tree's for the shop," she pointed out logically as they pulled in front of the house. "So the shop bought the tree. Just as it buys the stock and pays the electric bill." Noting that he was annoyed, Shane walked around the truck to kiss him. "You're sweet, Vance, and I do appreciate it. Buy me something else."

He gave her a long, considering look. "What?"

"Oh, I don't know. I've always had a fancy for something frivolous and extravagant…like chinchilla earmuffs."

With difficulty, he maintained his gravity. "It would

serve you right if I did buy you some. Then you'd have to wear them."

She rose on her toes, inviting another kiss. As he bent down, Shane slipped the handful of snow she'd been holding down his back. When he swore pungently, she made a dash for safety. Shane fully expected the snowball that bashed into the back of her head, but she didn't expect to be agilely tackled so that she landed facedown in the snow.

"Oh! You really aren't a gentleman," she muttered, hampered by a mouthful of snow. Vance sat back, roaring with laughter while she struggled to sit up, wiping at her face.

"Snow looks even better on you than mud," he told her.

Shane lunged at him, catching him off-balance so that he toppled onto his back. She landed with a soft thud on his chest. Before she could deposit the snow she held in his face, he rolled her over and pinned her. Resigned, she closed her eyes and waited. Instead of the cold shock of snow, she felt his lips crush down on hers. In immediate response, she pulled him closer, answering hungrily.

"Give?" he demanded.

"No," she said firmly, and dragged him back again.

The urgency of her response made him forget they were lying in the snow in the middle of the afternoon. He no longer felt the wet flakes that drifted down the back of his neck, though he could taste others on her skin. He fretted against the bulky clothes that kept the shape of her from him, against the gloves that prevented him from feeling the softness of her skin. But he could taste, and he did so greedily.

"God, I want you," he murmured, savaging her small, avid mouth again and again. "Right here, right now." Lifting his head, he looked down on her, but whatever he would have said was cut off by the sound of an approaching car. "If I'd had any sense I'd have taken you to my house," he mumbled, then helped her to her feet.

Hugging him, she whispered in his ear, "I close in two hours."

While Shane dealt with a straggle of customers who touched everything and bought nothing, Vance made himself useful by setting up the tree. Pat's lighthearted chatter helped cool the blood Shane had so quickly heated. Following Shane's instructions, he found the boxes of ornaments in the dusty attic.

Dusk was falling before they were alone again. Because she was still looking pale, Vance bullied her into a quick meal before they began to sort through the ornaments. They made do with cold meat from the rib roast neither of them had touched the night before.

But as well as alleviating her hunger, the meal reminded her forcibly of her mother's visit. She struggled to push away the depression, or at least to conceal it. Her chatter was bright and mindless and entirely too strained.

Vance caught her hand, stopping her in midsentence. "Not with me, Shane," he said quietly.

Not bothering to pretend she didn't understand, Shane squeezed his hand. "I'm not dwelling on it, Vance. It just sneaks up on me sometimes."

"And when it does, I'm here. Lean on me, Shane, when you need to." He lifted her hand to his lips. "God knows, I'll lean on you."

"Now," she said shakily. "Just hold me a minute."

He drew her into his arms, pressing her head to his heart. "As long as you want."

She sighed, relaxing again. "I hate being a fool," she murmured. "I suppose I hate that worse than anything."

"You're not being a fool," he said, then drew her away as he came to a decision. "Shane, I went to see your mother this morning."

"What?" The word came out in a whisper.

"You can be angry if you like, but I won't stand by and watch you be hurt again. I made it very clear that if she bothered you again, she'd have me to deal with."

Shaken, she turned away from him. "You shouldn't—"

"Don't tell me what I shouldn't have done," he interrupted angrily. "I love you, damn it. You can't expect me to do nothing while she puts you through the wringer."

"I can deal with it, Vance."

"No." Taking her shoulders, he turned her around. "With an amazing number of things, yes, but not with this. She turns you inside out." His grip lightened to a caress. "Shane, if it had been me hurting, what would you have done?"

She opened her mouth to speak, but only released a pent-up breath. Taking his face in her hands, she pulled it down to hers. "I hope I'd have done the same thing. Thank you," she said, kissing him gently. "I don't want to know what was said," she added with more firmness. "No more problems tonight, Vance."

He shook his head, acknowledging another delay in making everything known to her. "All right, no more problems."

"We'll trim the tree," she stated decisively. "Then you're going to make love to me under it."

He grinned. "I suppose I could do that." He allowed her

to pull him down the stairs. "What if I make love to you under it, then we trim it?"

"There's nothing festive in that," she said gravely as she began unpacking ornaments.

"Wanna bet?"

She laughed, but shook her head. "Absolutely not. There's an order to these things, you know. Lights first," she announced, pulling out a neatly coiled string.

It took well over an hour as Shane shared her memories about nearly every ornament she unpacked. As she took out a red felt star, she recalled the year she had made it for her grandmother. It brought both a sting and a warmth. She'd been dreading Christmas. It hadn't seemed possible to celebrate the holiday in that house without the woman who had always shared it with her. Gran would have reminded her that there was a cycle, but Shane knew she would have found a tree and tinsel unbearable had she been alone.

She watched Vance carefully arranging a garland. How Gran would have loved him, she thought with a smile. And he her. Somehow she found it didn't matter that the two people she loved most in the world had never met. She knew both of them, and the link was formed. Shane was ready to give herself to him completely.

If he doesn't ask me to marry him soon, she mused, I'll just have to ask him. When he glanced over, she sent him a saucy smile.

"What are you thinking?" he demanded.

"Oh, nothing," she said innocently, stepping back to view the results. "It's perfect, just as I knew it would be." She gave a satisfied nod before taking out the old silver star that would adorn the top.

Vance accepted it from her, then eyed the top branch. "I'm not going to be able to get this on there without knocking half of everything else off. We need a ladder."

"Oh no, that's okay. Let me up on your shoulders."

"There's a stepladder upstairs," he began.

"Oh, don't be so fussy." Shane jumped nimbly onto his back, hooking her legs around his waist for balance. "I'll be able to reach it without any trouble," she assured him, then began scooting up to his shoulders. Vance felt every line of her body as if he'd run his hands over it. "There," she said, settled. "Hand it to me and I'll stick it on."

He obliged, then gripped her knees as she leaned forward. "Damn it, Shane, not so far; you're going to fall into the tree."

"Don't be silly," she said lightly as she secured the star. "I have terrific balance. There!" Putting her hands on her hips, she surveyed the results. "Step back a bit so I can see the whole thing." When he had, Shane gave a long sigh, then kissed the top of his head. "It's beautiful, isn't it? Just smell the pine." Carelessly, she linked her ankles against his chest.

"It'll look better with the overhead lights off." Still carrying her, he moved to flick the wall switch. In the dark, the colored lights on the tree seemed to jump into life. They shimmered against garland and tinsel, glowed warmly against pine.

"Oh yes," Shane breathed. "Just perfect."

"Not quite yet," Vance disagreed.

With a deft move, he pulled her around into his arms as she slid down from his shoulders. "This," he told her as he laid her on the rug, "is perfect."

The lights danced on her face as she smiled up at him. "It certainly is."

His hands weren't patient tonight, but neither were hers. They undressed each other quickly, laughing and swearing a bit at buttons or snaps. But when they were naked, the urgency only intensified. Their hands sought to touch, their mouths hurried to taste—everywhere. She marveled again at his taut, corded muscles. He filled himself again on the flavor and fragrance of her skin. They paid no more notice to the warmth of the lights or the tang of pine than they had to the chill of the snow. They were alone. They were together.

Chapter 13

It wasn't easy for Shane to keep her mind on her work the next day. Though she made several sales, among them the tilt-top table she had so painstakingly refinished, she was distracted throughout the morning. Distracted enough that she never noticed the discreet Sold sign Pat had attached to the Hepplewhite set in lieu of a price tag. She could think of little else but Vance. Once or twice during the morning, she caught herself glancing at the Christmas tree and remembering. In all of her dreams, in all of her wishes, she had never imagined it could be this way. Each time they made love it was different, a new adventure. Yet somehow it was as though they had been together for years.

Every time she touched him it was like making a fresh discovery, and still Shane felt she had known him for a lifetime rather than a matter of three short months. When he kissed her, it was just as thrilling and novel as the first time. The recognition she had felt the instant she had seen him had deepened into something much more abiding. Faith.

Without doubt, she was certain that the excitement and the learning would go on time after time over the comfortable core of honest love. There was no need to romanticize what was real. She had only to look at him to know what they shared was special and enduring. With another glance at the tree, she realized she'd never been happier in her life.

"Miss!" The customer considering the newly caned ladder-back chair called impatiently for Shane's attention.

"Yes, ma'am, I'm sorry." If the smile Shane gave her was a bit dreamy, the woman didn't seem to notice. "It's a lovely piece, isn't it? The seat's just been redone." Calling herself to order, Shane turned the chair over to show off the workmanship.

"Yes, I'm interested." The woman poked at the caning a moment. "But the price…"

Recognizing the tone, Shane settled down to bargain.

It was just past noon when things began to quiet down. The morning's profits weren't extraordinary, but solid enough to help Shane stop worrying over the large chunk of her capital that she had given to her mother. The wolf wasn't at the door yet, she told herself optimistically. And with luck—and the Christmas rush—she could hold him off for quite some time. Two or three good sales would keep her books from dipping too deeply into the red. Professionally, she wanted little more at the moment than to calmly tread water. Personally, she knew precisely what she wanted, and she had every intention of seeing to it quickly.

She was going to marry Vance, and it was time she told

him so. If he was too proud to ask her because he didn't yet have a steady job, she would simply have to persuade him to see things differently. Shane had made up her mind to take a firm stand that very day. There was an excitement bubbling inside her, a sense of purpose. Today, she thought, almost giddy from it, nothing could hurt her. She was going to propose to the man she loved. And she wasn't going to take no for an answer.

"Pat, can you handle things if I go out for an hour?"

"Sure, it's slow now anyway." Pat glanced up from the table she was polishing. "Are you going to another auction?"

"No," Shane told her blithely. "I'm going on a picnic."

Leaving Pat staring behind her, Shane raced upstairs.

It took her less than ten minutes to fill the wicker basket. There was a cold bottle of Chablis inside it, which she had splurged on madly. It might be a bit rich for the peanut butter sandwiches, but Shane's mind wasn't on proprieties. As she raced out the back door, she was already picturing spreading the checked tablecloth in front of Vance's living-room fire.

Wet, slushy snow sloshed over her boots as she stepped off the porch onto the lawn. The perfect day for a picnic, she decided, letting the hamper swing. The air was absolutely still. Melted snow dripped from the roof with a musical patter. The fast water in the creek broke through thin sheets of ice with an excited hissing and bubbling. Shane paused to listen a moment, enjoying the mixture of sounds. The feeling of euphoria built. She found it the most exquisite of days, with the sky coldly blue, the snow-laced mountains rising and the naked trees slick with wet.

Then the low purr of an engine intruded. She looked back, then stopped as she recognized Anne pulling up in the drive. All of her joy in the afternoon slipped quietly away. She hardly noticed the fingers of tension that crept up to the base of her neck.

With her faultless grace, Anne picked her way over the melting snow in calfskin boots. She wore a trim fox-fur hat now to match her coat, and a small, smug smile. There were ruby studs, or clever imitations, glinting at her ears. Though her daughter stood rigid as a stone, she glided up to greet her with the customary brush of cheeks. Without speaking, Shane set the hamper down on the bottom step of the porch.

"Darling, I had to drop by before I left." Anne beamed at her with a cold gleam in her eye.

"Going back to California?" Shane asked flatly.

"Yes, of course, I have the most marvelous script. Of course, I'll probably be weeks on location, but…" She gave a gay shrug. "But that's not why I dropped by."

Shane studied her, marveling. It was as though the ugly scene between them had never taken place. She has no feelings, she realized abruptly. It meant less than nothing to her. "Why did you come by, Anne?"

"Why, to congratulate you, of course!"

"Congratulate me?" Shane lifted a brow. It was easier somehow knowing that the woman in front of her was simply a stranger. A few shared genes didn't make a bond. It was love that did that, or affection. Or at the very least, respect.

"I admit I didn't think you had it in you, Shane, but I'm pleasantly surprised."

Shane then surprised both of them by giving an impatient sigh. "Will you get to the point, Anne? I was on my way out."

"Oh, now, don't be cross," she said placatingly. "I'm really thrilled for you, catching yourself a man like that."

Shane's eyes chilled. "I beg your pardon?"

"Vance Banning, darling." She gave a slow, appreciative smile. "What a catch!"

"Strange, I never thought about it quite that way." Bending, Shane prepared to pick up the hamper again.

"The president of Riverton Construction isn't just a mild triumph, sweetheart, it's a downright *coup*."

Shane's fingers froze on the handle. Straightening, she looked Anne dead in the eye. "What are you talking about?"

"Only your fantastic luck, Shane. After all, the man's *rolling* in it. I imagine you'll be able to turn this little shop of yours into an antique palace if you want a hobby." She gave a quick, brittle laugh. "Leave it to cute little Shane to land herself a millionaire the first time around. If I had a bit more time, darling, I'd insist on hearing the details of how you managed it."

"I don't know what you're talking about." Cold panic was beginning to rush through her. She wanted to turn and run away, but her legs were stiff and unyielding.

"God knows why he decided to dump himself in this town," Anne went on mildly. "But it's your good fortune he did, and right next door too. I suppose he means to keep it for a little hideaway once the two of you move to D.C." *A fabulous house,* she thought on a flash of envy. *Servants, parties.* Carefully, she kept her tone gay. "I can't tell you how thrilled I was to learn you'd hooked up with the man who owns virtually the biggest construction firm in the country."

"Riverton," Shane repeated numbly.

"Very prestigious, darling Shane. It does give me cause to wonder how you'll fit in, but…" She shrugged this off and aimed her coup de grâce. "It's a shame about that nasty scandal though." Shane merely shook her head and stared at Anne blankly. "His first wife, you know. A terrible tangle."

"Wife?" Shane repeated faintly. She felt the nausea rising in her stomach. "Vance's wife?"

"Oh, Shane, don't tell me he didn't mention it!" It was exactly what she'd hoped for. Anne shook her head and sighed. "That's disgraceful of him, really. Isn't it just like a man to expect some wide-eyed girl to take everything on face value." She clucked her tongue in disapproval, thinking with inner appreciation that Vance Banning was going to take his knocks on this one. She didn't think of Shane at all.

"Well, the very least he might have done was tell you he was married before," she continued primly. "Even if he didn't go into the nasty business."

"I don't…" Shane managed to swallow the sickness and continue. "I don't understand."

"A spicy little scandal," Anne told her. "His wife was a raving beauty, you know. Perhaps too much so." Anne paused delicately. "One of her lovers put a bullet in her heart. At least that's what the Bannings would have everyone believe." The shock in Shane's eyes gave Anne another surge of gratification. Oh yes, she thought grimly, Vance Banning was going to get back some of his now. "Hushed it up rather quickly too," she added, then brushed the matter away with the back of an elegantly gloved hand. "An odd business. Well, I must run, don't want to miss my plane. *Ciao,* darling, and don't let that handsome gold mine slip away from you. There are plenty of women just dying to catch him." Pausing, she touched Shane's cap of curls with a finger. "For God's sake, Shane, find a decent hairdresser. I suppose he thinks you're…refreshing. Get the ring on your finger before he gets bored." She brushed Shane's cold cheek with hers, then dashed off, satisfied she'd paid Vance back for his threats.

Shane stood perfectly still, staring after her. But she didn't see her. She saw nothing. Trapped in the ice of shock, the pain was dormant. That would have surprised Anne had she given it any thought. As a woman who knew nothing of emotional pain, she would assume Shane would feel only fury. But the fury was surrounded by pain, and the pain lay waiting to spring out.

The sun bounced glaringly off the melting snow. A breeze, chill and sharp, whipped through her carelessly unbuttoned coat. In a flash of scarlet, a cardinal swooped over the ground to roost comfortably on a low branch. Shane stood absolutely still, noticing nothing. Sluggishly, her mind began to work.

It wasn't true, she told herself. Anne had made it up for some unexplainable purpose of her own. *President of Riverton?* No, he said he was a carpenter. He *was,* she thought desperately. She'd seen his work herself… He'd…he'd worked for her. Taken the job she had offered. Why would he—how could he—if he was everything Anne had said? *His first wife.*

Shane felt the first stab of pain. No, it couldn't be, he would have told her. Vance loved her. He wouldn't lie or pretend. He wouldn't make a fool of her by letting her think he was out of work when he was the head of one of the biggest construction firms in the country. He wouldn't have said he loved her without telling her who he really was. *His first wife.* Shane heard a soft, despairing moan without realizing it was hers.

When she saw him coming down the path, she stared blankly. As she watched him, her whirling thoughts came to a sudden halt. She knew then she'd been a fool.

Spotting her, Vance smiled in greeting and increased his pace. He was still several yards away when he recognized the expression on her face. It was the same stricken look he'd seen in the moonlight only a few nights before.

"Shane?" He came to her quickly, reaching for her. Shane stepped back.

"Liar," she said in a broken whisper. "All lies." Her eyes both accused and pleaded. "Everything you said."

"Shane—"

"No, don't!" The panic in her voice was enough to halt the hand he held out to her. He knew that somehow she had learned everything before he could tell her himself.

"Shane, let me explain."

"Explain?" She dragged shaking fingers through her hair. "Explain? How? How can you explain why you let me think you were something you're not? How can you explain why you didn't bother to tell me you were president of Riverton, that you—that you'd been married before? I *trusted* you," she whispered. "God, how could I have been such a fool!"

Anger he could have met and handled. Vance faced despair without any notion of how to cope with it. Impotently he thrust his hands into his pockets to keep from touching her. "I would have told you, Shane. I intended—"

"Would have?" She gave a quick, shaky laugh. "When? After you'd gotten bored with the joke?"

"There was never any joke," he said furiously, then clamped down on his panic. "I wanted to tell you, but every time—"

"No joke?" Her eyes glittered now with the beginnings of anger, the beginnings of tears. "You let me give you a job. You let me pay you six dollars an hour, and you don't think that's funny?"

"I didn't want your money, Shane. I tried to tell you. You wouldn't listen." Frustrated, he turned away until he had himself under control. "I banked the checks in an account under your name."

"How dare you!" Wild with pain, she shouted at him, blind and deaf to everything but the sense of betrayal. "How dare you play games with me! *I believed you.* I believed everything. I thought—I thought I was helping you, and all the time you were laughing at me."

"Damn it, Shane, I never laughed at you." Pushed beyond endurance, he grabbed her shoulders. "You know I never laughed at you."

"I wonder how you managed not to laugh in my face. God, you're clever, Vance." She choked on a sob, then swallowed it.

"Shane, if you'd try to understand why I came, why I didn't want to be connected with the company for a little while…" None of the words he needed would come to him. "It had nothing to do with you," he told her fiercely. "I didn't expect to get involved."

"Did it keep you from being bored?" she demanded, struggling against his hold. "Amusing yourself with a stupid little country girl who was so gullible she'd believe anything you said? You could play the poor working man and be entertained."

"It was never like that." Enraged by the words, he shook her. "You don't really believe that."

The tears gushed out passionately, strangling her voice. "And I was so willing to fall into bed with you. You knew it!" She sobbed, pushing desperately at him. "Right from the first I had no secrets from you."

"I had them," he admitted in a tight voice. "I had reasons for them."

"You knew how much I loved you, how much I wanted you. You *used* me!" On a moan, she covered her face with her hands. "Oh God, I left myself wide open."

She wept with the same honest abandon he'd seen when she laughed. Unable to do otherwise, he crushed her against him. He thought if he could only calm her down, he could make her understand. "Shane, please, you have to listen to me."

"No, no, I don't." She pulled in breath after jerky breath as she struggled for release. "I'll never forgive you. I'll never believe anything you say again. Damn you, let me go."

"Not until you stop this and hear what I have to say."

"No! I won't listen to any more lies. I won't let you make a fool of me again. All this time, all this time when I was giving you everything, you were lying and laughing at me. I was just something to keep the nights from being dull while you were on vacation."

He jerked her back, his face rigid with fury. "Damn it, Shane, you know better than that."

Her struggles ceased abruptly. As he watched, the tears seemed to turn to ice. Without expression, she stared up at him. Nothing she had said so far had struck him to the core like that one cool look.

"I don't know you," she said quietly.

"Shane—"

"Take your hands off me." The command was devoid of passion. Vance felt his stiff fingers loosen. Freed, Shane stepped back until they were no longer touching. "I want you to go away and leave me alone. Stay away from me," she added flatly, still looking directly into his eyes. "I don't want to see you again."

Turning, she walked up the steps and to the door. After its final click came absolute silence.

Far beneath the window, the streets were packed with traffic. The steady fall of snow increased the confusion. Beneath the overhang of the department store across the street, a red-cheeked Santa rang his bell, ho-hoing when someone dropped a coin into his bucket. The scene below was played in pantomime. The thick glass of the window and well-constructed walls allowed no street sounds to intrude. Vance kept his back to his plush, spacious office and continued to watch.

He'd made his obligatory appearance at the company Christmas party. It was still going on, with enthusiasm, in a large conference room on the third floor. When it broke up, everyone would go home to spend Christmas Eve with their families or friends. He'd refused more than a dozen invitations for the evening since his return to Washington. It was one thing to do his duty as the head of the company, and another to put himself through hours of small talk and celebrating. *She wouldn't be there,* he thought, staring down at the snowy sidewalk.

Two weeks. In two weeks, Vance had managed to straighten out a few annoying contractual tangles, plot out a bid for a new wing to a hospital in Virginia and head a heated board meeting. He'd dealt with paperwork, and some minor corporate intrigue he might have found amusing if he'd been sleeping properly. But he wasn't sleeping properly any more than he was forgetting. Work wasn't an elixir this time. As she had from the very first moment, Shane haunted him.

Turning from the window, Vance took his place behind the massive oak desk. It was clear of papers. In a fury of frustrated energy, he'd taken care of every letter, memo and contract, putting his secretary and assistants through an orgy of work over the last two weeks. Now, he had nothing but an empty desk and a clear calendar. He considered the possibility of flying to Des Moines to supervise the progress of a condominium development. That would throw the Iowa branch into a panic, he thought with a quick laugh. Hardly fair to upset their applecart because he was restless. He brooded at the far wall, wondering what Shane was doing.

He hadn't left in anger. It would have been easier for Vance if that had been the case. He had left because Shane had wanted it. He didn't blame her, and that too made it impossibly frustrating. Why should she listen to him, or understand? There had been enough truth in what she had flung at him to make the rest difficult to overturn. He had lied, or at the very least, he hadn't been honest. To Shane, one was the same as the other.

He'd hurt her. He had put that look of helpless despair on her face. That was unforgivable. Vance pushed away from the desk to pace over the thick stone-colored carpet. But damn it, if she'd just listened to him! If she'd only given him a moment. Going to the window again, he scowled out. Laughed at her? Made fun of her? No, he thought with the first true fury he'd felt in two weeks. No, by God, he'd be damned if he'd stand quietly aside while she turned the most important thing in his life into a joke.

She'd had her say, Vance told himself as he headed for the door. Now he was going to have his.

"Shane, don't be stubborn." Donna followed her through the doorway from the museum into the shop.

"I'm not being stubborn, Donna, I really have a lot to do." To prove her point, Shane leafed through a catalog to price and date her latest stock. "With the Christmas rush, I've really fallen behind on the paperwork. I've got invoices to file, and if I don't get the books caught up before the quarter, I'm going to be in a jam."

"Baloney," Donna said precisely, flipping the catalog closed.

"Donna, please."

"No, I don't please." She stuck her hands on her hips. "And it's two against one," she added, indicating Pat with a jerk of her head. "We're not having you spend Christmas Eve alone in this house, and that's all there is to it."

"Come on, Shane." Pat joined ranks with her sister-in-law. "You should see Donna and Dave chase after Benji when he heads for the tree. And as Donna's putting on a little weight," she added, grinning at the expectant mother, "she isn't as fast as she used to be."

Shane laughed, but shook her head. "I promise I'll come by tomorrow. I've got a very noisy present for Benji. You'll probably never speak to me again."

"Shane." Firmly, Donna took her by the shoulders. "Pat's told me how you've been moping around. And," she continued, ignoring the annoyed glance Shane shot over her shoulder at the informant, "anyone can take one look at you and see you're worn-out and miserable."

"I'm not worn-out," Shane corrected.

"Just miserable?"

"I didn't say—"

Donna gave her a quick affectionate shake. "Look, I don't know what happened between you and Vance—"

"Donna…"

"And I'm not asking," she added. "But you can't expect me to stand by while my best friend is unhappy. How much fun can I have, thinking about you here all alone?"

"Donna." Shane gave her a fierce hug then drew away. "I appreciate it, really I do, but I'm lousy company now."

"I know," Donna agreed mercilessly.

That made Shane laugh and hug her again. "Please, take Pat and go back to your family."

"So speaks the martyr."

"I'm not—" Shane began furiously, then broke off, seeing the gleam in Donna's eyes. "That won't work," she told her. "If you think you can make me mad so I'll come just to prove you wrong—"

"All right." Donna settled herself in a rocker. "Then I'll just sit here. Of course, poor Dave will spend Christmas Eve without me, and my little boy won't understand where his mother could be, but…" She sighed and folded her hands.

"Oh, Donna, really." Shane dragged her hand through her hair, caught between laughter and tears. "Talk about martyrs."

"I'm not complaining for myself," she said in a long-suffering tone. "Pat, run along and tell Dave I won't be home. Dry little Benji's tears for me."

Pat gave a snort of laughter, but Shane rolled her eyes. "I'll be sick in a minute," she promised. "Donna, go home!" she insisted. "I'm closing the shop."

"Good, go get your coat. I'll drive."

"Donna, I'm not…" She trailed off as the shop door opened. Seeing her friend pale, Donna turned her head to watch Vance walk in.

"Well, we have to run," she stated, springing quickly to her feet. "Come on, Pat, Dave's probably at his wit's end keeping Benji from pulling over the tree. Merry Christmas, Shane." She gave Shane a quick kiss before grabbing her coat.

"Donna, wait…"

"No, we just can't stay," she claimed, making the reversal without blinking an eye. "I've got a million things to do. Hi, Vance, nice to see you. Let's go, Pat." They were out the door before Shane could fit in another word.

Vance lifted a brow at the hasty exit but made no comment. Instead, he studied Shane as the silence grew long and thick. The anger that had driven him there melted. "Shane," he murmured.

"I—I'm closing."

"Fine." Vance turned and flicked the lock on the door. "Then we won't be disturbed."

"I'm busy, Vance. I have…" She searched desperately for something important. "Things to do," she finished lamely. When he neither spoke nor moved, she sent him a look of entreaty. "Please go away."

Vance shook his head. "I tried that, Shane. I can't." He slipped off his coat and dropped it on the chair Donna had vacated. Shane stared at him, thrown off-balance by his appearance in a trimly tailored suit and silk tie. It brought it home to her again that she didn't know him. And, God help her, she loved him anyway. Turning, she began to fiddle with an arrangement of cut glass.

"I'm sorry, Vance, but I have a few things to finish up here before I leave. I'm supposed to go to Donna's tonight."

"She didn't seem to expect you," he commented as he walked to her. Gently, he laid his hands on her shoulders. "Shane—"

She stiffened immediately. "Don't!"

Very slowly, he took his hands from her, then dropped them to his sides. "All right, damn it, I won't touch you." The words came out savagely as he whirled away.

"Vance, I told you I'm busy."

"You said that you loved me."

Shane spun around, white with anger. "How can you throw that in my face?"

"Was it a lie?" he demanded.

She opened her mouth, but closed it again before any impetuous words could be spoken. Lifting her chin, she looked at him steadily. "I loved the man you pretended to be."

He winced, but he didn't back away. "Direct hit, Shane," he said quietly. "You surprise me."

"Why, because I'm not as stupid as you thought I was?"

Anger flashed into his eyes, then dulled. "Don't."

Shaken by the pain in the single word, she turned away. "I'm sorry, Vance. I don't want to say spiteful things. It would be better for both of us if you just went away."

"The hell it would, if you've been half as miserable as I've been. Have you been able to sleep, Shane? I haven't."

"Please," she whispered.

He took a deep breath as his hands clenched into fists.

He'd come prepared to fight with her, to bully her, to plead with her. Now, it seemed he could do nothing but try to fumble through an explanation. "All right, I'll go, but only if you listen to me first."

"Vance," she said wearily, "what difference will it make?"

The finality of her tone had fear twisting in his stomach. With a strong effort, he kept his voice calm. "If that's true, it won't hurt you to listen."

"All right." Shane turned back to face him. "All right, I'll listen."

He was quiet for a moment, then began to pace as though whatever ran through him wouldn't allow him to keep still. "I came here because I had to get away, maybe even hide. I'm not sure anymore. I was still very young when I took over the company. It wasn't what I wanted." He stopped for a moment to send her a direct look. "I'm a carpenter, Shane, that was the truth. I'm president of Riverton because I have to be. *Why* doesn't really matter at this point, but a title, a position, doesn't change who I am." When she said nothing, he began to pace again.

"I was married to a woman you'd recognize very quickly. She was beautiful, charming and pure plastic. She was totally self-consumed, emotionless, even vicious." Shane's brows drew together as she thought of Anne. "Unfortunately, I didn't recognize the last of those qualities until it was too late." He stopped because the next words were difficult. "I married the woman she pretended to be." Because his back was to her, Vance didn't see the sudden change in Shane's expression. Pain rushed into her eyes, but it wasn't for herself. It was all for him.

"For all intents and purposes, the marriage was over

very soon after it had begun. I couldn't make a legal break at first because too many things were involved. So, we lived together in mutual distaste for several years. I involved myself in the company to the point of obsession, while she began to take lovers. I wanted her out of my life more than I wanted anything. Then, when she was dead, I had to live with the knowledge that I'd wished her dead countless times."

"Oh, Vance," Shane murmured.

"That was over two years ago," he continued. "I buried myself in work…and bitterness. I'd come to a point where I didn't even recognize myself anymore. That's why I bought the house and took a leave of absence. I needed to separate myself from what I'd become, try to find out if that was all there was to me." He dragged an agitated hand through his hair. "I brought the bitterness with me, so that when you popped up and started haunting my mind, I wanted nothing more than to be rid of you. I looked…I searched," he corrected, turning to her again, "for flaws in you. I was afraid to believe you could really be so…generous. The truth was, I didn't want you to be because I'd never be able to resist the woman you are." His eyes were suddenly very dark, and very direct on hers. "I didn't want you, Shane, and I wanted you so badly I ached. I loved you, I think, from the very first minute."

On a long breath, he moved away again to stare at the flickering lights of the tree. "I could have told you—should have—but at first I had a need for you to love me without knowing. Unforgivably selfish."

She remembered the secrets she had seen in his eyes. Remembered too, telling herself they were his until he shared them with her. Still, she felt the hurt of not being trusted. "Did you really think any of it would have mattered to me?"

Vance shook his head. "No."

"Then why did you hide it all from me?" Confused, she lifted her hands palms up.

"I never intended to. Circumstances—" He broke off, no longer sure he could make her understand. "The first night we were together, I was going to tell you, but I didn't want any past that night. I told myself it wasn't too much to ask, and that I'd explain things to you the next day. God, Shane, I swear to you I would have." He took a step toward her, then stopped himself. "You were so lost, so vulnerable after Anne had left, I couldn't. How could I have dumped all this on you when you already had that to deal with?"

She remained silent, but he knew she listened very carefully. He didn't know she was remembering very clearly the things he had said to her their first night together, the tension in him, the hints of things yet to be told. And she remembered too his compassion the next evening.

"You needed my support that night, not my problems," Vance went on. "From the very first, you gave everything to me. You brought me back, Shane, and I knew that I took much more than I gave. Until that night, you'd never asked me for anything."

She gave him a puzzled look. "I never gave you anything."

"Nothing?" he countered with a baffled shake of his head. "Trust, understanding. You made me laugh at myself again. Maybe you don't see just how important that is because you've never lost it. If I could give you nothing else, I thought that for a few days I could give you some peace of mind. I tried to tell you again when we argued about that damned dining-room set." Pausing, he sent her a narrowed look. "I bought it anyway."

"You—"

"There's not a thing you can do about it," he stated, cutting off her astonished exclamation. "It's done."

She met the angry challenge in his eyes. "I see."

"Do you?" He let out a quick, rough laugh. "Do you really? The only thing you see when you lift your chin up like that is your own pride." He watched her mouth open, then close again. "It's just as well," he murmured. "It would be difficult if you were perfect." He moved to her then but was careful not to touch her. "I never set out to deceive you, but I deceived you nonetheless. And now I have to ask you to forgive me, even if you can't accept who and what I am."

Shane lowered her eyes to her hands a moment. "It's not accepting so much as understanding," she said quietly. "I don't know anything about the president of Riverton. I knew the man who bought the old Farley place, you see." She lifted her eyes again. "He was rude, and nasty, with a streak of kindness he did his best to overcome. I loved him."

"God knows why," Vance replied, thinking over her description. "If that's who you want, I can promise I'm still rude and nasty."

With a small laugh, she turned away. "Vance, it's all hit me, you see. Maybe if I had time to get used to it, to think it through…I don't know. When I thought you were just…" She made an uncharacteristically helpless gesture with her hands. "It all seemed so easy."

"Did you only love me because you thought I was out of work?"

"No!" Frustrated, she tried to explain herself. "I haven't

changed though," she added thoughtfully. "I'm still exactly what I seem. What would the president of Riverton do with me? I can't even drink martinis."

"Don't be absurd."

"It's not absurd," she corrected. "Be honest. I don't fit in. I'd never be elegant if I had years to practice."

"What the hell's wrong with you?" Suddenly angry, he spun her around. "*Elegant!* In the name of God, Shane, what kind of nonsense is that? I had my share of elegance the way you mean. I'll be damned if you're going to put me off because you've got some twisted view of the life I lead. If you can't accept it, fine. I'll resign."

"W-what?"

"I said I'll resign."

She studied him with wide, astonished eyes. "You mean it," she said wonderingly. "You really do."

He gave her an impatient shake. "Yes, I mean it. Can you really believe the company means more to me than you do? God, you're an idiot!" Furious, he gave her an unlover-like shove and strode away. "You don't yell at me for anything I've done. You don't demand to hear all the filthy details of my first marriage. You don't make me crawl as I was damn well ready to do. You start spouting nonsense about martinis and elegance." After swearing rudely, he stared out the window.

Shane swallowed a sudden urge to laugh. "Vance, I—"

"Shut up," he ordered. "You drive me crazy." With a quick jerk, he pulled his coat from the chair. Shane opened her mouth, afraid he was about to storm out, but he only pulled an envelope out of the pocket before he flung the coat down again. "Here." He stuck it out to her.

"Vance," she tried again, but he took her hand and slapped the envelope into her palm.

"Open it."

Deciding a temporary retreat was advisable, Shane obeyed. She stared in silent astonishment at two round-trip tickets to Fiji.

"Someone told me it was a good place for a honeymoon," Vance stated with a bit more control. "I thought she might still think so."

Shane looked up at him with her heart in her eyes. Vance needed nothing more to pull her into his arms, crushing the envelope and its contents between them as he found her mouth.

Shane's answer was wild and unrestricted. She clung to him even as she demanded, yielded even as she aroused. She couldn't get enough of him, so that the desperate kisses incited only more urgent needs. "Oh, I've missed you," she murmured. "Make love to me, Vance. Come upstairs and make love to me."

He buried his face against her neck. "Uh-uh. You haven't said you're taking me to Fiji yet." But his hands were already searching under her sweater. As his fingers skimmed over her warm, soft skin, he groaned, pulling her to the floor.

"Oh, Vance, your suit!" Laughing breathlessly, Shane struggled against him. "Wait until we go upstairs."

"Shut up," he suggested, then assured himself of her obedience by crushing his mouth on hers. It only took a moment to realize her trembling came from laughter, not from passion. Lifting his head, Vance studied her amused eyes. "Damn you, Shane," he said in exasperation. "I'm trying to make love to you."

"Well, then at least take off that tie," she suggested, then buried her face against his shoulder and laughed helplessly. "I'm sorry, Vance, but it just seems so funny. I mean, there you are asking if I'll take you to Fiji before I've even gotten around to asking you to marry me, and—"

"*You* asking *me?*" he demanded, eyeing her closely.

"Yes," she continued blithely. "I've been meaning to, though I thought I'd have to overcome some silly ego thing. You know, I thought you were out of work."

"Ego thing," he repeated.

"Yes, and of course, now that I know you're such an important person… Oh, this tie is *silk!*" she exclaimed after she had begun to struggle with the knot.

"Yes." He allowed her to finger it curiously. "And now that you know I'm such an important person?" he prompted.

"I'd better snap you up quick."

"Snap me up?" He bit her ear painfully.

Shane only giggled and linked her arms around his neck. "And even if I refuse to drink martinis or be elegant, I'll make an extremely good wife for a…" She paused a moment, lifting a brow. "What are you?"

"Insane."

"A corporate president," Shane decided with a nod. "No, I don't suppose you could do any better. You're making a pretty good deal now that I think about it." She gave him a noisy kiss. "When do we leave for Fiji?"

"Day after tomorrow," he informed her before he rose and dumped her over his shoulder.

"Vance, what are you doing?"

"I'm taking you upstairs to make love with you."

"Vance," she began with a half laugh. "I told you before

I won't be carted around this way. This is no way for the fiancée of the president of Riverton to be treated."

"You haven't seen anything yet," he promised her.

Exasperated, Shane gave him a hearty thump on the back. "Vance, I mean it, put me down!"

"Am I fired?"

He heard the telltale choke of laughter. "Yes!"

"Good." He tucked his arm firmly around her knees and carried her up the stairs.

* * * * *

BLITHE IMAGES

To Ron's Patience…

Chapter 1

The girl twisted and turned under the lights, her shining black hair swirling around her as various expressions flitted across her striking face.

"That's it, Hillary, a little pout now. We're selling the lips here." Larry Newman followed her movements, the shutter of his camera clicking rapidly. "Fantastic," he exclaimed as he straightened from his crouched position. "That's enough for today."

Hillary Baxter stretched her arms to the ceiling and relaxed. "Good, I'm beat. It's home and a hot tub for me."

"Just think of the millions of dollars in lipstick your face is going to sell, sweetheart." Switching off lights, Larry's attention was already wavering.

"Mind-boggling."

"Mmm, so it is," he returned absently. "We've got that

shampoo thing tomorrow, so make sure your hair is in its usual gorgeous state. I almost forgot." He turned and faced her directly. "I have a business appointment in the morning. I'll get someone to stand in for me."

Hillary smiled with fond indulgence. She had been modeling for three years now, and Larry was her favorite photographer. They worked well together, and as a photographer he was exceptional, having a superior eye for angles and detail, for capturing the right mood. He was hopelessly disorganized, however, and pathetically absentminded about anything other than his precious equipment.

"What appointment?" Hillary inquired with serene patience, knowing well how easily Larry confused such mundane matters as times and places when they did not directly concern his camera.

"Oh, that's right, I didn't tell you, did I?" Shaking her head, Hillary waited for him to continue. "I've got to see Bret Bardoff at ten o'clock."

"*The* Bret Bardoff?" Hillary demanded, more than a little astonished. "I didn't know the owner of *Mode* magazine made appointments with mere mortals—only royalty and goddesses."

"Well, this peasant's been granted an audience," Larry returned dryly. "As a matter of fact, Mr. Bardoff's secretary contacted me and set the whole thing up. She said he wanted to discuss plans for a layout or something."

"Good luck. From what I hear of Bret Bardoff, he's a man to be reckoned with—tough as nails and used to getting his own way."

"He wouldn't be where he is today if he were a pushover," Larry defended the absent Mr. Bardoff with a shrug. "His father may have made a fortune by starting *Mode,* but Bret Bardoff made his own twice over by expanding and developing other magazines. A very successful businessman, and a good photographer—one that's not afraid to get his hands dirty."

"You'd love anyone who could tell a Nikon from a Brownie," Hillary accused with a grin, and pulled at a lock of Larry's disordered hair. "But his type doesn't appeal to me." A delicate and counterfeit shudder moved her shoulders. "I'm sure he'd scare me to death."

"Nothing scares you, Hil," Larry said fondly as he watched the tall, willowy woman gather her things and move for the door. "I'll have someone here to take the shots at nine-thirty tomorrow."

Outside, Hillary hailed a cab. She had become quite adept at this after three years in New York. And she had nearly ceased to ponder about Hillary Baxter of a small Kansas farm being at home in the thriving metropolis of New York City.

She had been twenty-one when she had made the break and come to New York to pursue a modeling career. The transition from small-town farm girl to big-city model had been difficult and often frightening, but Hillary had refused to be daunted by the fast-moving, overwhelming city and resolutely made the rounds with her portfolio.

Jobs had been few and far between during the first year, but she had hung on, refusing to surrender and escape to the familiar surroundings of home. Slowly, she had constructed a reputation for portraying the right image for the right product, and she had become more and more in demand. When she had begun to work with Larry, everything had fallen into place, and her face was now splashed throughout magazines and, as often as not, on the cover. Her life was proceeding according to plan, and the fact that she now commanded a top model's salary had enabled her to move from the third-floor walk-up in which she had started her New York life to a comfortable high-rise near Central Park.

Modeling was not a passion with Hillary, but a job. She had not come to New York with starry-eyed dreams of fame and glamour, but with a resolution to succeed, to stand on her own. The choice of career had seemed inevitable, since she possessed a natural grace and poise and striking good looks. Her coal black hair and high cheekbones lent her a rather exotic fragility, and large, heavily fringed eyes in deep midnight blue contrasted appealingly with her golden complexion. Her mouth was full and shapely, and smiled beautifully at the slightest provocation. Along with her stunning looks, the fact that she was inherently photogenic added to her current success in her field. The uncanny ability to convey an array of images for the camera came naturally, with little conscious effort on her part. After being told the type of woman she was to portray, Hillary became just that— sophisticated, practical, sensuous—whatever was required.

Letting herself into her apartment, Hillary kicked off her shoes and sank her feet into soft ivory carpet. There was no date to prepare for that evening, and she was looking forward to a light supper and a few quiet hours at home.

Thirty minutes later, wrapped in a warm, flowing azure robe, she stood in the kitchen of her apartment preparing a model's feast of soup and unsalted crackers. A ring of the doorbell interrupted her far-from-gourmet activities.

"Lisa, hi." She greeted her neighbor from across the hall with an automatic smile. "Want some dinner?"

Lisa MacDonald wrinkled her nose in disdain. "I'd rather put up with a few extra pounds than starve myself like you."

"If I indulge myself too often," Hillary stated, patting a flat stomach, "I'd be after you to find me a job in that law firm you work for. By the way, how's the rising young attorney?"

"Mark still doesn't know I'm alive," Lisa complained as she flopped onto the couch. "I'm getting desperate, Hillary. I may lose my head and mug him in the parking lot."

"Tacky, too tacky," Hillary said, giving the matter deep consideration. "Why not attempt something less dramatic, like tripping him when he walks past your desk?"

"That could be next."

With a grin, Hillary sat and lifted bare feet to the surface of the coffee table. "Ever hear of Bret Bardoff?"

Lisa's eyes grew round. "Who hasn't? Millionaire, incredibly handsome, mysterious, brilliant businessman and still fair game." These attributes were counted off carefully on Lisa's fingers. "What about him?"

Slim shoulders moved expressively. "I'm not sure. Larry has an appointment with him in the morning."

"Face to face?"

"That's right." Amusement dawned first, then dark blue eyes regarded Lisa with curiosity. "Of course, we've both done work for his magazines before, but I can't imagine why the elusive owner of *Mode* would want to see a mere photographer, even if he is the best. In the trade, he's spoken of in reverent whispers, and if gossip columns are to be believed, he's the answer to every maiden's prayer. I wonder what he's really like." She frowned, finding herself nearly obsessed with the thought. "It's strange, I don't believe I know anyone who's had a personal dealing with him. I picture him as a giant phantom figure handing out monumental corporate decisions from *Mode*'s Mount Olympus."

"Maybe Larry will fill you in tomorrow," Lisa suggested, and Hillary shook her head, the frown becoming a grin.

"Larry won't notice anything unless Mr. Bardoff's on a roll of film."

Shortly before nine-thirty the following morning, Hillary used her spare key to enter Larry's studio. Prepared for the shampoo ad, her hair fell in soft, thick waves, shining and full. In the small cubicle in the rear she applied her makeup with an expert hand, and at nine forty-five she was impatiently switching on the lights required for indoor shots. As minutes slipped by, she began to entertain the annoying suspicion that Larry had neglected to arrange for a substitute. It was nearly ten when the door to the studio opened, and Hillary immediately pounced on the man who entered.

"It's about time," she began, tempering irritation with a small smile. "You're late."

"Am I?" he countered, meeting her annoyed expression with raised brows.

Pausing a moment, she realized how incredibly handsome the man facing her was. His hair, the color of corn silk, was full and grew just over the collar of his casual polo-necked gray sweater, a gray that exactly matched large, direct eyes. His mouth was quirked in a half smile, and there was something vaguely familiar about his deeply tanned face.

"I haven't worked with you before, have I?" Hillary

asked, forced to look up to meet his eyes since he was an inch or more over six feet.

"Why do you ask?" His evasion was smooth, and she felt suddenly uncomfortable under his unblinking gray glance.

"No reason," she murmured, turning away, feeling compelled to adjust the cuff of her sleeve. "Well, let's get to it. Where's your camera?" Belatedly, she observed he carried no equipment. "Are you using Larry's?"

"I suppose I am." He continued to stand staring down at her, making no move to proceed with the task at hand, his nonchalance becoming thoroughly irritating.

"Well, come on then, let's not be all day. I've been ready for half an hour."

"Sorry." He smiled, and she was struck with the change it brought to his already compelling face. It was a carelessly slow smile, full of charm, and the thought passed through her mind that he could use it as a deadly weapon. Pivoting away from him, she struggled to ignore its power. She had a job to do. "What are the pictures for?" he asked her as he examined Larry's cameras.

"Oh, Lord, didn't he tell you?" Turning back to him, she shook her head and smiled fully for the first time. "Larry's a tremendous photographer, but he is the most exasperatingly absentminded man. I don't know how he remembers to get up in the morning." She tugged a lock of raven hair before giving her head a dramatic toss. "Clean, shiny, sexy hair," she explained in the tone of a commercial. "Shampoo's what we're selling today."

"Okay," he returned simply, and began setting equipment to rights in a thoroughly professional manner that did much to put Hillary's mind at ease. *At least he knows his* job, she assured herself, for his attitude had made her vaguely uneasy. "Where is Larry, by the way?" The question startled Hillary out of her silent thoughts.

"Didn't he tell you anything? That's just like him." Standing under the lights, she began turning, shaking her head, creating a rich black cloud as he clicked the camera, crouching and moving around her to catch different angles. "He had an appointment with Bret Bardoff," she continued, tossing her hair and smiling. "Lord help him if he forgot that. He'll be eaten alive."

"Does Bret Bardoff consume photographers as a habit?" the voice behind the camera questioned with dry amusement.

"Wouldn't be surprised." Hillary lifted her hair above her head, pausing for a moment before she allowed it to fall back to her shoulders like a rich cloak. "I would think a ruthless businessman like Mr. Bardoff would have little patience with an absentminded photographer or any other imperfection."

"You know him?"

"Lord, no." She laughed with unrestrained pleasure. "And I'm not likely to, far above my station. Have you met him?"

"Not precisely."

"Ah, but we all work for him at one time or another, don't we? I wonder how many times my face has been in one of his magazines. Scillions," she calculated, receiving a raised-brow look from behind the camera. "Scillions," she repeated with a nod. "And I've never met the emperor."

"Emperor?"

"How else does one describe such a lofty individual?" Hillary demanded with a gesture of her hands. "From what I've heard, he runs his mags like an empire."

"You sound as though you disapprove."

"No," Hillary disagreed with a smile and a shrug. "Emperors just make me nervous. I'm plain peasant stock myself."

"Your image seems hardly plain or peasant," he remarked, and this time it was her brow that lifted. "That should sell gallons of shampoo." Lowering his camera, he met her eyes directly. "I think we've got it, Hillary."

She relaxed, pushed back her hair, and regarded him curiously. "You know me? I'm sorry, I can't quite seem to place you. Have we worked together before?"

"Hillary Baxter's face is everywhere. It's my business to recognize beautiful faces." He spoke with careless simplicity, gray eyes smoky with amusement.

"Well, it appears you have the advantage, Mr.—?"

"Bardoff, Bret Bardoff," he answered, and the camera clicked to capture the astonished expression on her face. "You can close your mouth now, Hillary. I think we've got enough." His smile widened as she obeyed without thinking. "Cat got your tongue?" he mocked, pleasure at her embarrassment obvious.

She recognized him now, from pictures she had seen of him in newspapers and his own magazines, and she was busily engaged in cursing herself for the stupidity she had just displayed. Anger with herself spread to encompass the man in front of her, and she located her voice.

"You let me babble on like that," she sputtered, eyes and cheeks bright with color. "You stood there taking pictures you had no business taking and just let me carry on like an idiot."

"I was merely following orders." His grave tone and sober expression added to her mounting embarrassment and fury.

"Well, you had no right following them. You should have

told me who you were." Her voice quavered with indignation, but he merely moved his shoulders and smiled again.

"You never asked."

Before she could retort, the door of the studio opened
and Larry entered, looking harassed and confused. "Mr.
Bardoff," he began, advancing on the pair standing under
the lights. "I'm sorry. I thought I was to meet you at your
office." Larry ran a hand through his hair in agitation.
"When I got there, I was told you were coming here. I don't
know how I got it so confused. Sorry you had to wait."

"Don't worry about it," Bret assured him with an easy
smile, "The last hour's been highly entertaining."

"Hillary." Her existence suddenly seeped into Larry's
consciousness. "Good Lord, I knew I forgot something.
We'll have to get those pictures later."

"No need." Bret handed Larry the camera. "Hillary and
I have seen to them."

"You took the shots?" Larry looked at Bret and the
camera in turn.

"Hillary saw no reason to waste time." He smiled and
added, "I'm sure you'll find the pictures suitable."

"No question of that, Mr. Bardoff." His voice was tinged
with reverence. "I know what you can do with a camera."

Hillary had an overwhelming desire for the floor to
open up and swallow her. She had to get out of there
quickly. Never before in her life had she felt such a fool.
Of course, she reasoned silently, it was his fault. The nerve
of the man, letting her believe he was a photographer! She
recalled the fashion in which she had ordered him to begin,
and the things she had said. She closed her eyes with an
inward moan. All she wanted to do now was disappear, and

with luck she would never have to come face to face with Bret Bardoff again.

She began gathering her things quickly. "I'll leave you to get on with your business. I have another session across town." Slinging her purse over her shoulder, she took a deep breath. "Bye, Larry. Nice to have met you, Mr. Bardoff." She attempted to brush by them, but Bret put out his hand and captured hers, preventing her exit.

"Goodbye, Hillary." She forced her eyes to meet his, feeling a sudden drain of power by the contact of her hand in his. "It's been a most interesting morning. We'll have to do it again soon."

When hell freezes over, her eyes told him silently, and muttering something incoherent, she dashed for the door, the sound of his laughter echoing in her ears.

Dressing for a date that evening, Hillary endeavored, without success, to block the events of the morning from her mind. She was confident that her path would never cross Bret Bardoff's again. After all, she comforted herself, it had only been through a stupid accident that they had met in the first place. Hillary prayed that the adage about lightning never striking twice would hold true. She had indeed been hit by a lightning bolt when he had casually disclosed his name to her, and her cheeks burned again, matching the color of her soft jersey dress as her careless words played back in her mind.

The ringing of the phone interrupted her reflections, and she answered, finding Larry on the other end. "Hillary, boy, I'm glad I caught you at home." His excitement was tangible over the wire, and she answered him quickly.

"You just did catch me. I'm practically out the door. What's up?"

"I can't go into details now. Bret's going to do that in the morning."

She noted the fact that *Mr. Bardoff* had been discarded since that morning and spoke wearily. "Larry, what are you talking about?"

"Bret will explain everything in the morning. You have an appointment at nine o'clock."

"What?" Her voice rose and she found it imperative to swallow twice. "Larry, what are you talking about?"

"It's a tremendous opportunity for both of us, Hil. Bret will tell you tomorrow. You know where his office is." This was a statement rather than a question, since everyone in the business knew *Mode*'s headquarters.

"I don't want to see him," Hillary argued, feeling a surge of panic at the thought of those steel gray eyes. "I don't know what he told you about this morning, but I made a total fool of myself. I thought he was a photographer. Really," she continued, with fresh annoyance, "you're partially to blame, if—"

"Don't worry about all that now," Larry interrupted confidently. "It doesn't matter. Just be there at nine tomorrow. See you later."

"But, Larry." She stopped, there was no purpose in arguing with a dead phone. Larry had hung up.

This was too much, she thought in despair, and sat down heavily on the bed. How could Larry expect her to go through with this? How could she possibly face that man after the things she had said? Humiliation, she decided, was simply something for which she was not suited. Rising from the bed, she squared her shoulders. Bret Bardoff probably wanted another opportunity to laugh at her for her stupidity. Well, he wasn't going to get the best of Hillary Baxter, she told herself with firm pride. She'd face him without cringing. This peasant would stand up to the emperor and show him what she was made of!

Hillary dressed for her appointment the next morning with studious care. The white, light wool cowl-necked dress was beautiful in its simplicity, relying on the form it covered to make it eye-catching. She arranged her hair in a loose bun on top of her head in order to add a businesslike air to her appearance. Bret Bardoff would not find her stammering and blushing this morning, she determined, but cool and confident. Slipping on soft leather shoes, she was satisfied with the total effect, the heels adding to her height. She would not be forced to look up quite so high in order to meet those gray eyes, and she would meet them straight on.

Confidence remained with her through the taxi ride and all the way to the top of the building where Bret Bardoff had his offices. Glancing at her watch on the elevator, she was pleased to see she was punctual. An attractive brunette was seated at an enormous reception desk, and Hillary stated her name and business. After a brief conversation on a phone that held a prominent position on the large desk, the woman ushered Hillary down a long corridor and through a heavy oak door.

She entered a large, well-decorated room where she was greeted by yet another attractive woman, who introduced herself as June Miles, Mr. Bardoff's secretary. "Please go right in, Miss Baxter. Mr. Bardoff is expecting you," she informed Hillary with a smile.

Walking to a set of double doors, Hillary's eyes barely had time to take in the room with its rather fabulous decor before her gaze was arrested by the man seated at a huge oak desk, a panoramic view of the city at his back.

"Good morning, Hillary." He rose and approached her. "Are you going to come in or stand there all day with your back to the door?"

Hillary's spine straightened and she answered coolly. "Good morning, Mr. Bardoff, it's nice to see you again."

"Don't be a hypocrite," he stated mildly as he led her to a seat near the desk. "You'd be a great deal happier if you never laid eyes on me again." Hillary could find no comment to this all-too-true observation, and contented herself with smiling vaguely into space.

"However," he continued, as if she had agreed with him in words, "it suits my purposes to have you here today in spite of your reluctance."

"And what are your purposes, Mr. Bardoff?" she demanded, her annoyance with his arrogance sharpening her tone.

He leaned back in his chair and allowed his cool gray eyes to travel deliberately over Hillary from head to toe. The survey was slow and obviously intended to disconcert, but she remained outwardly unruffled. Because of her profession, her face and form had been studied before. She was determined not to let this man know his stare was causing her pulses to dance a nervous rhythm.

"My purposes, Hillary—" his eyes met hers and held "—are for the moment strictly business, though that is subject to change at any time."

This remark cracked Hillary's cool veneer enough to bring a slight blush to her cheeks. She cursed the color as she struggled to keep her eyes level with his.

"Good Lord." His brows lifted with humor. "You're blushing. I didn't think women did that anymore." His grin widened as if he were enjoying the fact that more color leaped to her cheeks at his words. "You're probably the last of a dying breed."

"Could we discuss the business for which I'm here, Mr. Bardoff?" she inquired. "I'm sure you're a very busy man, and believe it or not, I'm busy myself."

"Of course," Bret agreed. He grinned reflectively. "I remember—'*Let's not waste time.*' I'm planning a layout for *Mode,* a rather special layout." He lit a cigarette and offered Hillary one, which she declined with a shake of her head. "I've had the idea milling around in my mind for some time, but I needed the right photographer and the right woman." His eyes narrowed as he peered at her speculatively, giving Hillary the sensation of being viewed under a microscope. "I've found them both now."

She squirmed under his unblinking stare. "Suppose you give me some details, Mr. Bardoff. I'm sure it's not usual procedure for you to interview models personally. This must be something special."

"Yes, I think so," he agreed suavely. "The idea is a layout—a picture story, if you like—on the Many Faces of Woman." He stood then and perched on the corner of the desk, and Hillary was affected by his sheer masculinity, the power and strength that exuded from his lean form clad in a fawn-colored business suit. "I want to portray all the facets of womanhood: career woman, mother, athlete, sophisticate, innocent, temptress, et cetera—a complete portrait of Eve, the Eternal Woman."

"Sounds fascinating," Hillary admitted, caught up in the backlash of his enthusiasm. "You think I might be suitable for some of the pictures?"

"I know you're suitable," he stated flatly, "for *all* of the pictures."

Finely etched brows raised in curiosity. "You're going to use one model for the entire layout?"

"I'm going to use *you* for the entire layout."

Struggling with annoyance and the feeling of being submerged by very deep water, Hillary spoke honestly. "I'd be an idiot not to be interested in a project like this. I don't think I'm an idiot. But why me?"

"Come now, Hillary." His voice mirrored impatience, and he bent over to capture her surprised chin in his hand. "You do own a mirror. Surely you're intelligent enough to know that you're quite beautiful and extremely photogenic."

He was speaking of her as if she were an inanimate object rather than a human being, and the fingers, strong and lean on her chin, were very distressing. Nevertheless, Hillary persisted.

"There are scores of beautiful and photogenic models in New York alone, Mr. Bardoff. You know that better than anyone. I'd like to know why you're considering me for your pet project."

"Not considering." He rose and thrust his hands in his pockets, and she observed he was becoming irritated. She found the knowledge rewarding. "There's no one else I would consider. You have a rather uncanny knack for getting to the heart of a picture and coming across with exactly the right image. I need versatility as well as beauty. I need honesty in a dozen different images."

"In your opinion, I can do that."

"You wouldn't be here if I weren't sure. I never make rash decisions."

No, Hillary mused, looking into his cool gray eyes, you calculate every minute detail. Aloud, she asked, "Larry would be the photographer?"

He nodded. "There's an affinity between the two of you that is obvious in the pictures you produce. You're both superior alone, but together you've done some rather stunning work."

His praise caused her smile to warm slightly. "Thank you."

"That wasn't a compliment, Hillary—just a fact. I've given Larry all the details. The contracts are waiting for your signature."

"Contracts?" she repeated, becoming wary.

"That's right," he returned, overlooking her hesitation. "This project is going to take some time. I've no intention of rushing through it. I want exclusive rights to that beautiful face of yours until the project's completed and on the stands."

"I see." She digested this carefully, unconsciously chewing on her bottom lip.

"You needn't react as if I've made an indecent proposal, Hillary." His voice was dry as he regarded her frowning concentration. "This is a business arrangement."

Her chin tilted in defiance. "I understand that completely, Mr. Bardoff. It's simply that I've never signed a long-term contract before."

"I have no intention of allowing you to get away. Contracts are obligatory, for you and for Larry. For the next few months I don't want you distracted by any other jobs. Financially, you'll be well compensated. If you have any complaints along those lines, we'll negotiate. However, my rights to that face of yours for the next six months are exclusive."

He lapsed into silence, watching the varied range of expressions on her face. She was working out the entire platform carefully, doing her best not to be intimidated by his overwhelming power. The project appealed to her, although the man did not. It would be fascinating work, but she found it difficult to tie herself to one establishment for any period of time. She could not help feeling that signing her name was signing away liberation. A long-term contract equaled a long-term commitment.

Finally, throwing caution to the winds, she gave Bret one of the smiles that made her face known throughout America.

"You've got yourself a face."

Chapter 2

Bret Bardoff moved quickly. Within two weeks contracts had been signed, and the shooting schedule had been set to begin on a morning in early October. The first image to be portrayed was one of youthful innocence and unspoiled simplicity.

Hillary met Larry in a small park selected by Bret. Though the morning was bright and brisk, the sun filtering warm through the trees, the park was all but deserted. She wondered a moment if the autocratic Mr. Bardoff had arranged the isolation. Blue jeans rolled to mid-calf and a long-sleeved turtleneck in scarlet were Hillary's designated costume. She had bound her shining hair in braids, tied them with red ribbons, and had kept her makeup light, relying on natural, healthy skin. She was the essence of honest, vibrant youth, dark blue eyes bright with the anticipation.

"Perfect," Larry commented as she ran across the grass to meet him. "Young and innocent. How do you manage it?"

She wrinkled her nose. "I am young and innocent, old man."

"Okay. See that?" He pointed to a swing set complete with bars and a slide. "Go play, little girl, and let this old man take some pictures."

She ran for the swing, giving herself over to the freedom of movement. Stretching out full length, she leaned her head to the ground and smiled at the brilliant sky. Climbing on the slide, she lifted her arms wide, let out a whoop of uninhibited joy, and slid down, landing on her bottom in the soft dirt. Larry clicked his camera from varying angles, allowing her to direct the mood.

"You look twelve years old." His laugh was muffled, his face still concealed behind the camera.

"I am twelve years old," Hillary proclaimed, scurrying onto the crossbars. "Betcha can't do this." She hung up by her knees on the bar, her pigtails brushing the ground.

"Amazing." The answer did not come from Larry, and she turned her head and looked directly into a pair of well-tailored gray slacks. Her eyes roamed slowly upward to the matching jacket and farther to a full, smiling mouth and mocking gray eyes. "Hello, child, does your mother know where you are?"

"What are you doing here?" Hillary demanded, feeling at a decided disadvantage in her upside-down position.

"Supervising my pet project." He continued to regard her, his grin growing wider. "How long do you intend to hang there? The blood must be rushing to your head."

Grabbing the bar with her hands, she swung her legs

over in a neat somersault and stood facing him. He patted her head, told her she was a good girl, and turned his attention to Larry.

"How'd it go? Looked to me as if you got some good shots."

The two men discussed the technicalities of the morning's shooting while Hillary sat back down on the swing, moving gently back and forth. She had met with Bret a handful of times during the past two weeks, and each time she had been unaccountably uneasy in his presence. He was a vital and disturbing individual, full of raw, masculine power, and she was not at all sure she wanted to be closely associated with him. Her life was well ordered now, running smoothly along the lines she designated, and she wanted no complications. There was something about this man, however, that spelled complications in capital letters.

"All right." Bret's voice broke into her musings. "Setup at the club at one o'clock. Everything's been arranged." Hillary rose from the swing and moved to join Larry. "No need for you to go now, little girl—you've an hour or so to spare."

"I don't want to play on the swings anymore, Daddy," she retorted, bristling at his tone. Picking up her shoulder bag, she managed to take two steps before he reached out and took command of her wrist. She rounded on him, blue eyes blazing.

"Spoiled little brat, aren't you?" he murmured in a mild tone, but his eyes narrowed and met the dark blue blaze with cold gray steel. "Perhaps I should turn you over my knee."

"That would be more difficult than you think, Mr. Bardoff," she returned with unsurpassable dignity. "I'm twenty-four, not twelve, and really quite strong."

"Are you now?" He inspected her slim form dubiously. "I suppose it's possible." He spoke soberly, but she recognized the mockery in his eyes. "Come on, I want some coffee." His hand slipped from her wrist, and his fingers interlocked with hers. She jerked away, surprised and disconcerted by the warmth. "Hillary," he began in a tone of strained patience. "I would like to buy you coffee." It was more a command than a request.

He moved across the grass with long, easy strides, dragging an unwilling Hillary after him. Larry watched their progress and automatically took their picture. They made an interesting study, he decided, the tall blond man in the expensive business suit pulling the slim, dark woman-child behind him.

As she sat across from Bret in a small coffee shop, Hillary's face was flushed with a mixture of indignation and the exertion of keeping up with the brisk pace he had set. He took in her pink cheeks and bright eyes, and his mouth lifted at one corner.

"Maybe I should buy a dish of ice cream to cool you off." The waitress appeared then, saving Hillary from formulating a retort, and Bret ordered two coffees.

"Tea," Hillary stated flatly, pleased to contradict him on some level.

"I beg your pardon?" he returned coolly.

"I'll have tea, if you don't mind. I don't drink coffee; it makes me nervous."

"One coffee and one tea," he amended before he turned

back to her. "How do you wake up in the morning without the inevitable cup of coffee?"

"Clean living." She flicked a pigtail over her shoulder and folded her hands.

"You certainly look like an ad for clean living now." Sitting back, he took out his cigarette case, offering her one and lighting one before going on. "I'm afraid you'd never pass for twenty-four in pigtails. It's not often one sees hair that true black—certainly not with eyes that color." He stared into them for a long moment. "They're fabulous, so dark at times they're nearly purple, quite dramatic, and the bone structure, it's rather elegant and exotic. Tell me," he asked suddenly, "where did you get that marvelous face of yours?"

Hillary had thought herself long immune to comments and compliments on her looks, but somehow his words nonplussed her, and she was grateful that the waitress returned with their drinks, giving her time to gather scattered wits.

"I'm told I'm a throwback to my great-grandmother." She spoke with detached interest as she sipped tea. "She was an Arapaho. It appears I resemble her quite strongly."

"I should have guessed." He nodded his head continuing his intense study. "The cheekbones, the classic bone structure. Yes, I can see your Indian heritage, but the eyes are deceiving. You didn't acquire eyes like cobalt from your great-grandmother."

"No." She struggled to meet his penetrating gaze coolly. "They belong to me."

"To you," he acknowledged with a nod, "and for the next six months to me. I believe I'll enjoy the joint ownership." The focus of his study shifted to the mouth that moved in a frown at his words. "Where are you from, Hillary Baxter? You're no native."

"That obvious? I thought I had acquired a marvelous New York varnish." She gave a wry shrug, grateful that the intensity of his examination appeared to be over. "Kansas—a farm some miles north of Abilene."

He inclined his head, and his brows lifted as he raised his cup. "You appear to have made the transition from wheat to concrete very smoothly. No battle scars?"

"A few, but they're healed over." She added quickly, "I hardly have to point out New York's advantages to you, especially in the area of my career."

His agreement was a slow nod. "It's very easy to picture you as a Kansas farm girl or a sophisticated New York model. You have a remarkable ability to suit your surroundings."

Hillary's full mouth moved in a doubtful pout. "That makes me sound like I'm no person on my own, sort of…inconspicuous."

"Inconspicuous?" Bret's laughter caused several heads to turn, and Hillary stared at him in dumb amazement. "Inconspicuous," he said again, shaking his head as if she had just uttered something sublimely ridiculous. "What a beautiful statement. No, I think you're a very complex woman with a remarkable affinity with her surroundings. I don't believe it's an acquired talent, but an intrinsic ability."

His words pleased Hillary out of all proportion, and she made an issue of stirring her tea, giving it her undivided attention. Why should a simple, impersonal compliment wrap around my tongue like a twenty-pound chain? she wondered, careful to keep a frown from forming. I don't think I care for the way he always manages to shift my balance.

"You do play tennis, don't you?"

Again, his rapid altering of the conversation threw her into confusion, and she stared at him without comprehension until she recalled the afternoon session was on the tennis court of an exclusive country club.

"I manage to hit the ball over the net once in a while." Annoyed by his somewhat condescending tone, she answered with uncharacteristic meekness.

"Good. The shots will be more impressive if you have the stance and moves down properly." He glanced at the gold watch on his wrist and drew out his wallet. "I've got some things to clear up at the office." Standing, he drew her from the booth, again holding her hand in his oddly familiar manner, ignoring her efforts to withdraw from his grip. "I'll put you in a cab. It'll take you some time to change from little girl to female athlete." He looked down at her, making her feel unaccustomedly small at five foot seven in her sneakers. "Your tennis outfit's already at the club, and I assume you have all the tricks of your trade in that undersized suitcase?" He indicated the large shoulder bag she heaved over her arm.

"Don't worry, Mr. Bardoff."

"Bret," he interrupted, suddenly engrossed with running his hand down her left pigtail. "I don't intend to stop using your first name."

"Don't worry," she began again, evading his invitation. "Changing images is my profession."

"It should prove interesting," he murmured, tugging the braid he held. Then, shifting to a more professional tone he said, "The court is reserved for one. I'll see you then."

"You're going to be there?" Her question was accompanied by a frown as she found herself undeniably distressed at the prospect of dealing with him yet again.

"My pet project, remember?" He nudged her into a cab, either unaware of or unconcerned by her scowl. "I intend to supervise it very carefully."

As the cab merged with traffic, Hillary's emotions were in turmoil. Bret Bardoff was an incredibly attractive and distracting man, and there was something about him that disturbed her. The idea of being in almost daily contact with him made her decidedly uneasy.

I don't like him, she decided with a firm nod. He's too self-assured, too arrogant, too… Her mind searched for a word. *Physical*. Yes, she admitted, albeit unwillingly, he was a very sexual man, and he unnerved her. She had no desire to be disturbed. There was something about the way he looked at her, something about the way her body reacted whenever she came into contact with him. Shrugging, she stared out the window at passing cars. She wouldn't think of him. Rather, she corrected, she would think of him only as her employer, and a temporary one at that—not as an individual. Her hand still felt warm from his, and glancing down at it, she sighed. It was imperative to her peace of mind that she do her job and avoid any more personal dealings with him. Strictly business, she reminded herself. Yes, their relationship would be strictly business.

The tomboy had been transformed into the fashionable tennis buff. A short white tennis dress accented Hillary's long, slender legs and left arms bare. She covered them, as she waited on the court, with a light jacket, since the October afternoon was pleasant but cool. Her hair was tied away from her face with a dark blue scarf, leaving her delicate features unframed. Color had been added to her eyes, accenting them with sooty fringes, and her lips were tinted deep rose. Spotless white tennis shoes completed her outfit, and she held a lightweight racket in her hands. The pure white of the ensemble contrasted well with her golden skin and raven hair, and she appeared wholly feminine as well as capable.

Behind the net, she experimented with stances, swinging the racket and serving the balls to a nonexistent partner while Larry roamed around her, checking angles and meters.

"I think you might have better luck if someone hit back."

She spun around to see Bret watching her with an amused gleam in his eyes. He too was in white, the jacket of his warm-up suit pushed to the elbows. Hillary, used to seeing him in a business suit, was surprised at the athletic appearance of his body, whipcord lean, his shoulders broad, his arms hard and muscular, his masculinity entirely too prevalent.

"Do I pass?" he asked with a half smile, and she flushed, suddenly aware that she had been staring.

"I'm just surprised to see you dressed that way," she muttered, shrugging her shoulders and turning away.

"More suitable for tennis, don't you think?"

"We're going to play?" She spun back to face him, scowling at the racket in his hand.

"I rather like the idea of action…shots," he finished with a grin. "I won't be too hard on you. I'll hit some nice and easy."

With a good deal of willpower, she managed not to stick

out her tongue. She played tennis often and well. Hillary decided, with inner complacency, that Mr. Bret Bardoff was in for a surprise.

"I'll try to hit a few back," she promised, her face as ingenuous as a child. "To give the shots realism."

"Good." He strode over to the other side of the court, and Hillary picked up a ball. "Can you serve?"

"I'll do my best," she answered, coating honey on her tongue. After glancing at Larry to see if he was ready, she tossed the ball idly in the air. The camera had already replaced Larry's face, and Hillary moved behind the fault line, tossed the ball once more, connected with the racket, and smashed a serve. Bret returned her serve gently, and she hit back, aiming deep in the opposite corner.

"I think I remember how to score," she called out with a thoughtful frown. "Fifteen-love, Mr. Bardoff."

"Nice return, Hillary. Do you play often?"

"Oh, now and again," she evaded, brushing invisible lint from her skirt. "Ready?"

He nodded, and the ball bounced back and forth in an easy, powerless volley. She realized with some smugness that he was holding back, making it a simple matter for her to make the return for the benefit of Larry's rapidly snapping camera. But she too was holding back, hitting the ball lightly and without any style. She allowed a few more laconic lobs, then slammed the ball away from him, deep in the back court.

"Oh." She lifted a finger to her lips, feigning innocence. "That's thirty-love, isn't it?"

Bret's eyes narrowed as he approached the net. "Why do I have this strange feeling that I'm being conned?"

"Conned?" she repeated, wide-eyed, allowing her lashes to flutter briefly. He searched her face until her lips trembled with laughter. "Sorry, Mr. Bardoff, I couldn't resist." She tossed her head and grinned. "You were so patronizing."

"Okay." He returned her grin somewhat to Hillary's relief. "No more patronizing. Now I'm out for blood."

"We'll start from scratch," she offered, returning to the serving line. "I wouldn't want you to claim I had an unfair advantage."

He returned her serve with force, and they kept each other moving rapidly over the court in the ensuing volley. They battled for points, reaching deuce and exchanging advantage several times. The camera was forgotten in the focus of concentration, the soft click of the shutter masked by the swish of rackets and thump of balls.

Cursing under her breath at the failure to return a ball cleanly, Hillary stooped to pick up another and prepared to serve.

"That was great." Larry's voice broke her concentration, and she turned to gape at him. "I got some fantastic shots. You look like a real pro, Hil. We can wrap it up now."

"Wrap it up?" She stared at him with incredulous exasperation. "Have you lost your mind? We're at deuce." She continued to regard him a moment as if his brain had gone on holiday, and shaking her head and muttering, she resumed play.

For the next few minutes, they fought for the lead until Bret once more held the advantage and once more placed the ball down the line to her backhand.

Hillary put her hands on her hips and let out a deep breath after the ball had sailed swiftly past her. "Ah, well, the agony of defeat." She smiled, attempted to catch her wind, and approached the net. "Congratulations." She offered both hand and smile. "You play a very demanding game."

He accepted her hand, holding it rather than shaking it. "You certainly made me earn it, Hillary. I believe I'd like to try my luck at doubles, with you on my side of the net."

"I suppose you could do worse."

He held her gaze a moment before his eyes dropped to the hand still captive in his. "Such a small hand." He lifted it higher and examined it thoroughly. "I'm astonished it can swing a racket like that." He turned it palm up and carried it to his lips.

Odd and unfamiliar tingles ran up her spine at his kiss, and she stared mesmerized at her hand, unable to speak or draw away. "Come on." He smiled into bemused eyes, annoyingly aware of her reaction. "I'll buy you lunch." His gaze slid past her. "You too, Larry."

"Thanks, Bret." He was already gathering his equipment. "But I want to get back and develop this film. I'll just grab a sandwich."

"Well, Hillary." He turned and commanded her attention. "It's just you and me."

"Really, Mr. Bardoff," she began, feeling near to panic at the prospect of having lunch with him and wishing with all her heart that he would respond to the effort she was currently making to regain sole possession of her hand. "It's not necessary for you to buy me lunch."

"Hillary, Hillary." He sighed, shaking his head. "Do you always find it difficult to accept an invitation, or is it only with me?"

"Don't be ridiculous." She attempted to maintain a casual

tone while she became more and more troubled by the warmth of his hand over hers. She stared down at the joined hands, feeling increasingly helpless as the contact continued. "Mr. Bardoff, may I please have my hand back?" Her voice was breathless, and she bit her lip in vexation.

"Try Bret, Hillary," he commanded, ignoring her request. "It's easy enough, only one syllable. Go ahead."

The eyes that held hers were calm, demanding, and arrogant enough to remain steady for the next hour. The longer her hand remained in his, the more peculiar she felt, and knowing that the sooner she agreed, the sooner she would be free, she surrendered.

"Bret, may I please have my hand back?"

"There, now, we've cleared the first hurdle. That didn't hurt much, did it?" The corner of his mouth lifted as he released her, and immediately the vague weakness began to dissipate, leaving her more secure.

"Nearly painless."

"Now about lunch." He held up his hand to halt her protest. "You do eat, don't you?"

"Of course, but—"

"No buts. I rarely listen to buts or nos."

In short order Hillary found herself seated across from Bret at a small table inside the club. Things were not going as she had planned. It was very difficult to maintain a businesslike and impersonal relationship when she was so often in his company. It was useless to deny that she found him interesting, his vitality stimulating, and he was a tremendously attractive man. But, she admonished herself, he certainly wasn't her type. Besides, she didn't have time for entanglements at this point of her life. Still, the warning signals in her brain told her to tread carefully, that this man was capable of upsetting her neatly ordered plans.

"Has anyone ever told you what a fascinating conversationalist you are?" Hillary's eyes shot up to find Bret's mocking gaze on her.

"Sorry." Color crept into her face. "My mind was wandering."

"So I noticed. What will you have to drink?"

"Tea."

"Straight?" he inquired, his smile hovering.

"Straight," she agreed, and ordered herself to relax. "I don't drink much. I'm afraid I don't handle it well. More than two and I turn into Mr. Hyde. Metabolism."

Bret threw back his head and laughed with the appearance of boundless pleasure. "That's a transformation I would give much to witness. We'll have to arrange it."

Lunch, to Hillary's surprise, was an enjoyable meal, though Bret met her choice of salad with open disgust and pure masculine disdain. She assured him it was adequate, and made a passing comment on the brevity of overweight models' careers.

Fully relaxed, Hillary enjoyed herself, the resolution to keep a professional distance between herself and Bret forgotten. As they ate, he spoke of the next day's shooting plans. Central Park had been designated for more outdoor scenes in keeping with the outdoor, athletic image.

"I've meetings all day tomorrow and won't be able to supervise. How do you exist on that stuff?" He changed the trend of conversation abruptly, waving a superior finger at Hillary's salad. "Don't you want some food? You're going to fade away."

She shook her head, smiling as she sipped her tea, and he muttered under his breath about half-starved models before resuming his previous conversation. "If all goes according to schedule, we'll start the next segment Monday. Larry wants to get an early start tomorrow."

"Always," she agreed with a sigh. "If the weather holds."

"Oh, the sun will shine." She heard the absolute confidence in his voice. "I've arranged it."

Sitting back, she surveyed the man across from her with uninhibited curiosity. "Yes." She nodded at length, noting the firm jaw and direct eyes. "I believe you could. It wouldn't dare rain."

They smiled at each other, and as the look held, she experienced a strange, unfamiliar sensation running through her—something swift, vital, and anonymous.

"Some dessert?"

"You're determined to fatten me up, aren't you?" Grateful that his casual words had eliminated the strange emotion, she summoned up an easy smile. "You're a bad influence, but I have a will of iron."

"Cheesecake, apple pie, chocolate mousse?" His smile was wicked, but she tossed her head and lifted her chin.

"Do your worst. I don't break."

"You're bound to have a weakness. A little time, and I'll find it."

"Bret, darling, what a surprise to see you here." Hillary turned and looked up at the woman greeting Bret with such enthusiasm.

"Hello, Charlene." He granted the shapely, elegantly dressed redhead a charming smile. "Charlene Mason, Hillary Baxter."

"Miss Baxter." Charlene nodded in curt greeting, and green eyes narrowed. "Have we met before?"

"I don't believe so," Hillary returned, wondering why she felt a surge of gratitude at the fact.

"Hillary's face is splashed over magazines covers everywhere," Bret explained. "She's one of New York's finest models."

"Of course." Hillary watched the green eyes narrow further, survey her, and dismiss her as inferior merchandise. "Bret, you should have told me you'd be here today. We could have had some time."

"Sorry," he answered with a casual move of his shoulders. "I won't be here long, and it was business."

Ridiculously deflated by his statement, Hillary immediately forced her spine to straighten. *Didn't I tell you not to get involved?* she reminded herself. *He's quite right, this was a business lunch.* She gathered her things and stood.

"Please, Miss Mason, have my seat. I was just going." She turned to Bret, pleased to observe his annoyance at her hasty departure. "Thanks for lunch, Mr. Bardoff," she added politely, flashing a smile at the frown that appeared at her use of his surname. "Nice to have met you, Miss Mason." Giving the woman occupying the seat she had just vacated a professional smile, Hillary walked away.

"I didn't realize taking employees to lunch was part of your routine, Bret." Charlene's voice carried to Hillary as she made her exit. Her first instinct was to whirl around and inform the woman to mind her own business, but grasping for control, she continued to move away without hearing Bret's reply.

* * *

The following day's session was more arduous. Using the brilliant fall color in Central Park for a backdrop, Larry's ideas for pictures were varied and energetic. It was a bright, cloudless day, as Bret had predicted, one of the final, golden days of Indian summer. Gold, russet, and scarlet dripped from the branches and covered the ground. Against the varied fall hues, Hillary posed, jogged, threw Frisbees, smiled, climbed trees, fed pigeons, and made three costume changes as the day wore on. Several times during the long session she caught herself looking for Bret, although she knew he was not expected. Her disappointment at his absence both surprised and displeased her, and she reminded herself that life would run much more smoothly if she had never laid eyes on a certain tall, lean man.

"Lighten up, Hil. Quit scowling." Larry's command broke into her musings. Resolutely, she shoved Bret Bardoff from her mind and concentrated on her job.

That evening she sank her tired body into a warm tub, sighing as the scented water worked its gentle magic on aching muscles. Oh, Larry, she thought wearily, with a camera in your hands you become Simon Legree. What you put me through today. I know I've been snapped from every conceivable angle, with every conceivable expression, in every conceivable pose. Thank heavens I'm through until Monday.

This layout was a big assignment, she realized, and there would be many more days like this one. The project could be a big boost to her career. A large layout in a magazine of *Mode*'s reputation and quality would bring her face to international recognition, and with Bret's backing she would more than likely be on her way to becoming one of the country's top models.

A frown appeared from nowhere. Why doesn't that please me? The prospect of being successful in my profession has always been something I wanted. Bret's face entered her mind, and she shook her head in fierce rejection.

"Oh, no you don't," she told his image. "You're not going to get inside my head and confuse my plans. You're the emperor, and I'm your lowly subject. Let's keep it that way."

Hillary was seated with Chuck Carlyle in one of New York's most popular discos. Music filled every corner, infusing the air with its vibrancy, while lighting effects played everchanging colors over the dancers. As the music washed over them, Hillary reflected on her reasoning for keeping her relationship with Chuck platonic.

It wasn't as though she didn't enjoy male companionship, she told herself. It wasn't as though she didn't enjoy a man's embrace or his kisses. A pair of mocking gray eyes crept into her mind unbidden, and she scowled fiercely into her drink.

If she shied away from more intimate relationships, it was only because no one had touched her deeply enough or stirred her emotions to a point where she felt any desire to engage in a long-term or even a short-term affair. Love, she mused, had so far eluded her, and she silently asserted that she was grateful. With love came commitments, and commitments did not fit into her plans for the immediate future. No, an involvement with a man would bring complications, interfere with her well-ordered life.

"It's always a pleasure to take you out, Hillary."

Thoughts broken, she glanced over to see Chuck grin and look pointedly down at the drink she had been nursing ever since their arrival. "You're so easy on my paycheck."

She returned his grin and pushed soul-searching aside. "You could look far and wide and never find another woman so concerned about your financial welfare."

"Too true." He sighed and adopted a look of great sadness. "They're either after my body or my money, and you, sweet Hillary, are after neither." He grabbed both of her hands and covered them with kisses. "If only you'd marry me, love of my life, and let me take you away from all this decadence." His hand swept over the dance floor. "We'll find a vine-covered cottage, two-point-seven kids, and settle down."

"Do you know," Hillary said slowly, "if I said yes, you'd faint dead away?"

"When you're right, you're right." He sighed again. "So instead of sweeping you off your feet to a vine-covered cottage, I'll drag you back to the decadence."

Admiring eyes focused on the tall, slim woman with the dress as blue as her eyes. Hillary's skirt was slit high to reveal long, shapely legs as she turned and spun with the dark man in his cream-colored suit. Both dancers possessed a natural grace and affinity with the music, and they looked spectacular on the dance floor. They ended the dance with Chuck lowering Hillary into a deep, dramatic dip, and when she stood again, she was laughing and flushed with the excitement of the dance. They wove their way back to their table, Chuck's arm around her shoulders, and Hillary's laughter died as she found herself confronted with the gray eyes that had disturbed her a short time before.

"Hello, Hillary." Bret's greeting was casual, and she was grateful for the lighting system, which disguised her change of color.

"Hello, Mr. Bardoff," she returned, wondering why her stomach had begun to flutter at the sight of him.

"You met Charlene, I believe."

Her eyes shifted to the redhead at his side. "Of course, nice to see you again." Hillary turned to her partner and made quick introductions. Chuck pumped Bret's hand with great enthusiasm.

"Bret Bardoff? *The* Bret Bardoff?" Hillary cringed at the undisguised awe and admiration.

"The only one I know," he answered with an easy smile.

"Please—" Chuck indicated their table "—join us for a drink."

Bret's smile widened as he inclined his head to Hillary, laughter lighting his eyes as she struggled to cover her discomfort.

"Yes, please do." She met his eyes directly, and her voice was scrupulously polite. She was determined to win the silent battle with the strange, uncommon emotions his mere presence caused. Flicking a quick glance at his companion, her discomfort changed to amusement as she observed Charlene Mason was no more pleased to share their company than she was. Or perhaps, Hillary thought idly as they slid behind the table, she was not pleased with sharing Bret with anyone, however briefly.

"A very impressive show the two of you put on out there," Bret commented to Chuck, indicating the dance floor with a nod of his head. His gaze roamed over to include Hillary. "You two must dance often to move so well together."

"There's no better partner than Hillary," Chuck declared magnanimously, and patted her hand with friendly affection. "She can dance with anyone."

"Is that so?" Bret's brows lifted. "Perhaps you'll let me borrow her for a moment and see for myself."

An unreasonable panic filled Hillary at the thought of dancing with him and it was reflected in her expressive eyes.

She rose with a feeling of helpless indignation as Bret came behind her and pulled out her chair without waiting for her assent.

"Stop looking like such a martyr," he whispered in her ear as they approached the other dancers.

"Don't be absurd," she stated with admirable dignity, furious that he could read her so effortlessly.

The music had slowed, and he turned her to face him, gathering her into his arms. At the contact, an overpowering childish urge to pull away assailed her, and she struggled to prevent the tension from becoming noticeable. His chest was hard, his basic masculinity overwhelming, and she refused to allow herself the relief of swallowing in nervous agitation. The arm around her waist held her achingly close, so close their bodies seemed to melt together as he moved her around the floor. She had unconsciously shifted to her toes, and her cheek rested against his, the scent of him assaulting her senses, making her wonder if she had perhaps sipped her drink too quickly. Her heart was pounding erratically against his, and she fought to control the leaping of her pulses as she matched her steps to his.

"I should have known you were a dancer," he murmured against her ear, causing a fresh flutter of her heartbeat.

"Really," she countered, battling to keep her tone careless and light, attempting to ignore the surge of excitement of his mouth on the lobe of her ear. "Why?"

"The way you walk, the way you move. With a sensuous grace, and effortless rhythm."

She intended to laugh off the compliment and tilted her head to meet his eyes. She found herself instead staring wordlessly into their gray depths. His hold on her did not lessen as they faced, their lips a breath apart, and she found the flip remark she had been about to make slip into oblivion.

"I always thought gray eyes were like steel," she murmured, hardly aware she was voicing her thoughts. "Yours are more like clouds."

"Dark and threatening?" he suggested, holding her gaze.

"Sometimes," she whispered, caught in the power he exuded. "And others, warm and soft like an early mist. I never know whether I'm in for a storm or a shower. Never know what to expect."

"Don't you?" His voice was quiet as his gaze dropped to her lips, tantalizingly close to his. "You should by now."

She struggled with the weakness invading her at his softly spoken retort and clutched for sophistication. "Really, Mr. Bardoff, are you attempting to seduce me in the middle of a crowded dance floor?"

"One must make use of what's available," he answered, then lifted his brow. "Have you somewhere else in mind?"

"Sorry," she apologized, and turned her head so their faces no longer met. "We're both otherwise engaged, and," she added, attempting to slip away, "the dance is over."

He did not release her, pulling her closer and speaking ominously in her ear. "You'll not get away until you drop that infuriatingly formal Mr. Bardoff and use my name." When she did not reply, he went on, an edge sharpening his voice. "I'm perfectly content to stay like this. You're a woman who was meant for a man's arms. I find you suit mine."

"All right," Hillary said between her teeth. "Bret, would you please let me go before I'm crushed beyond recognition?"

"Certainly." His grip slacked, but his arm remained around her. "Don't tell me I'm really hurting you." His smile was wide and triumphant as he gazed into her resentful face.

"I'll let you know after I've had my X-rays."

"I doubt if you're as fragile as all that." He led her back to the table, his arm still encircling her waist.

They joined their respective partners, and the group spoke generally for the next few minutes. Hillary felt unmistakable hostility directed toward her from the other woman, which Bret was either blissfully unaware of or ignored. Between frosty green eyes and her own disquieting awareness of the tall, fair man whose arms had held her so intimately, Hillary was acutely uncomfortable. It was a relief when the couple rose to leave, and Bret refused Chuck's request that they stay for another round. Charlene looked on with undisguised boredom.

"Charlene's not fond of discos, I'm afraid," Bret explained, grinning as he slipped an arm casually around the redhead's shoulders, causing her to look up at him with a smile of pure invitation. The gesture caused a sudden blaze of emotions to flare in Hillary that she refused to identify as jealousy. "She merely came tonight to please me. I'm thinking of using a disco background for the layout." Bret gazed down at Hillary with an enigmatic smile. "Wasn't it a stroke of luck that I was able to see you here tonight. It gives me a much clearer picture of how to set things up."

Hillary's gaze narrowed at his tone, and she caught the gleam of laughter in his eyes. Luck nothing, she thought suddenly, realizing with certainty that Bret rarely depended on luck. Somehow he had known she would be here tonight, and he had staged the accidental meeting. This layout must be very important to him, she mused, feeling unaccountably miserable. What other reason would he have for seeking her out and dancing with her while he had the obviously willing Charlene Mason hanging all over him?

"See you Monday, Hillary," Bret said easily as he and his lady made to leave.

"Monday?" Chuck repeated when they were once more alone. "Aren't you the fox." His teeth flashed in a grin. "Keeping the famous Mr. Bardoff tucked in your pocket."

"Hardly," she snapped, irritated by his conclusion. "Our relationship is strictly business. I'm working for his magazine. He's my employer, nothing more."

"Okay, okay." Chuck's grin only widened at her angry denial. "Don't take my head off. It's a natural mistake, and I'm not the only one who made it."

Hillary looked up sharply. "What are you talking about?"

"Sweet Hillary," he explained in a patient tone, "didn't you feel the knives stabbing you in the back when you were dancing with your famous employer?" At her blank stare, he sighed deeply. "You know, even after three years in New York, you're still incredibly naive." The corners of his mouth lifted, and he lay a brotherly hand on her shoulder. "A certain redhead was shooting daggers into you from her green eyes the entire time you were dancing. Why, I expected you to keel over in a pool of blood at any second."

"That's absurd." Hillary swirled the contents of her glass and frowned at them. "I'm sure Miss Mason knew very well Bret's purpose in seeing me was merely for research, just background for his precious layout."

Chuck regarded her thoroughly and shook his head. "As I said before, Hillary, you are incredibly naive."

Chapter 3

Monday morning dawned cool, crisp, and gray. In the office of *Mode,* however, threatening skies were not a factor. Obviously, Hillary decided, Bret had permitted nature to have a tantrum now that shooting had moved indoors.

At his direction, she was placed in the hands of a hairdresser who would assist in the transformation to smooth, competent businesswoman. Jet shoulder-length hair was arranged in a sleek chignon that accented classic bone structure, and the severely tailored lines of the three-piece gray suit, instead of appearing masculine, only heightened Hillary's femininity.

Larry was immersed in camera equipment, lighting, and angles when she entered Bret's office. Giving the room a quick survey, she was forced to admit it was both an elegant and suitable background for the morning's session. She watched with fond amusement as Larry, oblivious to her presence, adjusted lenses and tested meters, muttering to himself.

"The genius at work," a voice whispered close to her ear, and Hillary whirled, finding herself staring into the eyes that had begun to haunt her.

"That's precisely what he is," she retorted, furious with the way her heart began to drum at his nearness.

"Testy this morning, aren't we?" Bret observed with a lifted brow. "Still hung over from the weekend?"

"Certainly not." Dignity wrapped her like a cloak. "I never drink enough to have a hangover."

"Oh, yes, I forgot, the Mr. Hyde syndrome."

"Hillary, there you are." Larry interrupted Hillary's search for a suitable retort. "What took you so long?"

"Sorry, Larry, the hairdresser took quite some time."

The amused gleam in Bret's eyes demanded and received her answer. As their gaze met over Larry's head with the peculiar intimacy of a shared joke, a sweet weakness washed over her, like a soft, gentle wave washing over a waiting shore. Terrified, she dropped her eyes, attempting to dispel the reaction he drew from her without effort.

"Do you always frighten so easily?" Bret's voice was calm, with a hint of mockery, the tone causing her chin to lift in defiance. She glared, helplessly angry with his ability to read her thoughts as if they were written on her forehead. "That's better," he approved fending off the fire with cool composure. "Anger suits you. It darkens your eyes and puts rose in your cheeks. Spirit is an essential trait for women and—" his mouth lifted at the corner as he paused "—for horses."

She choked and sputtered over the comparison, willing her temper into place with the knowledge that if she lost it she would be powerless against him in a verbal battle. "I suppose that's true," she answered carelessly after swallowing the words that had sprung into her head. "In my observation, men appear to fall short of the physical capacity of one and the mental capacity of the other."

"Well, that hairstyle certainly makes you look competent." Larry turned to study Hillary critically, oblivious to anything that had occurred since he had last spoken. With a sigh of defeat, Hillary gazed at the ceiling for assistance.

"Yes," Bret agreed, keeping his features serious. "The woman executive, very competent, very smart."

"Assertive, aggressive, and ruthless," Hillary interrupted, casting him a freezing look. "I shall emulate you, Mr. Bardoff."

His brows rose fractionally. "That should be fascinating. I'll leave you then to get on with your work, while I get on with mine."

The door closed behind him, and the room was suddenly larger and strangely empty. Hillary shook herself and got to work, attempting to block out all thoughts of Bret Bardoff from her mind.

For the next hour Larry moved around the room, clicking his camera, adjusting the lighting, and calling out directions as Hillary assumed the poses of a busy woman executive.

"That's a wrap in here." He signaled for her to relax, which she did by sinking into a soft leather chair in a casual, if undignified, pose.

"Fiend!" she cried as he snapped the camera once more,

capturing her as she sprawled, slouched in the chair, legs stretched out in front of her.

"It'll be a good shot," he claimed with an absent smile. "Weary woman wiped-out by woesome work."

"You have a strange sense of humor, Larry," Hillary retorted, not bothering to alter her position. "It comes from having a camera stuck to your face all the time."

"Now, now, Hil, let's not get personal. Heave yourself out of that chair. We're going into the boardroom, and you, my love, can be chairman of the board."

"Chairperson," she corrected, but his mind was already involved with his equipment. Groaning, she stood and left him to his devices.

The remainder of the day's shooting was long and tedious. Dissatisfied with the lighting, Larry spent more than half an hour rearranging and resetting until it met with his approval. After a further hour under hot lights, Hillary felt as fresh as week-old lettuce and was more than ready when Larry called an end to the day's work.

She found herself searching for Bret's lean form as she made her way from the building, undeniably disappointed when there was no sign of him and angry with her own reaction. Walking for several blocks, she breathed in the brisk autumn air, determined to forget the emotions stirred by the tall man with sharp gray eyes. Just a physical attraction, she reasoned, tucking her hands in her pockets and allowing her feet to take her farther down the busy sidewalk. Physical attraction happens all the time; it would pass like a twenty-four-hour virus.

A diversion was what she required, she decided—something to chase him from her mind and set her thoughts back on the track she had laid out for herself. Success in the field she had chosen, independence, security—these were her priorities. There was no room for romantic entanglements. When the time came for settling down, it certainly would not be with a man like Bret Bardoff, but with someone safe, someone who did not set her nerves on end and confuse her at every encounter. Besides, she reminded herself, ignoring the sudden gloom, he wasn't interested in her romantically in any case. He seemed to prefer well-proportioned redheads.

Shooting resumed the next morning, once again in *Mode*'s offices. Today, dressed in a dark blue shirt and boot-length skirt of a lighter shade, Hillary was to take on the role of working girl. The session was to take place in Bret's secretary's office, much to that woman's delight.

"I can't tell you how excited I am, Miss Baxter. I feel like a kid going to her first circus."

Hillary smiled at the young woman whose eyes were alight with anticipation. "I'll admit to feeling like a trained elephant from time to time—and make it Hillary."

"I'm June. This is all routine to you, I suppose." Her head shook, causing chestnut curls to bounce and sway. "But it seems very glamorous and exciting to me." Her eyes drifted to where Larry was setting up for the shooting with customary absorption. "Mr. Newman's a real expert, isn't he? He's been fiddling with all those dials and lenses and lights. He's very attractive. Is he married?"

Hillary laughed, glancing carelessly at Larry. "Only to his Nikon."

"Oh." June smiled, then frowned. "Are you two, ah, I mean, are you involved?"

"Just master and slave," Hillary answered, seeing Larry as an attractive, eligible man for the first time. Looking back at June's appealing face, she smiled in consideration. "You know the old adage, 'The way to a man's heart is through his stomach.' Take my advice. The way to that man's heart is through his lenses. Ask him about f-stops."

Bret emerged from his office. He broke into a slow, lazy smile when he saw Hillary. "Ah, man's best friend, the efficient secretary."

Ignoring the pounding of her heart, Hillary forced her voice into a light tone. "No corporate decisions today. I've been demoted."

"That's the way of the business world." He nodded understandingly. "Executive dining room one day, typing pool the next. It's a jungle out there."

"All set," Larry announced from across the room. "Where's Hillary?" He turned to see the trio watching him and grinned. "Hello, Bret, hi, Hil. All set?"

"Your wish is my command, O master of the thirty-five millimeter," Hillary said, moving to join him.

"Can you type, Hillary?" Bret inquired cheerily. "I'll give you some letters, and we can kill two birds with one stone."

"Sorry, Mr. Bardoff," she replied, allowing herself to enjoy his smile. "Typewriters and I have a longstanding agreement. I don't pound on them, and they don't pound on me."

"Is it all right if I watch for a while, Mr. Newman?" June requested. "I won't get in the way. Photography just fascinates me."

Larry gave an absent assent, and, after casting his secretary a puzzled look, Bret turned to reenter his office. "I'll need you in a half hour, June—the Brookline contract."

The session went quickly with Larry and Hillary progressing with professional ease. The model followed the photographer's instructions, often anticipating a mood before he spoke. After a time, June disappeared unobtrusively through the heavy doors leading to Bret's office. Neither Hillary nor Larry noticed her silent departure.

Sometime later, Larry lowered his camera and stared fixedly into space. Hillary maintained her silence, knowing from experience this did not signal the end, but a pause while a fresh idea formed in his mind.

"I want to finish up with something here," he muttered, staring through Hillary as if she were intangible. His face cleared with inspiration. He focused his eyes. "I know. Change the ribbon in the typewriter."

"Surely you jest." She began an intense study of her nails.

"No, it'll be good. Go ahead."

"Larry," she protested in patient tones. "I haven't the foggiest notion how to change a ribbon."

"Fake it," Larry suggested.

With a sigh, Hillary seated herself behind the desk and stared at the typewriter.

"Ever harvested wheat, Larry?" she hazarded, attempting to postpone his order. "It's a fascinating process."

"Hillary," he interrupted, drawing his brows together.

With another sigh, she surrendered to artistic temperament. "I don't know how to open it," she muttered, pushing buttons at random. "It has to open, doesn't it?"

"There should be a button or lever under it," Larry returned patiently. "Don't they have typewriters in Kansas?"

"I suppose they do. My sister... Oh!" she cried, and grinned, delighted out of all proportion, like a small child completing a puzzle, when the release was located. Lifting the lid, she frowned intently at the inner workings. "Scalpel," she requested, running a finger over naked keys.

"Keep going, Hil," Larry commanded. "Just pretend you know what you're doing."

She found herself falling into the spirit of things and attacked the thin black ribbon threaded through various guides with enthusiasm. Her smooth brow was puckered in concentration as she forgot the man and his camera and gave herself over to the job of dislodging ribbon from machine. The more she unraveled, the longer the ribbon became, growing with a life of its own. Absently, she brushed a hand across her cheek, smearing it with black ink.

An enormous, ever-growing heap tangled around her fingers. Realization dawned that she was fighting a losing battle. With a grin for Larry, she flourished the mess of ribbon as he clicked a final picture.

"Terrific," he answered her grin as he lowered his camera. "A classic study in ineptitude."

"Thanks, friend, and if you use any of those shots, I'll sue." Dumping the mass of loose ribbon on the open typewriter, she expelled a long breath. "I'll leave it to you to explain to June how this catastrophe came about. I'm finished."

"Absolutely." Bret's voice came from behind, and Hillary whirled in the chair to see both him and June staring at the chaos on the desk. "If you ever give up modeling, steer clear of office work. You're a disaster."

Hillary attempted to resent his attitude, but one glance at the havoc she had wrought brought on helpless giggles.

"Well, Larry, get us out of this one. We've been caught red-handed at the scene of the crime."

Bret closed the distance between them with lithe grace and gingerly lifted one of Hillary's hands. "Black-handed, I'd say." Putting his other hand under her chin, he smiled in the lazy way that caused Hillary's reluctant heart to perform a series of somersaults. "There's quite a bit of evidence on that remarkable face as well."

She shook off the sweet weakness invading her and peered down at her hands. "Good Lord, how did I manage that? Will it come off?" She addressed her question to June, who assured her soap and water would do the trick. "Well, I'm going to wash away the evidence, and I'm leaving you—" she nodded to Larry "—to make amends for the damage." She encompassed June's desk with a sweeping gesture. "Better do some fast talking, old man," she added in a stage whisper, and gave June the present of her famous smile.

Reaching the door before her, Bret opened it and took a few steps down the long hall beside her. "Setting up a romance for my secretary, Hillary?"

"Could be," she returned enigmatically. "Larry could do with more than cameras and darkrooms in his life."

"And what could you use in yours, Hillary?" His question was soft, putting a hand on her arm and turning her to face him.

"I've…I've got everything I need," she stammered, feeling like a pinned butterfly under his direct gaze.

"Everything?" he repeated, keeping her eyes locked on his. "Pity I've an appointment, or we could go into this in more detail." Pulling her close, his lips brushed hers, then formed a crooked smile that was devastatingly appealing. "Go wash your face—you're a fine mess." Turning, he strode down the hall, leaving Hillary to deal with a mixture of frustration and unaccustomed longing.

She spent her free afternoon shopping, a diversionary tactic for soothing jangled nerves, but her mind constantly floated back to a brief touch of lips, a smile lighting gray eyes. The warmth seemed to linger on her mouth, stirring her emotions, arousing her senses. A cold blast of wind swirling in her face brought her back to reality. Cursing her treacherous imagination, she hailed a cab. She would have to hurry in order to make her dinner date with Lisa.

It was after five when Hillary entered her apartment and dumped her purchases on a chair in the bedroom. She released the latch on the front door for Lisa's benefit and made her way to the bath, filling the tub with hot, fragrant water. She intended to soak for a full twenty minutes. Just as she stepped from the tub and grabbed a towel, the bell sounded at the front door.

"Come on in, Lisa. Either you're early, or I'm late." Draping the towel saronglike around her slim body, she walked from the room, the scent of strawberries clinging to her shining skin. "I'll be ready in a minute. I got carried away in the tub. My feet were…" She stopped dead in her tracks, because instead of the small, blond Lisa, she was confronted by the tall, lean figure of Bret Bardoff.

"Where did you come from?" Hillary demanded when she located her voice.

"Originally or just now?" he countered, smiling at her confusion.

"I thought you were Lisa."

"I got that impression."

"What are you doing here?"

"Returning this." He held up a slim gold pen. "I assumed it was yours. The initials H.B. are engraved on it."

"Yes, it's mine," she concurred, frowning at it. "I must have dropped it from my bag. You needn't have bothered. I could have gotten it tomorrow."

"I thought you might have been looking for it." His eyes roamed over the figure scantily clad in the bath towel and lingered on her smooth legs, then rested a moment on the swell of her breast. "Besides, it was well worth the trip."

Hillary's eyes dropped down to regard her state of disarray and widened in shock. Color stained her cheeks as his eyes laughed at her, and she turned and ran from the room. "I'll be back in a minute."

Hastily, she pulled on chocolate brown cords and a beige mohair sweater, tugged a quick brush through her hair, and applied a touch of makeup with a deft hand. Taking a deep breath, she returned to the living room, attempting to assume a calm front that she was far from feeling. Bret was seated comfortably on the sofa, smoking a cigarette with the air of someone completely at home.

"Sorry to keep you waiting," she said politely, fighting back the embarrassment that engulfed her. "It was kind of you to take the trouble to return the pen to me." He handed it to her and she placed it on the low mahogany table. "May I...would you..." She bit her lip in frustration, finding her poise had vanished. "Can I get you a drink? Or maybe you're in a hurry—"

"I'm in no hurry," he answered, ignoring her frown. "Scotch, neat, if you have it."

Her frown deepened. "I may have. I'll have to check." She retreated to the kitchen, searching through cupboards for her supply of rarely used liquor. He had followed her, and she turned, noting with a quickening of pulse how his presence seemed to dwarf the small room. She felt an intimacy that was both exciting and disturbing. She resumed her search, all too conscious of his casual stance as he leaned against the refrigerator, hands in pockets.

"Here." Triumphantly, she brandished the bottle. "Scotch."

"So it is."

"I'll get you a glass. Neat, you said?" She pushed at her hair. "That's with no ice, right?"

"You'd make a marvelous bartender," he returned, taking both bottle and glass and pouring the liquid himself.

"I'm not much of a drinker," she muttered.

"Yes, I remember—a two-drink limit. Shall we go sit down?" He took her hand with the usual familiarity, and her words of protest died. "A very nice place, Hillary," he commented as they seated themselves on the sofa. "Open, friendly, colorful. Do the living quarters reflect the tenant?"

"So they say."

"Friendliness is an admirable trait, but you should know better than to leave your door unlatched. This is New York, not a farm in Kansas."

"I was expecting someone."

"But you got someone unexpected." He looked into her eyes, then casually swept the length of her. "What do you think would have happened if someone else had come across that beautiful body of yours draped in a very insufficient towel?" The blush was immediate and impossible to control, and she dropped her eyes. "You should keep your door locked, Hillary. Not every man would let you escape as I did."

"Yes, O mighty emperor," Hillary retorted before she could bite her tongue, and his eyes narrowed dangerously. He captured her with a swift movement, but whatever punishment he had in mind was postponed by the ringing of the phone. Jumping up in relief, Hillary hurried to answer.

"Lisa, hi. Where are you?"

"Sorry, Hillary." The answering voice was breathless. "The most wonderful thing happened. I hope you don't mind, but I have to beg off tonight."

"Of course not—what happened?"

"Mark asked me to have dinner with him."

"So you took my advice and tripped him, right?"

"More or less."

"Oh, Lisa," Hillary cried in amused disbelief, "you didn't really!"

"Well, no," she admitted. "We were both carrying all these law books and ran smack into each other. What a beautiful mess."

"I get the picture." Her laughter floated through the room. "It really has more class than a mugging."

"You don't mind about tonight?"

"Do you think I'd let a pizza stand in the way of true love?" Hillary answered. "Float along and have fun. I'll see you later."

She replaced the receiver and turned to find Bret regarding her with open curiosity. "I must admit that was the most fascinating one-ended conversation I've ever heard." She flashed him a smile with full candlepower and told him briefly of her friend's long unrequited love affair.

"So your solution was to land the poor guy on his face at her feet," he concluded.

"It got his attention."

"Now you're stood up. A pizza, was it?"

"My secret's out," she said, carefully seating herself in a chair across from him. "I hope I can trust you never to breathe a word of this, but I am a pizza junkie. If I don't have one at well-ordered intervals, I go into a frenzy. It's not a pretty sight."

"Well, we can't have you foaming at the mouth, can we?" He set down his empty glass and stood with a fluid motion. "Fetch a coat, I'll indulge you."

"Oh, really, there's no need," she began with quick panic.

"For heaven's sake, let's not go through this again. Get a coat and come on," he commanded, pulling her from her chair. "I could do with some food myself."

She found herself doing his bidding, slipping on a short suede jacket as he picked up his own brown leather. "Got your keys?" he questioned, reengaging the latch and propelling her through the door.

Soon they were seated in the small Italian restaurant that Hillary had indicated. The small table was covered with the inevitable red and white checkered cloth, a candle flickering in its wine bottle holder.

"Well, Hillary, what will you have?"

"Pizza"

"Yes, I know that," he countered with a smile. "Anything on it?"

"Extra cholesterol."

White teeth flashed as he grinned at her. "Is that all?"

"I don't want to overdo—these things can get out of hand."

"Some wine?"

"I don't know if my system can handle it." She considered, then shrugged. "Well, why not, you only live once."

"Too true." He signaled the waiter and gave their order. "You, however," he continued when they were once more alone, "look as though you had lived before. You are a reincarnation of an Indian princess. I bet they called you Pocahontas when you were a kid."

"Not if they were smart," Hillary returned. "I scalped a boy once for just that."

"Do tell?" Bret's attention was caught, and he leaned forward, his head on his hands as his elbows rested on the table. "Please elaborate."

"All right, if you can handle such a bloodthirsty subject over dinner." Pushing back her hair with both hands, she mirrored his casual position. "There was this boy, Martin Collins. I was madly in love with him, but he preferred Jessie Winfield, a cute little blond number with soulful brown eyes. I was mad with jealousy. I was also too tall, skinny, all eyes and elbows, and eleven years old. I passed them one day, devastated because he was carrying her books, and he called out 'Head for the hills, it's Pocahontas.' That did it, I was a woman scorned. I planned my revenge. I went home and got the small scissors my mother used for mending, painted my face with her best lipstick, and returned to stalk my prey.

"I crept up behind him stealthily, patiently waiting for the right moment. Springing like a panther, I knocked my quarry to the ground, holding him down with my body and cutting off as much hair as I could grab. He screamed, but I showed no mercy. Then my brothers came and dragged me off and he escaped, running like the coward he was, home to his mother."

Bret's laughter rang out as he threw back his head. "What a monster you must have been!"

"I paid for it." She lifted the glass of wine that Bret had poured during her story. "I got the tanning of my life, but it was worth it. Martin wore a hat for weeks."

Their pizza arrived, and through the meal their conversation was more companionable and relaxed than Hillary would have believed possible. When the last piece was consumed, Bret leaned back and regarded her seriously.

"I'd never have believed you could eat like that."

She grinned, relaxed by the combination of wine, good food, and easy company. "I don't often, but when I do, I'm exceptional."

"You're a constant amazement. I never know what to expect. A study of contradictions."

"Isn't that why you hired me, Bret?" She used his name for the first time voluntarily without conscious thought. "For my versatility?"

He smiled, lifted his glass to his lips, and left her question unanswered.

Hillary felt her earlier nervousness return as they walked down the carpeted hall toward her apartment. Determined to remain calm, she bent her head to fish out her keys, using the time to assume a calm veneer.

"Would you like to come in for coffee?"

He took the keys from her hand, unlocked the door, and gave her a slow smile. "I thought you didn't drink coffee."

"I don't, but everyone else in the world does, so I keep some instant."

"With the Scotch, no doubt," he said leading her into the apartment.

Removing her jacket, Hillary assumed the role of hostess. "Sit down. I'll have coffee out in a minute."

He had shed his own coat, carelessly dropping it down over the arm of a chair. Once more she was aware of the strong build beneath the dark blue rib-knit sweater and close-fitting slacks. She turned and made for the kitchen.

Her movements were deft and automatic as she set the kettle on the burner and removed cups and saucers from cupboards. She set a small sugar bowl and creamer on the glass and wicker tray, and prepared tea for herself and coffee for the man in her living room. She moved with natural grace to the low table, to set the ladened tray down. She smiled with professional ease at the tall man who stood across the room leafing casually through her collection of record albums.

"Quite an assortment." He addressed her from where he stood, looking so at ease and blatantly masculine that Hillary felt her veneer cracking rapidly and fought back a flutter of panic. "Typical of you though," he went on, sparing her from the necessity of immediate comment. "Chopin when you're romantic, Denver when you're homesick, B. B. King when you're down, McCartney when you're up."

"You sound like you know me very well." She felt a strange mixture of amusement and resentment that he had pinpointed her mood music with such uncanny accuracy.

"Not yet," he corrected, putting down an album and coming over to join her. "But I'm working on it."

Suddenly, he was very close, and there was an urgent

need in Hillary to be on a more casual footing. "Your coffee's getting cold." She spoke quickly and bent to remove the clutter from the tray, dropping a spoon in her agitation. They bent to retrieve it simultaneously, his strong, lean fingers closing over her fine-boned hand. At the contact a current of electricity shot down her arm and spread through her body, and her eyes darkened to midnight. She raised her face to his.

There were no words as their eyes met, and she realized the inevitability of the movement. She knew they had been drifting steadily toward this since the first day in Larry's studio. There was a basic attraction between them, an undefinable need she did not pause to question as he lifted her to her feet, and she stepped into his arms.

His lips were warm and gentle on hers as he kissed her slowly, then with increasing pressure, his tongue parted her lips, and his arms tightened around her, crushing her breasts against the hardness of his chest. Her arms twined around his neck. She responded as she had never responded to any man before. The thought ran through her clouded brain that no one had ever kissed her like this, no one had ever held her like this. Then all thought was drowned in a tidal wave of passion.

She made no resistance as she felt herself lowered onto the cushions of the couch, her mouth still the captive of his. The weight of his body pushed hers deep into the sofa as his legs slid between hers, making no secret of his desire. His mouth began to roam, exploring the smooth skin of her neck. The fire of a new and ageless need raged through her veins. She felt the thudding of a heart—hers or his, she could not tell—as his lips caressed her throat and face before meeting hers with possessing hunger. His hand moved under her sweater to cup the breast that swelled under his touch. She sighed and moved under him.

She was lost in a blaze of longing such as she had never known, responding with a passion she had kept buried until that moment, as his lips and hands moved with expertise over her warm and willing body.

His hands moved to the flatness of her stomach, and when she felt his fingers on the snap of her pants, she began to struggle against him. Her protests were ignored, his mouth devouring hers, then laying a trail of heat along her throat.

"Bret, please don't. You have to stop."

He lifted his head from the curve of her neck to look into the deep pools of her eyes, huge now with fear and desire. His own breathing was ragged. She knew a sharp fear that the decision to stop or go on would be taken out of her hands.

"Hillary," he murmured, and bent to claim her lips again, but she turned her head and pushed against him.

"No, Bret, no more."

A long breath escaped from his lips as he removed his body from hers, standing before removing a cigarette from the gold case he had left on the table. Hillary sat up, clutching her hands together in her lap, keeping her head lowered to avoid his eyes.

"I knew you were many things, Hillary," he said after expelling a swift and violent stream of smoke. "I never thought you were a tease."

"I'm not!" she protested, her head snapping up at the harshness of his tone. "That's unfair. Just because I stopped, just because I didn't let you…" Her voice broke.

She was filled with confusion and embarrassment, and a perverse longing to be held again in his arms.

"You are not a child," he began with an anger that caused her lips to tremble. "What is the usual outcome when two people kiss like that, when a woman allows a man to touch her like that?" His eyes were dark with barely suppressed fury, and she sat mutely, having been unprepared for the degree his temper could reach. "You wanted me as much as I wanted you. Stop playing games. We've both been well aware that this would happen eventually. You're a grown woman. Stop behaving like an innocent young girl."

The remark scored, and the telltale flush crept to her cheeks before she could lower her lashes to conceal painful discomfort. Bret gaped at her, anger struggling with stunned disbelief. "Good heavens, you've never been with a man before, have you?"

Hillary shut her eyes in humiliation, and she remained stubbornly silent.

"How is that possible?" he asked in a voice tinged with reluctant amusement. "How does a woman reach the ripe old age of twenty-four with looks like yours and remain as pure as the driven snow?"

"It hasn't been all that difficult," she muttered, and looked anywhere in the room but at him. "I don't normally let things get so out of hand." She made a small, helpless shrug.

"You might let a man know of your innocence before things get out of hand," he advised caustically, crushing out his cigarette with undue force.

"Maybe I should paint a red V for virgin on my forehead—then there'd be no confusion." Hillary flared, lifting her chin in bold defiance.

"You know, you're gorgeous when you're angry." He spoke coolly, but the steel vibrated in his tone, casual elegance wrapped around a volatile force. "Watch yourself, or I'll have another go at changing your status."

"I don't think you would ever stoop to forcing a woman," she retorted as he moved to pick up his jacket.

Pausing, he turned back to her, gray eyes narrowing into slits as he hauled her to her feet, possessing her again until her struggles had transformed into limp clinging.

"Don't count on it." His voice was deadly soft as he gave her a firm nudge back onto the couch. "I make a point of getting what I want." His eyes moved lazily over her slim body, pausing on the lips still soft from his. "Make no mistake," he went on as she began to tremble under his prolonged gaze. "I could have you here and now without forcing, but—" he moved to the door "—I can afford to wait."

Chapter 4

For the next few weeks shooting moved along with few complications. Larry was enthusiastic about the progress that was being made and brought Hillary a file of work prints so that she could view the fruits of their labor.

Studying the pictures with a professional objectivity, she admitted they were excellent, perhaps the best work Larry and she had done together or separately. There was a touch of genius in his choice of angles and lighting, using shadows and filters with a master hand. Added to this was Hillary's ability to assume varied roles. The pictures were already beginning to form a growing study of womanhood. They were nearly halfway through the planned shooting. If everything continued to go as well, they would be finished ahead of schedule. Bret was now planning a crash publication, which would put the issue on the stands in early spring.

Sessions would resume following the Thanksgiving weekend, while the art director and staff, with Bret's approval, began the selection of what would be printed in the final copy. Hillary was grateful for the time off, not only for the rest, but for the separation from the man who filled her thoughts and invaded her dreams.

She had expected some constraint between them when she returned to work after their evening together, but Bret had greeted her in his usual way, so casually, in fact, that she thought for a moment that she had imagined the feel of his lips on hers. There was no mention of their meal together or the scene that followed, while he slipped with apparent ease into the partly professional, partly mocking attitude he invariably directed toward her.

It was not as simple a task for Hillary to mirror his nonchalance after the emotions he had awakened in her—emotions that had laid sleeping within her until his touch had brought them to life—but outwardly she displayed a casualness at odds with her inner turmoil.

All in all, the remainder of the shooting time passed easily, and if Larry was forced to admonish her from time to time to relax and not to scowl, he was characteristically preoccupied and saw nothing amiss.

Hillary stood staring from the window of her apartment, her state of mind as bleak as the scene that greeted her. The late November sky was like lead, casting a depressing spell over the city, the buildings and skyscrapers taking on a dismal hue. Leaves had long since deserted the trees, leaving them naked and cheerless, and the grass, where sidewalks made room for it, had lost its healthy green tone, looking instead a sad, dreary yellow. The somberness of the day suited her mood precisely.

A sudden wave of homesickness washed over her, a strong desire for golden wheat fields. Moving to the stereo, she placed a Denver album on the turntable, halting in her movements when the image of Bret standing in the very spot she now occupied swept through her mind. The memory of the hardness of his body against hers and the intimacy briefly shared filled her with a painful longing, replacing homesickness. With a flash of insight, she realized that her attraction for him was more than physical. She switched on the player, filling the room with soft music.

Falling in love had not been in her plans, she reminded herself, and falling for Bret was out of the question, now or ever. That road would lead nowhere but to disaster and humiliation. But she could not quiet the voice that hammered in her brain telling her it was already too late. She sank down in a chair, confusion and depression settling over her like a fog.

It had grown late when Hillary let herself into her apartment after having joined Lisa and Mark for Thanksgiving dinner. The meal had been superb, but she had hidden her lack of appetite under the guise of keeping a careful watch on her figure. She had hidden her depression and concentrated on appearing normal and content. As she closed the door behind her, she breathed a sigh of relief, at last removing the frozen smile and relaxing. Before she could move to the closet to hang up her coat, the phone rang.

"Hello." Her voice reflected her weariness and annoyance.

"Hello, Hillary. Been out on the town?"

There was no need for the caller to identify himself.

Hillary recognized Bret immediately, glad that the thumping of her heart was not audible over the wire.

"Hello, Mr. Bardoff." She schooled her voice to coolness. "Do you always call your employees so late?"

"Grouchy, aren't we?" He seemed unperturbed. The thrill of hearing his voice warred with irritation at his composure. "Did you have a nice day?"

"Lovely," she lied. "I'm just home from having dinner with a friend. And you?"

"Spectacular. I'm very fond of turkey."

"Did you call to compare menus or was there something on your mind?" Her voice grew sharp at the picture of Bret and Charlene enjoying a beautifully catered dinner in elegant surroundings.

"Oh, yes, I've something on my mind. To begin with, I had thought to share a holiday drink with you, if you still have that bottle of Scotch."

"Oh." Her voice cracked, panic-filled. Clearing her throat, she stumbled on. "No, I mean, yes, I have the Scotch, but it's late and…"

"Afraid?" he interrupted quietly.

"Certainly not," she snapped. "I'm just tired. I'm on my way to bed."

"Oh, really?" She could hear the amusement in his voice.

"Honestly." To her disgust, she felt herself blushing. "Must you continually make fun of me?"

"Sorry." His apology lacked conviction. "But you will insist on taking yourself seriously. Very well, I won't dip into your liquor supply." Pausing, he added, "Tonight. I'll see you Monday, Hillary, sleep well."

"Good night," she murmured, filled with regret as she

replaced the receiver. Glancing around the room, she felt a swift desire to have him there, filling the emptiness with the excitement of his presence. She sighed and pushed at her hair, realizing she could hardly call him back and issue the invitation had she known where to reach him.

It's better this way, she rationalized, better to avoid him whenever possible. If I'm going to get over this infatuation, distance is my best medicine. He'll tire soon enough without encouragement. I'm sure he gets an ample supply of it from other quarters. Charlene is more his style, she went on, digging at the wound. I could never compete with her sophistication, I haven't the knack. She probably speaks French and knows about wines and can drink more than one glass of champagne before she starts to babble.

On Saturday Hillary met Lisa for lunch, hoping the short outing would boost her flagging spirits. The elegant restaurant was crowded. Spotting Lisa at a small table, Hillary waved and made her way through the room.

"Sorry, I know I'm late," Hillary apologized, picking up the menu set before her. "Traffic was dreadful, and I had a terrible time getting a cab. Winter's definitely on its way. It's freezing out there."

"Is it?" Lisa grinned. "It feels like spring to me."

"Love has apparently thrown you off balance. But," she added, "even if it's affected your brain, it's done wonders for the rest of you. I believe you could glow in the dark."

The blissful smile that lighted Lisa's face was a heart-catching sight, and Hillary's depression evaporated.

"I know my feet haven't touched the ground in weeks. I guess you're sick of watching me float around."

"Don't be silly. It's given me a tremendous lift watching you light up like a neon sign."

The two women ordered their meal, slipping into the easy camaraderie they enjoyed.

"I really should find a friend with warts and a hooked nose," Lisa commented.

Hillary's fork paused on its journey to her mouth. "Come again?"

"The most fascinating man just came in. I might as well be invisible for all the attention he paid me. He was too busy staring at you."

"He's probably just looking for someone he knows."

"He's got someone he knows hanging on to his arm like an appendage," Lisa declared, staring boldly at the couple across the room. "His attention, however, is riveted on you. No, don't turn around," she hissed as Hillary started to turn her head. "Oh, good grief, he's coming over. Quick," she whispered desperately, "look natural."

"You're the one standing on her head, Lisa," Hillary returned calmly, amused by her friend's rapid capitulation.

"Well, Hillary, we just can't keep away from each other, can we?"

Hillary heard the deep voice and her wide eyes met Lisa's startled ones before she looked up to meet Bret's crooked smile. "Hello." Her voice was oddly breathless. Her glance took in the shapely redhead on his arm. "Hello, Miss Mason, nice to see you again," she said quietly.

Charlene merely nodded. From the expression in her frosty green eyes, it was apparent she couldn't have disagreed more. There was a short pause. Bret raised his brow in inquiry.

"Lisa MacDonald, Charlene Mason and Bret Bardoff," Hillary introduced quickly.

"Oh, you're *Mode* magazine," Lisa blurted out, her eyes shining with excitement. Hillary looked in vain for a hole to open up and swallow her.

"More or less."

Hillary watched, helpless, as Bret turned his most charming smile on Lisa.

"I'm a great fan of your magazine, Mr. Bardoff," Lisa bubbled. She appeared to be unaware of the darts shooting at her from Charlene's narrowed eyes. "I can barely wait for this big layout of Hillary's. It must be very exciting."

"It's been quite an experience so far." He turned to Hillary with an annoying grin. "Don't you agree, Hillary?"

"Quite an experience," she agreed carelessly, forcing her eyes to remain level.

"Bret," Charlene interrupted. "We really must get to our table and let these girls get on with their lunch." Her eyes swept both Hillary and Lisa, dismissing them as beneath notice.

"Nice to have met you, Lisa. See you later, Hillary." His lazy smile had Hillary's heart pounding in its now familiar way. But she managed to murmur goodbye. Nervously, she reached for her tea, hoping Lisa would not discuss the encounter.

Lisa stared at Bret's retreating back for several seconds. "Wow," she breathed, turning huge brown eyes on Hillary. "You didn't tell me he was so terrific! I was literally liquified when he smiled at me."

Dear heaven, Hillary thought wearily, does he affect all

women that way? Aloud, she spoke with mock censure. "Shame on you—your heart's supposed to be taken."

"It is," Lisa affirmed. "But I'm still a woman." Looking at Hillary, she went on shrewdly, "Don't tell me he leaves you unmoved. We know each other too well."

A deep sigh escaped. "I'm not immune to Mr. Bardoff's devastating charm, but I'll have to develop some kind of antidote during the next couple of months."

"Don't you think the interest might be mutual? You're not without substantial charm yourself."

"You did notice the redhead clinging to him like ivy on a brick wall?"

"Couldn't miss her." Lisa grimaced. "I had the feeling she expected me to rise and curtsy. Who is she, anyway? The Queen of Hearts?"

"Perfect match for the emperor," Hillary murmured.

"What?"

"Nothing. Are you done? Let's get out of here." Rising without waiting for an answer, Hillary gathered her purse and the two women left the restaurant.

The following Monday Hillary walked to work. She lifted her face to the first snow of the season. Cold flakes drifted to kiss her upturned face, and she felt a thrill of anticipation watching soft white swirl from the lead-colored sky. Snow brought memories of home, sleigh rides, and snow battles. Sluggish traffic was powerless against her mood of excitement, and Hillary arrived at Larry's studio as bright and exuberant as a child.

"Hi, old man. How was your holiday?" Wrapped in a calf-length coat, a matching fur hat pulled low over her head, and cheeks and eyes glowing with the combination of cold and excitement, she was outrageously beautiful.

Larry paused in his lighting adjustment to greet her with a smile. "Look what the first snow blew in. You're an ad for winter vacations."

"You're incorrigible." She slipped out of her outdoor clothing and wrinkled her nose. "You see everything cropped and printed."

"Occupational hazard. June says my eye for a picture is fascinating," he added smugly.

"*June* says?" Delicate brows raised inquiringly.

"Well, yeah, I've, uh, been teaching her a little about photography."

"I see." The tone was ironic.

"She's, well, she's interested in cameras."

"Ah, her interest is limited to shutter speeds and wide-angle lenses," Hillary agreed with a wise nod.

"Come on, Hil," Larry muttered, and began to fiddle with dials.

Gliding over, she hugged him soundly. "Kiss me, you fox. I knew you had it in you somewhere."

"Come on, Hil," he repeated, disentangling himself. "What are you doing here so early? You've got half an hour."

"Amazing, you noticed the time." She batted her eyes, received a scowl, and subsided. "I thought I might look over the work prints."

"Over there." He indicated his overloaded desk in the back corner of the room. "Go on now and let me finish."

"Yes, master." She retreated to search out the file filled with the prints of the layout. After a few moment's study, she drew out one of herself on the tennis court. "I want a copy of this," she called to him. "I look fiercely competitive." Receiving no response, she glanced over, seeing him once more totally involved and oblivious to her presence. "Certainly, Hillary, my dear," she answered for him. "Anything you want. Look at that stance," she continued with deep enthusiasm, glancing back at the picture in her hands. "The perfect form and intense concentration of a champion. Look out, Wimbledon, here I come. You'll tear them apart, Hil." She again assumed Larry's role. "Thanks, Larry. All that talent and beauty too. Please, Larry, you're embarrassing me."

"They lock people up for talking to themselves," a deep voice whispered in her ear. Hillary jumped. The picture dropped from her hands to the pile on the desk. "Nervous, too—that's a bad sign."

She whirled and found herself face to face with Bret— so close, in fact, she took an instinctive step in retreat. The action did not go unnoticed, and the corner of his mouth twitched into a disarmingly crooked smile.

"Don't creep up on me like that."

"Sorry, but you were so engrossed in your dialogue." His shoulders moved eloquently, and he allowed his voice to trail away.

A reluctant smile hovered on Hillary's lips. "Sometimes Larry lets the conversation drag a mite, and I'm obliged to carry him." She gestured with a slender hand. "Just look at that. He doesn't even know you're here."

"Mmm, perhaps I should take advantage of his preoccupation." He tucked a silky strand of hair behind her ear. The warmth of his fingers shot through her as he made the disturbingly gentle gesture, and her pulse began to jump at an alarming rate.

"Oh, hi, Bret. When did you get in?"

At Larry's words, Hillary let out a sigh, unsure whether it was born of relief or frustration.

December was slipping slowly by. Progress on the layout was more advanced than expected, and it appeared that actual shooting would be completed before Christmas. Hillary's contract with Bret ran through March, and she speculated on what she would do when the shooting stage was over and she was no longer needed. It was possible that Bret would release her, though she admitted this was highly unlikely. He would hardly wish her to work for a competitor before his pet project was on the stands.

Maybe he'll find some other work for me through the next couple of months, she theorized during a short break in a session. Or maybe she could be idle for a time. Oddly, the latter prospect appealed to her, and this surprised her. She enjoyed her work, didn't she? Hard work, yes, but rarely boring. Of course she enjoyed her work. It was enough for her, and she intended to keep it first in her life for the next few years. After that, she could retire if she liked or take a long vacation, travel—whatever. Then, when everything was in order, there would be time for a serious romance. She'd find someone nice, someone safe, someone she could marry and settle down with. That was her plan, and it made perfect sense. Only now, when thought through, it sounded horribly cold and dull.

Larry's studio was more crowded than usual during the second week of December. This particular morning, voices and bodies mingled in the room in delightful chaos. In this shooting, Hillary was sharing the spotlight with an eight-month-old boy as she portrayed the young mother.

A small section of the room was set to resemble part of a living area. When Hillary emerged from the hairdresser's hands, Larry was busy double-checking his equipment. Bret worked with him, discussing ideas for the session, and she chided herself for staring at his strong, lean back.

Leaving the men to their duties, she went over to meet the young mother and the child who would be hers for a few minutes in front of the camera. She was both surprised and amused by the baby's resemblance to her. Andy, as his mother introduced him, had a tuft of hair as dark and shining as Hillary's, and his eyes, though not as deep as hers, were startlingly blue. She would be taken without question for his mother by any stranger.

"Do you know how hard it was to find a child with your looks?" Bret asked, approaching from across the room to where Hillary sat with Andy on her lap. Bret stopped in front of her as she laughed and bounced the baby on her knee, and both woman and child raised deep blue eyes. "A person could be struck blind by all that brilliance. Perhaps you two should turn down the wattage."

"Isn't he beautiful?" Her voice was warm as she rubbed her cheeks against the soft down of his hair.

"Spectacular," he agreed. "He could be yours."

A shadow clouded over dark blue, and Hillary lowered her lashes on the sudden longing his words aroused. "Yes, the resemblance is amazing. Are we ready?"

"Yes."

"Well, partner." She stood and rested Andy on her hip. "Let's get to work."

"Just play with him," Larry instructed. "Do what comes naturally. What we're looking for is spontaneity." He looked down at the round face, and Andy's eyes met his levelly. "I think he understands me."

"Of course," Hillary agreed with a toss of her head. "He's a very bright child."

"We'll keep the shots candid and hope he responds to you. We can only work with children a few minutes at a time."

And so they began, with the two dark heads bent near each other as they sat on the carpeted area with Hillary building alphabet blocks and Andy gleefully destroying her efforts. Soon both were absorbed in the game and each other, paying scant attention to Larry's movements or the soft click of the camera. Hillary lay on her stomach, feet in the air, constructing yet another tower for ultimate demolition. The child reached out, diverted by a strand of silky hair. His stubby fingers curled around the softness, tugging on it and bringing it to his mouth wrapped in a small fist.

Rolling on her back, she lifted the child over her head, and he gurgled in delight at the new game. Setting him on her stomach, he soon became enchanted by the pearl buttons on her pale green blouse. She watched his concentration, tracing his features with her fingertip. Again, she felt the pull of sudden longing. She lifted the baby over her body, making the sounds of a plane as she swayed him over her. Andy squealed in delight and she stood him on her stomach, letting him bounce to his own music.

She stood with him, swinging him in a circle before hugging him against her. This is what I want, she realized suddenly, holding the child closer. A child of my own, tiny arms around my neck, a child with the man I love. She closed her eyes as she rubbed her cheek against Andy's round one. When she opened them again, she found herself staring up into Bret's intense gaze.

She held her eyes level a moment as it drifted over her quietly that this was the man she loved, the man whose child she wanted to feel in her arms. She had known the truth for some time, but had refused to acknowledge it. Now, there was no denying it.

Andy's none-too-gentle tug on her hair broke the spell, and Hillary turned away, shaken by what she had just been forced to admit to herself. This was not what she had planned. How could this happen? She needed time to think, time to sort things out. Right now she felt too confused.

She was profoundly relieved when Larry signaled the finish. With a supreme effort, Hillary kept her professional smile in place while inside she trembled at her new awareness.

"Outstanding," Larry declared. "You two work together like old friends."

Not work, Hillary corrected silently, a fantasy. She had been acting out a fantasy. Perhaps her entire career was a fantasy, perhaps her entire life. A hysterical giggle bubbled inside her, and she choked it back. She could not afford to make a fool of herself now. She could not allow herself to think about the feelings running through her or the questions buzzing inside her brain.

"It's going to take some time to break down and set up for the next segment, Hil." Larry consulted his watch. "Go grab a bite before you change. Give it an hour."

Hillary assented with a wave of relief at the prospect of some time alone.

"I'll go with you."

"Oh, no," she protested, picking up her coat and hurrying out. His brow lifted at her frantic tone. "I mean, don't bother. You must have work to do. You must have to get back to your office or something."

"Yes, my work never ceases," he acknowledged with a heavy dose of mockery. "But once in a while I have to eat."

He took her coat to help her with it. His hands rested on her shoulders, their warmth seeping through the material and burning her skin, causing her to stiffen defensively. His fingers tightened and he turned her to face him.

"It was not my intention to have *you* for lunch, Hillary." The words were soft, at odds with the temper darkening his eyes. "Will you never cease to be suspicious of me?"

The streets were clear, but there was a light covering of white along the sidewalks and on the cars parked along the curb. Hillary felt trapped in the closed car sitting so close to the man who drove, long fingers closed over the steering wheel of the Mercedes. He skirted Central Park, and she endeavored to ease her tension and slow the incessant drumming of her heart.

"Look, it's beautiful, isn't it?" She indicated the trees, their bare branches now robed in white, glittering as if studded with diamonds. "I love the snow," she chattered on, unable to bear the silence. "Everything seems clean and fresh and friendly. It makes it seem more like…"

"Home?" he supplied.

"Yes," she said weakly, retreating from his penetrating gaze.

Home, she thought. Home could be anywhere with this man. But she must not reveal her weakness. He must never know the love that rushed through her, tossing her heart like the winds of a tornado that swept through Kansas in late spring.

Sitting in a small booth, Hillary babbled about whatever innocuous subject came to mind. Chattering to avoid a lull where he might glimpse the secret she held within her, securely locked like a treasure in a fortress.

"Are you okay, Hillary?" Bret asked suddenly when she paused to take a breath. "You've been very jumpy lately." His eyes were sharp and probing, and for a terrifying moment Hillary feared they would penetrate her mind and read the secret written there.

"Sure, I am." Her voice was admirably calm. "I'm just excited about the layout." She grasped at the straw of an excuse. "We'll be finished soon, and the issue will be on the stands. I'm anxious about the reception."

"If it's only business that bothers you," he said abruptly, "I believe I'm qualified to predict the reaction will be tremendous." His eyes reached out and held hers. "You'll be a sensation, Hillary. Offers will come pouring in—magazines, television, products for your endorsement. You'll be in a position to pick and choose."

"Oh" was all that she could manage.

His brows knitted dangerously. "Doesn't it excite you? Isn't that what you've always wanted?" he asked brusquely.

"Of course it is," she stated with a great deal more enthusiasm than she was feeling. "I'd have to be demented not to be thrilled, and I'm grateful for the opportunity you gave me."

"Save your gratitude." He cut her off curtly. "This project has been a result of teamwork. Whatever you gain from it, you've earned." He drew out his wallet. "If you're finished, I'll drop you back before I return to the office."

She nodded mutely, unable to comprehend what she had said to arouse his anger.

The final phase of shooting was underway. Hillary changed in the small room off Larry's main studio. Catching sight of her reflection in the full-length mirror, she held her breath. She had thought the negligee lovely but uninspired when she had lifted it from its box, but now, as it swirled around her, she was awed by its beauty. White and filmy, it floated around her slim curves, falling in gentle folds to her ankles. It was low cut, but not extreme, the soft swell of her breasts merely hinted at above the neckline. Yes, Hillary decided as she moved, the drifting material following in a lovingly lazy manner, it's stunning.

Earlier that day, she had modeled an exquisite sable coat. She remembered the feel of the fur against her chin and sighed. Larry had captured the first expression of delight and desire as she had buried her face against the collar. But Hillary knew now that she would rather have this negligee than ten sables. There was something special about it, as though it had been created with her in mind.

She walked from the dressing room and stood watching as Larry completed his setup. He has outdone himself this time, she mused with admiration. The lighting was soft and gentle, like a room lit with candles, and he had set up back-lighting, giving the illusion of moonlight streaming. The effect was both romantic and subtle.

"Ah, good, you're ready." Larry turned from his task, then, focusing on her directly, let out a low whistle. "You're gorgeous. Every man who sees your picture will be dying for love of you, and every woman will be putting herself in your place. Sometimes you still amaze me."

She laughed and moved to join him as the studio door opened. Turning, the gown drifting about her, she saw Bret enter the room with Charlene on his arm. Blue eyes locked with gray before his traveled slowly over her with the intensity of a physical caress.

He took his time in bringing his eyes back to her face. "You look extraordinary, Hillary."

"Thanks." She swallowed the huskiness of her voice and her gaze moved from his to encounter Charlene's icy stare. The shock was like a cold shower and Hillary wished with all her heart that Bret had not chosen to bring his shapely companion with him.

"We're just getting started." Larry's matter-of-fact tone shattered the spell, and three heads turned to him.

"Don't let us hold things up," Bret said easily. "Charlene wanted to see the project that's been keeping me so busy."

His implication that Charlene had a stake in his life caused Hillary's spirits to plummet. Shaking off encroaching depression, she reminded herself that what she felt for Bret was strictly one-sided.

"Stand here, Hil," Larry directed, and she drifted to the indicated spot.

Muted lighting lent a glow to her skin, as soft on her cheek as a lover's caress. Soft backlighting shone through the filmy material, enticingly silhouetting her curves.

"Good," Larry stated, and, switching on the wind machine, he added, "perfect."

The easy breeze from the machine lifted her hair and rippled her gown. Picking up his camera, Larry began to shoot. "That's good, now lift your hair. Good, good, you'll drive them crazy." His instructions came swiftly, and her expressions and stances changed in rapid succession. "Now, look right into the camera—it's the man you love. He's coming to take you into his arms." Her eyes flew to the back of the studio where Bret stood linked with Charlene. Her eyes met his and a tremor shook her body. "Come on, Hillary, I want passion, not panic. Come on now, baby, look at the camera."

She swallowed and obeyed. Slowly, she allowed her dreams to take command, allowed the camera to become Bret. A Bret looking at her not only with desire, but with love. He came to her with love and need. He was holding her close as she remembered him holding her. His hands moved gently over her as his lips claimed hers after he whispered the words she longed to hear.

"That does it, Hillary."

Lost in her own world, she blinked and stared at Larry without comprehension.

"That was great. I fell in love with you myself."

Letting out a deep breath, she shut her eyes a moment and sighed at her own imagination. "I suppose we could get married and breed little lenses," she murmured as she headed for the dressing room.

"Bret, that negligee is simply marvelous." Charlene's words halted Hillary's progress. "I really must have it, darling. You can get it for me, can't you?" Charlene's voice was low and seductive as she ran a well-manicured hand along Bret's arm.

"Hmm? Sure," he assented, his eyes on Hillary. "If you want it, Charlene."

Hillary's mouth fell open with astonishment. His casual gift to the woman at his side wounded her beyond belief. She stared at him for a few moments before fleeing to her dressing room.

In the privacy of the dressing room, she leaned against the wall battling the pain. How could he? she cried inwardly. The gown was special, it was hers, she belonged in it. She closed her eyes and stifled a sob. She had even imagined him holding her in it, loving her, and now…it would be Charlene's. He would look at Charlene, his eyes dark with desire. His hands would caress Charlene's body through the misty softness. Now a fierce anger began to replace the pain. If that was what he wanted, well, they were welcome to it—both of them. She stripped herself from frothy white folds and dressed.

When she left the dressing room, Bret was alone in the studio, sitting negligently behind Larry's desk. Summoning all her pride, Hillary marched to him and dropped the large box on its cluttered surface.

"For your friend. You'll want to have it laundered first."

She turned to make her exit with as much dignity as possible, but was outmaneuvered as his hand closed over her wrist.

"What's eating you, Hillary?" He stood, keeping his grip firm and towering over her.

"Eating me?" she repeated, glaring up at him. "Whatever do you mean?"

"Drop it, Hillary," he ordered, the familiar steel entering both voice and eyes. "You're upset, and I mean to know why."

"Upset?" She tugged fiercely at her arm. As her efforts for liberation proved fruitless, her anger increased. "If I'm upset, it's my own affair. It's not in my contract that I'm obliged to explain my emotions to you." Her free hand went to his in an attempt to pry herself free, but he merely transferred his hold to her shoulders and shook her briskly.

"Stop it! What's gotten into you?"

"I'll tell you what's gotten into me," she snapped as her hair tumbled around her face. "You walk in here with your redheaded girlfriend and just hand over that gown. She just bats her eyes and says the word, and you hand it over."

"Is that what all this is about?" he demanded, exasperated. "Good heavens, woman, if you want the damn thing, I'll get you one."

"Don't you patronize me," she raged at him. "You can't buy my good humor with your trinkets. Keep your generosity for someone who appreciates it and let me go."

"You're not going anywhere until you calm down and we get to the root of the problem."

Her eyes were suddenly filled with uncontrollable tears. "You don't understand." She sniffed as tears coursed down her cheeks. "You just don't understand anything."

"Stop it!" He began to brush her tears away with his hand. "Tears are my downfall. I can't handle them. Stop it, Hillary, don't cry like that."

"It's the only way I know how to cry," she said, weeping miserably.

He swore under his breath. "I don't know what this is

all about. A nightgown can't be worth all this! Here, take it—it's obviously important to you." He picked up the box, holding it out to her. "Charlene has plenty." The last words, uttered in an attempt to lighten her mood, had precisely the reverse effect.

"I don't want it. I don't ever want to see it again," she shouted, her voice made harsh by tears. "I hope you and your lover thoroughly enjoy it." With this, she whirled, grabbed her coat, and ran from the studio with surprising speed.

Outside, she stood on the sidewalk, stomping her feet against the cold. Stupid! she accused herself. Stupid to get so attached to a piece of cloth. But no more stupid than getting attached to an arrogant, unfeeling man whose interests lay elsewhere. Spotting a cab, she stepped forward to flag it down when she was spun around to face the buttons on Bret's leather coat.

"I've had enough of your tantrums, Hillary, and I don't tolerate being walked out on." His voice was low and dangerous, but Hillary tilted back her head to meet his gaze boldly.

"We have nothing more to say."

"We have plenty more to say."

"I don't expect you to understand." She spoke with the exaggerated patience an adult uses when addressing a slow-witted child. "You're just a man."

She heard the sharp intake of his breath as he moved toward her.

"You're right about one thing, I am a man," she heard him whisper before he pulled her close, crushing her mouth in an angry kiss, forcing her lips to open to his demands. The world emptied but for his touch, and the two stood locked together, oblivious to the people who walked the sidewalk behind them.

When at last he freed her, she drew back from him, her breath coming quickly. "Now that you've proven your masculinity, I really must go."

"Come back upstairs. We'll finish our discussion."

"Our discussion is finished."

"Not quite." He began to drag her back toward the studio.

I can't be alone with him now, she thought wildly. Not now, when I'm already so vulnerable. He could see too much too easily.

"Really, Bret." She was proud of the calmness of her voice. "I do hate to create a scene, but if you continue to play the caveman I shall be forced to scream. And I can scream very loud."

"No, you wouldn't."

"Yes," Hillary corrected, digging in her heels. "I would."

"Hillary." He turned, maintaining possession of her arm. "We have things to clear up."

"Bret, it's gotten blown out of proportion." She spoke sweetly, ignoring the weakness in her legs. "We've both had our outburst of temper—let's just leave it at that. The entire thing was silly anyway."

"It didn't seem silly to you upstairs."

The slender hold on her control was slipping rapidly, and she looked up at him in a last ditch attempt. "Please, Bret, drop it. We're all temperamental sometimes."

"Very well," he agreed after a pause. "We'll drop it for the time being."

Hillary sighed tremulously. She felt that if she stayed any longer she ran the risk of agreeing to whatever he asked. Out of the corner of her eye she glimpsed a passing cab, and she put her fingers to her mouth to whistle it down.

Bret's mouth lifted in irrepressible amusement. "You never cease to surprise me."

Her answer was lost as she slammed the cab door behind her.

Chapter 5

Christmas was approaching, and the city was decorated in its best holiday garb. Hillary watched from her window as cars and people bustled through the brightly lit streets. The snow fell upon city sidewalks, the drifting white adding to her holiday mood. She watched the huge flakes float to earth like down from a giant pillow.

Shooting of the layout was complete, and she had seen little of Bret in the past few days. She would be seeing less of him, she realized, a shaft of gloom darkening her cheerful mood. Now that her part in the project was over, there would be no day-to-day contact, no chance meetings. She sighed and shook her head. I'm going home tomorrow, she reminded herself, home for Christmas.

That was what she needed, she told herself, closing her eyes on the image of Bret's handsome features. A complete change of scene. Ten days to help heal her heart, time to reevaluate all the plans she had laid out, which now seemed hopelessly dull and unsatisfying.

The knock on the door caused her to remove her face, which had been pressed against the glass. "Who is it?" she called as she placed her hand on the knob.

"Santa Claus."

"B-Bret?" she stammered, thrown off balance. "Is that you?"

"Just can't fool you, can I?" After a slight pause, he asked, "Are you going to let me in, or do we have to talk through the door?"

"Oh, sorry." She fumbled with the latch and opened the door, staring at his lean form, which leaned negligently against the frame.

"You're locking up these days." His eyes swept her pearl-colored velour housecoat before he brought them back to hers. "Are you going to let me in?"

"Oh, sure." Hillary stood back to let him enter, desperately searching for lost composure. "I, ah, I thought Santa came down the chimney."

"Not this one," he returned dryly, and removed his coat. "I could use some of your famous Scotch. It's freezing out there."

"Now I'm totally disillusioned. I thought Santa thrived on cookies and milk."

"If he's half the man I think he is, he's got a flask in that red suit."

"Cynic," she accused, and retreated to the kitchen. Finding the Scotch easily this time, she poured a measure into a glass.

"Very professional." Bret observed from the doorway. "Aren't you going to join me in some holiday cheer?"

"Oh, no." Hillary wrinkled her nose in disgust. "This stuff tastes like the soap I had my mouth washed out with once."

"You've got class, Hillary," he stated wryly, and took the glass from her hand. "I won't ask you what your mouth was washed out for."

"I wouldn't tell you anyway." She smiled, feeling at ease with the casual banter.

"Well, have something, I hate to drink alone."

She reached into the refrigerator and removed a pitcher of orange juice.

"You do live dangerously, don't you?" he commented as she poured. She raised the glass in toast and they returned to the living room.

"I heard you're off to Kansas in the morning," he said as he seated himself on the sofa. Hillary strategically made use of the chair facing him.

"That's right, I'll be home until the day after New Year's."

"Then I'll wish you both a Merry Christmas and a Happy New Year early." He lifted his glass to her. "I'll think of you when the clock strikes twelve."

"I'm sure you'll be too busy to think of me at the stroke of midnight," she retorted, and cursed herself for losing the calm, easy tone.

He smiled and sipped his Scotch. "I'm sure I'll find a minute to spare." Hillary frowned into her glass and refrained from a comment. "I've something for you, Hillary." He rose and, picking up his jacket, removed a small package from its pocket. Hillary stared at it dumbly, then raised her expressive eyes to his.

"Oh, but…I didn't think…that is…I don't have anything for you."

"Don't you?" he asked lazily, and color rushed to her cheeks.

"Really, Bret, I can't take it. I wouldn't feel right."

"Think of it as a gift from the emperor to one of his subjects." He took the glass from her hand and placed the package in its stead.

"You have a long memory." She smiled in spite of herself.

"Like an elephant," he said, then, with a touch of impatience: "Open it. You know you're dying to."

She stared at the package, conceding with a sigh. "I never could resist anything wrapped in Christmas paper." She tore the elegant foil away, then caught her breath as she opened the box and revealed its contents. Earrings of deep sapphire stones blinked up from their backing of velvet.

"They reminded me of your eyes, brilliantly blue and exquisite. It seemed a crime for them to belong to anyone else."

"They're beautiful, really very beautiful," she murmured when she found her voice. Turning her sapphire eyes to his, she added, "You really shouldn't have bought them for me, I—"

"I shouldn't have," he interrupted, "but you're glad I did."

She had to smile. "Yes, I am. It was a lovely thing to do. I don't know how to thank you."

"I do." He drew her from the chair, his arms slipping around her. "This will do nicely." His lips met hers and, after a moment's hesitation, she responded, telling herself she was only showing her gratitude for his thoughtfulness. As the kiss lingered, her gratitude was forgotten. He lifted his mouth, and dazedly she made to move from the warm circle of his arms. "There are two earrings, love." His mouth claimed possession again, now more demanding, and her lips parted beneath his insistence. Her body seemed to melt against his, her arms twining around his neck, fingers tangling in his hair. She was lost in the feel of him, all thought ceasing, her only reality his mouth on hers, and his hard body blending with her yielding softness.

When at last their lips separated, he looked down at her, his eyes darkened with emotion. "It's a pity you've only got two ears." His voice was husky, and his head lowered toward hers.

She dropped her forehead to his chest and attempted to catch her breath. "Please, Bret," she whispered, her hands slipping from his neck to his shoulders. "I can't think when you kiss me."

"Can't you now?" His mouth tarried a moment in her hair. "That's very interesting." He brought his hand under her chin and lifted her face, his eyes moving over her features slowly. "You know, Hillary, that's a very dangerous admission. I'm tempted to press my advantage." He paused, continuing to study the fragile, vulnerable face. "Not this time." He released her, and she checked the impulse to sway toward him. Walking to the table, he downed the remainder of his Scotch and lifted his coat. At the door, he turned, giving her his charming smile. "Merry Christmas, Hillary."

"Merry Christmas, Bret," she whispered at the door he closed behind him.

The air was brisk and cold, carrying the clean, pure scent that meant home, the sky brilliantly blue and naked of clouds. Hillary let herself into the rambling farmhouse and for a moment gave in to memories.

"Tom, what are you doing coming in all the way around the front?" Sarah Baxter bustled from the kitchen, wiping her hands on a full white apron. "Hillary." She stopped as she caught sight of the slim, dark woman in the center of the room. "Well, time's just gotten away from me."

Hillary ran and enveloped her mother in a fierce hug. "Oh, Mom, it's good to be home."

If her mother noticed the desperate tone of Hillary's words, she made no comment, but returned the embrace with equal affection. Standing back, she examined Hillary with a mother's practiced eye. "You could use a few pounds."

"Well, look what the wind blew in all the way from New York City." Tom Baxter entered through the swinging kitchen door and caught Hillary in a close embrace. She breathed deeply, reveling in the smell of fresh hay and horses that clung to him. "Let me look at you." He drew her away and repeated his wife's survey. "What a beautiful sight." He glanced over Hillary's head and smiled at his wife. "We grew a real prize here, didn't we, Sarah?"

Later, Hillary joined her mother in the large kitchen that served the farm. Pots were simmering on a well-used range, filling the air with an irresistible aroma. Hillary allowed her mother to ramble about her brothers and their families, fighting back the deep longing that welled inside her.

Her hand went unconsciously to the blue stones at her ears, and Bret's image flooded her mind, bringing him almost close enough to touch. She averted her face, hoping that the bright tears that sprung to her eyes would not be observed by her mother's sharp glance.

* * *

On Christmas morning, Hillary woke with the sun and snuggled lazily in her childhood bed. She had fallen into the bed late the night before, but, having slipped between the covers, had been unable to sleep. Tossing and turning, she had stared at a dark ceiling until the early hours. Bret had remained in her mind no matter how strenuously she had tried to block him out. His image broke through her defenses like a rock through plate glass. To her despair, she found herself aching to be close to him, the need an ache deep inside her.

In the morning, in the clear light of day, she once more stared at the ceiling. There's nothing I can do, she realized hopelessly. I love him. I love him and I hate him for not loving me back. Oh, he wants me all right—he's made no secret of that—but wanting's not loving. How did it happen? Where did all my defenses go? He's arrogant, she began, mentally ticking off faults in an effort to find an escape hatch in her solitary prison. He's short tempered, demanding, and entirely too self-assured. Why doesn't any of that matter? What's happened to my brain? Why can't I stop thinking about him for more than five minutes at a time?

It's Christmas, she reminded herself, shutting her eyes against his intrusion. I am not going to let Bret Bardoff spoil my day!

Rising, she threw back the quilt, slipped on a fleece robe, and hurried from the room.

The house was already stirring, the quiet morning hush vanishing into activity. For the next hour, the scene around the Christmas tree was filled with gaiety, exclamations for the gifts that were revealed, and the exchange of hugs and kisses.

Later Hillary slipped outside, the thin blanket of frost crunching under her boots as she pulled her father's worn work jacket tighter around her slimness. The air tasted of winter, and the quiet seemed to hang like a soft curtain. Joining her father in the barn, she automatically began to measure out grain, her movements natural, the routine coming back as if she had performed the tasks the day before.

"Just an old farm hand after all, aren't you?" Though the words had been spoken in jest, Hillary halted and looked at her father seriously.

"Yes, I think I am."

"Hillary." His tone softened as he noticed the clouding of her eyes. "What's wrong?"

"I don't know." She let out a deep sigh. "Sometimes New York seems so crowded. I feel closed in."

"We thought you were happy there."

"I was...I am," she amended, and smiled. "It's a very exciting place, busy and filled with so many different kinds of people." She forced back the image of clear gray eyes and strong features. "Sometimes I just miss the quiet, the openness, the peace. I'm being silly." She shook her head and scooped out more grain. "I've been a bit homesick lately, that's all. This layout I just finished was fascinating, but it took a lot out of me." Not the layout, she corrected silently, but the man.

"Hillary, if you're unhappy, if there's anything on your mind, I want to help you."

For a moment, she longed to lean on her father's shoulder and pour out her doubts and frustrations. But what good would it do to burden him? What could he do about the fact that she loved a man who saw her only as a temporary diversion, a marketable commodity for selling magazines? How could she explain that she was unhappy because she had met a man who had broken and captured her heart unknowingly and effortlessly? All these thoughts ran through her brain before she shook her head, giving her father another smile.

"It's nothing. I expect it's just a letdown from finishing the layout. Postphotography depression. I'll go feed the chickens."

The house was soon overflowing with people, echoing with mixed voices, laughter, and the sound of children. Familiar tasks and honest affection helped to erase the ache of emptiness that still haunted her….

When only the echoes of the holiday lingered, Hillary remained downstairs alone, unwilling to seek the comfort of her bed.

Curled in a chair, she stared at the festive lights of the tree, unable to prevent herself from speculating on how Bret had celebrated his holiday. A quiet day with Charlene, perhaps, or a party at the country club? Right now they were probably sitting in front of a roaring fire, and Charlene was snuggled in his arms draped in that beautiful negligee.

A pain shot through her, sharp as the point of an arrow, and she was enveloped by a tortuous combination of raging jealousy and hopeless despair. But the image would not fade.

The days at home went quickly. They were good days, following a soothing routine that Hillary dropped into gratefully. Kansas wind blew away a portion of her depression. She took long, quiet walks, gazing out at the rolling hills and acres of winter wheat.

People from the city would never understand, she mused. How could they comprehend this? Her arms were lifted wide as she spun in a circle. In their elegant apartments looking out at steel and concrete they could never feel the exuberation of being a part of the land. The land; she surveyed its infinity with wondering eyes. The land is indomitable; the land is forever. There had been Indians here, and plainsmen and pioneers and farmers. They came and went, lived and died, but the land lived on. And when she was gone, and another generation born, wheat would still wave in the bright summer sun. The land gave them what they needed, rich and fertile, generously giving birth to acres of wheat year after year, asking only for honest labor in return.

And I love it, she reflected, hugging herself tightly. I love the feel of it in my hands and under my bare feet in the summer. I love the rich, clean smell of it. I suppose, for all my acquired sophistication, I'm still just a farm girl. She retraced her steps toward the house. What am I going to do about it? I have a career; I have a place in New York as well. I'm twenty-four. I can't just throw in the towel and come back to live on the farm. No. She shook her head vigorously, sending her hair swirling in a black mist. I've got to go back and do what I'm qualified to do. Firmly, she ignored the small voice that asserted her decision was influenced by another resident of New York.

The phone jangled on the wall as she entered the house, and, slipping off her jacket, she lifted it.

"Hello."

"Hello, Hillary."

"Bret?" She had not known pain could come so swiftly at the sound of a voice.

"Very good." She heard the familiar mockery and pressed her forehead to the wall. "How are you?"

"Fine, I'm just fine." She groped for some small island of composure. "I...I didn't expect to hear from you. Is there a problem?"

"Problem?" he returned in a voice that mirrored his smile. "No permanent one in any case. I thought you might be needing a reminder of New York about now. We wouldn't want you to forget to come back."

"No, I haven't forgotten." Taking a deep breath, she made her voice lightly professional. "Have you something in mind for me?"

"In mind? You might say I had one or two things in mind." There was a slight pause before he continued. "Anxious to get back to work?"

"Uh, yes, yes, I am. I wouldn't want to get stale."

"I see."

You couldn't see through a chain-link fence, she thought with growing frustration.

"We'll see what we can do when you get back. It would be foolish not to put your talents to use." He spoke absently, as though his mind was already formulating a suitable project.

"I'm sure you'll think of something advantageous for both of us," she stated, trying to emulate his businesslike tone.

"Mmm, you'll be back at the end of the week?"

"Yes, on the second."

"I'll be in touch. Keep your calendar clear." The order was casual, confident, and brisk. "We'll get you in front of the camera again, if that's what you want."

"All right. I...well...thanks for calling."

"My pleasure. I'll see you when you get back."

"Yes. Bret…" She searched for something to say, wanting to cling to the small contact, perhaps just to hear him say her name one more time.

"Yes?"

"Nothing, nothing." Shutting her eyes, she cursed her lack of imagination. "I'll wait to hear from you."

"Fine." He paused a moment, and his voice softened. "Have a good time at home, Hillary."

Chapter 6

The first thing Hillary did upon returning to her New York apartment was to put a call through to Larry. When greeted by a feminine voice, she hesitated, then apologized.

"Sorry, I must have the wrong number…"

"Hillary?" the voice interrupted. "It's June."

"June?" she repeated, confused, then added quickly. "How are you? How were your holidays?"

"Terrific to both questions. Larry told me you went home. Did you have a good time?"

"Yes, I did. It's always good to get home again."

"Hang on a minute. I'll get Larry."

"Oh, well, no, I'll…"

Larry's voice broke into her protestations. She immediately launched into an apology, telling him she would call back.

"Don't be dumb, Hil, June's just helping me sort out my old photography magazines."

It occurred to Hillary that their relationship must be moving along at light speed for Larry to allow June to get her hands on his precious magazines. "I just wanted you to know I was back," she said aloud. "Just in case anything comes up."

"Mmm, well, I guess you really should get in touch with Bret." Larry considered. "You're still under contract. Why don't you give him a call?"

"I won't worry about it," she returned, striving to keep her tone casual. "I told him I'd be back after the first." Her voice dropped. "He knows where to find me."

Several days passed before Bret contacted Hillary. Much of the interim she spent at home because of the snow, which seemed to fall unceasingly over the city, alternating with a penetrating, bitter sleet. The confinement, coming on the heels of the open freedom she had experienced in Kansas, played havoc with her nerves, and she found herself staring down from her window at ice-covered sidewalks with increasing despair.

One evening, as the sky dropped the unwelcome gift of freezing rain, Lisa arranged to have dinner and spend a few hours in Hillary's company. Standing in the kitchen, Hillary was separating a small head of lettuce when the phone rang. Looking down at her wet, leaf-filled hands, she rubbed her nose on her shoulder and asked Lisa to answer the ring.

Lifting the receiver, Lisa spoke into it in her most formal voice. "Miss Hillary Baxter's residence, Lisa MacDonald speaking. Miss Baxter will be with you as soon as she gets her hands out of the lettuce."

"Lisa." Hillary laughed as she hurried into the room. "I just can't trust you to do anything."

"It's all right," she announced loudly, holding out the receiver. "It's only an incredibly sexy male voice."

"Thanks," Hillary returned with deep sincerity, and rescued the phone. "Go, you're banished back into the kitchen." Pulling a face, Lisa retreated, and Hillary gave her attention to her caller. "Hello, don't mind my friend, she's just crazy."

"On the contrary, that's the most interesting conversation I've had all day."

"Bret?" Until that moment, Hillary had not realized how much she needed to hear his voice.

"Right the first time." She could almost see the slow smile spread across his features. "Welcome back to the concrete jungle, Hillary. How was Kansas?"

"Fine," she stammered. "It was just fine."

"Mmm, how illuminating. Did you enjoy your Christmas?"

"Yes, very much." Struggling to regain the composure that had fled at the sound of his voice, she spoke quickly. "And you? Did you have a nice holiday?"

"Delightful, though I'm sure it was a great deal quieter than yours."

"Different anyway," Hillary rejoined, annoyed.

"Ah, well, that's behind us now. Actually, I'm calling about this weekend."

"Weekend?" Hillary repeated dumbly.

"Yes, a trip to the mountains."

"Mountains?"

"You sound like a parrot," he said shortly. "Do you have anything important scheduled from Friday through Sunday?"

"Well, I…ah…"

"Lord, what an astute conversationalist you are." His voice reflected growing annoyance.

Swallowing, she attempted to be more precise. "No. That is, nothing essential. I—"

"Good," he interrupted. "Ever been skiing?"

"In Kansas?" she retorted, regaining her balance. "I believe mountains are rather essential for skiing."

"So they are," he agreed absently. "Well, no matter. I had an idea for some pictures of a lovely lady frolicking in the snow. I've a lodge in the Adirondacks near Lake George. It'll make a nice setting. We can combine business with pleasure."

"We?" Hillary murmured weakly.

"No need for panic," he assured her, his words heavy with mockery. "I'm not abducting you to the wilderness to ravish you, although the idea does have some interesting angles." He paused, then laughed outright. "I can feel you blushing right through the phone."

"Very funny," she retorted, infuriated that he could read her so easily. "I'm beginning to recall an urgent engagement for the weekend, so—"

"Hold on, Hillary," he interrupted again, his words suddenly brooking no argument. "You're under contract. My rights hold for a couple more months. You wanted to get back to work; I'm putting you back to work."

"Yes, but—"

"Read the fine print if you like, but keep this weekend clear. And relax," he continued as she remained silent.

"You'll be well protected from my dishonorable advances. Larry and June will be coming with us. Bud Lewis, my assistant art director, will be joining us later."

"Oh," she replied inadequately, unsure whether she was relieved or disappointed.

"I—the magazine, that is—will provide you with suitable snow gear. I'll pick you up at seven-thirty Friday morning. Be packed and ready."

"Yes, but—" Hillary stared at the dead receiver with a mixture of annoyance and trepidation. He had not given her the opportunity to ask questions or formulate a reasonable excuse to decline. Hanging up, she turned around, her face a study in bewilderment.

"What was all that? You look positively stunned." Lisa regarded her friend from the kitchen doorway.

"I'm going to the mountains for the weekend," she answered slowly, as if to herself.

"The mountains?" Lisa repeated. "With the owner of that fascinating voice?"

Hillary snapped back and attempted to sound casual. "It's just an assignment. That was Bret Bardoff. There'll be plenty of others along," she added.

Friday morning dawned clear and cloudless and cold. Hillary was packed and ready as instructed, sipping a second cup of tea, when the doorbell sounded.

"Good morning, Hillary," Bret said as she opened the door. "Ready to brave the uncharted wilderness?"

He looked quite capable of doing just that in a hip-length sheepskin jacket, heavy corded jeans, and sturdy boots. Now he appeared rugged, not the cool, calculating businessman to whom she had grown accustomed.

Gripping the doorknob tightly, she maintained a cool exterior and invited him in.

Assuring him she was quite ready, she walked away to place the empty cup in the sink and fetch her coat. Slipping her coat over her sweater and jeans, she pulled a dark brown ski hat over her hair. Bret looked on silently.

"I'm ready." Suddenly aware of his intense regard, she moistened her lips nervously with her tongue. "Shall we go?"

Inclining his head, he bent to pick up the case she had waiting beside the sofa, his movements coinciding with hers. Straightening with a jerk, she flushed awkwardly. His brow lifted with his smile as he captured her hand and led her to the door.

They soon left the city as Bret directed the Mercedes north. He drove quickly and skillfully along the Hudson, keeping up a light conversation. Hillary found herself relaxing in the warm interior, forgetting her usual inhibition at being in close contact with the man who stirred her senses. As they began to pass through small towns and villages, she could hardly believe they were still in New York, her experience with the state having been limited exclusively to Manhattan and the surrounding area. Ingenuously, she voiced her thoughts, pulling off her hat and shaking out her rich fall of hair.

"There's more in New York than skyscrapers," he informed her with a crooked smile. "Mountains, valleys, forests—it has a bit of everything. I suppose it's time we changed your impression."

"I've never thought of it except as a place to work," she admitted, shifting in her seat to face him more directly. "Noisy, busy, and undeniably exciting, but draining at times because it's always moving and never seems to sleep.

It always makes the sound of the silence at home that much more precious."

"And Kansas is still home, isn't it?" He seemed to be thinking of something else as he asked, his expression brooding on the road ahead. Hillary frowned at his change of mood, then gave her attention to the scenery without answering.

They continued northward, and she lost track of time, intoxicated by the newness and beauty of her surroundings. At her first glimpse of the Catskills, she let out a small cry of pleasure, spontaneously tugging on Bret's arm and pointing. "Oh, look—mountains!"

Turning her eyes from the view, she gave him her special smile. He returned the smile, and her heart did a series of acrobatics. She turned back to the scene out the window. "I suppose I must seem terribly foolish, but when you've only known acres of wheat and rolling hills, this is quite a revelation."

"Not foolish, Hillary." His voice was gentle, and she turned to face him, surprised at the unfamiliar tone. "I find you utterly charming."

Picking up her hand, he turned it upward and kissed her palm, sending shooting arrows of flame up her arm and down to her stomach. Dealing with his mockery and amusement was one thing, she pondered dizzily, she was quite used to that by now. But these occasional gentle moods turned her inside out, making her spark like a lighted match. This man was dangerous, she concluded, very dangerous. Somehow she must build up an impregnable defense against him. But how? How could she fight both him and the part of herself that wanted only to surrender?

"I could do with some coffee," Bret said suddenly, bringing Hillary back from her self-interrogation. "How about you?" He turned to her and smiled. "Want some tea?"

"Sure," she answered casually.

The Mercedes rolled into the small village of Catskill and Bret parked in front of a cafe. He opened his door and stepped from the car, and she quickly followed suit before he circled the front and joined her on the curb. Her eyes were fixed on the overpowering encircling mountains.

"They look higher than they are," Bret commented. "Their bases are only a few hundred feet above sea level. I'd love to see the expression on that beautiful face of yours when you encounter the Rockies or the Alps."

Interlocking his hand with hers, he led her out of the cold and into the warmth of the cafe. When the small table was between them, Hillary shrugged out of the confines of her coat, concentrating on the view, attempting to erect a wall of defense between herself and Bret.

"Coffee for me and tea for the lady. Are you hungry, Hillary?"

"What? Oh, no,…well, yes, actually a little." She grinned, remembering the lack of breakfast that morning.

"They serve an outstanding coffee cake here." He ordered two slices before Hillary could protest.

"I don't usually eat that kind of thing." She frowned, thinking of the half grapefruit she had had in mind.

"Hillary, darling," Bret broke in with exaggerated patience. "One slice of cake is hardly likely to affect your figure. In any case," he added with irritating bluntness, "a few pounds wouldn't hurt you."

"Really," she retorted, chin rising with indignation. "I haven't had any complaints so far."

"I'm sure you haven't, and you'll get none from me. I've become quite enchanted with tall, willowy women. Though," he continued, reaching over to brush a loose strand of hair from her face, "the air of frailty is sometimes disconcerting."

Hillary decided to ignore both gesture and remark. "I don't know when I've enjoyed a drive more," she said, determined to remain casual. "How much farther do we have to go?"

"We're at the halfway point." Bret added cream to his coffee. "We should arrive around noon."

"How is everyone else coming? I mean, are they driving together?"

"Larry and June are coming up together." He smiled and ate a forkful of cake. "I should say Larry and June are accompanying Larry's equipment. I'm amazed he allowed her to travel in the same car with his precious cameras and lenses."

"Are you?" Hillary questioned, grinning into her tea.

"I suppose I shouldn't be," he admitted wryly. "I have noticed our favorite photographer's increasing preoccupation with my secretary. He seemed inordinately pleased to have her company on the drive."

"When I phoned him the other day, he was actually allowing her to sort out his photography magazines." Hillary's voice was tinged with disbelief. "That's tantamount to a bethrothal." She gestured with her fork. "It might even be binding. I'm not sure of the law. I still can't believe it." She swallowed a piece of cake and looked at Bret in amazement. "Larry's actually serious about a flesh-and-blood woman."

"It happens to the best of us, love," Bret agreed gently. But would it ever to Bret? She could not meet his eyes.

* * *

On the road once more, Hillary contented herself with the scenery as Bret kept up a general conversation. The warmth of the Mercedes' interior and its smooth, steady ride had lulled her into a state of deep relaxation, and leaning back, she closed her suddenly heavy lids as they crossed the Mohawk River. Bret's deep voice increased her peaceful mood, and she murmured absently in response until she heard no more.

Hillary stirred restlessly as the change in road surface disturbed her slumber. Her eyes blinked open, and after a moment's blankness, reality returned. Her head was nestled against his shoulder, and, sitting up quickly, she turned her sleep-flushed face and heavy dark eyes to him.

"Oh, I'm sorry. Did I fall asleep?"

"You might say that," he said, glancing over as she pushed at tumbled hair. "You've been unconscious for an hour."

"Hour?" she repeated, attempting to clear the cobwebs. "Where are we?" she mumbled, gazing around her. "What did I miss?"

"Everything from Schenectady on, and we're on the road that leads to my lodge."

"Oh, it's beautiful." She came quickly awake as she focused on her surroundings.

The narrow road they traveled was flanked with snow-covered trees and rugged outcroppings of rock. Snow draped the green needles of pine, and what would have been dark, empty branches glistened with icicles and pure, sparkling white. Dense and thick, they seemed to be everywhere, rising majestically from a brilliant virgin blanket.

"They're so many." She scooted in her seat to experiment with the view from Bret's window, her knees brushing his thigh.

"The forest is full of them."

"Don't make fun." She punched his shoulder and continued to stare. "This is all new to me."

"I'm not making fun," he said, rubbing his shoulder with exaggerated care. "I'm delighted with your enthusiasm."

The car halted, and Hillary turned from Bret to look out the front window of the car. With a cry of pleasure, she spotted the large A-frame dwelling nestled in a small clearing so much a part of the surroundings it might have grown there. Picture windows gleamed and glistened in the filtered sunlight.

"Come get a closer look," Bret invited, stepping from the car. He held his hand out to her, and she slipped hers into his grasp as they began to crunch through the untouched snow. An ice-crusted stream tumbled swiftly on the far side of the house and, like a child wishing to share a new toy, Hillary pulled Bret toward it.

"How marvelous, how absolutely marvelous," she proclaimed, watching water force its way over rocks, its harsh whisper the only disturbance of peace. "What a fabulous place." She made a slow circle. "It's so wild and powerful, so wonderfully untouched and primitive."

Bret's eyes followed her survey before staring off through a dense outcropping of trees. "Sometimes I escape here, when my office begins to close in on me. There's such blessed peace—no urgent meetings, no deadlines, no responsibilities."

Hillary regarded him in open amazement. She had never imagined his needing to escape from anything or seeking deliberate solitude in a place so far from the city and its comforts and pleasures. To her, Bret Bardoff had represented the epitome of the efficient businessman, with employees rushing to do his bidding at the snap of his imperious finger. Now, she began to see another aspect of his nature, and she found the knowledge brought her a swift rush of pleasure.

He turned and encountered her stare, locking her eyes to his with a force that captured her breath. "It's also quite isolated," he added, in such a swift change of mood it took her a moment to react.

Blue eyes deepened and widened and she looked away, staring at the trees and rocks. She was here in the middle of nowhere, she realized, unconsciously chewing on her lip. He had told her the others were coming, but there was only his word. She had not thought to check with Larry. What if he had made the whole thing up? She would be trapped with him, completely alone. What would she do if…

"Keep calm, Hillary." Bret laughed wryly. "I haven't kidnapped you, the others will be along to protect you." He had deliberately provoked her reaction, and Hillary whirled to tell him what she thought of him, but he went on before she could speak, "That is, if they can find the place," he muttered, his brow creasing before his features settled in a wide smile. "It would be a shame if my directions were inadequate, wouldn't it?" Taking her hand once more, he led a confused and uneasy Hillary toward the lodge.

The interior was spacious, with wide, full windows bringing the mountains inside. The high ceiling with exposed beams added to the openness. Rough wooden stairs led to a balcony that ran the length of the living room. A stone fireplace commanded an entire wall, with furniture arranged strategically around it. Oval braid rugs graced the dark pine floor, their bright colors the perfect accent for the rustic, wood-dominated room.

"It's charming," Hillary said with delight as she gazed about her. She walked over to the huge expanse of glass. "You can stand here and be inside and out at the same time."

"I've often felt that way myself," Bret agreed, moving to join her and slipping her coat from her shoulders. "What is that scent you wear?" he murmured, his fingers massaging the back of her neck, their strength throbbing through her. "It's always the same, very delicate and appealing."

"It's, ah, it's apple blossom." She swallowed and kept her eyes glued to the window.

"Mmm, you mustn't change it, it suits you.... I'm starving," he announced suddenly, turning her to face him. "How about opening a can or something, and I'll start the fire? The kitchen's well stocked. You should be able to find something to ward off starvation."

"All right," she agreed, smiling. "We wouldn't want you to fade away. Where's the kitchen?" He pointed, and leaving him still standing by the window, she set off in the direction he indicated.

The kitchen was full of old-fashioned charm, with a small brick fireplace of its own and copper-bottomed pots hanging along the wall. The stove itself Hillary regarded doubtfully, thinking it resembled something her grandmother might have slaved over, until she observed that it had been adapted for modern use. The large pantry was well stocked, and she located enough cans for an adequate midday meal. Not precisely a gourmet feast, she reflected as she opened a can of soup, but it will have to do. She was spooning soup into a pan when she heard Bret's footsteps behind her.

"That was quick!" she exclaimed. "You must have been a terrific Boy Scout."

"It's a habit of mine to set the fire before I leave," he explained, standing behind her as she worked. "That way all I have to do is open the flue and light a match."

"How disgustingly organized," Hillary observed with a sniff, and switched the flame under the soup.

"Ah, ambrosia," he proclaimed, slipping his arms around her waist. "Are you a good cook, Hillary?"

The hard body pressed into her back was very distracting. She struggled to remain cool. "Anyone can open a can of soup." The last word caught in her throat as his hand reached up to part the dark curtain of her hair, his lips warm as they brushed the back of her neck. "I'd better make some coffee." She attempted to slip away, but his arms maintained possession, his mouth roaming over her vulnerable skin. "I thought you were hungry." The words came out in a babbling rush as her knees melted, and she leaned back against him helplessly for support.

"Oh, I am," he whispered, his teeth nibbling at her ear. "Ravenous."

He buried his face in the curve of her neck, and the room swayed as his hands slid upward under her sweater.

"Bret, don't," she moaned as a rush of desire swept over her, and she struggled to escape before she was lost.

He muttered savagely and spun her around, roughly crushing her lips under his.

Though he had kissed her before, demanding, arousing

kisses, there had always been a measure of control in his lovemaking. Now it was as if the wildness of their surroundings had entered him. Like a man whose control has been too tightly bound, he assaulted her mouth, parting hers and taking possession. His hands pressed her hips against him, molding them together into one form. She was drowning in his explosion of passion, clinging to him as his hands roamed over her, seeking, demanding, receiving. The fire of his need ignited hers, and she gave herself without reservation, straining against him, wanting only to plunge deeper into the heat.

The sound of a car pulling up outside brought a muffled curse from Bret. Lifting his mouth from hers, he rested his chin on top of her head and sighed.

"They found us, Hillary. Better open another can."

Chapter 7

Voices drifted through the building, June's laughter and Larry's raised tones in some shared joke. Bret moved off to greet them, leaving Hillary battling to regain some small thread of composure. The urgent demand of Bret's lovemaking had awakened a wild, primitive response in her. She was acutely aware that, had they been left undisturbed, he would not have held back, and she would not have protested. The need had been too vital, too consuming. The swift beginning and sudden end of the contact left her trembling and unsteady. Pressing hands to burning cheeks, she went back to the stove, to attend to soup and coffee, hoping the simple mechanical tasks would restore her equilibrium.

"So, he's got you slaving away already." June entered the kitchen, arms ladened with a large paper bag. "Isn't that just like a man?"

"Hi." Hillary turned around, showing a fairly normal countenance. "It appears we've both been put in our places. What's in the bag?"

"Supplies for the long, snowbound weekend." Unpacking the bag, June revealed milk, cheese, and other fresh goods.

"Always efficient," Hillary stated, and, feeling the tension melt away, flashed her smile.

"It is difficult being perfect," June agreed with a sigh. "But some of us are simply born that way."

Meal preparations complete, they carried bowls and plates into the adjoining room to a large, rectangular wooden table with long benches running along each side. The group devoured the simple meal as though months had passed since they had seen a crust of bread. Mirroring Bret's now casual manner was at first difficult, but, summoning all her pride, Hillary joined in the table talk, meeting his occasional comments with an easy smile.

She retreated with June upstairs as the men launched into a technical discussion on the type of pictures required, and found the room they would share as charmingly rustic as the remainder of the house. The light, airy room with a breathtaking view of forest and mountains held two twin beds covered in patchwork quilts. Again wood predominated, the high sloping ceiling adding to the space. Brass lamps ensured soft lighting once the sun had descended behind the peaks outside.

Hillary busied herself with the case containing her wardrobe for the photo session as June threw herself heavily on a bed.

"Isn't this place fantastic?" Stretching her arms to the ceiling, June heaved a deep sigh of contentment. "Far from the maddening crowd and typewriters and telephones. Maybe it'll snow like crazy, and we'll be here until spring."

"We'd only be able to stick it out if Larry brought enough film for a couple of months. Otherwise, he'd go into withdrawal," Hillary commented. Removing a red parka and bibbed ski pants from the case, she studied them with a professional eye. "Well, this should stand out in the snow."

"If we painted your nose yellow, you'd look like a very large cardinal," June commented, clasping her hands behind her head. "That color will look marvelous on you. With your hair and complexion, and the snow as a backdrop, you'll be smashing. The boss never makes a mistake."

The sound of a car caught their attention, and they moved to the window looking down as Bud Lewis assisted Charlene from the vehicle. "Well—" June sighed and grimaced at Hillary "—maybe one."

Stunned, Hillary stared at the top of Charlene's glossy red head. "I didn't…Bret didn't tell me Charlene was coming." Infuriated by the intrusion on her weekend, Hillary turned from the window and busied her hands with unpacking.

"Unless I'm very much mistaken, he didn't know." Scowling, June turned and leaned against the windowsill. "Maybe he'll toss her out in the snow."

"Maybe," Hillary countered, relieving some of her frustration by slamming the top of her suitcase, "he'll be glad to see her."

"Well, we won't find out anything standing around up here." June started toward the door, grabbing Hillary's arm along the way. "Come on, let's go see."

Charlene's voice drifted to Hillary as she descended the stairs. "You really don't mind that I came to keep you company, do you, Bret? I thought it would be such a lovely surprise."

Hillary entered the room in time to see Bret's shrug. He was seated on a love seat in front of the blazing fire, Charlene's arm tucked possessively through his. "I didn't think the mountains were your style, Charlene." He gave her a mild smile. "If you'd wanted to come, you should have asked instead of spinning a tale to Bud about my wanting him to drive you up."

"Oh, but, darling, it was just a little fib." Tilting her head, she fluttered darkened lashes. "A little intrigue is so amusing."

"Let's hope your 'little intrigue' doesn't lead you to 'a lot of boredom.' We're a long way from Manhattan."

"I'm never bored with you."

Soft and coaxing, the voice grated on Hillary's nerves. Perhaps she made some small sound of annoyance for Bret's eyes shifted to where she stood with June in the doorway. Charlene followed his gaze, her lips tightening for a moment before settling into a vague smile.

There followed an unenthusiastic exchange of greetings. Opting for distance, Hillary seated herself across the room with Bud as Charlene again gave Bret her full attention.

"I thought we'd never get here," Charlene complained with a petulant pout. "Why you would own a place in this godforsaken wilderness is beyond me, darling." She glanced up at Bret with cool green eyes. "All this snow, and nothing but trees and rocks, and so cold." With a delicate shiver, she huddled against him. "Whatever do you find to do up here all alone?"

"I manage to find diversions," Bret drawled, and lit a cigarette. "And I'm never alone—the mountains are teeming with life." He gestured toward the window. "There are squirrels, chipmunks, rabbits, foxes—all manner of small animal life."

"That's not precisely what I meant by company," Charlene murmured, using her most seductive voice. Bret granted her a faint smile.

"Perhaps not, but I find them entertaining and undemanding. I've often seen deer pass by as I stood by that window, and bear."

"Bears?" Charlene exclaimed, and tightened her hold on his arm. "How dreadful."

"Real bears?" Hillary demanded, eyes bright with adventure. "Oh, what kind? Those huge grizzlies?"

"Black bear, Hillary," he corrected, smiling at her reaction. "But big enough just the same. And safely in hibernation at the moment," he added with a glance at Charlene.

"Thank heaven," she breathed with genuine feeling.

"Hillary's quite taken to the mountains, haven't you?"

"They're fabulous," she agreed with enthusiasm. "So wild and untamed. All this must look nearly the same as it did a century ago, unspoiled by buildings and housing developments. Nothing but undisturbed nature for miles and miles."

"My, my, you are enthusiastic," Charlene observed.

Hillary shot her a deadly glance.

"Hillary grew up on a farm in Kansas," Bret explained, observing danger signals in dark blue eyes. "She'd never seen mountains before."

"How quaint," Charlene murmured, lips curving in a smile. "They grow wheat or something there, don't they? I would imagine you're quite accustomed to primitive conditions coming from a little farm."

The superior tone had Hillary bristling with anger, her rising temper reflected in her voice. "The farm is hardly little or primitive, Miss Mason. Impossible, I suppose, for one of your background to visualize the eternity of wheat, the miles of gently rolling hills. Not as sophisticated as New York, perhaps, but hardly prehistoric. We even manage to have hot and cold running water right inside the house most of the time. There are those who appreciate the land and respect it in all forms."

"You must be quite the outdoor girl," Charlene said in a bored voice. "I happen to prefer the comforts and culture of the city."

"I think I'll take a walk before it gets dark." Hillary rose quickly, needing to put some distance between herself and the other woman before her temper was irrevocably lost.

"I'll go with you." Bud stood, moving to join her as she slipped on her outdoor clothing. "I've been cooped up with that woman all day," he whispered with a conspirator's smile. "I think the fresh air will do me a world of good."

Hillary's laughter floated through the room as she strolled through the door, arm in arm with Bud. She was oblivious of the frown that darkened the gray eyes that followed her.

Once outside, the two breathed deeply, then giggled like children at their private joke. By mutual consent, they headed for the stream, following its tumbling progress downstream as they ambled deeper into the forest. Sunlight winked sporadically through the trees, glistening on the velvet snow. Bud's easy conversation soothed Hillary's ruffled spirits.

They stopped and rested on a mound of rock for a moment of companionable silence.

"This is nice," Bud said simply, and Hillary made a small sound signifying both pleasure and agreement. "I begin to feel human again," he added with a wink. "That woman is hard to take. I can't imagine what the boss sees in her."

Hillary grinned. "Isn't it strange that I agree with you?"

They walked home in the subtle change of light that signified encroaching dusk. Again, they followed the stream, easily retracing the footsteps they had left in the pure, white snow. They were laughing companionably as they entered the A-frame.

"Don't either of you have more sense than to wander about the mountains after dark?" Bret asked them, scowling.

"Dark? Don't be silly." Hillary hopped on one foot as she pried off a boot. "We only followed the stream a little way, and it's barely dusk." Losing her balance, she collided with Bud, who slipped an arm around her waist to right her, keeping it there while she struggled with her other boot.

"We left a trail in the snow," Bud stated with a grin. "Better than bread crumbs."

"Dusk turns to dark quickly, and there's no moon tonight," Bret said. "It's a simple matter to get lost."

"Well, we're back, and we didn't," Hillary told him. "No need for a search party or a flask of brandy. Where's June?"

"In the kitchen, starting dinner."

"I better go help then, hadn't I?" She gave him a radiant smile and brushed past them, leaving Bud to deal with his boss's temper.

"A woman's work is never done," Hillary observed with a sigh as she entered the kitchen.

"Tell that to Miss Nose-in-the-Air." June wrinkled her

own as she unwrapped the steaks. "She was so fatigued from the arduous drive—" June placed a dramatic hand to her forehead "—she simply had to lie down before dinner."

"That's a blessing. Anyway," Hillary went on as she joined in the meal preparation, "who voted us in charge of kitchen duty? I'm quite sure it's not in my contract."

"I did."

"Voluntarily?"

"It's like this," June explained, searching through cupboards. "I've had a small example of Larry's talents, culinary talents, and I don't want another bout of ptomaine. The boss even makes lousy coffee. And as for Bud—well, he might be Chef Boy-Ar-Dee as far as I know, but I was unwilling to take the chance."

"I see what you mean."

In easy companionship they prepared the meal. The kitchen came to life with the clatter of dishes and sizzling of meat. Larry materialized in the doorway, breathing deeply.

"Ah, exquisite torture. I'm starving," he announced. "How much longer?"

"Here." June thrust a stack of dishes in his hands. "Go set the table—it'll keep your mind off your stomach."

"I knew I should have stayed out of here." Grumbling, he vanished into the adjoining room.

"I guess it's the mountain air," Hillary commented between bites as the group sat around the long table. "I'm absolutely ravenous."

The slow smile that drifted across Bret's face brought back the memory of the earlier scene in the kitchen, and warm color seeped into her cheeks. Picking up her glass containing a red wine Bret had produced from some mysterious place, she took a deep, impulsive swallow and firmly gave her attention to the meal.

The clearing up was confused and disorganized as the men, through design or innocence, served only to get in the way, causing June to throw up her hands and order them away.

"I'm the boss," Bret reminded her. "I'm supposed to give the orders."

"Not until Monday," June returned, giving him a firm shove. She watched with a raised brow as Charlene floated with him.

"Just as well," she observed, turning back to Hillary. "I probably couldn't have prevented myself from drowning her in the sink."

The party later spread out with lazy contentment in the living room. Refusing Bret's offer of brandy, Hillary settled herself on a low stool near the fire. She watched the dancing flames, caught up in their images, unaware of the picture she created, cheeks and hair glowing with flickering light, eyes soft and dreamy. Her mind floated, only a small portion of it registering the quiet hum of conversation, the occasional clink of glass. Elbows on knees, head on palms, she drifted with the fire's magic away from conscious thought.

"Are you hypnotized by the flames, Hillary?" Bret's lean form eased down beside her as he stretched out on the hearth rug. Tossed suddenly into reality, she started at his voice, then smiled as she brushed at her hair.

"Yes, I am. There're pictures there if you look for them," she answered, inclining her head toward the blaze. "There's a castle there with turrets all around, and there's a horse with his mane lifted in the wind."

"There's an old man sitting in a rocker," Bret said softly, and she turned to stare at him, surprised that he had seen the image too. He returned her look, with the intensity of an embrace, and she rose, flustered by the weakness his gaze could evoke.

"It's been a long day," she announced, avoiding his eyes. "I think I'll go up to bed. I don't want Larry to complain that I look washed out in the morning."

Calling her good nights, she went swiftly from the room without giving Bret the opportunity to comment.

The room was dim in early morning light when she awoke. She stretched her arms to the ceiling and sat up, knowing sleep was finished. When she had slipped under the blankets the night before, her emotions had been in turmoil, and she had been convinced the hours would be spent tossing and turning. She was amazed that she had slept not only immediately but deeply, and the mood with which she greeted the new day was cheerful.

June was still huddled under her quilt, the steady rhythm of her breathing the only sound in the absolute silence. Easing from the bed, Hillary began to dress quietly. She tugged a heavy sweater in muted greens over her head, mating it with forest green cords that fit with slim assurance. Forgoing makeup, she donned the snowsuit Bret had provided, pulling the matching ski cap over her hair.

Creeping down the stairs, she listened for the sounds of morning stirring, but the house remained heavy in slumber. Pulling on boots and gloves, Hillary stepped outside into the cold, clear sunlight.

The woods were silent, and she looked about her at the

solitude. It was as if time had stopped—the mountains were a magic fairyland without human habitation. Her companions were the majestic pines, robed in glistening ermine, their tangy scent permeating the air.

"I'm alone," she said aloud, flinging out her arms. "There's not another soul in the entire world." She raced through the snow, drunk with power and liberation. "I'm free!" She tossed snow high above her head, whirling in dizzying circles before flinging herself into the cold snow.

Once more, she contemplated the white-topped mountains and dense trees, realizing her heart had expanded and made room for a new love. She was in love with the mountains as she was with the free-flowing wheat fields. The new and old love filled her with jubilation. Scrambling up, she sped once more through the snow, kicking up mists of white before she stopped and fell on her back, the soft surface yielding beneath her. She lay, spread-eagle, staring up at the sky until a face moved into her view, gray eyes laughing down at her.

"What are you doing, Hillary?"

"Making an angel," she informed him, returning his smile. "You see, you fall down, and then you move your arms and legs like this." She demonstrated, and her smile faded. "The trick is to get up without making a mess of it. It requires tremendous ability and perfect balance." Sitting up carefully, she put her weight on her feet and started to stand, teetering on her heels. "Give me a hand," she demanded. "I'm out of practice." Grabbing his arm, she jumped clear, then turned back to regard her handiwork. "You see," she stated with arrogant pride, "an angel."

"Beautiful," he agreed. "You're very talented."

"Yes, I know. I didn't think anyone else was up," she added, brushing snow from her bottom.

"I saw you dancing in the snow from my window. What game were you playing?"

"That I was alone in all this." She whirled in circles, arms extended.

"You're never alone up here. Look." He pointed into the woods, and her eyes widened at the large buck that stared back at her, his rack adorning his head like a crown.

"He's magnificent." As if conscious of her admiration, the stag lifted his head before he melted into the cover of the woods. "Oh, I'm in love!" she exclaimed, racing across the snow. "I'm absolutely madly in love with this place. Who needs a man when you've got all this?"

"Oh, really?" A snowball thudded against the back of her head, and she turned to stare at him narrowly.

"You know, of course, this means war."

She scooped up a handful of snow, balling it swiftly and hurling it back at him. They exchanged fire, snow landing on target as often as it missed, until he closed the gap between them, and she engaged in a strategic retreat. Her flight was interrupted as he caught her, tossing her down and rolling on top of her. Her cheeks glowed with the cold, her eyes sparkled with laughter, as she tried to catch her breath.

"All right, you win, you win."

"Yes, I did," he agreed. "And to the victor go the spoils." He touched her mouth with his, his lips moving with light sensuality, stilling her laughter. "I always win sooner or later," he murmured, kissing her eyes closed. "We don't do this nearly often enough," he muttered against her mouth, deepening the kiss until her senses whirled. "You've snow all over your face." His mouth roamed to her cheek, his tongue gently removing flakes, instilling her with exquisite terror. "Oh, Hillary, what a delectable creature you are." Lifting his face, he stared into her wide, anxious eyes. He let out a deep breath and brushed the remaining snow from her cheeks with his hand. "The others should be stirring about now. Let's go have some breakfast."

"Stand over there, Hil." Hillary was once more out in the snow, but this time it was Larry and his camera joining her.

He had been taking pictures for what seemed to Hillary hours. Fervently, she wished the session would end, her mind lingering on the thought of steaming chocolate in front of the fire.

"All right, Hillary, come back to earth. You're supposed to be having fun, not floating in a daze."

"I hope your lenses freeze." She sent him a brilliant smile.

"Aw, cut it out, Hil," he mumbled, continuing to crouch around her.

"That'll do," he announced at last, and she fell over backwards in a mock faint. Larry leaned over her, taking still another picture. Shutting her eyes in amusement, she laughed up at him.

"Are the sessions getting longer, Larry, or is it just me?"

"It's you," he answered, shaking his head, allowing the camera to dangle by its strap. "You're over the hill, past your prime. It's all downhill from here."

"I'll show you who's over the hill." Hillary scrambled up, grabbing a handful of snow.

"No, Hil." Placing a protective hand over his camera,

Larry backed away. "Remember my camera, don't lose control." Turning, he ran through the snow toward the lodge.

"Past my prime, am I?" The snowball hit him full on the back as Hillary gave chase. Catching him, she leaped on his back, beating him playfully on the top of the head.

"Go ahead," he told her, carrying her without effort. "Strangle me, give me a concussion—just don't touch my camera."

"Hello, Larry." Bret strolled over as they approached the house. "All finished?"

Hillary noted with some satisfaction that, with the advantage of being perched on Larry's back, she could meet Bret's eyes on level.

"I shall have to speak to you, Mr. Bardoff, about a new photographer. This one has just inferred that I am over the hill."

"I can't help it if your career's shot," Larry protested. "I've been carrying you figuratively for months, and now that I've carried you literally, I think you're putting on weight."

"That does it," Hillary decided. "Now I have no choice—I have to kill him."

"Put it off for a while, would you?" June requested, joining them by the door. "He doesn't know it yet, but I'm dragging him off for a walk in the woods."

"Very well," Hillary agreed. "That should give me time to consider. Put me down, Larry—you've been reprieved."

"Cold?" Bret asked as Hillary began to strip off her outdoor clothing.

"Frozen. There are those among us who have developing fluid rather than blood in their veins."

"Modeling is not all glamour and smiles, is it?" he commented as she shook snow from her hair. "Are you content with it?" he asked suddenly, capturing her chin with his hand, his eyes narrowed and serious. "Is there nothing else you want?"

"It's what I do," she countered. "It's what I'm able to do."

"Is it what you *want* to do?" he persisted. "Is it *all* you want to do?"

"All?" she repeated, and, battling the urgent longing, she shrugged. "It's enough, isn't it?"

He continued to stare down at her before he mirrored her shrug and walked away. He moved, even in jeans, with a rather detached elegance. Puzzled, Hillary watched him disappear down the hall.

The afternoon passed in vague complacency. Hillary sipped the hot chocolate of her dreams and dozed in a chair by the fire. She watched Bret and Bud play a long game of chess, the three of them unconcerned by Larry's occasional, irrepressible intrusions with his camera.

Charlene remained stubbornly by Bret's side, following the contest with ill-concealed boredom. When the match was over, she insisted that he show her through the forest. It was apparent to Hillary that her mind was not on trees and squirrels.

The day drifted away into darkness. Charlene, looking disgruntled after her walk, complained about the cold, then stated regally that she would soak in a hot tub for the next hour.

Dinner consisted of beef stew, which left the redhead aghast. She compensated by consuming an overabundance of wine. Her complaints were genially ignored, and the meal passed with the casual intimacy characteristic of people who have grown used to each other's company.

Again accepting kitchen detail, Hillary and June worked in the small room, the latter stating she felt she was due for a raise. The job was near completion when Charlene strolled in, yet another glass of wine in her hand.

"Almost done with your womanly duties?" she demanded with heavy sarcasm.

"Yes. Your assistance was greatly appreciated," June answered, stacking plates in a cupboard.

"I should like to have a word with Hillary, if you don't mind."

"No, I don't mind," June returned, and continued to clatter dishes.

Charlene turned to where Hillary was now wiping the surface of the stove. "I will not tolerate your behavior any longer."

"Well, all right—if you'd rather do it yourself." Hillary offered the dishcloth with a smile.

"I saw you this morning," Charlene flung out viciously, "throwing yourself at Bret."

"Did you?" Hillary shrugged, turning back to give the stove her attention. "Actually, I was throwing snowballs. I thought you were asleep."

"Bret woke me when he got out of bed." The voice was soft, the implication all too clear.

Pain throbbed through Hillary. How could he have left one woman's arms and come so easily into hers? How could he degrade and humiliate her that way? She shut her eyes, feeling the color drain from her face. The simple fun and precious intimacy they had shared that morning now seemed cheap. Holding on to her pride desperately, she turned to face Charlene, meeting triumphant green eyes with blue ice. "Everyone's entitled to his own taste." She shrugged indifferently, tossing the cloth on the stove.

Charlene's color rose dramatically. With a furious oath, she threw the contents of her glass, splattering the red liquid over Hillary's sweater.

"That's going too far!" June exploded, full of righteous anger on Hillary's behalf. "You're not going to get away with this one."

"I'll have your job for speaking to me that way."

"Just try it, when the boss sees what you—"

"No more," Hillary broke in, halting her avenger. "I don't want any more scenes, June."

"But, Hillary."

"No, please, just forget it." She was torn between the need to crawl away and lick her wounds and the urge to pull out handfuls of red hair. "I mean it. There's no need to bring Bret into this. I've had it."

"All right, Hillary," June agreed, casting Charlene a disgusted look. "For your sake."

Hillary moved quickly from the room, wanting only to reach the sanctuary of her bedroom. Before she reached the stairs, however, she met Bret.

"Been to war, Hillary?" he asked, glancing at the red splatters on her sweater. "Looks like you lost."

"I never had anything to lose," she mumbled, and started to walk by him.

"Hey." He halted her, taking her arms and holding her in front of him. "What's wrong?"

"Nothing," she retorted, feeling her precious control slipping with each passing moment.

"Don't hand me that—look at you." His hand reached

out to tilt her chin, but she jerked back. "Don't do that," he commanded. His fingers gripped her face and held her still. "What's wrong with you anyway?"

"Nothing is the matter with me," she returned, retreating behind a sheet of ice. "I'm simply a bit weary of being pawed."

She watched, his eyes darkening to a thunderous gray. His fingers tightened painfully on her flesh. "You're darned lucky there're other people in the house, or I'd give you a fine example of what it's really like to be pawed. It's a pity I had a respect for fragile innocence. I shall certainly keep my hands off you in the future."

He relaxed his grip, and with chin and arm aching from the pressure, she pushed by him and calmly mounted the stairs.

Chapter 8

February had drifted into March. The weather had been as cold and dreary as Hillary's spirits. Since the fateful weekend in the Adirondacks, she had received no word from Bret, nor did she expect to.

The issue of *Mode* with Hillary's layout was released, but she could build up no enthusiasm as she studied the tall, slim woman covering the pages. The smiling face on the glossy cover seemed to belong to someone else, a stranger Hillary could neither recognize nor relate to. The layout was, nevertheless, a huge success, with the magazines selling as quickly as they were placed on the stands. She was besieged by offers as the weeks went by, but none of them excited her. She found the pursuit of her career of supreme indifference.

A call from June brought an end to her listlessness. The

call brought a summons from the emperor. She debated refusing the order, then, deciding she would rather face Bret in his office than to have him seek her out at home, she obeyed.

She dressed carefully for the meeting, choosing a discreetly elegant pale yellow suit. She piled her hair up from her neck, covering it with a wide-brimmed hat. After a thorough study, she was well pleased with the calm, sophisticated woman reflected in her mirror.

During the elevator ride to Bret's office, Hillary schooled herself to remain aloof and detached, setting her expression into coolly polite lines. He would not see the pain, she determined. Her vulnerability would be well concealed. Her ability to portray what the camera demanded would be her defense. Her years of experience would not betray her.

June greeted her with a cheery smile. "Go right on in." She pushed the button on her phone. "He's expecting you."

Swallowing fear, Hillary fixed a relaxed smile on her face and entered the lion's den.

"Good afternoon, Hillary," Bret greeted her, leaning back in his chair but not rising. "Come sit down."

"Hello, Bret." Her voice matched the polite tone of his. Her smile remained in place though her stomach had begun to constrict at the first contact with his eyes.

"You're looking well," he commented.

"Thank you, so are you." She thought giddily, What absurd nonsense!

"I've just been looking over the layout again. It's certainly been every bit as successful as we had hoped."

"Yes, I'm glad it worked out so well for everyone."

"Which of these is you, Hillary?" he muttered absently, frowning over the pictures. "Free-spirited tomboy, elegant socialite, dedicated career woman, loving wife, adoring mother, exotic temptress?" He raised his eyes suddenly, boring into hers, the power almost shattering her frail barrier.

She shrugged carelessly. "I'm just a face and body doing what I'm told, projecting the image that's required. That's why you hired me in the first place, isn't it?"

"So, like a chameleon, you change from one color to the next on command."

"That's what I'm paid to do," she answered, feeling slightly ill.

"I've heard you've received quite a number of offers." Once more leaning back in his chair, Bret laced his fingers and studied her through half-closed eyes. "You must be very busy."

"Yes," she began, feigning enthusiasm. "It's been very exciting. I haven't decided which ones to accept. I've been told I should hire a manager to sort things out. There's an offer from a perfume manufacturer—" she named a well-known company "—that involves a long-term contract— three years endorsing on TV and, of course, magazines. It's by far the most interesting, I think." It was at the moment the only one she could clearly remember.

"I see. I'd heard you'd been approached by one of the networks."

"Oh, yes." She made a dismissive gesture, racking her brains for the details. "But that involves acting. I have to give that a great deal of thought." I'd win an Oscar for this performance, she added silently. "I doubt if it would be wise to jump into something like that."

He stood and turned his back, staring out at the steel and glass. She studied him without speaking, wondering what was going on in his mind, noting irrelevantly how the sunlight combed his thick blond hair.

"Your contract with me is finished, Hillary, and though I'm quite prepared to make you an offer, it would hardly be as lucrative as a television contract."

An offer, Hillary thought, her mind whirling, and she was grateful his back was to her so that he could not observe her expression. At least she knew why he had wanted to see her—to offer her another contract, another piece of paper. She would have to refuse, even though she had no intention of accepting any of the other contracts. She could never endure continuous contact with this man. Even after this brief meeting, her emotions were torn.

She rose before answering, and her voice was calm, even professional. "I appreciate your offer, Bret, but I must consider my career. I'm more than grateful to you for the opportunity you gave me, but—"

"I told you before, I don't want your gratitude!" He spun to face her, the all-too-familiar temper darkening his eyes. "I'm not interested in perfunctory expressions of gratitude and appreciation. Whatever you receive as a result of this—" he picked up the magazine with Hillary's face on the cover "—you earned yourself. Take that hat off so I can look at you." He whipped the hat from her head and thrust it into her hands.

Hillary resisted the need to swallow. She met his angry, searching gaze without flinching.

"Your success, Hillary, is of your own making. I'm not responsible for it, nor do I want to be." He seemed to struggle for a measure of control and went on in calm, precise tones. "I don't expect you to accept an offer from me. However, if you change your mind, I'd be willing to negotiate. Whatever you decide, I wish you luck—I should like to think you're happy."

"Thank you." With a light smile, she turned and headed for the door.

"Hillary."

Hand on knob, she shut her eyes a moment and willed herself the strength to face him again. "Yes?"

He stared at her, giving her the sensation that he was filing each of her features separately in his brain. "Goodbye."

"Goodbye," she returned, and turning the knob, she escaped.

Shaken, she leaned her back against the smooth other side of the door. June glanced up from her work.

"Are you all right, Hillary? What's the matter?"

Hillary stared without comprehension, then shook her head. "Nothing," she whispered. "Oh, everything." With a muffled sob, she streaked from the room.

Hillary hailed a cab a few nights later with little enthusiasm. She had allowed herself to be persuaded by Larry and June to attend a party across town in Bud Lewis's penthouse apartment. She must not wallow in self-pity, cut off from friends and social activities, she had decided. It was time, she told herself, pulling her shawl closer against the early April breeze, to give some thought to the future. Sitting alone and brooding would not do the job.

As a result of her self-lecturing, she arrived at the already well-moving party determined to enjoy herself. Bud swung a friendly arm over her shoulders and, leading her to the well-stocked bar, inquired what was her pleasure. She started to request her usual well-diluted drink when a punch bowl filled with a sparkling rose pink liquid caught her eye.

"Oh, that looks nice—what is it?"

"Planter's punch," he informed her, already filling a glass.

Sounds safe enough, she decided as Bud was diverted by another of his guests. With a tentative sip, Hillary thought it remarkably good. She began to mingle with the crowd.

She greeted old and new faces, pausing occasionally to talk or laugh. She glided from group to group, faintly amazed at how light and content was her mood. Depression and unhappiness dissolved like a summer's mist. This is what she needed all along, she concluded—some people, some music, a new attitude.

She was well into her third glass, having a marvelous time, flirting with a tall, dark man who introduced himself as Paul, when a familiar voice spoke from behind her.

"Hello, Hillary, fancy running into you here."

Turning, Hillary was only somewhat surprised to see Bret. She had only agreed to attend the party when June had assured her Bret had other plans. She smiled at him vaguely, wondering momentarily why he was slightly out of focus.

"Hello, Bret, joining the peasants tonight?"

His eyes roamed over her flushed cheeks and absent smile before traveling down the length of her slim form. He lifted his gaze back to her face, one brow lifting slightly as he answered. "I slum it now and then—it's good for the image."

"Mmm." She nodded, draining the remainder of her glass and tossing back an errant lock of hair. "We're both good with images, aren't we?" She turned to the other man at her side with a brilliant smile that left him slightly dazed. "Paul, be a darling and fetch me another of these. It's the punch over there—" she gestured largely "—in that bowl."

"How many have you had, Hillary?" Bret inquired, tilting her chin with his finger as Paul melted into the crowd. "I thought two was your limit."

"No limit tonight." She tossed her head, sending raven locks trembling about her neck and shoulders. "I am celebrating a rebirth. Besides, it's just fruit punch."

"Remarkably strong fruit I'd say from the looks of you," he returned, unable to prevent a grin. "Perhaps you should consider the benefits of coffee after all."

"Don't be stuffy," she ordered, running a finger down the buttons of his shirt. "Silk," she proclaimed and flashed another smile up at him. "I've always had a weakness for silk. Larry's here, you know, and," she added with dramatic emphasis, "he doesn't have his camera. I almost didn't recognize him."

"It won't be long before you have difficulty recognizing your own mother," he commented.

"No, my mother only takes Polaroid shots on odd occasions," she informed him as Paul returned with her drink. Taking a long sip, she captured Paul's arm. "Dance with me. I really love to dance. Here—" she handed her glass to Bret "—hang on to this for me."

She felt light and free as she moved to the music and marveled how she had ever let Bret Bardoff disturb her. The room spun in time to the music, drifting with her in a newfound sense of euphoria. Paul murmured something in her ear she could not quite understand, and she gave an indefinite sigh in response.

When the music halted briefly, a hand touched her arm, and she turned to find Bret standing beside her.

"Cutting in?" she asked, pushing back tumbled hair.

"Cutting out is more what I had in mind," he corrected, pulling her along with him. "And so are you."

"But I'm not ready to leave." She tugged at his arm. "It's early, and I'm having fun."

"I can see that." He continued to drag her after him, not bothering to turn around. "But we're going anyway."

"You don't have to take me home. I can call a cab, or maybe Paul will take me."

"Like hell he will," Bret muttered, pulling her purposefully through the crowd.

"I want to dance some more." She did a quick spin and collided full in his chest. "You want to dance with me?"

"Not tonight, Hillary." Sighing, he looked down at her. "I guess we do this the hard way."

In one swift movement, he had her slung over his shoulder and began weaving his way through the amused crowd. Instead of suffering from indignation, Hillary began to giggle.

"Oh, what fun, my father used to carry me like this."

"Terrific."

"Here, boss." June stood by the door holding Hillary's bag and wrap. "Got everything under control?"

"I will have." He shifted his burden and strode down the hall.

Hillary was carried from the building and dumped without ceremony into Bret's waiting car. "Here." He thrust her shawl into her hands. "Put this on."

"I'm not cold." She tossed it carelessly into the back seat. "I feel marvelous."

"I'm sure you do." Sliding in beside her, he gave her one despairing glance before the engine sprang to life. "You've enough alcohol in your system to heat a two-story building."

"Fruit punch," Hillary corrected, and snuggled back against the cushion. "Oh, look at the moon." She sprang up to lean on the dash, staring at the ghostly white circle. "I love a full moon. Let's go for a walk."

He pulled up at a stoplight, turned to her, and spoke distinctly. "No."

Tilting her head, she narrowed her eyes as if to gain a new perspective. "I had no idea you were such a wet tire."

"Blanket," he corrected, merging with the traffic.

"I told you, I'm not cold." Sinking back into the seat, she began to sing.

Bret parked the car in the garage that serviced Hillary's building, turning to her with reluctant amusement. "All right, Hillary, can you walk or do I carry you?"

"Of course I can walk. I've been walking for years and years." Fumbling with the door handle, she got out to prove her ability. Funny, she thought, I don't remember this floor being tilted. "See?" she said aloud, weaving dangerously. "Perfect balance."

"Sure, Hillary, you're a regular tightrope walker." Gripping her arm to prevent a spill, he swept her up, cradled against his chest. She lay back contented as he carried her to the elevator, twining her arms around his neck.

"I like this much better," she announced as the elevator began its slow climb. "Do you know what I've always wanted to do?"

"What?" His answer was absent, not bothering to turn

his head. She nuzzled his ear with her lips. "Hillary," he began, but she cut him off.

"You have the most fascinating mouth." The tip of her finger traced it with careful concentration.

"Hillary, stop it."

She continued as if he had not spoken. "A nicely shaped face too." Her finger began a slow trip around it. "And I've positively been swallowed up by those eyes." Her mouth began to roam his neck, and he let out a long breath as the elevator doors opened. "Mmm, you smell good."

He struggled to locate her keys, hampered with the bundle in his arms and the soft mouth on his earlobe.

"Hillary, stop it," he ordered. "You're going to make me forget the game has rules."

At last completing the complicated process of opening the door, he leaned against it a moment, drawing in a deep breath.

"I thought men liked to be seduced," she murmured, brushing her cheek against his.

"Listen, Hillary." Turning his face, he found his mouth captured.

"I just love kissing you." She yawned and cradled her head against his neck.

"Hillary…for heaven's sake!"

He staggered for the bedroom while Hillary continued to murmur soft, incoherent words in his ear.

He tried to drop her down on the spread, but her arms remained around his neck, pulling him off balance and down on top of her. Tightening her hold, she once more pressed her lips to his.

He swore breathlessly as he struggled to untangle himself. "You don't know what you're doing." With a drowsy moan, she shut her eyes. "Have you got anything on under that dress?" he demanded as he removed her shoes.

"Mmm, a shimmy."

"What's that?"

She gave him a misty smile and murmured. Taking a deep breath, he shifted her over, released the zipper at the back of her dress, pulled the material over smooth shoulders, and continued down the length of the slimly curved body.

"You're going to pay for this," he warned. His cursing became more eloquent as he forced himself to ignore the honey skin against the brief piece of silk. He drew the spread over the inert form on the bed. Hillary sighed and snuggled into the pillow.

Moving to the door, he leaned wearily on the frame, allowing his eyes to roam over Hillary as she lay in blissful slumber. "I don't believe this. I must be out of my mind." His eyes narrowed as he listened to her deep breathing. "I'm going to hate myself in the morning." Taking a long, deep breath, he went to search out Hillary's hoard of Scotch.

Chapter 9

Hillary awoke to bright invading sunlight. She blinked in bewilderment attempting to focus on familiar objects. She sat up and groaned. Her head ached and her mouth felt full of grit. Placing her feet on the floor, she attempted to stand, only to sink back moaning, as the room revolved around her like a carousel. She gripped her head with her hands to keep it stationary.

What did I drink last night? she wondered, squeezing her eyes tight to jar her memory. What kind of punch was that? She staggered unsteadily to her closet to secure a robe.

Her dress was tossed on the foot of the bed, and she stared at it in confusion. I don't remember undressing, she thought. Shaking her head in bemusement, she pressed a hand against her pounding temple. Aspirin, juice, and a cold shower, she decided. With slow, careful steps, she walked toward the kitchen. She stopped abruptly and leaned against the wall for support as a pair of men's shoes and a jacket stared at her in accusation from her living room sofa.

"Good heavens," she whispered as a partial memory floated back. Bret had brought her home, and she had... She shuddered as she remembered her conduct on the elevator. But what happened? She could only recall bits and pieces, like a jigsaw puzzle dumped on the floor—and the thought of putting them together was thoroughly upsetting.

"Morning, darling."

She turned slowly, her already pale face losing all color as Bret smiled at her, clad only in slacks, a shirt carelessly draped over his shoulder. The dampness of his hair attested to the fact that he had just stepped from the shower. *My shower.* Hillary's brain pounded out as she stared at him.

"I could use some coffee, darling." He kissed her lightly on the cheek in a casual intimate manner that tightened her stomach. He strode past her into the kitchen, and she followed, terrified. After placing the kettle to boil, he turned and wrapped his arms around her waist. "You were terrific." His lips brushed her brow, and she knew a moment's terror that she would faint dead away. "Did you enjoy yourself as much as I did?"

"Well, I—I guess, I don't...I don't remember... exactly."

"Don't remember?" He stared in disbelief. "How could you forget? You were amazing."

"I was... Oh." She covered her face with her hands. "My head."

"Hung over?" he asked, full of solicitude. "I'll fix you up." Moving away, he rummaged in the refrigerator.

"Hung over?" she repeated, supporting herself in the doorway. "I only had some punch."

"And three kinds of rum."

"Rum?" she echoed, screwing up her eyes and trying to think. "I didn't have anything but—"

"Planter's punch." He was busily involved in his remedy, keeping his back toward her. "Which consists, for the most part, of rum—amber, white, and dark."

"I didn't know what it was." She leaned more heavily on the doorway. "I had too much to drink. I'm not used to it. You—you took advantage of me."

"I took advantage?" Glass in hand, he regarded her in astonishment. "Darling, I couldn't hold you off." He lifted his brow and grinned. "You're a real tiger when you get going."

"What a dreadful thing to say," she exploded, then moaned as her head hammered ruthlessly.

"Here, drink." He offered the concoction, and she regarded it with doubtful eyes.

"What's in it?"

"Don't ask," he advised. "Just drink."

Hillary swallowed in one gulp, then shivered as the liquid poured down her throat. "Ugh."

"Price you pay, love," he said piously, "for getting drunk."

"I wasn't drunk exactly," she protested. "I was just a little…a little muddled. And you—" she glared at him "—you took advantage of me."

"I would swear it was the other way around."

"I didn't know what I was doing."

"You certainly seemed to know what you were doing— and very well too." His smile prompted a groan from Hillary.

"I can't remember. I just can't remember."

"Relax, Hillary," he said as she began to sniffle. "There's nothing to remember."

"What do you mean?" She sniffed again and wiped her eyes with the back of her hand.

"I mean, I didn't touch you. I left you pure and unsullied in your virginal bed and slept on that remarkably uncomfortable couch."

"You didn't…we didn't…"

"No to both." He turned in response to the shrilling kettle and poured boiling water into a mug.

The first flood of relief changed into irritation. "Why not? What's wrong with me?"

He turned back to stare at her in amazement, then roared with laughter. "Oh, Hillary, what a contradiction you are! One minute you're desperate because you think I've stolen your honor and the next you're insulted because I didn't."

"I don't find it very funny," she retorted. "You deliberately led me to believe that I, that we—"

"Slept together," Bret offered, casually sipping his coffee. "You deserved it. You drove me crazy all the way from the elevator to the bedroom." His smile widened at her rapid change of color. "You remember that well enough. Now remember this. Most men wouldn't have left a tempting morsel like you and slept on that miserable couch, so take care with your fruit punch from now on."

"I'm never going to take another drink as long as I live," Hillary vowed, rubbing her hands over her eyes. "I'm never going to look at a piece of fruit again. I need some tea or some of that horrible coffee, *something*." The sound of the doorbell shrilled through her head, and she swore with unaccustomed relish.

"I'll fix you some tea," Bret offered, grinning at her fumbling search for obscenities. "Go answer the door."

She answered the summons wearily, opening the door to find Charlene standing at the threshold, taking in her disheveled appearance with glacial eyes.

"Do come right in," Hillary said, shutting the door behind Charlene with a force that only added to her throbbing discomfort.

"I heard you made quite a spectacle of yourself last night."

"Good news travels fast, Charlene—I'm flattered you were so concerned."

"You don't concern me in the least." She brushed invisible lint from her vivid green jacket. "Bret does, however. You seem to make a habit of throwing yourself at him, and I have no intention of allowing it to continue."

This is too much for anyone to take in my condition, Hillary decided, feeling anger rising. Feigning a yawn, she assumed a bored expression. "Is that all?"

"If you think I'm going to have a little nobody like you marring the reputation of the man I'm going to marry, you're very much mistaken."

For an instant, anger's heat was frozen in agony. The struggle to keep her face passive caused her head to pound with new intensity. "My congratulations to you, my condolences to Bret."

"I'll ruin you," Charlene began. "I'll see to it that your face is never photographed again."

"Hello, Charlene," Bret said casually as he entered the room, his shirt now more conventionally in place.

The redhead whirled, staring first at him, then at his jacket thrown carelessly over the back of the sofa. "What…what…are you doing here?"

"I should think that's fairly obvious," he answered, dropping to the sofa and slipping on his shoes. "If you didn't want to know, you shouldn't have taken it upon yourself to check up on me."

He's using me again, Hillary thought, banking down on shivering hurt and anger. Just using me to make her jealous.

Charlene turned on her, her bosom heaving with emotion. "You won't hold him! You're only a cheap one-night stand! He'll be bored with you within the week! He'll soon come back to me," she raved.

"Terrific," Hillary retorted, feeling her grip on her temper slipping. "You're welcome to him, I'm sure. I've had enough of both of you. Why don't you both leave? Now, at once!" She made a wild gesture at the door. "Out, out, out!"

"Just a minute," Bret broke in, buttoning up the last button of his shirt.

"You keep out of this," Hillary snapped, glaring at him. She turned back to Charlene. "I've had it up to the ears with you, but I'm in no mood for fighting at the moment. If you want to come back later, we'll see about it."

"I see no reason to speak to you again," Charlene announced with a toss of her head. "You're no problem to me. After all, what could Bret possibly see in a cheap little tramp like you?"

"Tramp," Hillary repeated in an ominously low voice. "Tramp?" she repeated, advancing.

"Hold on, Hillary." Bret jumped up, grabbing her around the waist. "Calm down."

"You really are a little savage, aren't you?" shot Charlene.

"Savage? I'll show you savage." Hillary struggled furiously against Bret.

"Be quiet, Charlene," he warned softly, "or I'll turn her loose on you."

He held the struggling Hillary until her struggles lost their force.

"Let me go. I won't touch her," she finally agreed. "Just get her out of here." She whirled on Bret. "And you get out too! I've had it with the pair of you. I won't be used this way. If you want to make her jealous, find someone else to dangle in front of her! I want you out—out of my life, out of my mind." She lifted her chin, heedless of the dampness that covered her cheeks. "I never want to see either of you again."

"Now you listen to me." Bret gripped her shoulders more firmly and gave her a brief but vigorous shake.

"No." She wrenched herself out of his grip. "I'm through listening to you. Through, finished—do you understand? Just get out of here, take your friend with you, and both of you leave me alone."

Picking up his jacket, Bret stared for a moment at flushed cheeks and swimming eyes. "All right, Hillary, I'll take her away. I'll give you a chance to pull yourself together, then I'll be back. We haven't nearly finished yet."

She stared at the door he closed behind him through a mist of angry tears. He could come back all right, she decided, brushing away drops of weakness. But she wouldn't be here.

Rushing into the bedroom, she pulled out her cases, throwing clothes into them in heaps. I've had enough!

she thought wildly, enough of New York, enough of Charlene Mason, and especially enough of Bret Bardoff. I'm going home.

In short order, she rapped on Lisa's door. Her friend's smile of greeting faded at the sight of Hillary's obvious distress.

"What in the world—" she began, but Hillary cut her off.

"I don't have time to explain, but I'm leaving. Here's my key." She thrust it into Lisa's hand. "There's food in the fridge and cupboards. You take it, and anything else you like. I won't be coming back."

"But, Hillary—"

"I'll make whatever arrangements have to be made about the furniture and the lease later. I'll write and explain as soon as I can."

"But, Hillary," Lisa called after her, "where are you going?"

"Home," she answered without turning back. "Home where I belong."

If Hillary's unexpected arrival surprised her parents, they asked no questions and made no demands. Soon she fell into the old, familiar pattern of days on the farm. A week drifted by, quiet and undemanding.

During this time it became Hillary's habit to spend quiet times on the open porch of the farmhouse. The interlude between dusk and sleep was the gentlest. It was the time that separated the busy hours of the day from the reflective hours of the night.

The porch swing creaked gently, disturbing the pure stillness of the evening, and she watched the easy movement of the moon, enjoying the scent of her father's pipe as he sat beside her.

"It's time we talked, Hillary," he said, draping his arm around her. "Why did you come back so suddenly?"

With a deep sigh, she rested her head against him. "A lot of reasons. Mostly because I was tired."

"Tired?"

"Yes, tired of being framed and glossed. Tired of seeing my own face. Tired of having to pull emotions and expressions out of my hat like a second-rate magician, tired of the noise, tired of the crowds." She made a helpless movement with her shoulders. "Just plain tired."

"We always thought you had what you wanted."

"I was wrong. It wasn't what I wanted. It wasn't all I wanted." She stood and leaned over the porch rail, staring into the curtain of night. "Now I don't know if I've accomplished anything."

"You accomplished a great deal. You worked hard and made a successful career on your own, and one that you can be proud of. We're all proud of you."

"I know I worked for what I got. I know I was good at my job." She moved away and perched on the porch rail. "When I left home, I wanted to see what I could do for myself by myself. I knew exactly what I wanted, where I was going. Everything was cataloged in neat little piles. First A, then B, and down the line. Now I've got something most women in my position would jump at, and I don't want it. I thought I did, but now, when all I have to do is reach out and take it, I don't want it. I'm tired of putting on the faces."

"All right, then it's time to stop. But I think there's more to your decision to come home than you're saying. Is there a man mixed up in all this?"

"That's all finished," Hillary said with a shrug. "I got in over my head, out of my class."

"Hillary Baxter, I'm ashamed to hear you talk that way."

"It's true." She managed a smile. "I never really fit into his world. He's rich and sophisticated, and I keep forgetting to be glamorous and do the most ridiculous things. Do you know, I still whistle for cabs? You just can't change what you are. No matter how many images you can slip on and off, you're still the same underneath." Shrugging again, she stared into space. "There was never really anything between us—at least not on his side."

"Then he must not have too many brains," her father commented, scowling at his pipe.

"Some might claim you're just a little prejudiced." Hillary gave him a quick hug. "I just needed to come home. I'm going up now. With the rest of the family coming over tomorrow, we'll have a lot to do."

The air was pure and sweet when Hillary mounted her buckskin gelding and set off on an early morning ride. She felt light and free, the wind blowing wildly through her hair, streaming it away from her face in a thick black carpet. In the joy of wind and speed, she forgot time and pain, and the clinging feeling of failure was lost. Reining in the horse, she contemplated the huge expanse of growing wheat.

It was endless, stretching into eternity—a golden ocean rippling under an impossibly blue sky. Somewhere a meadowlark heralded life. Hillary sighed with contentment. Lifting her face, she enjoyed the caressing fingers of sun on her skin, the surging scent of land bursting into life after its winter sleep.

Kansas in the spring, she mused. All the colors so real and vivid, the air so fresh and full of peace. Why did I ever leave? What was I looking for? She closed her eyes and let out a long breath. I was looking for Hillary Baxter, she thought, and now that I've found her, I don't know what to do with her.

"Time's what I need now, Cochise," she told her four-legged companion, and leaned forward to stroke his strong neck. "Just a little time to find all the scattered pieces and put them back together."

Turning the horse toward home, she set off in an easy, gentle lope, content with the soothing rhythm and the spring-softened landscape. As the farm and outbuildings came into view, however, Cochise pawed the ground, straining at the bit.

"All right, you devil." She tossed back her head and laughed, and with a touch of her heels sent the eager horse racing. The air vibrated with the sound of hooves on hard dirt. Hillary let her spirits fly as she gave the gelding his head. They cleared an old wooden jump in a fluid leap, touched earth, and streaked on, sending a flock of contented birds into a flurry of protesting activity.

As they drew nearer the house, her eyes narrowed as she spotted a man leaning on the paddock fence. She pulled back sharply on the reins, causing Cochise to rear in insult.

"Easy," she soothed, stroking his neck and murmuring soft words as he snorted in indignation. Her eyes were focused on the man. It appeared half a continent had not been big enough for a clean escape.

Chapter 10

"Quite a performance." Bret straightened his lean form and strode toward them. "I couldn't tell where the horse let off and the woman began."

"What are you doing here?" she demanded.

"Just passing by—thought I'd drop in." He stroked the horse's muzzle.

Gritting her teeth, Hillary slipped to the ground.

"How did you know where to find me?" She stared up at him, wishing she had kept her advantage astride the horse.

"Lisa heard me pounding on your door. She told me you'd gone home." He spoke absently, appearing more interested in making the gelding's acquaintance than enlightening her. "This is a fine horse, Hillary." He turned his attention from horse to woman, gray eyes sweeping over windblown hair and flushed cheeks. "You certainly know how to ride him."

"He needs to be cooled off and rubbed down." She felt unreasonably annoyed that her horse seemed so taken with the long fingers caressing his neck. She turned to lead him away.

"Does your friend have a name?" He fell into step beside her.

"Cochise." Her answer was short. She barely suppressed the urge to slam the barn door in his face as Bret entered beside her.

"I wonder if you're aware how perfectly his coloring suits you." He made himself comfortable against the stall opening. Hillary began to groom the gelding with fierce dedication.

"I'd hardly choose a horse for such an impractical reason." She kept her attention centered on the buckskin's coat, her back firmly toward the man.

"How long have you had him?"

This is ridiculous, she fumed, wanting desperately to throw the curry comb at him. "I raised him from a foal."

"I suppose that explains why the two of you suit so well."

He began to poke idly about the barn while she completed her grooming. While her hands were busy, her mind whirled with dozens of questions she could not find the courage to form into words. The silence grew deep until she felt buried in it. Finally she was unable to prolong the gelding's brushing. She turned to abandon the barn.

"Why did you run away?" he asked as they were struck with the white flash of sunlight outside.

Her mind jumped like a startled rabbit. "I didn't run away." She improvised rapidly. "I wanted time to think over the offers I've had—it wouldn't do to make the wrong decision at this point in my career."

"I see."

Unsure whether the mockery in his voice was real or a figment of her imagination, she spoke dismissively. "I've got work to do. My mother needs me in the kitchen."

The fates, however, seemed to be against her as her mother opened the back door and stepped out to meet them.

"Why don't you show Bret around, Hillary? Everything's under control here."

"The pies." Hillary sent out rapid distress signals.

Ignoring the silent plea, Sarah merely patted her head. "There's plenty of time yet. I'm sure Bret would like a look around before supper."

"Your mother was kind enough to ask me to stay, Hillary." He smiled at her open astonishment before turning to her mother. "I'm looking forward to it, Sarah."

Fuming at the pleasant first-name exchange, Hillary spun around and muttered without enthusiasm, "Well, come on then." Halting a short distance away, she looked up at him with a honey-drenched smile. "Well, what would you care to see first? The chicken coop or the pig sty?"

"I'll leave that to you," he answered genially, her sarcasm floating over him.

Frowning, Hillary began their tour.

Instead of appearing bored as she had expected, Bret appeared uncommonly interested in the workings of the farm, from her mother's vegetable garden to her father's gigantic machinery.

He stopped her suddenly with a hand on her shoulder and gazed out at the fields of wheat. "I see what you meant, Hillary," he murmured at length. "They're magnificent. A golden ocean."

She made no response.

Turning to head back, his hand captured hers before she could protest.

"Ever seen a tornado?"

"You don't live in Kansas for twenty years and not see one," Hillary said briefly.

"Must be quite an experience."

"It is," she agreed. "I remember when I was about seven, we knew one was coming. Everyone was rushing around, securing animals and getting ready. I was standing right about here." She stopped, gazing into the distance at memory. "I watched it coming, this enormous black funnel, blowing closer and closer. Everything was so incredibly still, you could feel the air weighing down on you. I was fascinated. My father picked me up, tossed me over his shoulder, and hauled me to the storm cellar. It was so quiet, almost like the world had died, then it was like a hundred planes thundering right over our heads."

He smiled down at her, and she felt the familiar tug at her heart. "Hillary." He lifted her hand to his lips briefly. "How incredibly sweet you are."

She began walking again, stuffing her hands strategically in her pockets. In silence, they rounded the side of the farmhouse, while she searched for the courage to ask him why he had come.

"You, ah, you have business in Kansas?"

"Business is one way to put it." His answer was hardly illuminating, and she attempted to match his easy manner.

"Why didn't you send one of your minions to do whatever you had in mind?"

"There are certain areas that I find more rewarding to

deal with personally." His grin was mocking and obviously intended to annoy. Hillary shrugged as if she were indifferent to the entire conversation.

Hillary's parents seemed to take a liking to Bret, and Hillary found herself irritated that Bret fit into the scene so effortlessly. Seated next to her father, on a firm first-name basis, he chatted away like a long-lost friend. The numerous members of her family might have intimidated anyone else. However, Bret seemed undaunted. Within thirty minutes, he had charmed her two sisters-in-law, gained the respect of her two brothers, and the adoration of her younger sister. Muttering about pies, Hillary retreated to the kitchen.

A few minutes later, she heard: "Such domesticity."

Whirling around, she observed Bret's entrance into the room.

"You've flour on your nose." He wiped it away with his finger. Jerking away, she resumed her action with the rolling pin. "Pies, huh? What kind?" He leaned against the counter as though settling for a comfortable visit.

"Lemon meringue," she said shortly, giving him no encouragement.

"Ah, I'm rather partial to lemon meringue—tart and sweet at the same time." He paused and grinned at her averted face. "Reminds me of you." She cast him a withering glance that left him undaunted. "You do that very well," he observed as she began rolling out a second crust.

"I work better alone."

"Where's that famous country hospitality I've heard so much about?"

"You got yourself invited to dinner, didn't you?" She

rolled the wooden pin over the dough as if it were the enemy. "Why did you come?" she demanded. "Did you want to get a look at my little farm? Make fun of my family and give Charlene a good laugh when you got back?"

"Stop it." He straightened from the counter and took her by the shoulders. "Do you think so little of those people out there that you can say that?" Her expression altered from anger to astonishment, and his fingers relaxed on her arms. "This farm is very impressive, and your family is full of warm, real people. I'm half in love with your mother already."

"I'm sorry," she murmured, turning back to her work. "That was a stupid thing to say."

He thrust his hands in the pockets of slim-fitting jeans and strolled to the screen door. "It appears baseball's in season."

The door slammed behind him, and Hillary walked over and looked out, watching as Bret was tossed a glove and greeted with open enthusiasm by various members of her family. The sound of shouting and laughter carried by the breeze floated to her. Hillary turned from the door and went back to work.

Her mother came into the kitchen and Hillary responded to her chattering with occasional murmurs. She felt annoyingly distracted by the activity outside.

"Better call them in to wash up." Sarah interrupted her thoughts, and Hillary moved automatically to the door, opening it and whistling shrilly. Her fingers retreated from her mouth in shock, and she cursed herself for again playing the fool in front of Bret. Stomping back into the kitchen, she slammed the screen behind her. Hillary found herself seated beside Bret at dinner, and ignoring the bats waging war in her stomach, she gave herself over to the table chaos, unwilling for him or her family to see she was disturbed in any way.

As the family gravitated to the living room, Hillary saw Bret once more in discussion with her father, and pointedly gave her attention to her nephew, involving herself with his game of trucks on the floor. His small brother wandered over and climbed into Bret's lap, and she watched under the cover of her lashes as he bounced the boy idly on his knee.

"Do you live with Aunt Hillary in New York?" the child asked suddenly, and a small truck dropped from Hillary's hand with a clatter.

"Not exactly." He smiled slowly at Hillary's rising color. "But I do live in New York."

"Aunt Hillary's going to take me to the top of the Empire State Building," he announced with great pride. "I'm going to spit from a million feet in the air. You can come with us," he invited with childlike magnanimity.

"I can't think of anything I'd rather do." Lean fingers ruffled dark hair. "You'll have to let me know when you're going."

"We can't go on a windy day," the boy explained, meeting gray eyes with six-year-old wisdom. "Aunt Hillary says if you spit into the wind you get your face wet."

Laughter echoed through the room, and Hillary rose and picked up the boy bodily, marching toward the kitchen. "I think there's a piece of pie left. Let's go fill your mouth."

The light was muted and soft with dusk when Hillary's brothers and their families made their departure. A few traces of pink bleeding from the sinking sun traced the horizon. She remained alone on the porch for a time, watching twilight drifting toward darkness, the first stars blinking into life, the first crickets disturbing the silence.

Returning inside, the house seemed strangely quiet. Only the steady ticking of the old grandfather clock disturbed the hush. Curling into a chair, Hillary watched the progress of a chess game between Bret and her father. In spite of herself, she found herself enchanted by the movements of his long fingers over the carved pieces.

"Checkmate." She started at Bret's words, so complete had been her absorption.

Tom frowned at the board a moment, then stroked his chin. "I'll be darned, so it is." He grinned over at Bret and lit his pipe. "You play a fine game of chess, son. I enjoyed that."

"So did I." Bret leaned back in his chair, flicking his lighter at the end of a cigarette. "I hope we'll be able to play often. We should find the opportunity, since I intend to marry your daughter."

The statement was matter-of-factly given. As the words passed from Hillary's ear to brain, her mouth opened, but no sound emerged.

"As head of the family," Bret went on, not even glancing in her direction, "I should assure you that financially Hillary will be well cared for. The pursuit of her career is, of course, her choice, but she need only work for her own satisfaction."

Tom puffed on his pipe and nodded.

"I've thought this through very carefully," Bret continued, blowing out a lazy stream of smoke. "A man reaches a time when he requires a wife and wants children." His voice was low and serious, and Tom met laughing gray eyes equally. "Hillary suits my purposes quite nicely. She is undoubtedly stunning, and what man doesn't enjoy beauty? She's fairly intelligent, adequately strong, and is apparently not averse to children. She is a bit on the skinny side," he added with some regret, and Tom, who had been nodding in agreement to Hillary's virtues, looked apologetic.

"We've never been able to fatten her up any."

"There is also the matter of her temper," Bret deliberated, weighing pros and cons. "But," he concluded with a casual gesture of his hand. "I like a bit of spirit in a woman."

Hillary sprang to her feet, unable for several attempts to form a coherent sentence. "How dare you?" she managed at length. "How dare you sit there and discuss me as if I were a—a brood mare! And you," she chastised her father, "you just go along like you were pawning off the runt of the litter. My own father."

"I did mention her temper, didn't I?" Bret asked Tom, and he nodded sagely.

"You arrogant, conceited, son of a—"

"Careful, Hillary," Bret cautioned, stubbing out his cigarette and raising his brows. "You'll get your mouth washed out with soap again."

"If you think for one minute that I'm going to marry you, you're crazy! I wouldn't have you on a platter! So go back to New York, and…and print your magazines," she finished in a rush, and stormed from the house.

After her departure, Bret turned to Sarah. "I'm sure Hillary would want to have the wedding here. Any close friends can fly in easily enough, but since Hillary's family is here, perhaps I should leave the arrangements to you."

"All right, Bret. Did you have a date in mind?"

"Next weekend."

Sarah's eyes opened wide for a moment as she imagined the furor of arrangements, then tranquilly returned to her knitting. "Leave it to me."

He rose and grinned down at Tom. "She should have cooled off a bit now. I'll go look for her."

"In the barn," Tom informed him, tapping his pipe. "She always goes there when she's in a temper." Bret nodded and strode from the house. "Well, Sarah." With a light chuckle, Tom resumed puffing on his pipe. "Looks like Hillary has met her match."

The barn was dimly lit, and Hillary stomped around the shadows, enraged at both Bret and her father. The two of them! she fumed. I'm surprised he didn't ask to examine my teeth.

With a groan, the barn door swung open, and she spun around as Bret sauntered into the building.

"Hello, Hillary, ready to discuss wedding plans?"

"I'll never be ready to discuss anything with you!" Her angry voice vibrated in the large building.

Bret smiled into her mutinous face unconcernedly. The lack of reaction incensed her further and she began to shout, storming around the floor. "I'll never marry you—never, never, never. I'd rather marry a three-headed midget with warts."

"But you will marry me, Hillary," he returned with easy confidence. "If I have to drag you kicking and screaming all the way to the altar, you'll marry me."

"I said I won't." She halted her confused pacing in front of him. "You can't make me."

He grabbed her arms and surveyed her with laconic arrogance. "Oh, can't I?"

Pulling her close, he captured her mouth.

"You let go of me," she hissed, pulling away. "You let go of my arms."

"Sure." Obligingly, he relinquished his hold, sending her sprawling on her back in a pile of hay.

"You—bully!" she flung at him, and attempted to scramble to her feet, but his body neatly pinned her back into the sweet-smelling hay.

"I only did what I was told. Besides," he added with a crooked smile, "I always did prefer you horizontal." She pushed against him, averting her face as his mouth descended. He contented himself with the soft skin of her neck.

"You can't do this." Her struggles began to lose their force as his lips found new areas of exploration.

"Yes, I can," he murmured, finding her mouth at last. Slow and deep, the kiss battered at her senses until her lips softened and parted beneath his, her arms circled his neck. He drew back, rubbing her nose with his.

"Wretch!" she whispered, pulling him close until their lips merged again.

"Now are you going to marry me?" He smiled down at her, brushing hair from her cheek.

"I can't think," she murmured and shut her eyes. "I can't ever think when you kiss me."

"I don't want you to think." He busied his fingers loosening her buttons. "I just want you to say it." His hand took possession of her breast and gently caressed it. "Just say it, Hillary," he ordered, his mouth moving down from her throat, seeking her vulnerability. "Say it, and I'll give you time to think."

"All right," she moaned. "You win, I'll marry you."

"Good," he said simply, bringing his lips back to hers for a brief kiss.

She fought the fog of longing clouding her senses and attempted to escape. "You used unfair tactics."

He shrugged, holding her beneath him easily. "All's fair in love and war, my love." His eyes lost their laughter as he stared down at her. "I love you, Hillary. You're in every part of my mind. I can't get you out. I love every crazy, beautiful inch of you." His mouth crushed hers, and she felt the world slip from her grasp.

"Oh, Bret." She began kissing his face with wild abandon. "I love you so much. I love you so much I can't bear it. All this time I thought... When Charlene told me you'd been with her that night in the mountains, I—"

"Wait a minute." He halted her rapid kisses, cupping her face with his hands. "I want you to listen to me. First of all, what was between Charlene and me was over before I met you. She just wouldn't let go." He smiled and brushed her mouth with his. "I haven't been able to think of another woman since the first day I met you, and I was half in love with you even before that."

"How?"

"Your picture—your face haunted me."

"I never thought you were serious about me." Her fingers began to tangle in his hair.

"I thought at first it was just physical. I knew I wanted you as I'd never wanted another woman. That night in your apartment, when I found out you were innocent, that threw me a bit." He shook his head in wonder and buried his face in the lushness of her hair. "It didn't take long for me to realize what I felt for you was much more than a physical need."

"But you never indicated anything else."

"You seemed to shy away from relationships—you panicked every time I got too close—and I didn't want to scare you away. You needed time. I tried to give it to you. Hanging on in New York was difficult enough." He traced the hollow of her cheek with a finger. "But that day in my lodge, my control slipped. If Larry and June hadn't come when they did, things would have progressed differently. When you turned on me, telling me you were sick of being pawed, I nearly strangled you."

"Bret, I'm sorry, I didn't mean it. I thought—"

"I know what you thought," he interrupted. "I'm only sorry I didn't know then. I didn't know what Charlene had said to you. Then I began to think you wanted only your career, that you didn't want to make room in your life for anything or anyone else. In my office that day, you were so cool and detached, ticking off your choices, I wanted to toss you out the window."

"They were all lies," she whispered, rubbing her cheek against his. "I never wanted any of it, only you."

"When June finally told me about the scene with Charlene at the lodge, and I remembered your reaction, I began to put things together. I came looking for you at Bud's party." He pulled up his head and grinned. "I intended to talk things out, but you were hardly in any condition for declarations of love by the time I got there. I don't know how I stayed out of your bed that night, you were so soft and beautiful…and so smashed! You nearly drove me over the edge."

He lowered his head and kissed her, his control ebbing

as his mouth conquered her. His hands began to mold her curves with an urgent hunger, and she clutched him closer, drowning in the pool of his desire.

"Good God, Hillary, we can't wait much longer." He removed his weight from her, rolling over on his back, but she went with him, closing her mouth over his. Drawing her firmly away, he let out a deep breath. "I don't think your father would think kindly of me taking his daughter in a pile of hay in his own barn."

He pushed her on her back, slipping his arm around her, cradling her head against his shoulder. "I can't give you Kansas, Hillary," he said quietly. She turned her head to look at him. "We can't live here—at least not now. I've obligations in New York that I simply can't deal with from here."

"Oh, Bret," she began, but he pulled her closer and continued.

"There's upper New York or Connecticut. There are plenty of places where commuting would be no problem. You can have a house in the country if that's what you want. A garden, horses, chickens, half a dozen kids. We'll come back here as often as we can, and go up to the lodge for long weekends, just the two of us." He looked down, alarmed at the tears spilling from wide eyes and over smooth cheeks. "Hillary, don't do that. I don't want you to be unhappy. I know this is home to you." He began to brush the drops from her face.

"Oh, Bret, I love you." She pulled his cheek against hers. "I'm not unhappy. I'm wonderfully, crazily happy that you care so much. Don't you know it doesn't matter where we are? Anyplace I can be with you is home."

He drew her away and regarded her with a frown. "Are you sure, love?"

She smiled and lifted her mouth, letting her kiss give him the answer.

* * * * *